SUICIDALLY
BEAUTIFUL
A Collection of Sport Stories

Edited by

Dennis F. Bormann
&
Stephen Taylor

MAIN STREET RAG PUBLISHING COMPANY
CHARLOTTE, NORTH CAROLINA

Copyright © 2012 Main Street Rag Publishing Company. Rights for individual stories revert to the author upon publication.

About the cover: Designed/created by M. Scott Douglass from a photograph courtesy of iStockphoto.com

Acknowledgments:

"Soccer Moms" was previously published in *Red Rock Review*
"Hog's Heart" previously appeared in *The Antioch Review*, *Best American Short Stories 1980* and in the book *Getting Serious* (University of Missouri Press, 1980)
"Digger" appeared in the now-defunct web zine *The Starry Night Review*
"In Dreams Begin" first appeared in *The Raleigh News & Observer*
"The Tools of Ignorance" first appeared in *Polonaise* (Southern Methodist University Press, 1999).
"Ropes" was previously published in *Short Story*.
"Golf in Pakistan" won the Crucible Prize for Fiction and appeared in the 1990 issue.

Library of Congress Control Number: 2011944904

ISBN: 978-1-59948-356-6

Produced in the United States of America

Mint Hill Books
Main Street Rag Publishing Company
PO Box 690100
Charlotte, NC 28227
www.MainStreetRag.com

Contents

Mark Pearson
    Ropes 1
Thomas E. Kennedy
    Turkey Shoot 6
Atar Hadari
    Where is Lion 21
Michael Duffy
    A Mutt Moment 36
Deirdre Murray-Homes
    Next Saturday 41
Gordon Weaver
    Hog's Heart 56
Michael Stigman
    Gunn and The Hammer. 78
Charles Rammelkamp
    What Did You Did 92
Mike Falcon
    Rontar. 106
Mark Pearson
    Eight Pounds of Sweat, or
    The Art of Dehydration 112
Colleen Shaddox
    Consummation: 2004 134
Jeanie Chung
    Spiderman vs. Superman 138
Demian Entrekin
    Winning .155
Frank Haberle
    Digger. 167
Carolyn P. Lawrence
    The Promised Land 178

William J. Francis
    Top of the Sixth 182
Jen McConnell
    Welcome, Anybody 193
William Torgerson
    Twilight 208
Lee Ann Robins
    My American Soccer Season 224
J. Weintraub
    The Year the Padres Won the Pennant. 232
Philip Gerard
    In Dreams Begin 242
Charles Blackburn
    Golf in Pakistan 247
Jane St. Clair
    Soccer Moms 272
Gaynell Gavin
    Yanks 283
Anthony Bukoski
    The Tools of Ignorance 289

Contributors 315

Introduction

In the fall of 1967 I was in a full leg cast for a medial collateral ligament tear and following my favorite football coach up the metal ladder that led to the roof of the school. It was from there we would spot for the game against Haverstraw H. S. This was a perspective I had never seen before.

The week before I would have been in the locker room hearing the muffled sound of the band. I was usually quiet before a game with my preparation. First in line to be taped. Well, to be honest, there was no line. I would have to wait on one of the coaches to get there. Then I'd go off by myself until it was time to get dressed out. Once uniformed the adrenaline would build. It was a rush.

But now, on the roof, I watched the influx of fans, some of the cheerleaders doing their thing, then the gathering of the band to blare the H.S. fight anthem, its music stolen years before from Notre Dame, ("bring out the whiskey, bring out the rye…"). It was crisp New York autumn air, breezy. The flags of the color guard beat time in this breeze. The panorama a vista of the fall climax. Coach Hoffman, a man we called "Coacheese" because of his florid complexion, nudged me with his forearm, then gestured with a nod of his head toward the view splayed out before us and said, "How can anyone not love a football game."

—Dennis F. Bormann

I probably didn't play center field half as brilliantly as I remember, but I'm not thinking about my own imagined prowess anyway. I'm thinking of a tee-ball game I stopped to watch like I do sometimes to smile and remember what sports are supposed to be. There was an outfielder in that game whose work was all done by sheer will. He didn't so much run as hop in a jerky sideways gallop like he was pretending to ride an imaginary horse. Something was wrong, of course, cerebral palsy maybe or some malformation of his hips. I remember him leaning forward as much as he could before each play, only a slight arch of his back—I don't think he could set his hands on his knees—but he popped his glove with his fist like he wanted the ball. It didn't take long to notice something else too. The coach of the team at bat was whispering to the on-deck batters, and you could see what he was telling them, because his head would turn a little toward right field, and the hitters turned their stances in that direction. It took a few minutes to believe it was actually happening, but there was no mistaking it, three, four, five balls in a row all hit to right. Some of us got mad, of course, when we were sure, but what we did or said doesn't matter. What matters is the kid galloping sideways after the ball regardless of how far it rolled. He never caught one on the fly—this wasn't fantasy—he had to slide to his knees even to pick up the ball, then sling it over his head like a hand grenade. And each time afterward that kid arched forward and popped his glove. It's that pop I want most to remember, the pop of the spirit.

— Stephen Taylor

Both of us, of course, turned to literature to summon the power of memory and hear the pop of the spirit. The title *Suicidally Beautiful* comes from a line in the James Wright poem "Autumn Begins in Martins Ferry, Ohio," which, as the poet contemplates the start of football season, conjures the psychic complexity, the grandeur, sacrifice, and delusion embodied in sports:

> *Therefore*
> *Their sons grow suicidally beautiful*
> *At the beginning of October,*
> *And gallop terribly against each other's bodies.*

The same, of course, now holds true for their daughters as well, and the range and quality of stories collected here powerfully amplify this complexity.

ROPES

Mark Pearson

He, once renowned for a murderous right and devastating jab, a man despised for laughing at his arrest for striking his wife and joking about the way she flew like a rag doll across the room, could not resist the chance to step into the ring one more time despite eroded skills and the passage of time so incomprehensible to him now.

And so, they came to the deteriorated concrete civic arena in a town that never hosted a name as big as his. Laughing, joking, smoking cigars, they paid ten dollars a ticket, twenty-five for ringside, to see the man get what he deserved. All he wanted: the Tennessee state professional heavyweight championship, not the world title he once held. Pathetic, the city newspaper had said: How hard a man can fall. How far! What did they know? He scoffed, he knew he was there because he loved every minute of it, from the sharp sound of the tape ripping as his fists were wrapped to the echoes of the ring announcer booming his name out into the darkness around the ring.

The crowd laughed as he climbed into the ring. He was paunchy, looking like a man who had not trained for months, years perhaps, covered in a sweat they joked about testing for alcohol, and cocaine. He had jowls. They shook when he spit as he entered the ring, hanging a bloody gob on the skirt of the ring. The front row crowd winced, and cursed him for the spit that sprayed them. He stepped through the ropes and entered the ring—a moment he relished, taking the stage, and standing above the crowd. Yes, those in the front rows would look up at him, and he loved that. His heels at eye level, black shoes shushing the bright blue and white canvas.

Time entered the ring with him, for there stripped of satin robe—his nickname Assassin embroidered across the back—he stood naked, revealed, a pretender to his former self. Every moment there, now measured. Three-minute rounds, one minute break between rounds. The referee ready, waiting to deliver his count. The lights bright enough to reveal the pores in his skin to the fans in row one.

The opponent in the opposite corner looked like dozens of others. He recognized him as one of them—the two hundred he faced in amateur and pro fights: young, wise cracking, foolish enough to think he had a career ahead of him. This opponent chosen as a walking target, limited in skill, and powerful, but born with the endurance of a trotting wolf on the trail of moose. He knew this one like the rest also desired all that he once had, the world titles and all rights and privileges pertaining thereto. The money, the women. Mostly the women.

The introduction. Ironic. Two men about to beat each other's brains out introduced to each other as if they were at a party about to converse. He laughed at the thought of it. How many times had he been through the routine and this had not occurred to him? He grinned. His opponent, perhaps thinking it was a mocking leer, shoved at his gloves when they raised them to touch, shouted incomprehensible threats through his mouthpiece. He saw the rabbit eyes, darting, and as the deep sweat pored from his limber body, he knew the kid was scared.

The fans waited for the bell too. He could see them, shifting, yelling. He had the urge to shout back at them like he'd done in the press and on the television: "I am who you all want to be and you hate me for it."

When the bell rang to start the opening round, he defied them. Round after round, the skills buried beneath the flab and disuse carried him to a lead on all cards. Moving in flashes as he once had, feet gliding inches above the canvas, in and out of the grasp of his opponent, who stumbling, amateurish, appeared as a gawking kid in the presence of a great artist. A lumbering boy, outmatched except in heart and strength. But, then as the rounds went on they wrestled. They did not box. He slipped in punches, frustrated the boy.

He grinned at the crowd between rounds as he looked out on their disappointed faces. They booed him, shouted insults. He taunted them, shaking a fist in the air as he returned to his corner. Using the old man's tactics, clinching, shoving, he conserved his energy. Oh, they hated him, his magnificent arrogance, and petulant demeanor. They hated him for crashing Rolls-Royces, Ferraris, wearing fur coats and fucking white women.

The punches came, artless attacks, but steady. They thudded off his forearms, slid off shoulders, and cut the thick air in front of his face. He blocked, slipped, clinched. One got through in the middle rounds, stung him. Lights flickered. The arena went silent. The crowd rose, sensed the moment at hand, but he held on, grabbed an arm for a crucial five seconds until his head cleared. The referee tried to pry them apart, issued a warning. When the bell rang to end the round he waved at the jeering crowd. A box of popcorn skidded across the ring in front of him. He kicked it into the front row.

Then it came, finally, and just as brutal as they hoped it would be. A slashing left to the body that brought his arms down enough to let in the right. And the right came in quickly, skimming the top of his red eight-ounce gloves, smacking his skin. The gloves hard, padding meant to protect fists, cracked the jawbone on impact, sent his head snapping back as if attached to a bungee cord not neck, bone, and muscle. Neck in arc, body falling backwards, slowly at first, as if a redwood crashing in the forest, first shaking free its roots, but gaining speed as it approached the top rope where it hit and then whiplashed.

The vein severed, leaking blood meant for the brain, flooding tissue not nourishing it, like a river that overran its banks. The referee drifted in a pool of light, waving his white-shirted arms as if swimming there. He was swimming too, backward and forward through time, trying to make sense of it. No longer angry but confused, a boy again, running across broken glass and shattered brick in the abandoned lots between ravaged tenements, on his way to the braided river where clear water mixed with mud. There, waiting for his turn to swing on the big rope, out over the merging waters and drop. How long had he waited there on that afternoon, any of them? The river unwound itself from the beginning of time, reached backward into the past and forward into the future. It moved beyond him then and now as if he was standing still, feet anchored in the muddy bank.

Was that his mother's voice, calling him to dinner, warning him, chastising him? I told you not to enter that ring. That's no place for a man with brains, unless he wants them beaten out of him, and him made into a mumbling slow-witted gardener, potting plants all day, lost in his dreams and nightmares, not sure of the time of day. But, she didn't understand what it meant to be a man, to stand in the middle of the ring and have his hand raised. Where else was that going to happen? And so he won and won and won, and each time she smiled and shook her head, and asked when he would have enough. When he said never, she knew he was right and she cried, served him the steak and eggs he'd bought with earnings from the latest fight, and let him eat alone. She would not move into the house he bought her, or drive the silver Cadillac he parked in the drive. I know where that river flows, she said. I know it up and down from source to mouth.

His turn came and he was out over the river, releasing the rough rope that bit into his palms and fingers, the burning feeling of holding on too long. He was soaring, above it all for those few seconds, free, taunting those landlocked souls standing on the banks. With a half-turn, a wave, and a shout, "sayonara suckers," he splashed into the river and sank down, the sunlight distorted above him, pouring down into the depths, kaleidoscopic, trees overhead, visible on the periphery of his vision, reduced to gray lines wavering on the watery surface. Breaking surface tension, looking for the muddy banks, the trees, he rose grinning, immortal.

TURKEY SHOOT

Thomas E. Kennedy

Late that afternoon, as soon as I get home from school, I close the door to my tiny room and sit at the old beat-up table I use for a desk and crack my English book. I'm supposed to read a poem by Edgar Alan Poe for tomorrow and need to get it done before I go out, but I can't concentrate on ravens; all I can think about is turkeys. I read the poem like twenty times but I'm still only thinking about turkeys. Then my mother calls me in to dinner, and I join her and Dad at the kitchen table.

He's got a Miller's and a shot of 4 Roses in front of him, and his meatloaf is untouched. He's staring at my mother. When she stands up to reach for the gravy pan off the stove, he cups his hand around her hip, but she shimmies away from his touch and, like, exclaims, "Hold off! Unhand me, graybeard loon!" Trying to make a joke out of it.

My Dad knocks back his rye and mutters, "Speak to me not of the albatross."

Another bird. But my head is still filled with visions of throwing a turkey, so I wolf down my meatloaf and mashed potatoes and peas, wash it down with a big glass of cold milk and rise from the beige metal table that we've been eating dinner at all my sixteen years.

"Where *you* going?" my Dad demands.

"Turkey Shoot," I say.

He snorts and looks at my mother again, says, "Know what, Glenda? You have truly elegant, beautiful shoulders," while I slip down the hall, shrug on my pea coat and hustle up the street, strewn with dirty snow skids, to Roosevelt.

Elmhurst Lanes is across Roosevelt Avenue in the shadow of the looming green iron structure of the IRT Elevated train that runs from the East River to Flushing Main Street. The Turkey Shoot is announced on the mimeographed sheet taped to the glass of the front door, just beneath the word *Bowling* in red neon script. WINNER TAKES ALL, it says above the fine print rules and regulations. The Shoot opens at seven this evening and runs to midnight, closing time. My friend Lenny says it's just a feeble attempt to draw business on a Thursday night, which is always slow, but so what? It costs five bucks to enter—five *1965* bucks—and whoever bowls three strikes in a row takes the pot. If more than one man throws a turkey the one who has the highest score in the overall game wins, unless one of them shoots *four* strikes in a row—that's better than a turkey. In case of a tie, there's a frame by frame play off.

I pause for a moment outside the door there, seeing my breath steam across the warm red neon script of the *Bowling* sign. It makes me feel welcome somehow, like I belong here.

Downstairs, bathed in the strange fluorescent lighting that illuminates the sixteen underground lanes, I pay Gus my five dollars and rent shoes from Mary, wave to John behind the food bar, and go to the far lower ball rack where I always stash my favorite marbleized red Brunswick, full weight. I love that ball. Nobody else seems to have noticed how beautiful it is, nobody ever gets to it before me. If they knew how good it is, they might, but they don't even notice. Armie Pinvill, Herman Heisse, Norman Halfpenny, and a few other guys are there already, tying their laces ahead of me. They're men and have their own shoes and balls and even their own towels and tubes of NuSkin. My friend Lenny is waiting there for me, too. He's not going to bowl—he doesn't want to risk Gus pocketing his cash; he's only here to keep score for me. Someone, maybe Lenny, has dropped a quarter in the juke and punched the same song three times; it keeps playing, the big hit that season, "1 2 3 It's So Easy (Like Taking Candy from a Baby)."

The other guys are already bowling now, but I take my time because I don't want to get feeling pressured. I tug on my shoes, tighten the laces, tie a double bow. That song is in my head now: *1 2 3 So easy...* Carefully, I wipe my palm dry with the towel tied to the scoring table and heft the ball in both my hands, like weighing it, like getting used to the weight all over again, before slipping my thumb and two fingers into the hole grips, take my position, breathe deep and start my approach. Three steps and I deliver the ball without a bump, following through with my whole body, watch the red Brunswick spin and hook left just where I want it to, into the pocket of the first two arrow-head spots, and I know it's home! Whack! Dead between the 1 and 3 pins. The pins jump in a tight dancing frenzy to that beautiful woody music of a strike!

"Nicely done!" says Lenny, behind me. He draws a fat black X in the little box on top of the first frame on the score sheet, then he strikes a match from his book and lights a Lucky, holds the pack out to me. I shake my head.

The men at the lanes to the right and left of me are aware my first ball was a strike, I can feel it. I glance to the left at Armie and Herman, who are rolling together, and right at Norman who's playing alone. I can hear, I can sense that no strikes have been thrown on either lane, maybe on none of the sixteen lanes, most of which are full. You can sense that kind of thing. And most of those guys have paid their five bucks. The pot is fat. The place is crowded now an very noisy and that song keeps playing, *1 2 3...so easy...*

Herman, a thin short man with an accent—he's like 40 or something and still works as a bicycle delivery boy for the German deli—looks at me with his mild eyes and says, "Hello hello hello." He always says that when someone gets a strike, three times hello—it's his way of saying congratulations. Herman is a leftie and throws a back-up ball that curves into the left pocket—when he's lucky. Neither Armie or Norman say a word. Norman looks pissed off. I watch him make his approach—he's a squat, strong, muscular guy but he can't bowl—he lofts the ball so it bounces on the wood when it lands. I can almost hear Gus grinding his teeth at the sound of Norman's ball hitting the lane. He bowls a straight ball and hits the head-pin dead-on, leaving a 7-10 split. I glance at Lenny, who meets my eyes, holding his fingers over his smiling lips as he puffs his Lucky. We don't care a whole hell of a lot for Norman, who once called me a snaggle-toothed little fink.

Breathing easy, I move slow to the ball return and palm the Brunswick. Glancing back over the benches, I glimpse Gus watching me from behind the cash register with his sharp eyes and tight smile. Elmhurst Lanes is owned by Gus and his wife, Mary, who's the sister of John—I don't know whether John is a partner or just works with them, but he's the only one I really like there, who really makes me feel like I belong here, am welcome here. He's been teaching me to spot bowl. I don't have a big brother, but I wish John was. Sometimes when it's really slow John clears the pins from one lane and turns off the automatic pin-setter and lets me practice spot bowling, just following the spots, watching them instead of the pins, and watching how I can vary the hook of my ball with the angle of my thumb and grip, how to deliver the ball smoothly but with power, throwing your shoulder into it, but with control. Too much head pin and you leave a near-impossible 7-10 split; too little and you leave a lonely 5 pin standing. I'm getting much better at hooking the ball just so, and I love to see the pins dance into a strike.

Gus is the main owner of the Lanes. There's something about him I don't much like—his slightly crouched posture, his sweaty hands, the tightness of his smile amidst his perennial five o'clock shadow, his dark sharp eyes—the way his clothes hang on his stooped frame, even the way he walks, with his toes kind of pointed to the sides.

But really, I wonder, are these reasons not to like someone? I know how it is not to be liked for something you can't help—there's a couple kids in school who call me Bucky because two of my front teeth stick out. Somehow it seems like if I allow myself to dislike Gus for his looks, then somehow I myself will be saying it's okay for those kids to mock me for my teeth.

From behind the bar, John sees me looking and smiles, gives me a thumbs up. He knows I threw a strike. He knows everything that happens on the lanes without even hardly looking. It seems weird to feel this about a guy, but I think John is beautiful. He has red hair and red eyebrows and eyelashes and his mouth is, well, pretty when he smiles—the same mouth that his sister Mary has, but Mary is not as nice as John. I mean it's not like I want to kiss him or anything, but I love him like a brother, like a big brother. I wave with my left hand, the ball cradled in my right arm, then turn my back to address the lane.

"Easy now," Lenny says to me, but I'm already easy, breathing evenly. I take my place, balancing the ball on my left palm, thumb and fingers comfortable in the holes. I look at the arrows, not the pins, like John taught me, breathe in and start to move. Three steps to the line and the ball leaves my hand as smooth as I could wish. I follow through, lifting my hand like a blade, all the way up, while I watch the red Brunswick hook 45 degrees left between the arrows, and by god, it's in the pocket! The pins dance in the air to the music of their own wood, and I pump my fist!

Lenny drawls, "Nicely fucking done!"

"Hey, watch your mouth, punk!" Norman snaps from the next lane, and Lenny smirks at him while he drags on his Lucky. You can see that Lenny's not afraid of him which makes Norman madder. He slams his bottle of Schaefer into the drink holder on his table and turns away. I once saw a cop slap Lenny across the face, and Lenny didn't even flinch—he looked at the cop and said, "Powerful fuck, ain't you?"

People are starting to drift over to my lane now, gathering behind the bench, the smell of a turkey in the air. The other three men at the lanes on either side have stopped bowling and are watching me. John is there, too, but Gus stays behind the cash register, and Mary is by the shoes. She's not smiling. Lenny says that she's the brains behind Gus. Lenny is a short, wiry, good-natured guy, though his eyes are always moving, trying to figure what's going on, and he's quick to anger if he thinks someone is trying to pull one on him. He's tough for his size, too, a lot tougher than me. He hasn't signed up for the Turkey Shoot because he read the rules and regulations and saw that if no one throws a turkey, all monies collected revert to the Elmhurst Lanes management.

"All fucking *monies*," Lenny muttered. Now he says with an evil smirk, "Bowl one more strike, and I guess all fucking monies are revertin' to you, huh?" Lenny has no qualms about hating Gus and I can see how much he is hoping that Gus will have to hand me the dough.

The reason Lenny gives for hating Gus is that he just doesn't like his face, but I'm pretty sure it's because of the flood me and all my friends helped keep clear of the lanes a couple months ago. I was down practicing spot bowling while there was a thunderstorm outside on the avenue and both bathrooms backed up. Water started flooding out of their doors. I got on the horn to all our friends—Lenny and Zack and Sam Cooke and Tony Pettetti and Vinnie and Carol, Kitty and Sandie… They all hurried over and started manning the mops and the floor cloths and buckets, and we kept the water from ever touching the wood of the lanes while we waited for the plumber to stop the leaks. That water could have ruined them. Only Gus and Mary were there that day—John was off duty—and afterwards, Gus called us all together and asked us to come in next day so he could express his appreciation. We figured maybe he'd let us all bowl a free game or maybe give free hamburgers, I don't know. But what he did when we showed up, he stood in front of us and said, "I'd like each and every one of you to know that my wife and me are deeply gratified to you all for what you done, and each and every one of you will always be welcome in our establishment."

And that was it. A lot of the kids stopped hanging around there after that, but really I don't think Gus cared. He didn't like teenagers hanging around. I overheard him once muttering to John, "They don't have no money. They bowl a line or two but that's it. They don't buy no food or drink, and they make the regular customers nervous. It's bad for business." John just looked at him like he couldn't even be bothered to argue. It hurt my feelings me that Gus didn't consider us "regular customers," and I figured okay Gus is cheap, but I knew from Joe Caccia who owns the record store on 82nd that it's hard to be a small businessman. "The average life of the American small business," Joe told me one day, "is seven years." He told me that because I said to him how nice it must be to own a record store, listen to music all day, get the latest releases, make your living selling something everybody likes, music, but Joe said, "It's a mutt's game. Stay in school. Go to college. You got a head. Get a good job. Don't buy no small-time record shop. Believe me." I figure Gus is just trying to make his business work and probably can't afford to let people bowl free of charge or give out free burgers.

Besides, I like this place and want it to survive. In a way it's like my new home. I get a good feeling when I cross

Roosevelt and see the glass door with the word *Bowling* written at a slant across it in that warm red neon script. Like it's a place I've found, a place where I'm welcome, a place where the owners know me and like me. It feels good.

There's a crowd of people behind me as I take the Brunswick from the return. I notice that Norman Halfpenny has stopped bowling completely—he's sitting on the bench, pretending to glare ahead, but it's clear he's watching me out of the corner of his eye, hoping I blow the turkey. There's a lot of people in the Shoot, must be a big pot by now, and everybody wants it, including Norman, but he's not going to shoot a turkey the wild way he lofts the ball like that, trying to do it with muscle instead of skill. He's got power but no control. He may be a grown up and I'm just a kid, but even I can see that.

But I'm not going to let his poison into my lungs. I'm breathing slow and even, just like John taught me to. John is behind the bench now, too, and he catches my eye and sort of lowers his lids and smiles, nodding, like he's saying, "You can do it, buddy."

I shoot the breath out my nostrils, trying to expel my nervousness, while I move from foot to foot and balance the ball in both hands against my chest. For a second I think about all that money, wonder how much there is, but then I shake my head a little to get those thoughts off my brain. This is not about money—it's about control. If I think about the money, I'll get sloppy, I'll screw up. I can feel the hush behind me, and for a second it feels good—like they're watching *me*, interested in what I'm going to do, like what I'm about to do is important. But then I become aware of myself feeling that, and I shake that off, too. I take another breath, slow and deep, get my thumb and two fingers into the grips and straighten my shoulders. I look at the pins, then I look at the spots, and adjust my wrist to the angle I want.

Another breath and three steps and I'm dipping into a crouch at the line, throwing my shoulder into the delivery as I set the ball down without a sound and lift my hand, straight up like a knife and hold it there at the height of my follow-through and watch that gorgeous red Brunswick roll and when it hooks through the arrowheads, I *know* it's in the pocket and I straighten as it rolls dead into the 1-3, just so, and *thwack!*

I wish I could have a still photograph of how the pins jump and shimmy when you hit them just right. It is so beautiful. Straightening my legs, I pump both fists, and the people behind me are clapping now. *Clapping!* It makes me feel shy, so I'm blushing when I turn to face them, but also smiling into their smiling faces. It's like they're glad, like I did something for them, too, like something good that happens makes us all believe that something good is *possible*. I look from face to face, and my smile gets firmer. That song is playing again—*1 2 3...so easy...* I look over their heads and see Gus and Mary behind the cash register. They're not smiling. In fact, it looks like they're arguing, very quietly, it's like the argument is more dangerous because it's so quiet. I just glimpse it for a second, but then John kind of leaps onto the wood beside the scoring table, where Lenny has now marked three black X's with a 30 in the first box, and I know the second box will be *at the very least* a 50. Fuck, I could bowl a perfect game! I could bowl a 300! Lenny is grinning with a butt pointing upwards between his lips, and John sort of leaps at me with his big bright red eye-browed smile and claps both my shoulders from the sides.

"You got that hook *down*, buddy!" he says. "You got that hook, and you got that arm!" He squeezes my bicep. "Come on. Make a muscle," he says, and I do, and he says, "*Man:* Like a *rock!*" I start blushing again I'm so pleased—I hate to blush, but I just feel so good it doesn't matter, and I take a cigarette from Lenny's pack and strike a book match, light up, take a couple drags, then rest it on the lip of the ashtray..

Before I turn back to finish the game, I catch a glimpse of Gus in the phone booth. He's not talking, looks like he's waiting for someone to answer. Lenny steps over to me and mutters, "What the fuck's he doin' in the phone booth? He's got a store phone right next to the register."

I say, "Maybe he's making a personal call."

"Yeah, I *bet* he's makin' a fuckin' personal call," Lenny says and looks at me like I should understand what he's saying, but I don't see anything in it. Lenny can be suspicious of everybody sometimes. I just don't see the problem. I already shot a turkey, and it's almost eight p.m,. and I can see all the way from here that there are at least thirty or forty names on the sign-up sheet taped to the wall, and I don't see anybody else bowling a triple or even a double. I'm gonna win this thing, so what's Lenny worried about? Thirty times five bucks means at least a yard and a half. The prospect of walking away with all that money is dizzying. I think of what I could do with it. I could buy a new corderoy suit (40 bucks on Main Street in Flushing), a fancy new pair of shoes (20 dollars at Florsheim's), a couple of shirts (five beans a pop at Field's). I could buy my own Brunswick bowling ball and bag and shoes and *still* have enough left to get my teeth capped by Dr. Scrivane, D.D.S., on 82nd Street in Jackson Heights.

I realize too late that it was not smart of me to start thinking about the money and what it could buy. My next frame is open—I leave a 5 pin and my second ball comes so close it wobbles the pin but it stays upright and I miss the spare—so my triple is only worth 78, and I only have 87 in the fourth frame with no spare. The rest of my game in no way builds on the promise of the first three frames. I throw a couple of strikes and a few spares, but the last frame is open again—I get a fucking eight. A fucking *eight*! And I end up with a 195. With that start I should have broken 200 easy, but I started thinking about the money, and I blew it. I'm too keyed up to bowl another game so I go over and check out the sign-up sheet. There's over forty people on it! More than two hundred bucks! And my name is the only one that has a turkey next to it—a shiny decal-like thing, looks like it should be licked and stuck on a Thanksgiving card, pasted next to my name, where my score is written, too: 195. No one else has shot a turkey yet.

Me and Lenny go over to the food bar and order two hamburgers. "I'm buyin'," I tell him. Mary looks at me like she tries to smile, but it's not really a smile. Which makes me feel a little funny—like I thought she'd be happy for me. We go over to a table and eat our burgers—they're not as good as Fat Sid makes over at the Hampton Luncheonette, but I figure I want to put some money into the Lanes, help keep them going. Anyway, to be truthful, I want to watch the other bowlers. I'm scared somebody's going to throw a turkey and rack up a better overall score than mine.

Lenny is thinking hard, I can see, glancing over at Gus every so often—he really hates Gus—and speculating why he used the phone booth to make a call earlier.

"Maybe he had something to say that was very private," I suggest, and Lenny looks flat at me with his green eyes. "That is exactly what I'm talking about," he says.

"*What*?" I say and hold up my empty hands, shrugging my shoulders.

Then I notice Gus and Mary and John over behind the cash register, and it looks like they're arguing, all three of them. Very quietly, but still... Then John comes over to tell me he has to go, he's sorry he can't stay to watch the finish. "But if you don't win," he says, "if someone else takes the pot, I want you to know I'm proud of you. You've become a damn good bowler this season. Damn good." Something about the way he says that makes the hamburger feel sick in my stomach.

As we watch John put on his ski jacket, Lenny says, "How come he suddenly has to leave? He's usually here all Friday night, so how come he suddenly has to leave?"

"Man, you are jumpy," I say. "You're jumpier than me."
"Well I don't trust these motherfuckers."
"Relax, man. Let's enjoy it."

Just to get away from his negativity I move over behind the benches and watch the various people bowl. Armie Pinvill throws two strikes but next frame he has a birthday cake of splits, and averages 154 for five games. Not bad really. Herman—who, if I had to lose, is the guy I'd hope to lose to—doesn't even bowl a double all night. I don't even watch Norman Halfpenny bowl—he'd probably just tell me to take off anyway, maybe call me snaggle-tooth again. The memory of how he called me that suddenly makes me glad I'm gonna win the pot and he's gonna lose. I'll spend his five bucks on something good, or maybe, *after* I get my teeth capped, I'll light a cigarette with it, right in front of him. Like, See this Norman? This is your five bucks.

I buy a couple more cokes for me and Lenny, and we sit at a table drinking them and listening to the juke—*1 2 3 ... like taking candy ...* —and watching the lanes thin out as people start going home with no turkeys. A couple of them wave as they come by, smile and say, "Nice work, buddy." Herman waves goodbye, saying, "Hello hello hello" again—even Armie Pinville smiles at me, like he wants me to win, like he's glad. Which makes me feel guilty at the stuff I thought about Norman Halfpenny before.

Then I'm sitting there thinking about the poem we had to read for homework today, "The Raven," by Edgar Alan Poe, and I get an idea. I look at Lenny and say, "Once upon a Thursday bowling, as I sent my Brunswick rolling..." I think a minute, or rather *wait* to see what else might come, and then go on, "Over many a strike zone of stupendous score..." I can see Lenny gets it and likes it. Finally he's stopped talking about Gus's phone call, but I can't think of any more lines. Then I skip ahead, "Ah distinctly I recall, it was on the second ball, and the score was one-four-four..." And then, "Quoth the judges: 'He fouled his score.'"

Lenny loves it. I can see he loves it, and he wants to add something himself but instead he just repeats what I said, "Once upon a Thursday bowling, as I sent my Brunswick rolling…"

The lanes are completely empty now, and it's past eleven, and the only people there are me and Lenny and Gus and Mary, and it seems highly unlikely that anyone else is coming in, and now I can see from where we're sitting that over 50 people are on the sign-up sheet—more than 250 bucks!—and only one shiny turkey decal, which is right next to my name!

Gus is back in the phone booth, but we don't hear him talking. He just dials and listens and hangs up. Plucks the dime out of the coin return chute, drops it back in the slot, and dials again and listens for a while and hangs up.

"Now who the *fuck* is that man tryin' a call?" Lenny asks.

Mary is washing dishes and looks like somebody pissed on her honey sandwich, and it's a quarter to twelve, and I'm starting to get hungry to stuff all those five dollar bills and tens and twenties and maybe even a couple of fifties in my jeans. I hope there's a couple fifties. I never had a fifty dollar bill before.

Now Gus is *talking* in the booth, like he finally got through. No, actually he's shouting, but cupping his hand over the mouthpiece, and I'm feeling confused.

"I don't fuckin' like this," Lenny says.

Gus comes out of the phone booth and joins Mary behind the food bar. She's still rinsing dishes, and he's leaning against the sink and talking quietly to her, and the minute hand on the big round clock over the cash register is like two notches away from midnight. Gus sees me looking at the clock and smiles and calls over, "That's always set a little fast."

Lenny holds up his wristwatch, pointing at the face of it, and says, "Mine ain't fast, and it says the same as that one. Two minutes to closin' time."

Gus doesn't seem to hear him. It's very quiet in the place because no one's bowling an there's no juke. It seems strange for it to be so quiet there. And then we hear footsteps jogging down the stairway from the street. Mary looks up from the sink, and Gus walks over to the door with his toes pointing to the sides and gets there just in time to meet a guy coming through. He's an older man and big with an underslung jaw, and he's wearing a hat and overcoat and suit jacket, and he's carrying a fancy black-and-white leather bowling bag.

He says, "I'm the guy who called down before and told you to write me up for the Shoot." He says it to Gus but loud enough that we can hear it.

Lenny turns his back to the others, but is facing me and mutters, "He's a fuckin' ringer."

I look at the clock. It's one minute past midnight. Gus smiles at me. Mary is smiling, too. Gus says, "He did call down before and asked me to sign him up, asked me to advance the five dollars. Which I did. I hope that's okay with you."

The three grown-ups are looking at me and smiling. Lenny is looking at me, too; his eyes are popping as he mouths the words, "Fuckin' ringer!"

I open my mouth and hear myself say, "Okay." And then it was said.

Fifteen minutes later, out beneath the El, Lenny and me wait to cross at the light even though there isn't any traffic on Roosevelt. I'm staring at a patch of dirty left-over snow which looks like burnt plastic along the curb.

"You *know* they fuckin' split the money," Lenny says. "*Your* money."

"I don't know," I say.

The big guy with the underslung jaw was like a machine, the way he threw four strikes in a row, four frames. We didn't even wait to see what his final score was. Didn't care.

Lenny turns to me, and his eyes are moving like crazy. We still haven't crossed the avenue, even though the light is green now and there's still no traffic. "You *are* a fuckin' idiot. I hope at least you know that."

"I just don't want to live like that," I say.

"Like *what* for fuck's sake?! What the *fuck* are you talkin' about?"

But I don't really know what I meant. I have to think about it. It has something to do with John, I think. I have to think about it. Maybe for a long time. Maybe I'll never stop thinking about it.

WHERE IS LION?

Atar Hadari

Teaching English started for me in the dining room when I was sitting there over my schnitzel and stewed greens and a voice hit me from the back. "It's you, isn't it? You're the boy from England? Leah," she said, moving from question to answer without a pause and sitting in the empty chair. I tended to regard time eating my lunch as private time, unlike nearly everyone else on kibbutz. Never having eaten a private meal in their lives, or not since escaping from Europe anyway, they were accustomed to being accosted over their vegetables. I was, at the time, enjoying a welcome break from one of my shifts at the dishwasher, when along came this shadow and fell across my plate. Actually she was rather more substantial than shadow, a woman the thickness of an oil drum, with glasses round as little coins across her face and a gappy smile, slightly buck-toothed. "I'm Leah, my husband is Yaakov," she said, "We're a matching set. You're from England, right? I learned English in England, on my way here, as a toddler. That's what I do here, I teach the children. After school. I teach the little kids, maybe you can teach the big kids? Eight and up? They already need more than the cards and letters I can show. Maybe you can come up with something? I've got lots of things to give you. If you want the job? Do you want the job? I understand you're working in the kitchen."

I went up to the little house where lessons were given, which turned out to be more or less sixty seconds walk, in a straight line across the grass, from our hut. I literally had to walk out my front door, dodge slightly right to avoid the bench and if I didn't turn left or right but kept on walking thirty seconds I couldn't help but be on time to start teaching the next little varmint. There actually weren't so many, and usually they were late, so I had time to take in the room.

The size of a little men's toilet, maybe, given that the whole building was just a shack, split off into three rooms. There was a back room where one of the Francophone kibbutz founders taught after school math, another room where an Auschwitz survivor offered counseling for kids. (She was a widow.) Leah had the little front room to herself, with a TV for educational videos and a blackboard (which was actually white, to use with felt tips) and a tiny table with the alphabet in plastic littered across it, plus playing cards with words on them, a pile of folders with student work spilling out on yellow legal pads, dog eared and crushed. I never really saw what Leah did with the little ones, beyond the occasional time I popped in to pick up a book I left behind. She just showed me the room, the little fridge where there was milk for my coffee and the cupboard where the huge tin of instant coffee sat. ("You never let the kids get in here, right? They'll drink every drop and leave the rest on the floor like I'm their mother. I'm not their mother."). And she gave me the keys and that was that.

My first victim was Itai, an architect's son. He came in, all staring eyes and buck teeth and turned out to be Leah's great grandson. If truth be told, I don't think I taught more than one or two children in that room that were not her distant relations. It occurs to me that Leah had managed to find a way to coerce both the kibbutz into ensuring that her grandchildren had better English and her grandchildren into accepting said improvement. Doubtless if she'd just offered, as Granny, to help them along they'd have said, "Thanks for the cookies but…") He walked in with his homework and asked me to do it for him.

I took a look. Something about how Spot runs, how many dots, where the tractor is and so on. "You can do that," I said.

"No I can't," he said. "What am I here for if you're not going to do my homework?"

"You're here so that I make sure you DO your homework."

He looked with some skepticism at this proposition.
"You're not going to answer the questions?" he said.
"What question?" I said.
"What does this mean?" he said.
"What does it say?"
"How many spots?"
"How many spots is right," I said.
"What does that mean?"
"Is there a picture?"
"Obviously there's a picture."
"What is it of?"
"A DOG, obviously. Are you mad or something?"
"And what does the dog have on him?"
"Spots?"
"I'm going to read my book. You do your homework."

There was a fifteen minute break while the first victim vacated the premises and the next victim arrived. Lessons began on the hour, more or less, depending when they tipped up on their bikes, and lasted forty five minutes. In between I was supposed to get a coffee, refresh my notes, check my lesson plan, dig out some educational theory to guide me in the next half hour, that sort of thing. More often than not I would avail myself of the proximity of my own hut and pop back to check if my wife was back from the dairy, grab a yoghurt, finish up something I'd tried to translate before but never managed to. I started work later than the other course students but kept working later too, and as winter set in I was often sitting there after dark, which they didn't do in their manual labor. As Itai left he sometimes overlapped with his cousin, Ohad.

Ohad was another grandchild of Leah's, but without the complementary buck teeth. A spindly boy with grim little coal black eyes, he looked as if he was sure you were going to give him the smallest portion of French fries. I tried him with a few of Leah's card games, did his homework with him, but after a little while Ohad actually caught on and started doing his homework himself before he got to the lessons (which I thought was less than sporting, since it prevented me from reading my book.) Eventually we settled into a routine of me setting up a board of mini-scrabble and him playing me short games of around twenty minutes, usually two games a lesson. At first he was stumped and needed a lot of help to make a word or two up but then he got the hang of it and started coming up with things himself and needing only the occasional nod for spelling. ("There's a c in duck, traditionally.") I would suggest words and he would look at me in wonder but they must have been there somewhere in the back of his head (he did have an English speaking grandmother) because after a while he started to come out with them himself. Leah reported that his teachers were pleased and he had stopped making a nuisance of himself in class, even though he still hung at the back with his cousin, Itai.

The last of my trio of eight years old was in no way whatsoever related to Leah. He was however the son of one of the course teachers, Ephraim, whom my wife and I nicknamed Extreme Ephraim for the energy with which he taught his one hour weekly lesson on the weekly bible portion. If Gadi was one of those kibbutznikim who shouted at God, Ephraim was one who shouted at everybody, at least everybody he was teaching. It was not ill-tempered shouting, just impatience to get the word out. ("Why did Abraham have to leave there? Because there were… IDOLS!!") And when he demonstrated how wicked keen Abraham was to get food for his angelic visitors he dashed around the tiny hut, leaping from one side of the flower filled bank of windows to the other so that his sneakers skidded along the floor.

Ephraim stood ram-rod straight in synagogue when the Torah portion was read, more or less the only one to do so amid a sea of sitting, lolling co-religionists, and his son Yonatan would come in dragging his bag as if stones were in it and hung around his neck. Yonatan had red hair, the same red hair that flamed across Ephraim's face, and small grey intelligent eyes and a way of flaring up in instantaneous anger, almost as explosive as his father's classroom style. The only common language I ever found with Yonatan was basketball. When trying to hit upon something he might like to read between lessons the only thing we could agree he might want to read in English was the basketball teams write up and their performance scores. The teams of the NBA were poetry in his ears and he chanted them like a devotee, priest of a cult from an antique land he had never laid eyes on. We went through the basketball words—hoop, basket, court, dribble etc.—more or less in one lesson. That left the words for teams, modes of attack and defense and opened up the field for all other terms for sportsmen, but he only really came alive when he talked about Kobe Bryant.

He knew his scores in every game, he knew where he went to college and who he played for after, knew the town he came from and where he was born. He didn't know anything about the life of a sportsman or what money was, because sometimes he didn't show for his lesson and I asked Leah about it and she said, of Ephraim, "He rides the boy too hard." I tried to explain to Yonatan one day by asking him about money.

"What about it?" he says.

"Do you know what twenty five dollars is?"

"Kobe Bryant earns that in twenty seconds."

"Probably less, but do you know how long it takes the kibbutz to earn it?"

"No idea, why?"

"Because that's what English lessons cost in Tel Aviv, for forty five minutes, and you're getting them here for free, but when you don't show up, the kibbutz is flushing twenty five dollars down the toilet, because that's what the forty five minutes is worth."

He thought about it and said he'd try to get there. Then he missed the next lesson again, then he came back with a list of sports related words he wanted to know the meaning of, things he'd read on the basketball websites, and that kept his interest going for a while.

I first knew there was a problem with Itai the day he refused to leave the classroom when Ohad came in. Itai had arrived late, so we were late starting, and then Ohad arrived on time and Itai wasn't done with his homework, so I said, "Take it with you, we'll finish the day after tomorrow."

"No I won't," Itai said. His little dark eyes looked round the room just like the first time he set foot in it. He looked like a little owl, with buck teeth. A hungry little owl.

"What's the matter?" I said.

"I'm not leaving," Itai said.

"Itai, come on, get outta here," Ohad said.

"He's always asking things," Itai said, "Nobody ever lets me stay anywhere."

"I'm going to get a coffee," I said, "You two talk among yourselves."

And I went out into the little tiny kitchen that Leah kept under lock and key (I let my own students go in and out of there at will, but not when we were running late). I poured milk into a polystyrene cup and added some coffee powder, hot water. By the time I was out of the kitchen Ohad was on the other side of the little teaching room's door and Itai was holding on to the handle from the inside, saying, at the top of his lungs. "You're not coming in here you bastard, it's my room, it's my room. You go away."

Ohad looked up at me, I looked at him.

"His mother is very busy," Ohad said, "She's on the committee for everything."

"So?" I said.

"His brother looks after him."

"His brother's no good?"

"I don't think he likes him very much."

"Do you want a milk chocolate?"

"That would be very nice."

Ohad went into the little kitchen to make himself a milk chocolate. I stood with my coffee outside the little office door. "Itai, do you have many more questions to do?"

"Five."

"Why don't you tell me what they are?"

By the time Ohad came back with his drink Itai was out and had his bag under his arm.

"See you in school?" he said to Ohad.

"See you," Ohad said.

I would see Itai sometimes, on Sabbath afternoons, prowling around the kibbutz with his architect father, trying to sidle up to some bird that had innocently alighted on a frond of date tree or clung to a limb of bush alive with flowers. His father, a huge bear of a man, short-sighted as a moth behind thick coke-bottle glasses, would keep up a running monologue about the mating habits of the birds, their habitations, their flight path from Asia minor, and that was the only time I ever saw Itai look happy. It was as if bird-watching with his father was real-life, the rest an unpleasant veil he had to drag his small face through. I never saw his mother with him, though I knew her by sight, would sometimes see her in the dining hall loading the food on trolleys. She was elected kibbutz secretary sometime in the spring, and I suppose Itai must have thrown his fit right around then. He didn't throw another fit, just found different ways to make his slow, small hoots of distress.

I drew a lion for Yonatan. When we got tired of basketball words one of the only things I could think of to keep him entertained was letting him draw on the black (actually white) board. He took the pens with relish, obviously something nobody ever countenanced letting him do in school. At first he drew a circle, with a furtive look over his shoulder at me, fully expecting me to stop him. I didn't stop him. I said he could draw, as long as he wrote things in between. So he wrote Kobe Bryant's name, and the name of all the other NBA meteors, rising and falling. I drew him a lion, with red felt-tip lines for a mane and a green muzzle, blue staring eyes. When we came in after a day or two, Leah had erased Kobe Bryant's name and that of all the other NBA players but left the lion, and written up her own lesson: "Dog, Dance, Doll". Then Yonatan started scribbling around the edges, drawing stars, "NBA" over and over, like a set of initials for his own gang. I came back from getting my coffee with the room open one afternoon and found Itai had slipped in quietly and wiped the board clean. It was clean and white as when I'd first started teaching there.

I looked at him.

"What did you do that for?"

"Nobody ever lets me stay anywhere," he said. "It's my blackboard."

Next lesson Yonatan came in and went immediately to the blackboard. "Where's the drawing?" he said.

I shrugged.

"Leah?" he said.

"I wasn't here when it happened," I said.

Yonatan took the felt tip, a red one, and wrote on the blackboard, without looking up to check spelling with me: "Where is lion?" He underlined the phrase three times, then he walked out. When he didn't come to the following lesson I sat there a while, reading, then got on the phone to call Leah.

She answered.

"Where's Yonatan?" I said.

"Oh, didn't I tell you?" she said, "Ephraim told me he wouldn't be coming anymore."

"He didn't tell me."

"Maybe he didn't want to hurt your feelings."

This was typical kibbutz. I asked, "Didn't he think he'd hurt your feelings?"

I could almost hear Leah shrug her shoulders, "I don't have any feelings about the French, just about some children. It's a shame about the boy. Well, more time to teach the others."

"Did he give any reason?" I said.

"I'll ask him," she said, "I never thought to ask."

A couple of days later I found an envelope in the conversion course mailbox with my name on it. I opened it. Inside was a print-out of a newspaper story from a U.S. based basketball website. Kobe Bryant had been arrested for rape. On the back of the story was written in small, meticulous Hebrew letters: "If he has to learn another language than Hebrew, I can teach him French."

Ephraim never said a word about it, naturally.

Ohad kept coming and Itai kept coming. Itai actually started coming twice a week after his mother got elected secretary (I guess she wasn't home after school). I kept refusing to do his homework and he kept saying I should and talking to himself, sometimes he would ask himself, quite irritably, "Who is Woody?" I ignored him, or at least those questions which weren't addressed directly to me, and sometimes saw Yonatan walking around on the kibbutz. I would say hello but he would keep on walking, never saying hello, never acknowledging that something may have been lost when he took the removal of the lion personally, and when Ephraim took his son's interests in idols with clay feet as a sign that it was time to limit the access to Babylon and its language.

I don't know if his English suffered, only that I didn't draw another lion on the blackboard because none of the other students seemed to merit it. They all were happy writing things on paper, or playing across a board, or even looking out the window as the dusk slowly settled into darkness and just saying words aloud in English. None of the others seemed to find the poetry in anything, let alone a man they never met the likes of, a man with skin not the colour of their own, thundering down the court to do something unheard of in mid-air under a shaking string basket.

"I'm ok, aren't I?" Itai said.

"You're fine," I said, "Aren't you fine?"

"I wonder sometimes," he said.

Then I would send him home and lock the little room up around the white board and go back to my wife who'd tell me what she learned by sneaking off to her own version of lessons, at the seminary by the plastic factory, where parents in Tel Aviv sent their girls away to learn about God.

I kept seeing Itai around kibbutz, stalking the birds on the trees and looking for somebody to tell him something other than flight paths, but I never saw Yonatan play basketball, and when I started taking adult students on, for Friday mornings, I told myself I didn't miss him. Just the picture of the lion that no-one else ever asked me to draw, and no one else could have mourned even for half a minute, whether their father cared or not, whether their father prayed or not, whether they liked the drawing itself or didn't, but just for the sake of a little color in the whiteness, something you could cheer for in a little room where nothing was said, just words, just the names of hopeful men and animals.

Summer came and I stopped teaching the boys, started working in the dining room, washing dishes, or rather taking them off of the conveyor belt that went through the industrial dish washer and washed them off. A couple of weeks after starting that I find a note in our pigeon hole mail slot asking me to stop in and see the kibbutz general secretary to discuss our residency contract.

I go to see the kibbutz secretary. This is now a two person job, split by the kibbutz since privatization went through. There is an internal kibbutz secretary, responsible for social matters and elected by the kibbutz from among its members, and as I had vaguely remembered it's the mother of one of my English students, Itai. I may even have seen her with him a day or so back, standing at the door to the new improved kibbutz secretary's office. I smiled at him. He smiled back then turned back to her. She was talking and not looking at anything. I see her in the office now and she's another huge woman, but kindly, wears glasses with crazy purple frames. She doesn't look like the mother of a terrified little owl, but I happen to know that she is, even though I've never actually seen her walking around the kibbutz with him on those long walks he takes on the Sabbath looking for birds to talk to.

The other secretary is Ilan, former secretary of a secular kibbutz down the road, now hired in to be a no-nonsense manager, somebody without any ties, the hatchet man. He's lanky and has acne scars on his cheeks, sprouts curly red hair and doesn't wear a yarmulke, though he carries one about with him in case he's asked to make up a minyan. My wife and I actually know him better than Ora because he gave us a lift once, from kibbutz to Afula and chatted about our various endeavors, musical and literary. Last time I saw him outside this building he turned to somebody he was talking to, somebody official, and said, "Hey, did you know that guy translates poetry?"

As I walk in this time though Ora greets me and says, "Ilan, why don't you start." Ora and Ilan are sitting on one side of the boardroom table. The empty chairs are echoey and large around us.

"We don't think your work is going to pan out here on kibbutz," Ilan says, "We'd like to know when you plan to leave."

"My wife works in the dairy," I said, "I was told there was no pressure to leave."

"We're reviewing the whole situation with non-member resident contracts," Ilan says, "And there's a shortage of flats. Gadi's daughter—is it Gadi's daughter, Ora?"

"Yes, Gadi's daughter. You know her?"

"I know her," I said.

"She's getting married. We need a flat for them. There are other couples coming, couples who are candidates for membership."

"What do they do for work?"

"Well, I think one of them is a neighbor of yours. A doctor?"

"Oh yes," I say. "They're nice."

"They are nice, aren't they?" Ora says.

"He might join the kibbutz," Ilan says. "We need you to clear your flat by June. Is there a problem with that?"

I ask how long we'd have if we didn't know where to go, Ilan is reluctant to stretch it beyond July. On my way back to our flat, I pass some kids playing in the street, the same kids who always run and shout and kid each other and have no time for adults who aren't their own, and always moved out of my way. This time, with the un-erring instinct of children for weakness, they actually throw a cheeky word or two at me. I can't remember what. I can't remember what the kid looked like. But I remember they all laughed and I remember saying to myself, "We don't live here anymore."

My wife took another pregnancy test, went into the bathroom with another white piece of plastic, came out holding it again and we waited and waited and the blue line again appeared, strong as a Conservative party manifesto gleaming up out of the little white box.

I told my wife to stop working at the dairy. I went down to the dairy to tell her boss, Joel. She didn't have the heart. He was a plump man sitting in front of a wall of photographs of much dourer people, most of them wearing grey beards. All the dead managers of the dairy. They seemed to frown at him every time he took a bite of his strudel. He took some papers out of his desk when he saw me coming.

"Look," he said, "I have your wife's new work contract. Now she's got citizenship we can employ her properly."

"She's pregnant," I said. "She can't work here anymore."

"She's pregnant?" he said. He looked like he was suddenly pinched in the stomach and shifted uncomfortably. He was the one person I met who seemed surprised to hear that we were going. The only one who acted like we might have been staying. He opened his drawer and threw her contract back inside it with a sigh. He shook my hand. As I left he looked at the remains of his strudel as if he no longer wanted anything to do with it.

Then the bleeding started. Slowly, but a drop when you're waiting for a baby to live is more than an ocean in a holiday photo. A drop, then another drop. I told her to lie down. She was already not going to work.

I took her in a cab into Afula. We didn't trust anybody's word about anything anymore, anywhere within a radius of twenty miles from the kibbutz and its surrounding settlements.

We sat in the waiting room of a small white building. The doctor opened the door and said "Come in" in Hebrew; he had blue black hair, slicked back like he combed it each morning in front of a mirror. He spoke a gentler Hebrew than any my wife had heard in the valley.

He listened to her talk slowly, ordered tests, scribbled on a pad.

"There's bleeding," my wife said. She looked at him.

"We'll see what we can see," he said. He smiled at her, gently.

The doctor came out of his door again and called us. We sat down in front of his desk.

"There is still a fetus," he said.

"What about the bleeding?" my wife said.

"There is bleeding, there is always bleeding in a pregnancy. There is still a fetus, and the fetus is alive."

"Thank God," my wife rocked, holding her stomach.

"Is there anything we can do?" I said.

"Pray," he said.

We packed all our things on the kibbutz lorry, that delivered plastic sheets. As we left, the little hut where we had sat for seven months started being torn down. They were expanding it. All I could see were the walls being torn and the windows that I watched teachers stand in front of being removed, one by one. Then they walked out with a huge book case made out of stripped pine. It was the length of the entire wall about to be knocked down. Gadi was standing next to me.

"I made that," he said. "By hand."

"What's going to happen to it?"

"You want it? Take it to Jerusalem."

We loaded Gadi's handiwork on to the kibbutz lorry. It made a kind of wall, next to the piles of boxes of books.

Our neighbor the doctor said he would drive us down. We packed the lorry and only left out toothbrushes, a few odds and ends—socks, a knife and fork, soap. The things you take inside a car, if your worldly goods are coming on a lorry. Then the doctor showed up at our house at nine o'clock in the morning and said his wife wouldn't let him drive that afternoon. She was nervous, he said, pregnant. I said goodbye and walked back into our little kibbutz flat, taking the keys out of the door.

I went into the office to see Ora and gave her the keys. "Oh, you're going?" she said. "It's only March. Where are you going?"

"Away," I said.

The bus to Jerusalem was late, but we loaded the last things on the truck and made our way onto the bus..

I saw Yonatan on a visit to the kibbutz, years later. He walked past me, looking straight down with his blue eyes hard as stones at the bottom of a pool. He was walking as fast as a man chasing after a basket ball that keeps bouncing just a little way out of his reach. I thought to say something, but after all, what could I say. He had the focused expression on his face his father used to have. And I thought about the lion he had so admired on that little white board and how he had asked where it had gone. That was the first question anyone asked about where we were going, before we even knew that we had started to be gone.

A MUTT MOMENT

Michael Duffy

Hoops. Night League Ball. Home game against the neighboring town of Sharon. Sharon, mostly Jews, with a black six-six center. Thoroughbreds every one, college-bound from the second the doctor slapped their lucky little asses. Even their uniforms (uniforms, for God's sake, in town-ball tournaments!) showed where they came from and where they were going. Smooth, well-practiced, well-coached. Frank's town team, Stoughton, tossed out its usual suspects—broken-nosed Micks, freckle-faced mulattoes, mix-breed mutts of all countries and continents. Scoring by ones, Frank's team was up twenty to nineteen. Victory at twenty-one; gotta win by two.

Forty-five minutes earlier, Frank had changed out of his work clothes, steel-toed boots and dungarees, behind a sprawling oak tree that afforded only the pretense of privacy. He knew junior high girls came to the games early, just to get spots along the Jones School fence nearest the tree, where they could peep and giggle as the guys hung it out while changing. But the guys didn't care. The game was more important than modesty. It was about pride, town pride, individual pride. The players would charge to the court directly from their various jobs—scraped knuckles, dirt packed under their nails—and go directly to the tree, the unofficial outdoor locker-room. Some used their cars but slipping behind the tree was faster, no nonsense. Time was the critical factor. The games started so early that the guys had no choice, not if they wanted to play. And everybody wanted to play. And if you didn't play, you came anyway. You came to watch because it was your town. Because it was Stoughton. Because it was summer. Because it was basketball.

The only thing that mattered to Frank, then or now, was Krieger. Jonathan Krieger. Gotta keep him from embarrassing me, Frank thought when he arrived and raced to the tree. He had turned his back to the giggles then, wondering if the ridicule was deserved, if the underwear he wore was the one with the two-inch rip in back. A surge of adolescent squealing confirmed that it was. He had flushed, more with anger than embarrassment, but now, thirty minutes later, it was a forgotten thing. Because now he was in the game. The game was the thing. The game. The stands were filled, and his team was up twenty-nineteen.

Krieger exploded forward, catching Frank flat-footed at the top of the key. As he blew past, Frank lost his balance. He pitched backwards, stretching as he fell, his long arm still focused, still trying to extend as he landed. Even falling he could hear someone laughing at him. But it didn't matter. The ball had caught the toe of Frank's sneaker and shot off at an angle out of bounds.

"Shit!" Krieger yelled. "Foul."

The ref shook his head, lifted his foot, and swung it back and forth. "Kickball." He dashed to the sideline and quickly retrieved the ball from a fan. All business, aware of the crowd by the focused way he ignored it, the ref planted himself—whistle in mouth, ball on hip—just out of bounds, waiting for Sharon to put the ball in play. Instead, they called a time-out.

Frank's team returned to their end of the court—there was no bench—and coach Fleming said, "Nice 'D' on that last play, Frank."

"Don't bust my chops, okay? I don't need that right now."

"Who's busting? Whether it was luck or intentional, it worked. That's all that matters, it worked. He had you jocked."

At one time, Bill Fleming was Frank's idol, the senior star when Frank was a freshman. He had graduated three years ago as team captain, left for a year of Single-A ball in the Pirates organization and then, to Frank's disappointment, returned home. It was a decision that forever diminished Bill in Frank's mind. Each time he saw him, Frank wondered why people like Bill came back to a place like Stoughton, even when blessed with the talent and the lungs to run away. Bill began poking each player in turn with a long bony finger, barking defensive placements and offensive possibilities. Frank noticed from his greater height that Bill's hair was thinning on top. Bill paid no attention to Frank. He knew Frank understood what needed to be done. At this point, they both realized it wasn't the coaching that was going to win or lose this game, it was the players. Bill was just filling the space Sharon's time-out had created.

Krieger caught the inbound pass. He was an erect dribbler, proud, never shielding the ball, daring his opponent to swipe. Frank had played him every summer for years. He knew Jonathan's tricks. He knew that if he shot out his hand, the ball would disappear the instant Frank shifted his balance. And Frank liked that. Because Krieger was the real thing—a ballplayer. A true baller. He was smart, played smart. And hard. Shoulders coming out, elbows flying. One flick at the tempting ball and Krieger would be three steps past before Frank could recover. Frank wouldn't bite. So Krieger came in.

He came directly at Frank, in the famous Krieger crouch, his knees pressing the long straight body down with each step like someone compressing a spring. Then he stutter-stepped, still coming forward, still face-on, still daring with the ball unprotected. Each bounce said come on, Frankie boy, here it is. Come and get it. Come and get it, mensch. He inched closer and closer. And then, crouching ridiculously low, Krieger began his trademark cross-body dribble. Instantly Frank could feel all around him the ripple of tension surging through the crowd. In the background, he could see more faces strain forward to line the court's edge.

The ball pounded hard off the court—hammer-hard!—boom-boom, boom-boom, as if Krieger was suddenly angry. One perfect Vee after another—boom-boom, boom-boom—left hand, right hand, left bounce, right bounce. The other players moved away, spreading it out.

It was one-on-one time.

Come and get it, come and get it, boom-boom, boom-boom. A metronome, a metronome on a wound-up spring. Along the sidelines and even deeper into the crowd, things grew quiet. Even the junior high girls became still. Boom-boom, boom-boom. This is what everyone came to see. Cocky. In-your-face. Basketball.

"What's the matter, Jonathan?" Frank called out, loud enough for all to hear, his voice piercing the thick summer air. "Leave your testes at home tonight?"

Deep in the crowd someone cackled, and Krieger was off. His body surged, as if going right. Head, shoulders, even the ball shot to the right. But his legs, his legs had other plans. The real cut was left, hard, to his weak side. This time, Frank's balance was solid. This time his hands were ready, waiting, poised, as if Frank knew what Krieger was going to do before Krieger knew himself, as if Frank had read the script beforehand. Frank's hands, his long delicate artistic hands, fired out. He didn't so much slap at the ball as snatch it. Outright. Off the ground. Right out of the dribble.

And then Frank was off. A long smooth sail.

There was no one in front of him. By the time his first dribble hit the court, the silence had exploded into a thunderous cheer. Frank pushed the ball far out in front of him, way out, almost beyond his grasp. He literally had to race to catch up to it. He wanted no one near him when he got to the basket. Six dribbles and he soared up, leaving the earth from just inside the foul line. His body stretched, arcing, the ball resting solidly in the meat of his right palm as he angled for the hoop. The crowd hushed, drawing breath, waiting along with the other straggling players for the indignity of the dunk. But then, as Frank's leap reached its apex, he relaxed. He could feel Krieger, close and closing. He adjusted himself just as the ball neared the rim and raised his other hand. He seemed to caress the leather, cup it, hold it, all in the briefest of seconds. Then he simply dropped it through, as Krieger's palm slapped against the backboard above his head. Frank was still descending when the crowd reacted. And that was it. Game over.

Mutts—one. Thoroughbreds—zero.

NEXT SATURDAY

Deirdre Murray-Holmes

That summer, my mother could not figure out for the life of her how to stop Jamie from going under the fence to play baseball with the zombies. Every Saturday morning about seven I'd hear him crawling down the trellis outside his window and pedaling off across the yard, his bat tied to his backpack with an old shoelace and slung across his back like a rifle.

People always knew Jamie and I were brothers right away because we looked so much alike even though he was five years older than me, but looks is where the similarity ended. He was brave and self-confident, I was shy and a little bit nerdy. In school, he got detention; I got the perfect attendance award. He played baseball and football and soccer and whatever else was on offer while I stuck to my books and the chess club. I told him over and over he was really screwing things up for himself, that he'd never get to college if he didn't change his way.

"Like you're ever going to accomplish anything playing chess! You can't even get a real person to play with you!" he'd shout. I'd give him my best very-hurt-feelings face, and we'd laugh, and sometimes he'd try to tackle me. I guess he thought he was being fun and brotherly, but I always yelled at him to stop, that he was hurting me. I'd never tell him, but I was so jealous I thought I'd die. I think he knew because sometimes he'd ask me if I wanted to play catch or watch the game with him. I tried to learn all the rules and pitches and funny phrases, but it was all over when I started trying to tell him how the sacrifice fly was like the Queen's Gambit.

For the longest time I had no idea where he was going every Saturday morning. I wondered if maybe he had a girlfriend and didn't want mom and me to know, or more likely didn't want her to meet us. It was the smell that finally gave him away. Dust, and the faint odor of corpse, especially if he'd had to slide or ram into the catcher trying to beat the throw home. Apparently this happened more often than might be expected—the zombies were slower than normal people and what might only amount to a double in a typical game could easily end up a home run when playing with the dead. I caught on to the whole scheme sooner than mom, but it was only a matter of time because she did our laundry.

"Why do your clothes always smell like moldy food?" she asked him one Sunday.

"I don't know" he shrugged, and went out the screen door crunching a green apple, and that seemed to be the end of it. But she must have asked around because it was only a few days later that she was sitting at the kitchen table, cup of burnt coffee and freshly lit cigarette in front of her, waiting for him when he got home.

"Jamie, I need to ask you something." She sighed, took a long drag on her cigarette and looked really serious. "Have you been spending time with zombies?"

He seemed to hesitate, and then got a sort of determined look on his face.

"Yeah. So?"

"So? So they're *zombies*, Jamie! You have lots of perfectly normal friends—why would you want to spend time with people like that?"

"People like *what*, mom? You don't even know any zombies! Have you ever even been on the reservation? Do you know *anything* about them?"

"I know they make your clothes stink. What on earth do you *do* out there?"

"We play baseball, mom. That's all. Just play baseball."

"Well that's just ridiculous. You can play baseball at school."

"They're my friends, mom! They actually want me around, which is more than I can say for you."

"What? You don't really believe that. Of course we want you around, right Tommy?"

They both turned toward me and I was suddenly terrified, but I'd rather have died than make Jamie mad at me.

"Well, maybe if he's just going out there to play baseball, it's not such a big deal."

"Of course it's a big deal! Everybody knows they're a terrible influence! They stink and they make you stink. It's a rotten way to live, and I feel sorry for them, but they choose to live that way and you can do much better."

Jamie was turning red. "See, you don't know anything! None of them chose to become zombies! Most of the stuff people say about zombies is just made up. TV only shows the bad stuff and tries to make everybody believe they're all like that. Well they're not, mom, they're not!"

"Whether that's true or not doesn't really matter, Jamie. As long as you live in my house, you're not going to spend time with those people. That's final."

She told him if he went there again he'd be grounded or she'd take away his phone or maybe both. But the next Saturday I heard his window slide open at 7am just like usual.

When he got home, mom had taken his mp3 player off his dresser, but he didn't say a word.

One day the next week I saw mom pacing back and forth in the kitchen, talking on her phone.

"Don't tell me this is just a phase, Tom! Are you even listening to me? This is our son I'm talking about. Playing baseball with zombies, for chrissake! Are you going to tell me you think that's okay?"

In the closest thing to yelling I ever heard from her, she told him she didn't want her son playing with those filthy creatures, and it should bother my dad just as much as it bothered her. But apparently it didn't, and she jabbed the off button and snapped her phone shut.

This went on week after week all summer: Jamie would sneak out Saturday morning, Mom would bust him when he came home in the late afternoon, they'd argue and say pretty much the same things about fairness and whose roof it was and how much extra detergent it was taking to get the smell out. Mom would ground him or unplug the wi-fi or confiscate his phone, he'd promise not to go again, and the whole thing would start over the next weekend.

After a few weeks, mom seemed to give up. She met him in the yard on his way out and told him if he wanted to go that much, he should just do what he wanted (he would anyway), she wouldn't stop him. He seemed shocked, but just nodded silently then got on his bike and rode off slowly toward the highway.

The next two weeks were awful. Mom drank pot after pot of coffee, making new ones when the old ones had burned down to a smelly black tar, and smoked a pack a day, and I couldn't figure out if she was mad or sad or what. Both of them came and went without saying a word to each other or me.

Late one Saturday a few weeks later I was up in my room reading "Pawn Strategies to a Better Endgame" when my door flew open and Jamie came crashing through. The stink was enough to knock you over, but he didn't even seem to notice.

"She was *there*, Tommy! She was *there*!"
"What? Who?"

"Mom!" he practically shrieked. "Mom showed up at the game today!"

It took everything I had not to burst out laughing, but I figured that would only make him angrier.

"No way!" was all I could manage.

"It would have been bad enough if she had just shown up and made me leave, but she *stayed*! And *cheered*! I was totally humiliated."

"Did you win?"

"Did I—did you hear me?! I said Mom was at my game!"

"Well, sometimes I think it would be nice if somebody came to watch me play chess. Wasn't it nice to have Mom there cheering for you?"

"Unbelievable! You're just as bad as her!" On his way out he slammed the door so hard the little wooden letter T nailed up on the outside fell off.

I didn't understand why he was so angry. I was trying to make him feel better, and now I felt like crying. But a second later I started to feel really mad. At him, for saying I was like mom. At mom, for going to the game without me. I ran and opened the door and shouted down the hallway "you'll never see me at one of your stupid games, ever!"

"Good!" he shouted back from downstairs. I picked up the little T and tried to put it back on the door, but the nail had fallen out and I couldn't find it.

Now I did cry. Just a little. I'd kept his secret for weeks before mom found out, and I'd stood up for him when she did. That should have counted for something. It wasn't fair. Just because he was 16 didn't mean he could do what he wanted all the time. And it didn't mean he could treat his brother like crap. He was supposed to be looking out for me, after all.

Mom bounced through the front door about half an hour later.

"Wow! What a day!" She glanced into the living room where Jamie was slouched on the floor leaning against the couch, scowling and rapidly punching buttons on the game controller.

"What a game! You should have seen it, Tommy!"

She was a blur of activity, unpacking the little red and white cooler with the leftovers of her lunch. "He's the pitcher, did you know that?" Leaning around the wall and aiming her voice directly into the living room, she called out "My son is the pitcher!"

Jamie jumped up and threw the controller down on the couch with a dramatic overhand swing.

"That's IT!" he yelled, and ran up the stairs to his room, slamming the door louder than ever.

Mom just watched him, a little smile turning up one corner of her mouth.

"Why'd you go today, mom? He's really mad."

Her smile seemed to fade a little. "I'm not really sure, sweetie. I just woke up with that same horrible feeling I had last Saturday, and the Saturday before that, and I knew I had to do something. Anything. The only thing I could think of was going to watch."

"I want to go." I half-mumbled.

"You do?"

"Um, yeah, I guess. Yeah."

"I think that's a great idea!" The smile returned to her face. "Next Saturday, we'll go together." She lit a cigarette and started making a pot of coffee, humming to herself.

I was overjoyed, and I didn't really know why. Yet somewhere deep inside I knew this wasn't going to end well.

Every day that week I got more and more excited. I dug out the glove Jamie had given me for my birthday a few years back to take in case there was a foul ball. It was stiff as a board but I rubbed it with Vaseline for five straight days until at least it didn't pinch my hand when I had it on. I practiced wearing it with one finger sticking out the back like the pros.

Jamie, meanwhile, spent the week avoiding us both. Mom would ask him if he wanted dinner and he'd snap "can't—homework" and head up the stairs, slamming his bedroom door as always.

But somehow mom and I kept our good mood about the whole thing in spite of Jamie. Day by day the picture in my head got bigger: at first I imagined a little dirt field, which over the next few days became a big, professional looking field with bright lights and a hot dog stand. Dirty zombies turned into guys with matching uniforms, even hats. My brother would hit six home runs, pitch a no-hitter, and his teammates would carry him around the field on their shoulders. By Friday I was about ready to explode. I didn't sleep all night, and when mom knocked on my door Saturday morning I shot up like it was Christmas.

"Ready?"

"Am I ever!" Best jeans, best t-shirt (Jamie wouldn't tell me their team colors but I was guessing green), and Dad's old Pirates cap.

We lived on about two acres of pretty much nothing but dried up knee-high weeds. Bunches of grasshoppers flew up in front of us with every step, and we crushed them by the dozen as we waded through the grass and crossed the highway into the trees on the other side. Soon I spotted Jamie's red Schwinn leaning against the chain link under a sign that said in large faded red letters "Do Not Enter" and in smaller black letters "Private Property of the Zombie Nation" and that weird, squiggly logo nobody could figure out. I wondered how we were going to get over the top, but mom walked right up to it and threw her stuff down like she was going to start climbing. Then I saw her push the cooler down through a hole someone had dug under the bottom, and she got down and wriggled through. I couldn't believe it. My mom crawling under a fence in the dirt? I think she could tell I was shocked, because I could hear her saying something like "I wasn't always a fat middle-aged housewife."

She stood on the other side dusting herself off for a few seconds, then said "are you coming or what?" I think I just kept staring, and finally she shrugged, picked up the cooler and walked away. I scrambled after her.

It was about a quarter of a mile before we came to the makeshift diamond. Somebody had scratched lines in the ground for the batter's box and scooped dirt together to make a tiny pitcher's mound. First base was a deteriorating old shoe, second looked like a piece of shirt or jacket, third was half a hubcap, and home plate was just that—a paper plate with a rock on it to keep it from blowing away. Jamie sat on the ground about where the home team dugout would have been, along with his team.

The pitcher was just entering his windup when we reached the treeline along third base. He threw the ball with surprising speed for something that usually has trouble even walking real fast. The batter just stood there as the ball went by, a solid *thwap* indicating the catcher had it. Whether the batter had a good eye or was just caught looking (assuming he still had eyes) I couldn't begin to guess. The umpire straightened up and slowly jabbed the air with a fist and the catcher returned the ball to the pitcher, all just like a real game.

We started looking for a good spot to watch just as the pitcher was letting loose his next pitch, and to our surprise the batter swung fairly hard and actually hit the ball, sending it high in the air toward right field. With that weird shuffle they have, the batter took off toward first as fast as his legs would carry him, which wasn't very fast, but the outfielders weren't getting to the ball very fast either. It plunked into the dirt and the right fielder reached it about ten seconds later. The batter was just about halfway to his base. It was going to be a close one.

With one hand the zombie picked up the ball and made a decent throw toward first, but it fell short and the first baseman had to walk out a few steps and lean down to pick it up. He turned back toward first and took the two steps to get there, his foot touching the old shoe at what looked like the same time as the runner. Everyone expectantly looked at the first base umpire, and it seemed like almost a full minute passed before he raised both arms in a waist high sweeping gesture. Safe.

"Yes! Woo hoo!" mom shouted, and that's when Jamie looked up and saw us. I'll never forget the look of utter horror in his eyes. He looked around at the other players to see if anyone else had seen us yet, and then scrambled to his feet and ran around the edge of the field in our direction.

"Mom, I told you not to come here! And why'd you bring him with you? That's great. That's just great." He was obviously furious, yet trying to keep his voice low to avoid drawing attention.

"But I had such a great time last week, and Tommy wanted to come! I think it's great we could get him away from that damn chess board for a while, don't you?" She beamed, and I looked at her incredulously as her last words sunk in. I thought she liked chess.

Jamie didn't seem to be buying any of it, and he turned and glared at me with such anger I was almost sort of scared.

"Jamie, I'm sorry, I…"

A dirty look was apparently all I was worth, because he turned right back to mom.

"You just came here to embarrass me in front of my friends! You're ruining everything!"

But mom just kept smiling. "I guess there's not really any stands, huh? Just as well, probably don't want to get too close anyway, huh? Whew!" She waved her hand in front of her nose, laughed and started spreading a checkered tablecloth out in the dirt. Jamie stared with disbelief while mom sat down and opened the little cooler and pulled out a triangle-shaped wedge of something wrapped in wax paper.

Mom thrust the sandwich toward him. "PBJ? It's your favorite!" He ignored her completely except for a low grunt. He kicked the dirt and stormed off toward his teammates, who kept playing and didn't even seem to have noticed they had visitors.

"I hate you! I wish I was dead!" he yelled back over his shoulder.

This caught the attention of the umpire, who walked over and stood in front of Jamie, made an elaborate (albeit slow) bunch of gestures, pointing toward himself, then miming biting something, then sweeping his arm out toward the other zombies.

"What? No, no, I don't really mean it. It's just something people say when they're mad."

They say zombies don't have feelings, but this one was doing a pretty fair imitation of looking hurt and confused. He scrunched up what was left of his face, lowered his head to his chest and shook it slowly.

"What's the score?" mom yelled out.

Jamie ignored her, but the umpire held up two fingers on his left hand and one on his right, so we took that to mean two to one.

"And what inning is it?" she yelled at him.

The zombie paused as if he had to think about it, and finally raised three fingers which we took to mean third, although it's possible he was just out of fingers.

The next at bat was pretty dull. Three pitches and no swings and the inning was over.

Jamie's team started walking to their positions, some faster than others. Jamie bounded up to the mound and started into a series of stretches and twists that looked just like the big leaguers. He ground the ball between his palms, socked it into his glove a few times, ground it a little more, tugged on his cap, licked his fingers, wiped them on his jeans, rolled his shoulders three or four times forward, then three or four back. He turned his head and spit, then took a big breath.

As mad as I was at him, I was mesmerized. I mean, I knew Jamie played baseball, and I knew he was a pitcher, but holy cow, he really knew his stuff. He looked like a real pro, leaning forward and staring intently at the catcher, probably getting signs.

By this time the other players were mostly in position, and the batter seemed ready. Jamie stood up straight, pulled up one knee, leaned back just a little and threw the ball. *Thwap!* and the catcher had it. The ump punched the air. Jamie's second pitch sailed right past the batter for another strike. On the third pitch, the batter took a big swing but only succeeded in spinning himself around and falling down.

It was pretty much the same story with the next two batters, and just like that there were three outs. It occurred to me that at this rate, it was going to be one of the fastest games ever.

But I hadn't accounted for the time Jamie wasn't pitching or batting. Zombie baseball, as it turns out, is all about patience. They all seemed to know exactly where they should be and what they should be doing, it just took them twice as long to do it. Plus all kinds of time gets wasted because body parts are loose, or falling off, or simply missing.

Still, they were getting by, so mom and I ate our sandwiches and drank our grape sodas and cheered for Jamie's team and booed their opponents. It was two full innings before it was Jamie's turn at bat, and I couldn't wait.

Once again, Jamie went though a big routine. Tapping the plate with the bat, crouching down and sort of bouncing a little, finally bringing the bat up and moving the end in four tiny circles over his head, then suddenly straightening up and putting a hand out behind him toward the ump to ask for time. Then he'd go through the whole thing one more time, until finally he was ready.

I never saw a pitcher honestly get one by him. About a third of the time they ended up in the dirt, and about another third they were so far out of the strike zone it was laughable. The rest of the time, if that ball was even a little hittable, Jamie would knock it sky high. And that's just what he did this time—a high fly that should have been easily caught by the right fielder, but the poor guy was still exhausted from that close call back in the third and the ball dropped about ten feet away from him. He made a huge effort to get to it, but Jamie was running full tilt and by the time the zombie got to the ball Jamie was rounding second and heading for third. The third base coach was windmilling his arms (*there's a potential disaster*, I thought) to say "keep going" and Jamie did. Right past third at top speed, the ball now in the hands of the second baseman.

Mom and I were both going wild, screaming and jumping up and down and clapping.

The second baseman drew back his arm and let go with a monster throw toward home, and the catcher stepped right across the plate and almost completely into the third base line. Jamie clearly wasn't slowing down for anybody, and just as the catcher reached out for the ball, Jamie plowed into him with all the force of a delivery truck.

Dust flew everywhere, and for a few seconds the only thing we could see was a tangle of arms and legs and a paper plate floating off toward the backfield. We had no idea what was happening. *He's gonna stink something fierce tonight* I remember thinking.

Then Jamie jumped to his feet and turned to the ump for the call. Again, the slow motion waist-high arms sweep to indicate "safe."

We screamed and cheered and high-fived each other, and I heard Jamie yell "yeah!" but then he caught my eye and his face went back to being angry.

Nobody had noticed that the catcher didn't seem to be getting up. Finally, several zombies went over and looked down at him, then one grabbed his collar and started dragging him away. Another zombie picked up the leg he'd left behind and absently threw it toward the treeline.

"If we could only get them to throw the ball like that." mom said, and then laughed at her own joke.

The rest of the game was sort of boring except when Jamie was playing. Everything seemed to be in slow motion except for sudden bursts of excitement when Jamie hit another home run or struck out another batter. In the end it was a slaughter, Jamie's team winning ten to one. After that last pitch, mom applauded like crazy and yelled "yeah" and "woo hoo" until she was hoarse.

When it was all over the players formed two lines in the middle of the field, Jamie in the lead, and slowly walked by high-fiving each other, brown dust going up in little puffs every time their hands met. I could just barely hear Jamie saying "good game, good game, good game." After the last zombie passed, Jamie grabbed up his bat and ball and glove and headed toward home, still looking angry.

"Great job, honey!" shouted mom. "See you at home!" She threw him a loud kiss. On the way home she kept up a steady monologue about the game—was I watching when this happened, did I see when that happened. I threw in a "yeah" or "uh huh" once or twice, but mostly I was thinking about whether Jamie was ever going to talk to me again.

The next Saturday mom packed the cooler as usual, and even though Jamie had acted mad all week I was still just as excited to see him play. But when we went out the front door, there was his bike leaning against the house. We went up the stairs and mom knocked gently on his door.

"Sweetie? Are we going to the game?"

"Go away! I'm sick!"

"But honey, aren't you supposed to pitch?"

"Go away!"

As awful as the whole situation had started out, I was still really disappointed. But I figured there was always next Saturday.

But next Saturday he was sick too, and the week after that. And then it just sort of wasn't discussed, and before I knew it school started and things were back to normal.

That fall Jamie (who now wanted to be called Jim) went to work for Mr. Hassett down at the hardware store and I signed up for student government and yearbook. If the subject of baseball came up we'd talk about the Pirates or the Indians or who was going to the series but never about those games out on the reservation. Mom never brought it up either, which struck me as a little weird since she was so into it for those few weeks, but who knows why adults do anything. Not long after, she joined a stop-smoking group and they started meeting in our living room. I never realized how bad burnt coffee smelled until I didn't have the odor of cigarettes to distract me.

In the end, it felt like that summer just sort of disappeared along with all the leaves, and as I watched Jaimie—Jim—go out the door to work in his bright yellow Hassett's Hardware vest, it kind of seemed like he'd disappeared too.

One chilly Saturday afternoon a couple of weeks later, I walked across the highway, crawled under the fence and looked for the place where we watched Jamie play. But every field I found looked the same, and none of them looked really familiar. Apparently even the zombies had moved on to something new. The sky was turning dark with gray autumn clouds and I was about to leave when I noticed someone standing in the trees across the field. After a while most zombies start to look alike, but I could have sworn it was the umpire from Jamie's game. He raised one hand in a little wave.

I waved back and after a minute we both started walking toward each other. When we met in the middle I realized I had no idea what to say or why I was even there, and we both stood in silence until he reached up and pointed at the logo on my jacket: a little embroidered chess piece with flames around it and the words "Rook n' Roll". I laughed, and he looked confused, and I motioned him to sit on the ground with me. From my backpack I dug out the little wooden game box I carried everywhere that had a chessboard on the inside. Opening it carefully, I unfolded the board and put it down between us. My new friend seemed fascinated, so I handed him a pawn. He slowly reached across and took it, and I pointed and he put it on the right square. The tiniest smile crossed his face, and I smiled a little too.

I wondered how hard it would be to teach a bunch of zombies to play chess. No harder than teaching them baseball, I figured. Plus it was more their speed. Next Saturday I'll come back, I thought, and teach a whole bunch of them. Next Saturday will be the start of something big.

HOG'S HEART

Gordon Weaver

Nor mouth had, no nor mind, expressed
What heart heard of, ghost guessed

It is everything and it is nothing. Hog says, "Different times, it's different feeling. Sometimes I feel like that it might could just be a feeling. Sometimes, I feel it is happening right then."

"Goddamnit, Hog," says Dr. Odie Anderson. Hog, perched on the edge of the examination table, cannot be more precise. He feels ridiculous, feet suspended above the floor like a child's, wearing a flimsy paper hospital gown that, like a dress, barely covers his scarred knees. Though the air conditioning sighs incessantly, he exudes a light sweat, pasting the gown to his skin, thighs and buttocks cemented to the table's chill metal surface. "Is it pains?" the doctor says. "Is it chest pain? Is it pain in your arm or shoulder? Is it pain you feel in your neck or your jaw?"

Says Hog, "It might could be I just imagine it sometimes." Dr. Odie Anderson, team physician, sits in his swivel chair, shabby lab coat thrown open, crumpled collar unbuttoned, necktie askew, feet up and crossed on his littered desk. Hog sees the holes in the soles of the doctor's shoes. Odie

Anderson's head lolls slightly, canted. His eyes, bulging and glossy, like a man with arrested goiter, roll. His tongue probes his cheeks and teeth, as if he seeks to dislodge a particle of his breakfast. He licks his lips, moistens the rim of scraggly beard around his open mouth; some say the doctor wears the beard to conceal chronic acne, but Hog thinks it is to hide a weak chin.

"Damn," says Dr. Anderson, "is it choking? Your breath hard to get? Sick to your stomach a lot? To avoid looking at him, Hog closes his eyes, wipes sweat from the lids with thumb and forefinger.

All like that. Sometimes." Hog turns his head to the window before opening his eyes. The rectangle of searing morning light dizzies him. He grips the edge of the table with both hands, tries not to hear the doctor, feels the trickle of sweat droplets course downward from the tonsure of hair above his jug ears, from the folds of flesh at his throat, the sausage rolls of fat at the back of his neck, from his armpits. He represses malarial shudders as the air conditioning blows on his bare back where the paper gown gaps.

"You-all want me to send you to Jackson to the hospital? You want all kind of tests, swallowing radioactivity so's they can take movies of your veins?" Almost touching the window pane, the leaves of a magnolia tree shine in the brilliant light as if filmed with a clear grease. One visible blossom looks molded of dull white wax, that it will surely melt and run if the sun's

rays reach it. Beyond the magnolia, a swath of campus greensward shimmers in the heat like green fire. The length of sidewalk Hog can see is empty. The cobbled street beyond is empty, stones buckled and broken.

"Not now," Hog says. "I got a season starting. I might could maybe go come spring if I can get off recruiting a while."

"Well now," Dr. Anderson is saying, "you *are* fat as a damn house, Hog, and your blood pressure is high. You might could be a classic case, except you don't smoke and last I heard your old daddy's still kicking up there to Hot Coffee.

"Daddy's fine. He's a little bitty man, though. I come by my size favoring Mama's people." A pulpcutter's truck, stacked high as a hayrick with pine logs, passes on the street, and then a flatbed truck loaded with stumps chained to the bed, on their way up to the Masonite plant at Laurel.

"You just as leave get dressed, Hog," the doctor says. "I can't find nothing wrong in there. Hell, damn it to hell, you strong as stump whiskey and mean as a yard dog!" Hog focuses on buttoning his shirt, zipping his fly to evade Dr. Anderson's leering cackle. He feels, he believes, the weight of the sodden air outside on the campus, pressure mounting, that it will shatter the window glass, crush the building, the room, the doctor and himself. "Damnit, you the Hog !" Odie Anderson says.

Sometimes it is everything. It is the sticky, brittle feel of sweat drying on his skin, the drafty breath of the air conditioning that makes him shudder in spasms, raises goose-bumps on his forearms. It is the late August morning's heat and humidity hovering like a cloud outside, waiting to drop on him, clutch him. It is the baked streets and sidewalks, the withering campus and lawns, everyone in Hattiesburg driven indoors until dusk brings relief from the glaring sun of south Mississippi.

"Say hey for me to Nyline and them big chaps," says Odie Anderson. It is his wife and four sons; it is the steaming campus of Mississippi Southern University, the athletic dormitory and stadium, the office where his senior assistants wait to review game films, the approach of the season opener at home against Alabama, this fourth year of his five-year contract, two-a-day workouts and recruiting trips across the Deep South and a pending NCAA investigation. It is all things now and up to now, Mama and Daddy and Brother-boy up at Hot Coffee, paying his dues coaching high school and junior college, his professional career cut short by injury in Canada, all things seeming to have come together to shape his conviction of his imminent demise from heart failure.

"We going to whip up on 'Bama, Hog?"

"We die trying," says Hog. They laugh. It is nothing.

Hog decides he is not dying, not about to, not subject to be dying. It is something that is probably nothing, and because he cannot define or express it, it is a terror there is no point in fearing. Hog decides it is himself, Hog Hammond, alive in Hattiesburg, Mississippi, in the blistering heat of late August, knowing he is alive, no more than naturally wondering about death.

Fraternity and sorority pep club banners limply drape the stadium walls. *Beat Bama. Roll Back The Tide. Go Southern. We Back Hog's Boys.* The stadium walls throw heat into Hog's face like the coils of a kiln. Pines and magnolias and live oaks droop in the humidity. The mockingbirds are silent. The painted letters of the banners swim before his eyes, air pressing him like a leaden mist. He begins to consciously reach, pull for each breath, fetid on his tongue. Awash with sweat, he lurches, wheezing, into the shade of the stadium entrance to his office.

Inside, the dimness of the hall leaves him light-blind, air conditioning a clammy shock, his heaving-echoing off the glossy tiles and paneling. Hog finds himself, eyes adjusting, before the Gallery of Greats, a wall-length display of photos and newspaper clippings, trophies and pennants, locked behind nonreflecting glass. This pantheon of Mississippi Southern's finest athletes, record-setters and holders, crowd-pleasers, semi-All-Americans, is a vanity he cannot resist.

His breathing slows and softens, sweat drying in his clothes, on his skin, as he steps closer. There he is, the great Hog Hammond in the prime of his prowess and renown. Three pictures of Hog: a senior, nineteen years ago, posed in half-crouch, helmet off to show his bullet head, cropped hair, arms raised shoulder-high, fingers curled like talons, vicious animal snarl on his glistening face; Hog, nineteen years ago, down in his three-point stance, right arm lifting to whip the shiver-pad into the throat of an imaginary offensive guard; Hog, snapped in action, the legendary Alabama game nineteen years ago, charging full-tilt, only steps away from brutally dumping the confused Alabama quarterback for a loss. Hog is motion, purpose, power; the Alabama quarterback is static, timid, doomed.

The newspaper clippings are curled at the edges, yellowing. *Southern Shocks Ole Miss. Southern Stalemates Mighty Tide. The Hog Signs For Canada Pros.*

Athletic Director Tub Moorman is upon him, comes up behind him silently, like an assassin with a garrote, the only warning the quick stink of the dead cigar he chews, laced with the candy odor of his talc and hair oil, like the perfume of a New Orleans streetwalker. Hog feels a catch in his throat, a twinge in his sternum, salivates.

"Best not live on old timey laurels, Hog," says Athletic Director Tub Moorman. A fluttering column of nausea rises from the pit of Hog's belly to his chest, tip swaying into his gullet like a cottonmouth's head. He swallows hard, tenses to hold his windpipe open. "Best look to this season," Tub Moorman says. Hog, pinned against the cool glass of the Gallery of Greats, gags, covers it with a cough.

"I'm directly this minute subject to review game films," he is able to say. Tub Moorman does not seem to hear. He is a butterball, head round as a cookpot, dirty-grey hair slicked with reeking tonic, florid face gleaming with aftershave. He dresses like a pimp, .white shoes, chartreuse slacks, loud blazer, gaudy jewel in his wide tie, gold digital watch, oversize diamond on his fat pinky, glossy manicured nails. His sour, ashy breath cuts through the carnival odor of his lotions. He limps slightly from chronic gout.

"This year four," Tub Moorman says. "Year one we don't much care do you win, play what you find when you come on board. Year two, year three, your business to scout the ridges and hollows for talent. Year four, we looking to see do you *produce*, see do we want to keep you-all in the family after year five. This year four, root hog or die, hear?" The athletic director speaks, laughs, without removing his unlit cigar from his mouth. Hog can see the slimey, chewed butt of the cigar, Tub Moorman's wet tongue and stained teeth.

Hog is able to say, "I'm feeling a touch puny today," before he must clamp his lips.

"You know we-all mighty high on you, Hog," Tub Moorman says, "you one of us and all." He flicks his lizard's eyes at the Gallery's pictures and clippings. "You a great one. Withouten you got injured so soon in Canada, you might could of been truly great as a professional. We fixing to build this program up great like in old timey days, Hog. Fixing to find the man can do it if you ain't him."

"I'm subject to give it all I got," Hog gasps, bile in his mouth.

"It's subject to take it," says the athletic director, "and maybe then some," and "Fact , you got to beat Alabama or Ole Miss or Georgia Tech or Florida, somebody famous, or we got to be finding us the man will."

"I might could," Hog is able to say without opening his jaws, and, "I got me a nigger place-kicker can be the difference."

Tub Moonnan's laugh is a gurgling, like the flush of a sewer. "We-all ain't particular," says Tub Moonnan, "but the NCAA is. Best not let no investigators find out your Cuba nigger got a forged transcript, son. Best forget old timey days, be up and doing now." Hurrying to the nearest toilet, the athletic director's stench clings to him, chest-thick with sickness, throat charged with acid, head swimming. Wretching into the closest commode, Hog blows and bellows like a teased bull, clears the residue of Tub Moonnan's smell from his nostrils.

Gordon Weaver

On the portable screen placed behind Hog's executive-size desk, Alabama routs Ole Miss before a record homecoming crowd at Oxford. Slivers of the sun penetrate the room at the edges of the blackout curtains, light enough for notetaking, an eery cast of illumniation on the accoustical ceiling. The projector chatters, the air conditioning chugs.

Only Sonny McCartney, Hog's coordinator, takes notes, writing a crabbed hand into manila folders, calling for freeze-frames and reruns whenever the significance of the action on the screen is obscure or ambiguous. Sonny McCartney reminds Hog frequently that national ranking is only a matter of planning, implementation of strategy, time.

Wally Everett, offensive assistant, mans the projector. Once a fleet wide receiver for the Tarheels of North Carolina, he wears a prim, disinterested and superior expression on his patrician face. Because he wears a jacket and necktie in even the warmest weather, he is sometimes mistaken by students for a professor. Believing there is no excuse for vulgar or obscene language, on or off the playing field, he is a frequent speaker at Fellowship of Christian Athletes banquets. He sits up straight in his chair, one leg crossed over the other at the knee, like a woman, hands, when not operating the projector's levers and buttons, folded in his lap.

Thumper Lee, Hog's defensive assistant, slouches in a chair at the back of the room. He played a rugged nose-guard for a small Baptist college in Oklahoma, looks like an aging ex-athlete should, unkempt, strong, moody, unintellectual. He shifts his weight in his chair, stamps his feet often as Alabama's three-deep-at-every-position squad shreds the Rebels on the screen, invincible. He snorts, says, "I seen two county fairs and a train, but I ain't never seen nothing like them! Them sumbitches *good*, Hog!"

"The problem," says Sonny McCartney, "is to decide what we can do best against them."

"They execute to perfection," says Wally Everett.

Wally rewinds the film for one more showing. Sonny rereads his notes. Gary Lee Stringer spits a stream of juice from his Red Man cud into the nearby wastebasket. The room is darker with the projector bulb off, the air conditioning louder in the greater silence. Hog holds tightly to the arms of his chair, sensing the formation of an awful formlessness in his chest.

It feels to him as if, at the very center of his heart, a hole, a spot of nothingness, appears. He braces himself. The hole at the center of his heart doubles in size, doubles again; his vital, central substance is disappearing, vanishing without a trace left to rattle against his ribs. He tries to hear the movement of his blood, but there is only the perpetual churning of the air conditioning, the click and snap of the projector being readied.

"Hog," says Thumper Lee, pausing to rise an inch off his chair, break wind with a hard vibrato, "Hog, they going to eat our lunch come opening day."

"Every offense has a defense," Sonny McCartney says.

"There is little argument with basic execution," Wally says.

Hog waits in his chair to die. It will grow, he believes, this void in his chest, until he remains, sitting, a hollow shell with useless arms, legs, head. At which point he will be dead. He will crumple, fall to the carpeted floor, be lifted, all but weightless, by his senior staff, carried to the campus infirmary, pronounced dead by Odie Anderson, transported to a Hattiesburg mortuary. Or he will crumble inward upon himself, collapse like a sucked egg. Or perhaps remain there, dead, in his chair through yet another viewing of the game film, like a store window dummy propped in place, an inflated rubber mannequin, his passing undiscovered until the film is over, lights turned on, his staff turning to him for discussion.

"Alabama don't know we got Fulgencio Carabajal ," Sonny says.

"Neither does the NC double-A. Yet," Wally says. "But they will if we 1et just one person close enough to speak to him."

"Is that tutoring learning him any English yet?" Thumper Lee asks.

"Again?" says Wally, finger on the projector's start-button.

"Ain't this a shame?" says Thumper, "Our best offense a nigger from Cuba don't talk no English."

"*I* did not forge his transcript ," Wally says.

"He can kick," says Sonny, and, "Hog?"

Hog, dying, rises from his chair. "You-all discuss this without me," he says, finds he can take a step toward the door. Another. "I got to get me some fresh air, I am feeling puny, boys," says Hog, reaches the door, opens it, leaves, walking slowly, carefully, afraid to bump anything, that he will break like a man made of blown glass, brittle sticks, no core left to him at all, no heart.

There is no reason Hog should wake in the still-dark hours of early morning, no stomach upset or troubling dream. He is simply sudden1y awake, fully awake in his king-size bed, Nyline asleep beside him. At first he is merely awake, Nyline beside him, and then his eyes focus, show him the lighter darkness, false dawn at the bedroom windows, and then he sees the textured ceiling, walls, furniture, the glow of the nightlight from the master bedroom's full bath, the light blanket covering him and his wife, Nyline in silhouette, her head turned away from him on the deep pillow, the back of her head studded with curlers. He hears the gentle growl of her faint snoring. He hears the high sighing of cooled air cycling through the house on which he holds a mortgage that runs past the year 2000.

He lies very still in the king-size bed, shuts out what he can see and hear, the rich smell of Nyline's Shalimar perfume in the cooled air, closes himself away, listens only to himself, then knows what has awakened him, so totally, from a deep sleep, so close to morning.

Now Hog hears, measures the rhythms, recognizes the bustle reduction in pace, tempo, intensity of his heartbeat. His heart is slowing, and this has awakened him, so that he can die knowing he is dying. The beat is still regular, but there comes a miniscule hesitation, a near-catch, a stutter before the muffled thump of each beat. He lies very still, holds his breath, the better to hear and feel. Then he inches his left hand free of the cover, moves it into position to press the declining pulse in his right wrist with his forefinger. His pulse is there, then vanishes under his finger.

His heart will stop, run down like a flywheel yielding up its motion to the darkness of the master bedroom. He will die, is dying here and now, at the moment of false dawn that shows him the shafts of pine trunks in his yard, the wrinkled texture of his new lawn of Bermuda grass. He will lie there, die, lie there dead, be discovered by Nyline when she wakes to the electric buzz of the alarm on her bedside table.

"Nyline ," Hog whispers, croaks. "Nyline." His voice surprises him; how long can a man speak, live, on the momentum of his last heartbeats. "Nyline." She groans, turns to him, puts out a hand, eyes shut, groping. Her arm comes across his chest, takes hold of his shoulder. She drags herself close to him, nuzzles his jaw, kisses him clumsily in her half sleep, presses her head into his throat, her curlers stabbing the soft flesh.

Hog says, "Nyline, I love you. I thank you for marrying me, when my people is just redneck pulpcutters and you are from fine high-type people in Biloxi. It is always a wonder to me why you married me when I was just a football player, and now coach, and you was runnerup Miss Gulf Coast and all. They is mortgage life insurance on the house, Nyline, so's you will have the house all paid for."

"Baby sweet ," his wife mumbles into his collarbone. "Lovey, Big sweet thing."

"No, Nyline," he says. "I do love you and thank you for giving me our boys. I am dying, Nyline, and it is just as good I do now, because we will not beat Alabama or Ole Miss nor nobody big-timey, and the NCAA will likely soon get me for giving a scholarship to a Cuba nigger has to have a interpreter to play football, and we will lose this house and all except I am dying and you will get it because of insurance."

"Sweetest old big old sweet thing," Ny1ine says, kisses his hairy chest, strokes his shoulder, his face, the slick bald crown of his head.

"No," Hog says. "Listen, Ny1ine. Tell me can you hear my heart going." She mutters as he turns her head gently, places her ear against his breast, then resumes her light growling snore.

Dying, Hog lifts her away to her side of the bed, throws back the cover, rises, pads out of the master bedroom, the sharp nap of the new carpet pleasant to the soles of his feet. Dying, he walks down the hall to the bedrooms where his four sons sleep the perfect sleep of children.

He can stand at the end of the hall, look into both bedrooms, see them sleeping, two to each room, his sons, and he stands, looking upon the future of his name and line, stands thinking of his wife and sons, how he loves them, in his wonderful new home with a mortgage that runs beyond the year 2000, thinking it is cruel to die when he can see the future sleeping in the two bedrooms, that it is hard to die knowing life in his name and with his blood will extend into time he cannot know.

It is the coming of true dawn, flaring in the windows of his sons' side-by-side bedrooms, that grants him a reprieve. True dawn comes, lights the trees and grass and shrubbery of his lawn, stirs a mockingbird to its first notes high in some pine tree, primes his flickering, weary heart to a fresh rhythm. He feels it kick into vigor like a refueled engine, then goes to the hall bathroom, sits, grateful, weeping, on the edge of the bathtub, staring at his blank-white toes and toenails, his white feet tinged with lavender, his heart resuming speed and strength for another day.

Nyline and his sons are somewhere outside with Daddy and Brother-boy, seeing the new machinery shed or feeding Brother-boy's catfish. Hog's mama serves him a big square of cornbread and a glass of cold buttermilk. "Mama, Mama," says Hog, "you are something special. I come to Hot Coffee for a visit and it's a new cake or fresh cornbread."

"Your mama will always have a sweet for her big boy when he comes to see his people, Euliss," his mama says.

The golden cornbread, straight from the oven, radiates heat like a small sun. Hog bites, chews, swallows, breaks into a film of sweat as he chills his mouth with buttermilk. Not hungry, he gives himself over to the duty of eating for her, bite, chew, swallow, drink, his mama's presence, watching him eat. He sweats more freely with the effort, feels a liquid warmth emerge in his belly, grow. Hog feigns gusto, moans, smacks his lips, slurps for her. A viscous heat squirts into his chest, as if a powerful spume played upon his heart, warming it.

"Nomore," he says as she reaches toward the pan with a knife to cut him another helping. "Oh, please, Mama, no," says Hog. He tries to smile. "I want to know what is the matter with my biggest boy ," she says. "You say you are feeling some puny, but I know my boy, Euliss. I think you are troubled in your spirit, son."

"I have worries, Mama," he tells her. "We got to play Alabama. I am just troubled with my work."

"Is it you and Nyline? Is it your family, Euliss, something with my grandbabies?"

"We all fine, Mama. Truly." He averts his eyes. She does not look right, not his old mama, in this modern kitchen, chrome and formica and plastic-covered chairs, double oven set in the polished brick wall, blender built into the counter-top, bronze-tone refrigerator large as two football lockers, automatic icecube maker, frostless, Masonite veneer on the cupboards; Hog remembers her cooking at an iron woodstove, chopping wood for it as skillfully as she took the head off a chicken while he clung to her long skirts, sucking a sugartit, remembers her buying fifty pound blocks of ice from the nigger wagon driver from Laurel, taking his tongs and carrying it into the house herself because she would not allow a nigger in her kitchen, until Hog was old enough to fetch and carry for her, his daddy out in the woods cutting pulp timber dawn to dusk.

Hog covers his eyes with his hand to hide the start of tears, hurt and joy mixing in him like a boiling pot, that his mama has this fine kitchen in this fine new brick home built by his daddy and Brother-boy on a loan secured by Hog's signature and Hog's life insurance, that his mama is old and will not ever again be 1ike he remembers her, that she will not be, 1ive forever.

"I do believe my boy is troubled in his souL" Mama says.

"Not my soul, Mama." Hog favors his mama's people, comes by his size from her daddy, a pulpcutter who died before Hog was born; Hog remembers her telling him how her daddy lacked four and one-half fingers from his two hands, cutting pulpwood for Masonite in Laurel all his life until a tree fell on him and killed him. Hog looks at her fingers, at his own.

"Are you right with Jesus, Euliss?" she says. She leans across the table, hands clenched in prayer now. "I pray to Jesus ," says his mama, "for my boy Euliss. I pray for him each day and at meeting particular." It is as if a dam bursts somewhere on the margins of Hog's interior, a deluge of tepidness rushing to drown his heart, the whole of his chest and belly sloshing.

"We go to church regular in Hattiesburg, Mama," he is able to say before this spill deprives him of words and will, his heart now a remoteness, muffled like the sound of children swimming in a far pond.

"Pray with me, Euliss," she says. "Oh, pray Jesus ease your trouble, drive doubt and Satan out! Oh, I am praying to You, Jesus, praying up my biggest boy to YOU!" Her locked hands shake, as if she tries to lift a weight too great for her wiry arms, her eyes squeezed shut to see only Blessed Jesus, lips puckered as though she drew the Holy Spirit into her lungs. Hog cannot look. It is his old mama, old now, who attends the Primitive Baptist Church of Hot Coffee, where she wrestles Satan until she falls, frothing, to the floor before the tiny congregation, where she washes the feet of elders, weeping. "Jesus, Jesus, speak to my boy Euliss," she prays in the fine, modern kitchen of the modern brick-ranch built with Hog's mortgage on land won by two generations of driving scrub cattle and pulpwood cutting.

Eyes brimming tears, nose clogged with sobbing, Hog's heart moves like a wellhouse pump lifting a thick, hot sweetness into his mouth. This death is sweet, filling, filled with Mama's love, all he feels of his memories of her, daddy, brother. "JesuspleaseJesusplease,"l she chants.

"Mama," says Hog, standing up, voice breaking on his lips like a bubble of honey, "I got to go find Daddy and Nyline and Brother-boy and those chaps. We got to be leaving back to Hattiesburg soon. Time flying, Mama." He flees the kitchen, the waters of her love receding in his wake, leaving her there, her prayer echoing damply in his ears.

Hog and his daddy pause at the electrified strand of fencing to admire the glossy Angus at the saltlick, the cattle clustering in the narrow shade of the old mule-driven mill where Hog helped his daddy crush cane for syrup. Hog sees the Angus melded with the scrubby mavericks he ran in the woods with razorbacks for his daddy, hears the squeak and crunch of the mill turning, snap of cane stalks. "Now see this, Eulliss ," says his daddy, a small man who has aged by shriveling, drying, hardening. "Don't it beat all for raising a shoat in a nigger-rigged crib?" his hardness glowing redly in the terrible sunshine, burnished with pride over the new cement floor of his pigpen. Hog, gasping, drowning, clucks appreciation for him. "Wait and see Brother-boy feed them fish!"his daddy says.

"Daddy ," Hog says, "how is it Mama so much for churching and you never setting foot in it, even for revival s?" Hog's daddy expertly blows his nose between thumb and forefinger, flicks snot into the grass as they pass the row of humming beehives, their stark whiteness conjuring the weathered stumps and gums Hog helped rob in his youth, wreathed in smoke, veiled.

"I never held to it," his daddy says, and would go on toward the pond, stopped by Hog's heavy hand on his shoulder.

"Why not? You didn't never believe in God? Ain't you never been so scared of dying or even of living so's you wanted to pray 1ike Mama?" He hears his own voice muffled, as if cushioned by water.

"I never faulted her for it, Euliss ," says his daddy. And, "And no man dast fault me for not. I'll tell you the why of it, Euliss. Son, a man don't get hardly no show in life, most of us. Now, not you, but me and Brother-boy and your mama. Most folks, 1ife wearies a man. So them as needs Jesus-ing to die quiet in bed or wherever, I say fine, like for Mama. Me nor mine never got no show, excepting you, naturally, Euliss, a famous player and coach and all. I guess I can die withouten I screech to Jesus to please let me not have to ."

"Daddy,"says Hog. Blood fills his chest, a steady seeping, a rich lake about his heart, pooling in the pit of his belly, pressing his lungs. "Daddy , when I was a chap, was I a good boy?"

"Now , Euliss," and his daddy embraces him there near the line of beehives, sinewy arms, the spread fingers of his horny hands clasping Hog's heaving sides. "Euliss, don't you know I have bragged on you since you was a chap?"I

"Are you proud of me still now I'm growed a man?" His daddy laughs, releases him, steps back.

"Oh, I recollect you then, son! You was a pistol for that football from the start. I recollect you not ten years old going out to lift the new calf day by day to build muscles for football playing!"

"Daddy." He feels a pleasant cleft in his breast widen, a tide of blood.

"Recollect the time I told you not to be blocking yourself into the gallery post for football practice? I had to frail you with a stick to teach you not. Oh, son, you was a pure pistol for that footballin! Your daddy been bragging on you since, Euliss!"

"Find Brother-boy, see them fish," Hog chokes with his last breath, heart and lungs and belly a sweet sea of blood, this death almost desirable to him. He staggers away, past Angus, new sty, modern brick-ranch home, pre-fabricated metal shed, suffocating in the fluid of his emotions.

"Brother," says Hog, "Brother-boy, are you resentful you stayed and lived your life here? Ain't you never wanted a wife and chaps of your own? Do you resent I went away to school for football and to Canada for my own life whiles you just stay working for Daddy like always?" Brother-boy looks like Hog remembers himself half a dozen years ago, less bald, less overweight. From a large cardboard drum, he scoops meal, sows it over the dark green surface

of the artificial pond. The catfish he farms swim to the top, thrash, feeding, rile the pond into bubbles and spray. "Was I a good brother to you? Is it enough I signed a note so's you can start a fish farm and all this cattle and stock of Daddy's?"

Brother-boy, sowing the meal in wide arcs over the pond, says, "I never grudged you all the fine things you got, Euliss. You was a special person, famous playing football in college and Canada, now a famous coach." His brother's voice dims, lost in the liquid whip of the pond's surface, the frenzied feeding of the catfish. "I am a happy enough man, Euliss," says Brother-boy. "I have things I do. Mama and Daddy need me. They getting old, Euliss. I don't need me no wife nor chaps, and I got a famous big brother was a famous player once and now a coach, and your sons are my nephews." Hog remembers Brother-boy, a baby wearing a shift, a chap following after him at chores, coming to see him play for Jones Agricultural Institute & Junior College in Laurel, for Mississippi Southern, once coming

by train and bus all the way up to Calgary, there to see Hog's career end in injury. "It is not my nature to resent nor grudge nobody nothing," says his brother, "It is my way to accept what is."

Hog lurches away, seeking an anchor for his heart, tossed in a wave of sweet blood. He thinks he will die now, or not die now, but soon, wishes he could wish to die here and now if he must die. But it is now here and now, and this knowing his death is yet to come is like a dry wind that evaporates the splash of love and memory within him, turning this nectar stale, then sour.

Seeking an overview of the last full drill in pads, Hog takes to a stubby knoll, shaded by a massive live oak tree, its snaking limbs so long they are supported by cables fastened to the tree's black trunk. From here, the practice field falls into neat divisions of labor.

At the far end of the field, parallel to the highway running toward Laurel and Hot Coffee, chimeric behind the rising heat waves, Fulgencio Carabajal placekicks ball after ball through jerry-built wooden goalposts, the first string center snapping, third team quarterback holding, two redshirts to shag balls for the Cuban, who takes a break every dozen or two dozen balls to talk with his interpreter. Hog watches Fulgencio's soccer-style approach, hears the hollow strike of the side of his shoe on the ball, the pock of this sound like a counterpoint to the beating of Hog's heart. He tries to follow the ball up between the uprights, loses it in the face of the sun that washes out the green of the dry grass.

Closest to Hog's shady knoll, the first and second team quarterbacks alternate short spot passes with long, lazy bombs to a self-renewing line of receivers who wait their turns casually, hands on hips. Catching balls in long fly patterns, receivers trot up to the base of Hog's knoll, cradling the ball loosely, showboating for him. He does not allow them to think he notices.

The slap of ball in receiver's hands comes as if deliberately timed to the throb of his heart, adding its emphasis to the twist of its constrictions.

At the field's center, Sonny McCartney coordinates, wears a gambler's green plastic eyeshade, clipboard and ballpoint in hand. Sonny moves from offense to defense in the shimmer of the heat like a man wading against a current. Hog squints to find Thumper Lee, on his knees to demonstrate firing off the snap to his noseguard, his jersey as sweated as any player's. Wally

Everett, as immobile as Hog, stands among his offensive players, stopping the drill frequently with his whistle, calling them close for short lectures, as unperturbed by the temperature and humidity as if he worked with chalk on blackboard in an air conditioned classroom. Hog feels Wally's whistle shrill in his veins, exciting his blood to speed.

The live oak's shade does not spare him. Hog's bald scalp is protected from burning by a billed cap, but seems to simmer under the flannel, the sweatband tightening at his temples. Sweat drenches the tonsure of his remaining hair, collects above his ears, rivulets to the folds of fat in his throat and at the back of his neck, overflows to course into pools in the shallow hollows behind his collarbones. His jersey is a second, wet skin. Sweat runs down his arms, catches in the grizzled hair above his wrists. Only the tun of his distended belly moves, a bellows struggling for oxygen in the clotted air. His great thighs glisten, the gnarled knobs of scar tissue at his knees shine pink. His delicate ankles and tiny feet, secret of his startling agility as a player, wrapped in soggy wool socks, burn, toes frying in his cleated shoes. His swollen hands tingle with quickening blood.

His heart picks up its pace, the intensity of each convulsion increasing to a thud, a bang. Now he cannot distinguish the echo of his accelerating heartbeat in the singing of his blood in his ears from the smack of pads down on the practice field, the slap of ball on sweaty palm, thumping of the tackling dummy , crash of shoulders against the blockinq sled, squealinq springs, the hollow pock of Fulgencio Carabajal's kicking.

Hog closes his eyes to die, digs with his cleats for a firmer stance on the knoll, prepared to topple into the dusty grass. He tenses his flesh, wonders why this raucous slamming of his heart does not shake him, why he does not explode into shards of flesh and bone. And wonders why he is not dead, still holding against his chest's vibrations, when he hears Sonny McCartney blow the final whistle to end the drill. Hog's heart subsides with the blood's song in his ears, like the fade of Sonny's whistle in the superheated air of late afternoon.

It is light. Light, falling upon Hog and his wife, still sleeping as he rises. Special, harder and brighter light while fixing himself a quick breakfast in the kitchen, chrome trim catching and displaying early morning's show of light to him while Nyline is dressing, his sons stirring in their bedrooms toward this new day. Light, the morning sky clear as creek water, climbing sun electric-white, overwhelming Hog's sense of trees, houses, streets, driving slowly through Hattiesburg to the stadium. And light, lighting his consciousness, pinning his attention in the gloom of the squad's locker room, the last staff strategy session, his talk to his players before they emerge into the light of the stadium.

Hog tells them, "It is not just football or playing a game. It is like life. It is mental toughness. Or you might could call it confidence. I do not know if you are as good as Alabama. Newspapers and TV is saying you are not, they will whip our butts. If it is, they is nothing any of us or you-all can do. We-all have to face that. It is Alabama we are playing today. Maybe it is like that you-all have to go out and play them knowing you will not have any show. It might could be I am saying mental toughness is just having it in you to do it even knowing they will whip up on your butt. I don't know no more to say. If He leads them, no cheering or spirit or charge in them, out into the light.

He sees, hears, registers it all, but all is suffused with this light, a dependency of light. The game flows like impure motes in perfect light. The game is exact, concrete, but still dominated by, a function of this light. The opening game against Alabama is a play of small shadows within the mounting intensity of light.

Hog takes his customary squat-stance, modified lineman's point, on the edge of the chalked boundary, notes the legendary figure of the opposing coach across the field, tall, chainsmoking cigarettes, houndstooth checked hat, coatless in the dense heat Hog does not feel. This light has no temperature for Hog, a light beyond heat or cold, transcending tangibility.

"They eating our damn lunch, Hog!" Thumper Lee screams in his ear when Alabama, starting on their twenty after Fulgencio Carabajal sends the kickoff into the endzone bleachers, drives in classic ground-game fashion for the first touchdown. "They taking it to our butts, Hog!" he screams, and to his defense lining up for the extra point, "Put your damn ears back or live with me when they done with you!" The snap is mishandled, the kick wide.

"I do declare we can run wide on them, Hog," says Wally Everett as Southern moves the ball in uneven spurts to the Crimson Tide thirty-seven where, stalled by a broken play, Fulgencio Caraba'al effortlessly kicks the the three-pointer. "I have seen teams field goaled to death," Wally says.

Late in the second quarter, Southern trails only 13-9 after Fulgencio splits the uprights from fifty-six yards out. "We *got* the momentum, Hog," says Sonny McCartney, earphones clamped on to maintain contact with the press-box spotters. "We can run wide, and pray Fulencio don't break a leg."

Thumper Lee, dancing, hugging the necks of his tackles, spits, screams, "I seen a train and a fair, but I ain't never seen *this* day before!"

"Notice the Bear's acting nervous over there?" Wally says, points to the excited assistants clustering in quick conference on the houndstooth hat across the field.

Says Hog, "You can't never tell a thing about nothing how it's going to be."

His death comes as light, all light, clarity, comprehensive and pervasive. There is nothing Hog does not see, hear, know. Everything is here, in this light, and not here. It is beyond all things, a moment obliterating moments, time or place.

He knows a possible myth, great legend is unfolding on the playing field, an astounding upset of Alabama's Crimson Tide. Hog knows he has come to this possible wonder, this time and place, by clear chronology, sequence of accident and design, peopled since the beginning with his many selves and those who have marked and made him who and what he is in this instant of his death. Light draws him in, draws everything together in him, Hog, the context of his death.

Dr. Odie Anderson sits on a campstool behind the players' bench, feet up on the bench, scratching his beard with both hands, rolling his bulged eyes at the game. Athletic Driector

Tub Moorman's face is wine-red with excitement, his unlit cigar chewed to pulpy rags. Thumper Lee drools tobacco juice when he shouts out encouragement to his stiffening defense. Wally Everett smirks as he counsels his quarterback. Sonny McCartney relays information from his spotters up in the press-box, where Nyline and the four sons of Hog watch the game through binoculars, drinking complimentary Coca-Colas. On the bench next to his chattering interpreter, Fulgencio Carabajal waits indifferently for his next field goal attempt. In the new modern kitchen in Hot Coffee, Mississippi, Hog's people, Mama, Daddy, Brother-boy listen to the radio broadcast, proud and praying. Only a little farther, folded into his memory like pecans in pralines, are the many Hogs that make him Hog: a boy in Hot Coffee lifting new calves to build muscle, football find at the Jones Agricultural Institute & Junior College, bonafied gridiron legendary Little All-American on this field, sure-fire prospect with Calgary's Stampeders in the Canadian Football League, career cut short by knee and ankle injuries, high school coach, defensive assistant, coordinator, Hog here and now, head coach at Mississippi Southern University, all these simultaneous in the marvel of his death's light.

Dying, Hog looks into the glare of the sun, finds his death is not pain or sweetness, finds totality and transcendence, dies as they rush to where he lies on the turf, dying, accepting this light that is the heart of him joining all light, Hog and not-Hog, past knowing and feeling or need and desire to say it is only light, dies hearing Fulgencio Carabajal say, *"Es muerte?"* gone into such light as makes light and darkness one.

GUNN AND THE HAMMER

Michael Stigman

On a Saturday, Gunn and Britches went to buy a new refrigerator. They had bet on a hockey game and agreed that the loser had to roll the fridge from the truck into the house. Gunn lost the bet, but that didn't stop him from enjoying the task of picking it out with Britches. When they had a salesperson's attention, they explained what they were looking for.

"Lots of drawers, and a big, self-defrosting freezer section," Gunn suggested.

"An automatic ice-maker," Britches chimed in.

"Or a Zamboni in the ice compartment," Gunn said.

The salesperson didn't laugh, but they did. They were in good spirits. Even Gunn. Later, he'd have to figure out a way to regain the upper hand. To him, it had always been about that. Gunn rooted for the Flyers, Britches for the Sabres. Up till now, here's how things had worked out:

In the NHL:	In Gunn's mind:
1975: Flyers beat Sabres 4 games to 2	The Flyers' win means Gunn has the upper hand in the relationship.

1976: Canadiens beat Flyers 4 games to 1	At least Gunn's team made it to the finals; Gunn has the upper hand.
1977: Canadiens beat Sabres 4 games to none	At least the Flyers had won one game against the Canadiens; Gunn retains the upper hand.
1978 to present: Neither the Flyers nor Sabres return to the Stanley Cup.	Gunn and Britches console each other, but Gunn worries often that they might not make the best match

After they'd been together a while, Gunn could say Britches was a good woman, even though she had her moments. Times Gunn had to try and knock a little sense into her. Times she got a little high on her horse, typically too big for her britches, he thought. Times like these didn't come often, but when they did the two of them tousled, and picture frames and little lamps broke and their tiny house shook as they knocked sense into each other.

Gunn thought of their fights as something like power plays in hockey, where the team with the man advantage tries to put on the pressure. It seemed to him that whoever had the man advantage, the upper hand, would find a way to kick the other when down, and when that happened it didn't take long for things to get bad. Their latest fight happened like the others, man advantage Gunn, except they both ended up in the emergency room. Gunn hadn't intended that much. He usually fought hard but under control. He never lost his head. That's why he spent more time than Britches in the emergency room. He didn't want to hurt her. He learned all this from his hero, The Hammer.

Gunn had a thing for Gary "The Hammer" Skovitz, a player for the Flyers. The Hammer wore a mean Fu-Manchu when a Fu-Manchu in the NHL meant you were a bad character. He taped his knuckles inside his gloves, and he fought anyone opposing the Flyers. Which was everybody back then. Night after night Gunn watched The Hammer turn his skates and coast toward some stranded sucker, and before The Hammer slung off his gloves, Gunn knew that the poor sucker would end up sorry he'd messed with the Flyers. Gunn watched The Hammer's fists, and they flew so quickly to all the poor sucker's thin skin and soft places. Ears, nose, eyes, chin, all so soft and hurt. The Hammer's fists did the work they set out to do, and Gunn watched. And he listened closely to the fists. He heard them pounding out and shaping a question: "You came to play hockey?" And an answer: "Mistake, mistake, mistake. Mistake." And to Gunn the fists said, "Watch out. Some think they can put one over on you. Don't, don't let them. Don't."

Having a thing for The Hammer meant, among other things, that Gunn kept scrapbooks. That made him The Hammer's number-one-fan, the way he saw it. He would have fought anyone who tried to challenge his position. But no one took him up on it because they knew it was true and they didn't want to fight over something they saw as ridiculous. Gunn didn't care what they thought. He figured that was the price a man paid for devotion. He loved The Hammer, and no one understood how much.

Not even Britches. Case in point: A week back, in the middle of the night, in the middle of his REM, Gunn woke from a hockey dream yelling, yelling, yelling. In the dream, Hammer and the Flyers and Gunn skated together, and when The Hammer got in a fight, Gunn tried to help out. That's where the yelling came in. In the morning, Gunn didn't want to explain it to Britches. So he didn't. But that didn't keep her from talking about it. Over breakfast, she described to him how he shot up in bed.

"Like a bolt of lightning. Like a bolt." She laughed, but Gunn didn't. Granted, it was a good dream as dreams go, but he didn't find her play-by-play as funny as she tried to make it. She only knew that Gunn had sat up in bed and let out a howl. In the way of explanations, the bolt of lightning was as close as she could get.

A hockey dream like Gunn's stays with you all day. Even after Britches had tried to make fun of him, Gunn felt good because of the dream. He went to the shop, and when he walked up to the entrance, he pulled open both doors so he could sweep through the foyer into his work bay. He felt ready to take on anybody who might step on his toes. After all, he'd fought alongside The Hammer, dream or not. He stepped into his bay, which he'd named "The Penalty Box," and hung his coat. Immediately, he noticed that a corner of his 1976 Flyers team poster was missing a thumbtack and had flopped forward. In Gunn's eyes, the corner of the poster looked like a dog's ear after a fight over a bitch in heat. It disarmed Gunn the way it would the dog. The dog doesn't really want to fight. It wants to hump. But that's where the poster stopped looking like the dog's ear. For Gunn there was nothing sexual about this. Someone had stolen one of his thumbtacks. He clenched his fists and thought to raise a stink about people messing with his personal effects. But then he stopped long enough to ask himself, What would The Hammer do in this situation? The Hammer fought only when he really needed to prove a point, and Gunn couldn't see the point he wanted to make. He only saw red. So he decided he'd count to ten and let it slide. He could let it slide because of the power of his dream.

When he felt hungry for lunch, he called Becker from the stockroom. Gunn sometimes ate lunch with Britches, but she had taken off work today and Gunn was pretty sure he didn't want to sit through both breakfast and lunch hearing her describe him as a bolt of lightning. On the loading dock stairs Becker and Gunn sat and ate and talked about Gunn's dream.

"Did anyone score?" Becker asked him.

"Some of us" Gunn said, pointing his thumb at his chest, "were too busy kicking ass."

"And you saved The Hammer from getting his head iced?"

"Yep. I remember yanking the guy's jersey over his head, and I remember punching a lot and saving The Hammer. That's about it."

They both imagined what Gunn described.

"What do you think the dream means?" Becker asked.

"What the hell do you mean 'What does it mean?' It means I fought side-by-side with The Hammer. It means I kept him from getting hurt." Sometimes Gunn couldn't believe he had a friend so dense as Becker. Why did he put up with such an idiot? Maybe lunch with Britches hadn't been such a bad idea. At least she understood the meaning of hockey.

She always had. She liked hockey and she liked the fights pretty well and that's how the two of them met. Stanley Cup, Flyers and Sabres. Britches had lived outside of Buffalo and so was a Sabres fan. Gunn, of course, was a Flyers fan. A shaky start for them. Gunn had always hated the Sabres for everything they were. He hated their mixed-up mascots—a buffalo and two swords crossed in front of it. To Gunn, the Sabres couldn't make up their minds which symbol would make a better mascot so they went with both. A bad choice. A buffalo on ice? Two swords? The Flyers, on the other hand, had a very clear message behind their team symbol—a wing flying around the ice with the puck. And kicking ass, what with The Hammer on the roster.

Despite the Sabres' mixed mascots, when Gunn saw Britches in the concession line, he forgot about all that. Looking back to see how the line grew, Gunn noticed her. He looked once and wanted to just look once, but then he looked over at her again, and once more, and then after he ordered his food he looked again. She was an ample woman, and tall. And Gunn liked the way she looked in her jersey, even if it was the Sabres. She wore it well, and each time he looked back Gunn noticed the way it hung on her body. He hated the buffalo but he adored the way its head and tail rose out of respect for Britches's breasts. And he adored the way the two sabres lay nestled in the middle of this abundance. The way he could still make out the shape of her ass below the Gilbert Perreault number 11.

Gunn kept looking down the concession line as if he were looking for someone who owed him money. When he'd done all the looking he could do without getting caught, he decided to make interesting conversation. He caught her eye and said, "Perreault can't fight for shit."

Britches smiled. "Who's your man?"

When he told her, she countered: "Skovitz can't shoot." She added, "For shit."

Gunn laughed. He couldn't imagine someone criticizing The Hammer for something he wasn't made for, especially when he was made so well for something else.

"Who cares?" he said. "There's more than one way to skin a cat."

"Skovitz wouldn't know the first thing about skinning a cat either." She moved closer to him and hissed, "What are we talking about here, anyway? I thought it was called 'hockey.'"

Before Gunn knew it, their argument had taken them out of the concession line and Britches had backed him up against a wall, pinning him there between her breasts. They continued to argue, back and forth. She argued for the purity of the sport and believed that guys like The Hammer sensationalized it.

"He's the reason people say, 'The other night I went to a fight and a hockey game broke out.'"

Gunn didn't know her from Adam's housecat, but he wanted to kiss her for that one. He loved the saying, he used it all the time, and to think that The Hammer might have brought the idea to the game made Gunn swell with pride, and something else, if the truth be told.

"For shame! For shame that this is what hockey has come to!" Britches said. She sounded like a preacher, bellowing angrily. She poked him repeatedly in the chest with each point she made. She made him nervous. Gunn felt the sweat build up on his palms and he thought he felt it puddle in his socks. He began to panic. He felt so afraid that she might hit him and so afraid that she might not, and he wanted so badly for something to happen that would make them never able to exist without each other, him a part of her and her a part of him. He didn't want the argument to stop. He wanted it to escalate forever and ever, in Jesus's name, amen. He wanted her to become ever angrier, and he wanted her to yell again, "For shame! For shame!" and he wanted to feel with conviction that it indeed was a shame that things had come to this.

Sometimes their friends asked Gunn what brought the two of them together, and he learned early on what to tell and what not to tell. Initially when he tried to describe what he felt, his friends just looked at him with faces that seemed pressed against Plexiglas. He understood their confusion, though. He'd felt it too. So in the end, he avoided trying to sort out the confusion. He told only one version of how they met, which focused on the good parts. With a finger stabbing the air or poking a table, he'd say: "We owe everything to hockey," or "I fell in love right then and there," even though he knew it was a copout. People said it was the sweetest love story they'd ever heard. He read in their faces that they saw the story as something sugary and special, but he never saw it as special even when he tried to tell it that way. He'd been scared shitless, and none of it was charted in the stars. Back when they met they weren't even rooting for the same team, and no one had ever called her Britches. Gunn and Britches just happened.

For $50 bucks, the appliance store would deliver a new refrigerator to your door. For $5, they'd lend you one of those serious, heavy-duty dollies. The salesperson raved about the dolly, saying, "It'll do most of the work for you!" At home, Gunn used the dolly to roll the refrigerator to the door, all the while reminding himself that it was supposed to do most of the work. As he crossed the threshold, maybe he misused the dolly. Maybe this kind of dolly retaliated if you tried to do more than your share of the work. He slipped on the welcome mat and threw out his back.

Britches took over for him. She stood the fridge upright just inside the door, and then she dragged Gunn over to the living room to an open spot on the floor. While she finished moving the fridge into place, Gunn watched and gave directions. Of course, for the rest of the night he didn't feel like doing much, so they finagled a scrapbook project to work on, one that Gunn had talked about wanting to complete. Britches laid out Flyers pictures and magazine cutouts and organized them into piles for another set of scrapbooks. She'd hold up a picture of one of the Flyers, and Gunn, flat on his back, would tell her which pile to put it in. He decided on two books for pictures of The Hammer, and after they worked through the pile, they began to paste in the pictures. From time to time, Britches maneuvered and adjusted two puck-shaped pillows under Gunn's back and fed him popcorn.

While they worked on the scrapbooks, they watched the Flyers against the Red Wings. And they talked about hockey, the history of hockey, and Britches commented on how these days everyone wears helmets and facemasks.

"And no one fights," Gunn said.

"Yes they do," Britches said. "Too much."

"No they don't. Everyone's too afraid to cut up his pretty little hands. It's bullshit."

"Well," Britches said. "So be it. It's the wave of the future. It's hockey finding itself. It's like us."

"What do you mean?" This sort of talk made Gunn uneasy.

"We're finding ourselves, don't you think?"

The last time Gunn had heard someone explain how she was finding herself, it was a woman who left her husband and kids. Yeah, she found herself. Found herself in the middle of a dirty little hippie commune. Gunn hated the phrase, and he hoped Britches didn't mean it the way the woman had.

"Finding ourselves. How so?"

"Well, Gunn. Don't get mad at me for saying so, but I'm handling myself better. And you're learning that things go better when you don't mess with me."

When she said this, Gunn's breath caught in his chest and he felt it running out of him elsewhere, as if he were not the one in charge of his breathing. Britches smiled, as if she were in control. As if she had sucked the breath from him, as if she had said all this just to get his goat, egg him on. She the buffalo, he the hen. Where were the Sabres?

When he caught his breath, he made a move to stand up, and Britches said, "Gunn. Maybe we shouldn't. Your back."

As soon as she said this, Gunn lost it. He slung the pile of pictures and the scrapbook at her, and then he lifted himself from the floor and rushed at her as she ran. He moved like a car with a bent frame, all cockeyed running down the road after her. She ran toward the kitchen, yelling "Gunn, let's not!" and "I don't want to hurt you, Honey!" He chased her around the corner, but as he did another rug moved on him, and he slipped and on pure momentum slid into the cabinets and crumpled. Britches only heard him fall, and then she began to move toward him. She waited in the doorway a distance from him and asked if he was all right. When he began to sniffle, she tiptoed over and laid his head in her lap and smoothed his hair against his head.

After a while of this, she rolled him onto the rug and pulled him back into the living room. She propped his head again with the pillows and covered him with a blanket. Neither spoke. She brought him his bottle of hydrocodone, fed him a few, and kissed his salty cheek. When she heard his breathing settle into a rhythm, she turned off the overhead lights in the living room, locked and chained the front door, and skated off to bed.

Gunn woke in the night to the sound of a repeated thumping. He wanted to ask Britches if she heard it, but he had forgotten that he still lay on the living room floor. It took him a long time to remember that. When he kept hearing the thumping and decided he wasn't imagining it, he tried to roll himself across the floor until he could see into the kitchen, where he thought the thumping came from. Moving was hard work. He felt heavy all over, as if the blanket covering him were made of lead. He moved like a skater on slushy ice. When he finally rolled himself to where he could see into the kitchen, he saw a man wearing a replica Hammer jersey with the name and number on the back. The man stood shooting a puck against the door of the new refrigerator. Gunn saw each shot by the black mark it made on the face of the fridge.

"Do you mind not shooting it like that?" he asked. "The marks."

The man turned around to face Gunn, and when Gunn realized it was The Hammer he felt badly for asking him to stop, as The Hammer's shooting game could always use some work. And then he wondered what The Hammer was doing in his house in the middle of the night. It surprised Gunn because it made The Hammer look shady. Gunn wondered how The Hammer could be a good person if he broke into people's houses to work on his wrist shot. And before he became angry, Gunn thought that what might matter was not whether The Hammer belonged there but why he was there.

The Hammer walked over, kneeled, and shook Gunn's hand. He apologized for the marks on the fridge, and he said, "Can we talk, Gunn? I want to talk with you."

This was odd, Gunn thought. The Hammer didn't seem much like himself. He didn't try to intimidate Gunn. He didn't try to manhandle him, the way The Hammer should have. He seemed nice, and he said "I want to talk with you" instead of "I got a bone to pick with you" or even "Let's shoot the shit." This troubled Gunn. He looked at The Hammer's hands, expecting to see telltale scars from his fights, but The Hammer's hands were clean with no visible scars. This surprised Gunn. He'd thought about The Hammer's hands a lot in the past. He imagined they'd end up battered for life, looking like ground hamburger or at least roast beef, but after seeing them Gunn figured the stickum and tape he wore for every game must have protected them pretty well. Even so, Gunn was disappointed that The Hammer didn't act like the bully Gunn knew him to be.

The Hammer propped up Gunn with another pillow, and then sat himself in the LazyBoy. But as he sat, he caught the front edge of the chair so that the backrest of the chair shot forward to accommodate his weight, and the doily that covered it flew forward and spread itself over The Hammer's head. Instantly, The Hammer's demeanor changed. For just a second he looked like an angel, but as soon as he snatched away the doily, he looked like The Hammer in the penalty box.

"How's it going, Gunn?" The Hammer asked.

"Not so well lately." He wanted to tell The Hammer about his fight with Britches, and about his back, and about feeling out-of-sorts. But just as he began, The Hammer waved his hands to stop him.

"That's what I wanted to talk to you about." He brought his hands together so that all his fingertips touched. "But first. About your dream—"

"What?"

"Gunn," The Hammer leveled his eyes. "C'mon."

Gunn felt his face wince. "Yeah, so I know that's not exactly how it happened. I just," Gunn said, and his brain didn't know what to send to his mouth, so he just stopped talking.

"It was really quite different from the way you tell it. I was shocked at how you embellished it." He tapped Gunn's chest with a finger and continued, "You were the one getting your ass kicked, not me."

"I know." Gunn felt his face flush.

"Besides, I'm not just a fighter." The Hammer's words floated out between them.

"You're a lover?"

"No. That's Michael Jackson. Don't ever confuse me with that poor bastard."

"Sorry," Gunn said.

"I just mean don't forget that I did score a few goals in my time."

Before he could stop himself, Gunn let out a laugh. Short and sharp like breath spent from an unexpected sucker punch to the belly, like one staccato syllable that, if multiplied, would've translated as "Yeah, right." Gunn looked at The Hammer's face to read it, but he couldn't. And then he looked to The Hammer's fists, which had turned to round, thick, lead-like lumps on the ends of his forearms. Gunn could hear the fists grumble and curse him. Faster than he'd ever thought himself capable, he felt sorry. He knew what was coming and he wished The Hammer hadn't picked him out, hadn't decided he was the one to take down. He closed his eyes and tried to pray. He tried to pray to his image of The Hammer, under his breath and in his heart. He wanted to say how sorry he was for laughing. He wanted to say he regretted it, he felt shame for it. He wanted his regret to show. He wanted to point to something that would show all this. What if he could build something, point to it, and say, "I'm sorry. Look. See?" But he said nothing, did nothing. He couldn't move. He opened his eyes. The Hammer still sat before him.

Hammer grimaced and flattened his hands out in front of him, and then he rubbed them together like a genie ready to grant a wish, a death wish. He rose, and he said, "Stand up, Gunn."

Gunn tried to explain that he couldn't, but the Hammer shushed him. And then Gunn felt his body upsurge from a force applied to the lapels of his bathrobe. He felt so light inside and about to pass out. The Hammer held him by his lapels until he gained his balance, and then he leaned toward Gunn, pinning his arms against his sides, and wrapped him in a bear hug. He raised Gunn off the floor, held him there, and then snapped him downward like a set of posthole diggers. At once, Gunn felt a shuddering ripple and a rippling shudder, like a shot to the funny bone turned up to eleven traveling down his spine. A moment later, Hammer released him but placed his hands on Gunn's shoulders. Gunn could tell that he had something to say but he looked as if he wasn't sure what. Gunn, feeling suddenly so sharp, thought to break the silence himself but Hammer shushed him again and brought his face very close to Gunn's, and when it looked to Gunn that Hammer wanted to plant a kiss on Gunn's cheek, Hammer whispered something.

"Britches is right, Gunn. It's not about fighting. It's not about the upper hand. It's different now, and you'd do well to change with it."

After The Hammer left, Gunn sat down. Between you and me, he cried again. For a full minute. And then he wiped his face with one of the puck-shaped pillows, and he let another minute pass. And then he looked up at the clock on the wall and watched most of three more minutes pass, and as the second hand swept toward the twelve, he looked over at his scrapbooks. When the second hand crossed the twelve, five minutes were up and Gunn started flipping through the scrapbooks he'd made of The Hammer because he wanted to look him in the face. He looked at The Hammer in each of the pictures, and something about his face looked different. A little less sure. Same jersey, same Fu-Manchu, but a soft, weak look to him. Gunn couldn't look at him the same way. That was it. Maybe he hadn't changed. Maybe he just wasn't The Hammer Gunn had thought him to be.

He began to make a different pile of all the individual photos of The Hammer that he'd collected. All of them. He thought to wake Britches and ask for her help. She'd be glad to, but then he thought better of it. He'd do this on his own. He could show her tomorrow, and she'd be just as happy. He took all of his Flyers' team pictures, and he cut out The Hammer's heads, and added these to the new pile until it started spilling on the floor.

If the house were equipped with a fireplace Gunn would've fired it up and thrown the pile into the flames. But it had no fireplace, so Gunn did the obvious. He swept the pictures and the severed Hammer heads into a plastic bag, tied a knot in the top, and brought it over to the fridge. He swung open the freezer door and watched the cold air blitz the warm air and then retreat. Gunn leaned his head into the freezer's opening and pushed the bag against the back of the freezer compartment.

With his head still inside, he felt the cold surround him. He closed his eyes and began to count. He wanted to see how long he could stand the cold pushing against his head, and while he waited to find out he wondered how much it would hurt. How much hurt he could take before he'd say, "I give."

WHAT DID YOU DID?

Charles Rammelkamp

"Opening day is for amateurs." The old man's voice comes as an assertive whine from behind the eight foot wall of lockers. Robert Duncavage, naked, still dripping from the shower, sits on the padded bench in front of his own locker at the Baltimore Athletic Club, listening to the disembodied voice develop its argument. "People who go to the opening day game won't go to another all year. Opening day is for amateur baseball fans the way New Year's Eve is for amateur drinkers."

Already Duncavage has arrayed proof that the argument is wrong. Specific cases. There is Bill Tawes, his former colleague. In the cubicle right next to his. With the calendar of Oriole home games next to the one with the babes in swimsuits. They used to get coffee together every morning, Bill yattering away like a machine gun about the Orioles, spitting out rapidfire statistics and predictions. Bill had been to something like twenty-five opening days in a row, and there was no way he'd miss today's game, the last opener in the old Memorial Stadium; next year the O's were moving downtown to Camden Yards. Bill lived the Orioles, went to maybe forty games a season. Which was probably why his wife had left him. Talk about a fan's sacrifice. Talk about dedication.

And then there was Marty Amberg. One aisle over in the cube next to the mail room. Good old Marty, Duncavage thinks, swallowing a lump in his throat. Wouldn't miss an opening day if his job depended on it, which it almost had once or twice. Always down on Thirty-third Street for the opening pitch of the season.

These were not amateurs. With a pang of nostalgia Duncavage envisions Marty in a seat along third base with an Orioles cap shading his eyes, trading baseball yarns with Bill Tawes. Marty's Frank Robinson three-run homer story for Bill's Eddie Murray grand slammer. Marty's Brooks Robinson game-saving diving catch at third base for Bill's Boog Powell towering line drive over the center field fence. Just like swapping baseball cards. The thought makes Duncavage's eyes burn, and he almost leaves his bench to correct the voice. Amateurs, indeed!

But of course Duncavage would never point any of this out to the retirees in the next aisle over. The old fellow, whoever he is, is simply justifying his own absence from the ballpark. From an habitual defensive posture. The voice of a henpecked husband or a younger brother. His voice rises with each word, shrill as a dogwhistle.

"I would have gone if McDonald'd been pitching," another voice chimes in. "Jack McDowell for the White Sox versus Ben McDonald for the Orioles. That would have been something. That would have been a real pitcher's duel. Remember Ben beat him one to nothing last year in his first major league start? But they went with Ballard instead. Ballard's a bum. You can't count on Ballard."

But now Duncavage has lost interest in the conversation and is absorbed in himself, deep in his own thoughts. He has just been laid off by the company for which he has worked for the past seven years as a technical writer. Just the Friday before. This is his first official day of idleness. Infodyne, his employer, had been purchased by a Canadian company called DataWorld, and the layoff had been rumored for months. The rumors and speculation had become so outrageous, like so many cheap horror film sequels, that when the hammer finally fell, Duncavage had a hard time really believing it.

Denial is always the first stage in accepting loss, he reflects, followed by anger, bargaining, depression and finally acceptance. Kubler-Ross. Well, he'd leapfrogged steps two and three and landed smack in the slough of despond where he'd been wallowing like a frog in a stagnant pool since last Friday.

His wife Renee had experienced the anger part for him. She was really pissed at management for dumping him; like a loyal spouse, she resented her husband's bosses. Why Robert and not that fat idiot, Louann Stark? He'd been complaining about her for years; she didn't do anything but take two-hour lunches and gossip all day long. They only kept her because she made twenty thousand less than he did. An exaggeration, but Renee had a point. The bastards. You could always depend on your spouse to defend you. There was some comfort in that.

His daughter was another matter. Cynthia was a precocious three-year old. She immediately pinned the blame on her old man.

"What did you did?" she asked in an accusing tone, only dimly comprehending that something was wrong. It made Robert and Renee laugh, but Cynthia pursued the point. "What did you did, Daddy?" she insisted.

"Daddy lost his job, but it wasn't his fault," the child's mother said. "It was all politics."

"But what did Daddy did?" Cynthia turned to Duncavage and asked again, "What did you did?"

What did you did?...What did you did?...What did you did? The question floats through Duncavage's mind, lazy as a fat gray cloud, full of portent, vaguely threatening. He pushes through the club door and into the parking lot, goes to his car, an ancient Toyota he will not be able to replace now any time soon. He glances at his wristwatch. One thirty. *What did you did?* More to the point, what should he do now? Renee is at work. Cynthia is in nursery school. Another routine Monday. The whole world is busy; everybody has some responsibility to attend do. Everybody, that is, except Duncavage.

And Bill Tawes and Marty Amberg, he thinks with sudden inspiration. The game begins at two o'clock. He can't get a ticket to see it at the stadium, but he can catch it on widescreen television at the Office.

The Office: How many bars are there with that name? A name as ubiquitous as the Dew Drop Inn, coming from the same wry impulse to pun, to joke around. Duncavage smiles wryly at the added irony. He really could call his wife and tell her he was "at the Office."

While the bar is only a few blocks from Duncavage's home, he has never actually been inside it in the five years they've lived in the neighborhood. But the sign out front advertizing widescreen TV has been stamped into his consciousness from countless glances driving by on his way to work, to Cynthia's school, to trips to the grocery, doctors' appointments, a thousand and one purposeful expeditions. He feels slightly self-conscious entering the dim lounge, and he stands there a moment to let his eyes adjust. It's a bright, warm day outside, but Duncavage thinks ruefully that seven years of staring at a CRT screen bathed in the fluorescent light of ceiling panels has ruined his eyesight. Diminished powers for which he is repaid by getting kicked out on his ass. Some thanks.

The Office is one spacious, warehouse-sized room with a long bar occupying most of one side. The widescreen television is angled into the corner nearest the bar. Square formica-topped tables seating four each are scattered throughout the room, maybe twenty of them, vaguely aimed toward the television like iron filings drawn to a magnet. Lamps in sconces on the walls provide what light there is, though Duncavage notices some of the overhead panels are the sort he recognizes from Infodyne. They're turned off now.

"Hey, look who's here," a throaty female voice says in the slightly mocking tone of a wiseguy. "I thought he was too good for us." Duncavage makes out a woman in a slinky dress with too much makeup on. All lipstick and rouge. He does not recognize her; her aggressiveness startles him.

"Cool it, Kitty," the bartender says sharply and then, turning to Duncavage, "Come in to watch the game? You're just in time. Have a seat. What'll it be? Sump'm to eat?" The bartender is a big beefy guy with a tough, meaty face. Something you might see sizzling on a grill. By the look of him he's the kind of guy used to putting up with feebs and felons. Savvy.

Duncavage orders a glass of beer and a Philadelphia cheesesteak sub. The lounge is fairly well filled with people here for the game, at least fifty. Most of them are young men. Lumpen proletariat types. The woman, Kitty, sits with a group of three of them and glances over at Duncavage often enough to make him feel nervous. A hunched-over man around sixty with obsidian eyeglasses, a hooked nose and a smooth bald head sits at her elbow like some giant pet parrot.

A funny smell taints the air, too, not what you'd expect in a bar. *What are the smells you'd expect in a bar?* Duncavage sniffs a few times but is unable to identify it, decides that at least it is not unpleasant, and focuses on the game, which is just getting underway.

It starts out well for the Orioles. With two out in the first inning, Cal Ripken singles up the middle into centerfield. Immediately afterward, the new Oriole slugger, Glenn Davis, slashes a double to left, and Ripken scores. Evans strikes out to end the inning, but the Orioles are leading one to nothing, and Duncavage idly compares himself with the team: its destiny is his. If the Orioles win, it is a sign he will soon get another job, that things will be looking up for him. Over the next fifteen minutes the fantasy becomes a conviction; Duncavage's fate will be determined by the Orioles' performance in this opening day game. Thus, with every pitch he becomes more and more anxious, on the edge of his seat, and as soon as he finishes his beer, he orders another. During his third or fourth draft, Duncavage gradually becomes aware of a new scent in the Office, but he cannot identify this one, either.

In the second inning, the White Sox get to Ballard for the first time. After the first out, Fisk singles to left. Then Snyder is safe on an error by Worthington at third. Two on, one out. Duncavage has a sick feeling of doom in the pit of his stomach, and when Sosa smashes a homer over the leftfield fence, he has the same sensation of emptiness, like a sucked-out balloon, that he'd experienced on Friday when he got his pink slip.

It is all downhill from then on. The Orioles can't quite get anything going against McDowell, and in the sixth the White Sox score five times, single after single chipping away at Duncavage's morale until, the final two runs knocked in by Fletcher's double to center, he knows the game is out of reach. He tries to tell himself it is only a game, but he is unable to convince himself his destiny has not been foretold. Meanwhile, he has been drinking beer after beer, muttering aloud to himself in despair. When he looks around during the seventh inning stretch, he notices the Office is practically deserted.

Kitty stands with her back to the bar, leaning towards him, one elbow supporting her weight against the bar, a magazine in her other hand.

"Reshape your future," she reads aloud in a sardonic voice.

Duncavage's head jerks up. He has been staring catatonically into his beer like a research scientist peering intently at the bacteriological culture of some exotic disease in a petri dish. Only, it is his fortune Duncavage has been trying to discern in the pattern of foam and bubbles. Now, his inhibitions relaxed, he speaks to this brassy woman who has evidently noticed him before though he does not recognize her.

"What about my future?"

"Can you believe it?" she says. "It's a come-on from a 'breast augmentation surgeon' in Washington, and the number you call is 1-800-BIGONES."

Duncavage looks away. For a moment he had thought that perhaps....

"What is that smell?" he blurts, the sound of his voice surprising him.

Kitty begins to laugh, and then, like a face looming up in a nightmare, the hunched-over bald guy swims into view at her side, perches on the stool beside her. The parrot. He laughs also.

"Marjoram," the hunchback says. "It's good for hypertension and nervousness." He and Kitty laugh together, as if at some private joke.

Kitty gestures with her head toward the back of the bar, and Duncavage notices a small, cream-white machine bubbling back there, the source of the aroma.

"An electric smell diffuser," the hunchback says. "Kenny got one for the place so he can pretend he's got one of those New Age yuppie bars in Federal Hill. Soothes the mind, heals the body, renews the spirit." Again, he and Kitty laugh, and Duncavage takes it he is mimicking the bartender.

"What was the other smell earlier?"

"You must mean the rosemary. It's a stimulant." The hunchback smiles to himself again, a stiletto-sharp thin-lipped grin slicing his lower face. "Would you like cedarwood instead? Or frankincense? They're good anti-depressants." He chuckles.

Kitty laughs, too, and as if this were some sort of signal, the hunchback shuffles over to Duncavage's table and offers his hand. The palm is damp and sponge-like when Duncavage takes it.

"My name is Mel Gholizadeh," he says, his voice somewhere between a chirp and a groan. Spittle foams at the corners of his mouth, a network fine as wrinkles. He seems to be salivating, rubbing his hands in anticipation. Or so Duncavage dimly thinks. "Is there something troubling you? Excuse me for asking, but I can tell when a guy's got troubles on his mind. Your wife cheating on you? Is that it?" A thin bloodless smile under the hook nose and the round dark lenses of his spectacles make Duncavage think of a predatory bird, a shrike, a vulture. He imagines the talons tearing his flesh, the beak at his neck.

He shrugs. "Lost my job."

The hunchback pirouettes on his heel. "Dja hear that, Kit? He lost his job. What did you say your name was, again?"

"Duncavage. Robert Duncavage." He suddenly wishes he'd said another name. Rick Taylor. Jim Richards. Panic seizes him and then relaxes its grip. In telling his name, he has only given information, right?

"Aw, Bobby," the woman says in mock sympathy, pushing herself away from the bar and tossing the magazine she'd been holding onto his table. It appears to be a New Age rag. It falls open to the advertisement for breast surgery with a photograph of a model in a black negligee, overhead view revealing enormous round breasts in a plunging neckline. "You lost your job?"

"It's no big deal, not these days," Duncavage mumbles, put off by the woman's savage mockery. *If only I hadn't mentioned my name!*

"Of course it is!" Mel says. "You lost your job, for cryin' out loud! Don't tell me it doesn't hurt!"

"Maybe we should burn some sandalwood." Kitty raises her eyebrows suggestively.

"What does that do?"

"Aphrodisiac."

"Come on, Kit! Give the guy a break!"

"That's what I'm trying to do, Mel!"

"That's not what he needs."

"You know what he needs? You think you know what he needs, Mel?"

"Hey, you two!" Kenny, the bartender, calls over. "Knock it off! Leave the guy alone!"

Duncavage waves at Kenny weakly, a gesture of thanks but also of reassurance. Don't worry about me. I'm OK. I can handle myself. Yet he gropes uncertainly for a clue to what their racket is, how he got involved with these two.

"Really, Bob," Mel says, oozing sympathy, "I've been through it before, too. I used to be in the teamsters, and I got canned. It wasn't my fault, but I sure got hurt."

"You do something stupid, Bobby? Steal from the cash register or something?"

Duncavage shakes his head. Nothing could be farther from the truth. "No," he tells Kitty. "It was the result of a merger. We saw it coming for months. I'm not the only one who lost his job."

"The bastards! The dirty rotten bastards!" Mel says. His vehemence amuses Duncavage. It also alarms him, makes him uneasy.

"Hey, I'm just as glad not to be there any more, to tell you the truth. Load off my mind. We used to spend the whole morning talking about going to work in Kuwait or Saudi Arabia, can you believe it? Like it was a serious option. You know, think of all the money you could make versus the prohibitions and the possibility of getting your hand chopped off. Shit like that. Whether there'd be any toilet paper, could you bring your own and if so, how much would you need. There were actually arguments about it.

People took sides and everything. It was depressing. Oh, and then there was the mania about lottery tickets...."

"Yeah, but still," Mel says. "You got a wife? Kids?" When Duncavage shrugs his shoulders to indicate yes, he does, but so what, Mel slaps the table so hard beer sloshes out of Duncavage's glass. "Those fuckin' bastards!"

"Yeah, I've seen his wife," Kitty says. "Stuck-up redheaded bitch with a rod up her butt."

"Hey, Christ. I don't even know you, lady. Why're you giving me so much shit? Ever since I stepped in here. You don't let up!"

"Well I know you!" Kitty rasps through her cigarette-abraded throat. "I know your type. A God damn crybaby is what you are. So you lost your job, so what? There a lot of people a helluva lot worse off than you are, mister! Why do you want us to feel sorry for *you*?"

"Hey, did I ever say —"

"Hey, Kit! Knock it off, will you? The man's just lost his job, can't you understand that?"

"Yeah, cool it, Kitty," the bartender says wearily. "Try and keep it down to a dull roar." Polishing the bar with a damp towel he looks over at them and shakes his head.

"Well excuse *me*, Mel! I didn't realize you were such a softy all of a sudden. I'll just leave you two fairies to yourselves." With a switch of her tail, Kitty goes back to the bar, parks herself on a stool, lights a cigarette and stares at the widescreen television through a blue cloud of smoke. The Orioles lost 9 to 1 what seems like hours ago by now. The television has been turned to an afternoon rerun of *The Cosby Show*. Cliff and Claire are trying to get some straight information from Theo about some possible misbehavior in which he has been involved. Duncavage wonders if the act before him starring Mel and Kitty is some version of good cop/bad cop. But what's in it for them? His head has started to ache and his throat feels dry. He signals to Kenny for another beer.

"Believe me, I know things must be pretty tough for you right now," Mel says in a low, confidential tone that invites confession. "Shit, don't I know it."

The bartender brings Duncavage the beer, and Duncavage asks Mel if he can get him anything to drink. On him. One drink, he figures, forming an indefinite plan, and he'll be out the door and headed home.

"Never thought you'd ask," Mel chuckles softly. "Bring me the bottle of Jim Beam, Kenny, would you?" Turning to Duncavage he assures: "It's practically empty, don't worry. One more drink, two tops."

Duncavage notices the bottle is still a quarter full when Kenny sets it before Mel with a shot glass. *So this is his scam*, Duncavage thinks with relief. *Cadging drinks.* He relaxes a bit, the insidious conspiracy exposed as a cheap hustle.

"Let me tell you about rough, though," Mel says, knocking back a shot of whiskey and refilling the glass. "I had a twin brother, lived in Chicago. Not identical, just fraternal. Still, our mother used to dress us alike and we had the same friends and all that. Well, Herb had bum kidneys. First one went, then the other. When the second was failing, he and his doctor approached me about giving him one of mine. Laid a guilt trip on me about how I got the good kidneys and all that. Not that I wouldn't give my *life* for my brother, you know, but it wasn't an easy decision."

"I bet not."

"Performed the surgery right here at Hopkins. Shit, we were both laid up for several months. This was back in the sixties, before they called it a 'procedure,' and it was all safe and simple. I mean, it was a critical operation. Took a lot out of me. Took a lot out of both of us."

"I bet so."

"Well, after Herb recovered, he went back to his family in Chicago. And you know what? The plane he flew back on had engine trouble and it crashed outside Indianapolis. Everybody was killed. Shit, and now I only have one kidney."

"Oh, wow," Duncavage says appreciatively, wondering if Mel has made the story up.

"So I know all about rough times, believe me. Did I ever tell you about my mother?" He looks at Duncavage expectantly, waiting for a reply. After a pause, Duncavage says he has not, and he wonders what sort of an answer Mel had expected. *Does this guy really think...?*

"My old man knocked her up when she was forty-five. This was a few years before the tragedy with my brother. Well, she didn't want to have the child, so she got a back alley abortion. Poor woman bled to death in her bedroom, afraid to go to the hospital, afraid they'd put her in jail." Mel belts back the whiskey and slams the glass down on the formica table so hard it makes a sharp crack. "The bastards! The fuckin' bastards! It makes you so angry you could just take a gun and shoot somebody, don't it? Doesn't it?"

"It could drive you mad," Duncavage concedes.

"Admit it, Bob. Don't you sometimes just want to rub the smug fuckin' smile off their faces? All of them?" Mel sweeps his arm in a vague, grand gesture. "See that look of terror in their eyes just before they die? That'd show them. The bastards! Scare the piss out of 'em, right out of their paisley neckties and Florsheim shoes." He raises the shot glass to his lips.

"Sometimes life seems unfair," Duncavage agrees lamely.

Mel spits the whiskey back into the glass, making a face. "Unfair! *That's* an understatement!"

"Let me have a drink of that," Duncavage says on impulse, wanting to finish off the bottle and get going.

Mel pours a generous splash into Duncavage's empty beer glass and then empties the bottle into his own.

"Here, take it."

Swaying in his seat, off-balance, Duncavage raises his eyebrows at Mel.

"The bottle. Take it."

"The bottle?"

"Go ahead. Take it," Mel says, and he forces it into Duncavage's hands.

"What do you want me to do with it?"

"Smash the fuckin' neck off the son of a bitch."

"Why?"

"Just to show 'em. Just to get the rage out. They can't walk all over us little guys forever! Just fuckin' blow off some of the steam, man. Show 'em you won't take it any more. Go ahead, Bob. Smash the fucker."

"But I don't—"

"Go ahead. I know how you feel! I know how all the broken bastards feel, Bob! Believe me, I *know*!"

"But I don't—I mean," Duncavage stammers, incited, nevertheless, by Mel's encouragement. Yes, why not one simple statement of violence? One gesture of despair, one lashing out at the injustice of his fate?

"Go ahead, Bob!"

Drunk, an automaton following orders, Duncavage raises the bottle over his head and brings it down on the side of the table. Its shattering is like an alarm clock, bringing him sober, awake.

"What the fuck is going on there!" Kenny roars from behind the bar. Duncavage has stood up by now and holds the broken bottle in his hand menacingly, bewildered, swaying drunkenly.

"Fucker's going to kill somebody! Call the police!" a voice shouts. Chairs scrape, a woman screams.

"Pathetic bastard! What a loser!" Duncavage hears Kitty say over the din. "Maybe we should have used chamomile in the smell diffuser."

Kenny leaps over the bar and pins Duncavage to the floor, disarming him by pounding the underside of his wrist with the buttend of a highball glass.

"Hey, it's all a mistake," Duncavage says. "I didn't mean anything! I don't—I mean, I'm not—! Just ask Mel! He can tell you! I wasn't trying t—" He looks around, but Mel is nowhere to be seen.

"Just pay for the drinks and get your ass out of here, mister," Kenny growls, bringing the highball glass down on Duncavage's wrist one more time. "And don't let me see you around here ever again."

Duncavage stands up unsteadily, removes his wallet from his rear pocket and begins to sort through the bills. Kenny yanks it out of his hand, grabs a wad and tosses the wallet back at Duncavage. It bounces off his forehead and onto the floor, cards and pictures scattering like leaves. He stoops over to gather them all up and feels a foot on his rear end push him to the floor.

"Get your shit and get out," Kenny says, turning back to the bar. After a moment, conversation picks up again in the bar, and Duncavage scrabbles around for his cards. Then he pushes himself up off the floor and staggers outside.

In the warm, pre-summer air, Duncavage leans against the brick wall of the Office and closes his eyes. A squirrel chatters somewhere nearby, and he is vaguely aware of birds twittering overhead. He is shaken, shamed, humiliated. He will never tell his wife about this. How can he? As he stands there in the growing twilight, Duncavage hears the anguished mental voice repeating endlessly, accusing him of moral crimes and spiritual shortcomings whose dimensions he can only guess. The deafening silent crepuscular swell fills him with the dizzying indictment of his character, his condemnation of his soul. *What did you did?...What did you did?...What did you did?*

RONTAR

Mike Falcon

Everything was so familiar to me, even as I stepped off the plane, that I instantly knew that Los Angeles and The Big Break were mine as surely as I knew my name. I had never laid eyes on a California Bungalow in person before, but I had seen so many of those tiny homes, the color of avocadoes, peaches, or sagebrush, on L.A.-based police series that I immediately knew one would be mine, just as I was convinced that at least one orange tree would be in the front yard. It had to be in the front because there would be a pool in the back, clear warm water bouncing tiny waves against its azure walls.

That I got both The Big Break and The Bungalow so quickly, in a matter of months, did not surprise me, either. The bungalow was not quite the shade I had imagined, and it was a lemon tree in the backyard instead. But remedies here are simple: If I didn't like the lemons, I could always squeeze them and add sugar and water, and Mann Brothers Paint on La Brea Avenue, with its crew of leftover sixties types who mixed exotic colors for studio set painters, would do the same for me. Even better, if I left them a joint. The interior of my apartment was precisely the same welcoming warm brown as the coliseum walls in Ben Hur.

"California is really surprisingly like it is here," explained my marketing professor at Northwest Iowa Community College, just before I left for the coast. "Only there *you*, as an actress, are the commodity, just like wheat, or corn, or milo." Although we were well into the late seventies, he didn't know the half of it. "Of course, they don't have silos, but even films are stored somewhere." But since he was the only man in town who had a foreign car *and* had been to a Bergman movie, that sort of expert analysis demanded attention, even though he found *The Seventh Seal* "a little short on action."

As was my first agent, whose advice was not even that reliable and who dismissed my late night bartending in an East Hollywood dive as "something Bacall would *never* do." Neither would she have retained the services of someone who globbed tablespoons of mayonnaise on his Canter's pastrami sandwiches or who had sent her to a total of two readings in six months, both cattle calls overflowing with young women as equally as star-struck, long and blond, and new to town as I was. "You got the part, didn't you?!," accused Marty when I called him to complain. "I mean, Jesus, Jane Russell had to sit at a soda fountain for months before anyone even noticed."

Maybe I was just lucky. No other woman from the tall corn state got called for, much less cast in, "The epic techno-space comedy of our generation" as the unit publicist billed the latest in a series of tax write-offs that would never see distribution entitled, I *swear* it, Rontar of Brooklyn. "Conceived in the cold reaches of outer space, hurled to earth by a galactic maelstrom, hatched in depths of the East River, neither earthling or alien, Rontar must …mate!" Perhaps Rontar's brief experience in L.A. partially explained why I stayed in the production so long—it was nice to know that the star of the show was new to town as well.

Added incentives included that I looked pretty good in purple Spandex, that I got to keep the very disco space outfit and wicked stiletto heels, and that *Rontar* was being filmed close to the bar. The manager let me slip out for night shoots, essential for this flick, since Rontar favored nocturnal arrivals. And, after all, if it hadn't been for this green man-lizard the size of a moving van I never would have got The Big Break, because I never would have met Luschan.

"You're the tall sex slave, aren't you?," she asked, wandering into my bar after a particularly difficult evening of filming—that scene where Rontar exchanges a harem of groveling earthlings for the heroine, played by my new acquaintance, still clad in the skimpy spacewear that convinced our monster to trade, a chrome-yellow hand towel and matching washcloth transformed into a reckless miniskirt and a plunging bra via a wizened seamstress from Poland, the director's mom.

I was surprised and flattered that the female lead recognized me out of costume, but taken aback after she watched me fumble through a couple of drinks and marched behind the counter like she owned the place. "This is the *only* way to mix a Sleepy Lagoon," directing me with a nod of her head to take the vacant barstool next to a puffy former leading man reduced to wincing in late night commercials for a discount hemorrhoid cream. "Listen. Glinda. If you can't do tropical drinks right, you might as well just head back to Oz."

"Iowa," I mumbled. I don't think she heard me over the dice she rattled like broken castanets in a rubber cup above her head. "And it's Michelle." Dice skittered across the wood. The actor slid her a five, shaking his head, the loss familiar.

The archetypal native Angeleno, half Jewish and half Mexican, the daughter of a commodities broker and a folk dance instructor, Luschan moved through this city like a Porsche with a radar detector. "I get to dub my own part for Latin America," she confided. "I'm the only who can say 'put down that blaster, you pig!' in Spanish." She also doubled as costumer for the flick, which is why she remembered me—there were few space helmets big enough for a six-foot farm girl. Add that she regularly beat the producer in poker, and you will immediately understand she was the only one around *Rontar* to take home more than rent money. Since she knew a fair amount about farm grains via her dad's commodities biz, we were a natural pair around the set. And then off it.

Until that time, I had spent few minutes in bars of any sort, but Luschan moved with seamless ease through outer space, boozy card tables in Gardena and Las Vegas, and bars with lots of football on the screens and little umbrellas in big drinks. I tagged along. And usually drove. She was the last of the last calls, closing every bar east of Western Avenue, leaving rivers of rum-laden soporifics and a wet trail of nodding lounge lizards behind her, once with a remark I both envied and despised, but have always remembered: "If they sent these rum bombs to Africa instead of that baby formula, we'd have a lot less dead kids." Dark.

But, in fairness to Luschan, she had a rather unhappy child of her own in some special place at the far reaches of the Mojave, so maybe it was just a way of compensating.

Certainly, her plot that would set us up in a two-bedroom dream bungalow was a gift that could never be repaid, and it was a treasure only she and Los Angeles, and only in concert, could bestow on a newcomer.

Although I think of watching football as the province of guys who are usually a little too fat and drunk, and a bit too lazy to do much more than a semiannual trimming of the oleanders, her appetite for anything that could be gambled on whetted my minimal interest. Expressions like "penetrating the goal line" and "shoving it in the end zone" seem to me a rapist's vocabulary under a full moon, and I've never watched another game since that fateful New Years Day. It's just another dimension I don't particularly want to be a part of. "This isn't sports," she was quick to add as she detailed the scheme. "It's not even gambling. All we're going to do is take the money."

No matter who you are, I'm convinced that if you have just a couple of odd talents that are utterly useless anywhere else, they can bring you some big bucks in Los Angeles. The apartment house down our street, for example, which houses a retired lion trainer, the requisite struggling actress, a Ferrari mechanic, the florist with four thumbs, and some guy with an tie-dyed eye patch who "balances energy" while you lie naked on a massage table and he sings words backwards, could exist only here. And only in L.A. would you find a health club that sells them on a family membership.

Take Lushcan's tropical drink expertise and gambling skills, add her football fanaticism, the money I had saved from bartending, the cash she won from *Rontar's* producer, and then toss in a little astrological coincidence—her birthday falls on January first—and it was obvious we were in line for cosmic intervention.

How else could you explain that early on New Years eve she stumbled out of a restaurant, tripped over a tall guy sitting on the curb, and flopped headlong into the border grass before demurely inquiring, "What the hell are you doing in the street!"

"I needed to talk to my parents." To a woman whose entire life was a non-sequitur, his response didn't seem like an entirely unreasonable reply. "I called five times." And there was something vaguely familiar about him. Rock band? Barboy? Go-fer? This encounter, as she related it to me later, did not strike me as unusual. I am forever bumping into people who I might almost know, as if I've seen their startled faces in a recent disaster epic.

Then she placed his face. Holy mother of God. Couldn't reach his parents? Were they stuck in a snowstorm? Phone lines down? Dead? Until that played out, she knew just the person he could talk to. Someone who would understand what he was going through. Someone from the Midwest, like him. Like me…

It was no problem for him and his best friend to slip past the coaches and hotel guards after curfew. After all, he had dodged swarms of jet-quick pursuers all season as he led his undefeated team to a unanimous number-one ranking and into the Rose Bowl. And all it took for us to make sure our bet paid off, at five-to-one odds *against* his team, the prohibitive favorite to waltz through the big game and into a national title, was to demonstrate the beauty of the 151 Rum Sea Snake before we boarded the daybreak flight to Las Vegas, carrying every cent we had and every buck we could borrow. He kept talking, I kept listening, Luschan kept pouring. So we knew that the next morning, just before kickoff, the country's premier college quarterback and future NFL number-one draft pick, was puking his brains out, all over his equally staggering pal, the kid who was supposed to *catch* the ball.

Just a half-dozen south sea drinks in a Los Angeles bar that looks like a set from *Tarzan*, and you can change the course of history. As Luschan so sagely observed the next day, watching the impossible upset unfold on our hotel television, when we knew for sure we would walk off with enough for the bungalow: "Hell, with six of those friggin' Sea Snakes in him, even that Goddamn Rontar would never have made it out of bed…much less, Brooklyn."

EIGHT POUNDS OF SWEAT, OR THE ART OF DEHYDRATION

Mark Pearson

When Ike Goodspeed walked outside into the snow-covered parking lot of the rest stop on I-80 East somewhere west of Elyria, Ohio, the first thing he noticed was that his ride was gone. Only the tracks remained in the snow where the dark blue team van had pulled straight back and turned abruptly to the east. The tracks led toward the gas pumps and the entry to the interstate, but they were quickly obscured by a multitude of other tracks that all led east in a tangle of rapidly disappearing ruts. He looked for the van at the gas pumps, but it wasn't there. As he peered through the dense snowfall for a sign of the van, a car pulled into the spot the van had vacated. Ike stepped back inside the glass doors of the rest stop to make a plan. He'd never been in this situation before, and he wasn't sure about what to do. What the hell had happened, he wondered, but he could picture it, everybody in the van was half asleep or just half dead from cutting weight, and Scotis was still telling the story about winning nationals for the first time. When they loaded up the van to leave, they didn't even check to see who was there and who wasn't. He went back inside where he was immediately swallowed by the dense smell of popcorn, hamburgers, and pizza. He asked the pizza shop for a cardboard box and a black marker. He wrote: "Left by bus need to get to Cleveland immediately," and then he went out front and stood at the entry ramp to the interstate. The snow kept falling, but it felt good. He was hot, dehydrated, and low on energy. The frozen world was calm, cold, and refreshing. It didn't take long to get a ride; a car abruptly pulled over and a young guy with shaggy hair and a young woman with a tie-die shirt looked out the car window at him. "That's where we're headed," she said. "We'll take you."

"Really?" Ike said, astonished at the sudden success of his sign. It felt like the first real break he'd had in days, weeks, months even.

He climbed into a new Saab; his father once had an old one that he drove Ike to wrestling practice in over ice-covered roads in the Appalachian foothills of eastern Pennsylvania where he grew up. He was thankful for it, because they were heavy front-wheel drive cars made for driving in the snow back in Sweden. The car would be OK in the snow that was growing steadily deeper. It seemed to plow through the snow as they pulled onto the highway. The storm raged, completely obliterating the horizon. They were students at Western Ohio University on their way home for the weekend. They introduced themselves, but Ike didn't quite catch their names; he thought he heard something like Gus and Serena. They were engaged. "What are you doing on the road in a blizzard like us?" they wondered. "We thought we got out ahead of the storm." Ike told them all about wrestling and Ohio Poly and Champ Scotis. They'd heard of Ohio Poly, but they didn't know who Scotis was and they looked at him like he'd just escaped from the state mental institution when he told them about having to cut weight and dehydrate. Eighteen-wheelers raced by, blowing snow everywhere, making it even harder to see. Wrestling didn't sound like too much fun to them. "Why do you do it? She asked. "I don't know," he said. "It's kind of crazy." He didn't feel like talking really because deep down it was tied to who he was and it seemed more violent than reasonable all of a sudden. You just have to like to fight, he was thinking to himself, but he doubted they'd understand that, most people didn't. On top of that, it had already been a crazy day and didn't really feel like talking much, but for some reason, perhaps energized by the serendipity of their offering him a ride, he felt compelled to explain it all, and he found his voice, despite the dehydration, despite the fatigue, and he spilled his guts to a pair of total strangers in an old Saab like his father once owned as they headed east on Interstate 80 in the worst snow storm in a quarter of a century. By that point it all seemed like an interminable hallucination.

He'd woken up at 4:30 a.m. that morning, stuck his head out a window into the night, and opened his mouth to eat snowflakes that appeared out of the black sky. They disintegrated against his face, and disappeared into his mouth. Tiny cold sparks lit his tongue. He imagined they quenched his thirst. The cold felt good. He walked the empty streets to the arena; snow and ice crunched underfoot as a light snow sifted around him. The town made no sounds. The cold night air bit at his throat and stung his shaved face. His last drink of water was eight hours before and it was hardly a drink; he allowed some water to trickle down his throat after he rinsed his mouth, and spit into a sink. He was a monk on the way to morning prayers, a mad aesthetic who had hardly eaten in days. He wondered why he was doing it. What was the point?

They were going to Cleveland to wrestle at the university there, but he had grown an inch taller and gained ten pounds since he arrived at college in September for his junior year, and making the weight now meant near starvation for a week. It meant walking around for days, light-headed with sparks floating in front of his eyes. When he told coach Scotis he couldn't make it, Scotis just looked at him and shook his head. Ike was on scholarship and felt the pressure.

Scotis stood there with his chin and chest thrust out trying to get all the height he could out of his five foot six frame. "We'll see about that," he said. Then he walked away, bow-legged, grinning, and mumbling something about kids these days.

"Name's Dunny Scotis," he'd say when he introduced himself. "Most people call me Champ."

"Mind over matter men, mind over matter," Champ Scotis loved to call out at the end of a hard practice when everybody was dragging ass around the room under the big sign that said. "In this world a man is either a hammer or an anvil. Which one are you?"

The first three months at school should have been filled with lectures and the library, but they were already doing two-a-days. Champ's team the year before had fallen apart at the conference meet and they'd failed to make the top twenty at nationals. Scotis was pissed about it. They'd done it to humiliate him as far as he was concerned, and he would have had all of their scholarships if the athletic director hadn't intervened to tell him that revoking scholarships on those grounds was against university policy.

Ike was up at five thirty every morning, so he could catch a bus from the dorm down to the gym then he dragged himself to class after an hour of running and drilling and a quick shower. He struggled to stay awake in class. After the four p.m. practice, he'd catch some sleep and try to study. His grades were in the shit-can. He had a professor who announced at the first class: If you're an athlete, don't expect any special treatment. It was an eight a.m. class. He woke up dreaming of sleep and stumbled to class. He sleepwalked through the rest of the day until afternoon practice.

The moment before Ike stepped on the scale the big needle was poised at zero. He stepped toward it as if he was made of air. His mind focused on that zero as if he weighed nothing at all. He had to weigh 145 pounds in five hours. It was five a.m. When his foot touched the scale, the needle jumped and spun wildly around the dial. His mind went with it. As the needle slowed, it lurched like a half dead man, and then came to rest, finally centered. He was eight pounds overweight. His body fat was 3.9 percent. No problem, he thought; he dropped more weight than that in a shorter time last week. He put on his sweats and ran around the arena concourse. He ran around and around, past empty concession stands with idle soda machines and hot dog cookers, through the lingering smell of popcorn. His footsteps echoed on the concrete. Every time he passed the popcorn machine his stomach cried. If he'd had any saliva left, his mouth would have watered. He did his laps, and headed for the sauna. It was his second home. He stripped to shorts and entered. In fifteen years, they'd ban saunas, and the dehydration.

One of Ike's teammates had dragged a stationary bike into the sauna and he squeezed by it to get to the benches. There were two rows of benches—one above the other. He twisted the electric timer and it started to tick. He smelled the heat as the stones got hot. It reminded him of an attic in summer; he found his father's scrapbook there and read about his success as a wrestler in the years before he was born. He poured a cup of water on the stones and a mushroom cloud of steam hissed upward. He gasped and his lungs burned. The temperature rose to 215. He rode the bike, and then he moved to the top bench where the hot air made him blink. His eyelids felt like sandpaper. If he were to speak, his words would rasp against his vocal chords, but it was only he alone in the sauna at that insane hour, and he didn't feel like talking anyway. If he felt like talking perhaps he would joke about the sauna—how the heat kills the sperm. He once told Wendy that and she laughed and threw a condom at him before she climbed on top of him in the hot box, their bodies so slick with sweat she nearly slipped off of him. He scraped his arm with a tongue depressor, clearing a dry swath of skin then he kept going, methodically scraping his arm then his torso. The wood stick slid across his back, but caught his ribs. He scraped the other arm and both legs. By the time he finished the sweat had beaded again, and turned into tiny streams that ran off his body. His skin was sore. The benches burned his legs. When he opened his mouth to breathe, his tongue stuck to the roof of his mouth. He sat with his hands pressed together as if he was praying, and counted the drops of sweat that fell from his fingertips. They gathered in a puddle that grew until he saw his gaunt reflection. He imagined the snowflakes he ate that morning somewhere in that puddle.

He cursed the day he learned about the sport. He cursed his coach. He cursed the sport. He cursed himself.

Ike remembered his father's words: "One day you may want to do something else. One day your life will no longer be defined by wrestling." He thought his father had lost his mind. He wondered if that time had come.

"Banty up," Medford, their heavyweight, would say when coach Scotis came in to a room.

It was a routine they got used to. Medford's sly "Banty up" followed by Coach Dunny "Champ" Scotis' bark: "Let's go cake-eaters. We got us some rasslin matches to win."

He'd scream at them while they were drilling; "Do it right, proper form. It don't matter if you do it a thousand times if it ain't right."

Medford started calling him "Chimp." "That's what you get when you mix a champ with a shrimp," he'd joke.

They all went there because they wanted to wrestle for Champ Scotis at the Ohio Polytechnical University in Starkville. Champ was a legend. He was the face of the sport; the kind of hero that high school wrestlers all over the country wanted to emulate. He'd won three national titles when he wrestled for Ohio Poly.

Even with all that Ike had some reservations. On his recruiting visit to Ohio Poly, Scotis drove him through Starkville; the car paused as crowds of students passed in the street around them. It was late April, a hint of green hung in the trees. Scotis parked the car and they walked around campus. "This is the Plaza, it's the center of campus and that's the undergrad library; it's the social center of campus." He looked at the old buildings and the crowds of people. Everyone seemed intent on going his or her own way. It was bigger than he imagined. His high school was small, and nearly everybody knew him. Faced with living his dream, he wasn't sure if I liked it. He was used to living in the middle of the woods, a small school, near a small town.

That night, Ike sat at the window of his hotel room, the highest building in town, and looked out at Starkville. He saw a crowd waiting in line for a movie, and a steady line of cars purred in the street. He became mesmerized by the constant flow of people and finally he went out of his room into the street where he merged with the crowd.

After practice when they were all beat, and slumped down on the sweat-slick mats, Scotis would tell them to "circle-up" and then he'd give us some wisdom: "Any rassler worth his salt is got to be running twenty five miles a week," he said in his Midwestern rasp. "We has got to be out working every other team in the nation. There just ain't no other way to be the best."

A few days before he Cleveland meet, he went up to Scotis's office to see if he could talk reasonably to him. It was the first big meet of the season, and they were ranked eighth in the country. Cleveland University was ranked tenth. Champ wanted to put some distance between them, let everybody know his team was for real. He was ashamed his team was ranked as low as eighth and he let everybody know it. "If you're satisfied with that then you don't belong in this room," he said when the rankings came out. A bunch of them thought that was pretty good. Except for the true believers, who hunkered down and obeyed the call to "speed it up" like workers on an assembly line. The whole business started to lose its shine. He began thinking about options; but, he hated to think of himself as a quitter and he would tell himself: you can make it. He'd spent his whole life dreaming about being right where he was. How many hours of sweat and pain had gone into it? He wasn't ready to throw it out the window, so he kept going.

Champ had a quote from Ephesians on the wall behind his desk that said: "For we wrestle not against the flesh and blood, but against the principalities, against the powers, against the world rulers of this present darkness, against the spiritual hosts of wickedness in the heavenly places." He had on a cowboy shirt and blue jeans and a pair of cowboy boots like he was headed out for a day on the range punching dogies instead of shuffling papers and making phone calls in the cinder block cubicle he called his office.

"I've got a Russian lit test tomorrow, I don't know if I can wrestle at Cleveland," Ike said.

"Damn right your rasslin. Let's get that straight right now. Drop that goddamn class. You came here to wrestle champ and that's what you're going to do."

"I don't know if I can make it," Ike said to Scotis. "I'm almost two inches taller than when I got here."

"You got to figure out a way to make it. You got to want it worse than anybody else. You got to be willing to go to the extreme. That's what it's all about. You figured that out yet? Everybody's hurting. It ain't a country club sport.

"Besides," he said. "Ain't nobody ever died from cutting weight that I heard of."

In fifteen years somebody would die from it.

It would all be worth it, Ike told himself, as the cedar boards in the blistering sauna creaked around him. Wouldn't it? It always had been worth it—that satisfied feeling of getting his hand raised after a win; the way his lungs heaved and burned after each match, the soreness that lingered after a bout. He remembered all those practices as a kid with his father. His father was an expert at the side roll and mat wrestling, "old school" technique, nearly lost by the time Ike was in high school.

Whatever it was that had convinced him as a kid that this was the road he wanted to follow was rapidly evaporating with the steam that hissed off the rocks each time he poured water on them. After an hour in the sauna, he went down to check his weight. He stripped down and toweled off and stepped on the scale. The needle danced around the dial and then quivered on a little line. He looked close. One fifty. He'd dropped three pounds in an hour. He still had five to go. When he got off the scale his legs cramped up and fell flat on his ass and rolled to his side to try to stand, but his hamstring had seized up and all he could do was lay there until it passed or wait until someone came by to help him up. He must have lay there for half an hour. When he got up he decided I'd had enough. Fuck it, I quit, he said, but as he spoke the words seemed to stick to his tongue, and there was no one there to hear them anyway. The cramp still tingled his hamstring. He showered and dressed and walked to his room. He had a plan: he would go back to his room, pack and leave Starkville for good. He had enough money to catch a Greyhound bus out of town. Which direction he would go, he wasn't sure. The sky was steel gray and a bitter wind gusted from the north. Snow flurries scattered on the ground, gathered in dust-like rivers and scattered again. It seemed like there had been snow lingering in steel clouds since late September when the last days of summer finally blew out of town. He'd been wrestling most of his life, but he'd had enough. The more he thought about it the more determined to get out of town he became. He got angry too; he got angry with Scotis for being a rock head, something he hadn't counted on when he recruited him; he got angry with himself for choosing Ohio Poly; he'd had other choices, but he'd turned them down.

Back at his room, Ike gathered his things quickly. He didn't want anybody to see him. He figured he would just take a few changes of clothes and leave the rest. He threw some jeans and shirts into a duffle bag and left. The Greyhound station was downtown. It took him about fifteen minutes to walk there. The snow came down harder as he walked and gathered on the streets and sidewalks. The air was clear and cold and it felt good to be walking away from it all. He felt certain about his decision, and he couldn't wait to get on the bus and watch Starkville disappear behind him. He had had enough of Scotis and his crap. He felt like he hated the sport ever since he'd arrived at Ohio Poly, and that made him a little sad. He remembered running home after school that day to tell his mother that the youth association was starting a wrestling team; how he couldn't wait for his father to get home to tell him; how he stood around the front door until his father pulled into the driveway, and then ran out to the car with the news.

The bus station was downtown and he smelled the black diesel exhaust when he was within a block of it. A few buses idled outside; the tracks in the snow they'd made on their arrival already disappearing. The snow at the bus station was dirty. A guy with a shovel had cleared the walkways and piles of blackened snow piled up on either side of the main entrance.

Some of the buses were delayed because of the snow. He wanted to catch the eastbound for Pittsburgh, transfer there and then head east, but the bus was coming from Chicago with the storm, and it was caught somewhere in the middle of it. There were other options: he could ride to Cleveland and transfer there; he could hitchhike, but he didn't want to do that in a snowstorm on the interstate. He sat down on a bench and set his bags beside him. His stomach rumbled and his tongue stuck to the roof of his mouth. He still hadn't eaten or had a drink since the night before. As soon as he bought his ticket he'd go down to the diner on the corner and order enough food to fill him up for a week. The bus station was hot, but not nearly as hot as the sauna. Hot air from a heating vent blew down on him, but after walking in the cold it felt good. Then he started to reconsider: maybe he was being rash. His mind raced back and forth between quitting and staying like a school of fish darting left then right. He had put a lot into wrestling and now he had actually made the team. He could still make the weight. If he could tolerate Scotis for the rest of the year, he could always transfer to another school. He picked up his bag and he started to walk back. The snow was heavier now and it grew deeper in the street, muffling the cars as they passed. It was almost silent. He went along for a while with his head tilted back, looking into the white abyss, eating snowflakes. Each one gave a little cold shock to his tongue. They were like little electrical shocks and he imagined they gave him energy. He felt restored in a way. He was going to go back and make the weight. He wasn't going to let Scotis or anybody else drive him away from what he wanted to do. He hefted the duffle, the strap bit into his shoulder, and he walked through the silent snow with his thoughts ringing in his head.

    He picked up a university bus at the corner of State Street and University and rode it to the gym. The bus was hot and he started to warm up by the time it pulled up to the gym. He was hot, but he was too dehydrated to sweat. Scotis was there. As he got off the bus, Scotis bobbed through the snow with his cocky cowboy gate. The only thing that seemed out of place was his briefcase. Every time he saw Scotis walking, he half-expected him to have a circle of rope slung over one shoulder. "Hey champ," Scotis said. That was another thing about Champ Scotis: he called everybody else champ too. It didn't necessarily mean he thought you were good. It was just a habit meant, Ike thought, to bring attention to the fact that Champ Scotis was the only true champ, so that everybody else would answer back, "Great, Champ. How's it going for you?" Then once the real champ was established, he'd puff up a little more and swagger on his way.

"How's the cut going?" Scotis said.

"Great," he said. "I'm almost there." Almost was relative, Ike thought.

"Way to go kid. I knew you had it in you." Kid was the other name Scotis called everybody. They used to say, Scotis didn't learn anybody's name until halfway through the year when he was fairly sure they'd make it—that they'd stick around, or were good enough—that he hadn't wasted valuable scholarship money on them.

"Its not so bad," Scotis said. But, Ike wasn't in the mood to talk. He just wanted to get the weight off and go wrestle. They still had a three-hour van ride across the top of Ohio to Cleveland ahead of them. Besides, it was bad, he just didn't want to admit it to Scotis because he didn't want Scotis to think he was weak. He felt about the worst he'd ever felt in his life. His head felt like it was filled with helium, and he kept seeing sparks float in front of his eyes as if they were dust motes or arctic bugs drifting through the icy air.

When he got to the locker room he stripped down and stepped on the scale; three pounds to go. After all that nonsense about walking to the bus station, and quitting, he dropped two pounds. He could drift a pound, maybe two on the ride to Cleveland, but he was already dehydrated so that might not happen either. He needed to take a little more off before they left just to be safe. That meant another couple miles around the gym concourse. The sauna would take its toll, so he wanted to avoid it. It took the life out of him with every drop of water. He'd be in danger of cramping up, especially during the match. By that point, he knew he might as well have been trying to drain liquid from a rock. He ran his fingers over his rib cage; he could have counted every rib. What was he doing? Why had he come back? He could have been on his way home by now. All the old doubts returned in a flash; he held them off: closed his eyes, concentrated. I can do it, he told himself. He slowed his breathing down, counted each breath, each inhalation, and each exhalation. He felt his heart pounding just under his skin.

Scotis walked in with his brief case sat down on the locker room bench and opened it in front of him. "Here's your meal money, Champ," he said.

Ike took it and stuffed it into his pants pocket. It would come in handy, later, of course, once he'd made the weight, and after he'd wrestled. He'd eat a full dinner before he had to think about doing it all over again for his next match.

On the way to Cleveland, Ike tried to get some sleep, but it was nearly impossible. They were packed into the van with their bags stuffed everywhere, under the seats, on the seats, and in the aisle. He rolled up a towel and stuck it between his head and the icy window. It worked for a little while, but his head slipped against the frozen window. The windshield wipers squeaked every time they slapped the snow away. The van was cramped. He shared the backseat with the massive Medford, their heavyweight, who at six foot six and two hundred and seventy five pounds, stretched more than halfway across the seat plus he had some heavyweight sized bags and a stack of accounting books that slid across the floor every time the van turned. Everybody else was cutting weight too, except for Medford, who just slept, so the ride was relatively quiet. Nobody had any tolerance for anything. Everybody, except Medford felt like shit. Nobody talked, except for Scotis, who was jawing to the trainer. Scotis had gotten on to his favorite subject, himself, and then his second favorite subject—reliving his first national championship during his sophomore year at Ohio Poly. He could hear him clearly all the way in the back of the van. By that point he'd heard the story so many times he could recite it word for word himself. It made the thought of accomplishing the same thing, any thing for that matter that Dunny Scotis had achieved seem like a stupid waste of time. By the time they pulled into a rest stop halfway to Cleveland, he felt so crappy and was so sick of hearing Scotis go on and on about how he'd pinned Bobby Burton with a guillotine, something he'd never attempted in a match before that he wrapped his towel around his ears. "I just sort of fell into it," Scotis was saying as he drove on through the snowstorm. He'd already heard that story four or five times by then, including the time Scotis told it to his parents and him when Scotis stopped by his house at the beginning of his senior year in high school on a recruiting visit. It seemed like a good story the first time he'd heard it, and it was a big deal because Champ Scotis had dropped by his house. But, by then it was like a song he'd heard too many times on the radio. He was ready to hitchhike back to school and pack his bags all over again, except by then the storm was a whiteout and there was no way he wanted to be thumbing it out on the highway in the middle of that mess.

He got out of the van to stretch with the rest of the team. One or two guys stayed in the van and slept, their heads melted circles in the frosted windows. The snow was drifting down slowly, but steadily, and the air was fresh with that clean snow smell even though cars spewed exhaust all around them. He was too dehydrated to piss, so he went into the snack shop and bought a pack of lifesavers—the kind with all the different flavors. They didn't weigh too much and they'd give him a little bit of an energy boost from the sugar. The first one was cherry and he held it up to admire its deep red color before he plopped it into his mouth. It stuck to his tongue for a minute before he could muster any saliva, but it tasted good. A popcorn machine sat in the glow of a yellow heat lamp and its smell filled the air. There were roast beef sandwiches, Italian subs, and ham and cheese sandwiches wrapped in shiny cellophane in the cooler next to chilled bottles of orange and apple juice and chocolate milk. The restaurant next to the snack shop served waffles and pancakes and he stopped for a minute to look at the colorful pictures of waffles and pancakes piled high with fruit and whipped cream. If we stopped there on the way home he would definitely order the Belgian waffles with either bananas or blueberries.

There were lots of things he never figured on when he went to Ohio Poly. Like how much he'd have to cut weight to make the team, and then turn around and bulk up in the summers only lose it all again the next winter like some manic aesthetic feasting before the famine. And then there was Burleson asking him to jam a needle in his ass loaded with Dianabol; it was part of his daily regimen; he also took mega doses of Winstrol and Anabol. Vitamins, he called them. He passed. Come on man, just do it, Burleson said. Stick it in and draw it a little, make sure there's no blood in the syringe. It's easy. Burleson started out as a 150 pounder, but he blew through three weight classes in a year until he started at 190. He lost in the All-American round at nationals last year. Not going to happen again, he said. He got ranked, but his back was an acne orchard, and he had a temper. That wasn't all: his face bloated and the acne rooted in his cheeks, but he was winning, and he won a lot. Scotis loved him like a son. Whatever it took to make it, Scotis was for. Ike wondered if Scotis knew it was the steroids, or if Scotis was just naïve, and thought Burleson was just outworking everybody else. Whatever it was, Scotis was impressed when Burleson picked up two big decisions on the Iowa swing—the year's toughest road trip. It got Burleson national attention, and he became Scotis's poster boy. You sure you don't want to try it,

Burleson said again. He shook his head, no, but he thought about it. Ike was a skinny kid in a world of muscle-bound freaks, and they weren't just strong, they could bend their bodies beyond recognition, and do the same to his. It was tempting. He had that dream too; the one he had since he was a kid—he wanted to win nationals. All that crap about it shrinking your balls is bullshit, Burleson said. I've never been harder. Man, you can go all night. I blew a load the other day that hit the ceiling. Besides, he said, nobody tests for it. Even if they did, they got chemists inventing new formulas every day to hide it. He wondered if he knew what he was talking about. Burleson wasn't exactly a Rhodes Scholar. In fact, if it weren't for wrestling Burleson wouldn't have been at Ohio Poly, he'd be humping buckets of rivets up a hundred stories, or in jail. But, Ike was glad he was there, because in the end, he was his friend. He might have been nuts, but Ike didn't give a shit, so was Ike in his own way, so were they all.

"I know a guy who can fix you up," Burleson said.

Ike thought about it; he thought about it again, because he was on a losing streak, three consecutive losses, and his last practice was a bust. That match stuck in his mind. But, the weird thing was, he even loved the sport after losing that last match. He'd fallen behind, but then he came back in a series of adrenaline charged flurries, only to lose 14-15; it ignited all the old feelings, and walking off the mat in defeat he knew he could make it; he knew he could succeed there.

But, next practice, he took a bad shot and broke his nose on a knee. Blood oozed down the back of his throat. The metallic taste lingered in his mouth, a full course meal of frustration and defeat. The same meal he'd eaten every year since he arrived at Ohio Poly. Scotis came over and looked right through him like he was counting the days until his scholarship expired, so he could recruit someone new.

"Get back out there," he screamed. "No rassler worth his salt ever let a bloody nose get in the way of finishing practice."

When practice was over, Ike stepped outside through a back door into the frozen air and steam rose from his body. He hadn't lived up to his own expectations. He went to Ohio with big dreams. Things got in the way, school, for one—he actually had to go to classes—and he nearly flunked Sociology, his own fault. And then, there was Wendy. Wendy didn't exactly get in the way. Wendy happened. Wendy was fun, a little bit crazy, a little bit kinky; she loved to fuck on the benches in the weight room at night (He had the key) when no one was there, her legs reaching for the racks. She was smart too; six months older than he was, but she already had a master's in comp lit., and he wasn't even done with undergrad, in fact, sometimes he thought would never finish. For a moment, he felt immune to the cold; it actually felt good, but the wind whipped up and cut through the veil of heat he emitted. He stayed outside for a minute more, and then returned to the stifling humidity of the wrestling room where he thought the lack of oxygen might make him stupid. Why not give the steroids a try? He always hated being a skinny kid anyway. What was it that Scotis said in the press guide? "Quick and scrappy, but needs to improve strength." This was his chance. Bulk up, put on that extra muscle that he needed to push himself over the top. But, he wondered about his chromosomes, his liver, his heart, and his brain. He knew he'd be fucking with things he had no clue about.

I like your body the way it is, Wendy said, and she stuck her tongue in his navel. "Why would you mess with it?" He writhed beneath the tip of her tongue, and her hair that spread across his chest and stomach. You guys are all the same, she said. I don't get it. Her ex played football; he did the chemicals and got named all conference. It worked. Everyone seemed to be doing it. What was the big deal? He could get the advantage for once. But, the questions persisted. He flip-flopped: it didn't seem worth it; Burleson's advice seemed good. Then, he decided: he wouldn't do the drugs. He wanted to do it on his own. Maybe he'd make it;

maybe he wouldn't; either way, he'd live with it. OK, OK, I won't do it, he said. She ran her fingernails lightly across his skin and he thought he could hit the ceiling too, even without the benefit of modern chemistry. He thought he was in love with her until the night he walked up to her room in the house she shared with some other girls and knocked on her door. "Wendy," he said. "It's me, Ike." Inside the door it was quiet and then a sudden rustling of sheets, and then a sound like a pile of books dumped on the floor, and someone slammed the door shut, and locked it. He just left, walked down the stairs and out the door into the bright summer day. He still thought about it; he still thought about her. It had been months since he'd seen her.

His mind churned with thoughts as he Saab purred onward through the heavy snow as the couple in the front seat sat quietly focused on his words, and the road ahead.

"That's all so crazy, the young woman said.

"I guess it is," Ike said.

After he stopped talking, they sat in silence for a long time as the car moved along steadily through the snow. He wondered where the team van was: how far ahead of him were they? He would get there, maybe a little late, but he would get there. They passed other cars, although they weren't going too fast; it was a comfortable ride. It was like being in a little cocoon. He calmed his mind; he let the thoughts go. The world outside was muffled and mild and tolerable and he was inside the warm car with smooth leather seats, power windows, and a stereo system that was playing the Grateful Dead as he talked to his new friends.

"I think this is our exit," the young man who was driving said. He hunched forward over the steering wheel, trying to look through the snow.

"That was pretty quick," Ike said as they passed a sign that said: Downtown Cleveland.

Then, the car slid sideways. At first it seemed OK because everything was muffled and seemed soft, but then they started an end around spin. They bounced off of something hard and a side window exploded. Glass, snow and cold air rushed through the shattered window. Ike covered his head with his arms as the seatbelt clamped him in place. The car became a refrigerator on wheels, and in a flash he saw them sitting upside down in a ditch, but it never happened, and a moment later, they were spinning more slowly. They drifted for what felt like an eternity; it would have seemed almost peaceful if they hadn't crashed into something. Ike kept his hands wrapped around the back of his head and his elbows nearly touched each other. He tried to lean forward but the seatbelt stopped him and kept him locked against the seat. The strap bit into the side of his neck. They must have slid off of the road onto the shoulder at some point. It was hard to tell where they were because the car was turning around and around like some children's ride at a fair before it came to a stop. He kept waiting for another violent hit, but it didn't happen, and as soon as they came to rest snowflakes drifted peacefully into the smashed window and disappeared on the seat.

The couple in the front seat looked stunned, but OK. She had her head down with her arms wrapped around her knees. He was staring straight ahead, white-faced, both hands clamped on the steering wheel.

"You OK?" the young man said.

I think so, Ike said. "You OK?"

Ike felt no pain. The cold air whipped in the window with the snow. It was strangely peaceful.

"I'm OK," Gus—was that his name?—said.

"Holy shit, Serena said. "What the hell happened?"

Gus started the engine, but the wheels just spun, and the car rocked forward and backward futilely in the ditch.

Soon, they were out walking. They went up the exit ramp toward a gas station sign they saw towering above the highway in the distance. For a while they just walked in a world silent except for the muffled crunch of the snow beneath their feet? Ike could feel the crunch before he heard it, and he walked on that way, waiting for the delayed sound after the crunch. Walking took his mind off his hunger, his dry mouth, and the pain in his side. He skimmed some fresh snow and ate it. He focused on every step. It was better that way, because the footing was unsure; it was hard to know where the edge of the road was, and he stumbled a few times. They passed cars buried in snow.

He wanted water. He told himself it would all pass soon, the pain in his stomach, the hunger, that dull hollow feeling that nagged at him, and that persistent question: why?

But, he knew the answer now. He loved it, not the weight cutting, but the sport itself, the adrenaline charge of walking into a match—little more than a fight with some rules so no one got maimed or killed. He loved it from the moment he was eight years old and he ran all the way home with the registration form for his parents to sign. From that point onward the person who he would become began to take shape. He loved that feeling of walking off the mat at the end of that one season that ended so perfectly: with thirty seconds to go in his finals match, his opponent got hurt and the match stopped. He went to his corner, and his coach asked him how he felt. His mouth was so dry he couldn't speak. He just wanted the match to start again. He was ahead 7-5. When they started again, his opponent shot, he caught him and threw him to his back and held him there. With eleven seconds left in the match, he clamped down hard and hung on, and watched the time tick off the big scoreboard, second by second, until the clock finally hit zero.

He loved it so much that he wanted the chance to catch that moment again. That one moment he realized might never come again.

Ike walked on through the snow as it brushed against his knees; it was hard going, slippery and cold. They walked in a line; Ike was in the lead, plowing through the knee-deep snow. It soaked his jeans and chilled his skin. The couple followed him up the exit ramp to a convenience store a few blocks from the exit. They asked directions at the convenience store, and Ike learned he had five miles to go. The young man called for a tow truck. "They're busy today," the store clerk said. "It'll be a while."

"We'll be OK," the young man said. "You better get going, if you want to make it to the university."

"Thanks for the ride," Ike said.

They stood for a moment outside the store, brushing the snow from their jackets, not sue what to say.

"Pretty crazy ride," she said.

"Hope you make your weight," he said.

"Maybe things will work out with Wendy," she said. "You never know."

She gave Ike a hug, and the young man extended his hand.

A cab idled in the store parking lot; a few moments later its driver emerged with a steaming cup of coffee. "Drive me to the university?" Ike said. "Sure thing," the driver said, pulling a black scarf away from his face to answer Ike and take a sip of his coffee. Ike paid for the ride with his meal money. They drove through the empty streets, following ruts in the snow. "You sure it won't be cancelled," the driver said.

"These things never get cancelled," Ike said.

When he got to the university gym, he found a scale and checked his weight. It was a balance scale, and he set the weight at one hundred forty-five. The arm of the scale dinged the top of the guide, then the bottom. It seemed to bounce for an interminable time until it steadied, and the indicator balanced evenly at one forty five. He marveled at how perfectly centered the arm of the scale was. He made it. The team hadn't arrived yet.

"You guys made it," the Cleveland coach said when he saw Ike leaving the locker room. "I thought we'd have to cancel." He kept running is hand over his bald head.

"They're coming," Ike said. "You know Scotis, he wouldn't miss a meet for anything."

"You guys will be in the visitor's locker room down the hall on the right."

"Thanks," Ike said. "I'll just wait for them to get here."

"What 're you going today," the coach asked.

"Forty-five," Ike said.

"Kind of tall for forty-five aren't you?"

"You could say that," Ike said. His mouth was dry and he felt light-headed.

"Must be a hard cut."

"Yeah," Ike said. "It's not easy."

The gym was nearly empty. A few Cleveland wrestlers were lying on a purple and white wrestling mat, or helping the maintenance man set up the purple and white team chairs. It was a small gym, more like a high school gym than a college gym. He thought about all he had gone through just to make it there. It made him laugh. All that, he thought, just to wrestle in an empty gym. He waited almost an hour before he saw the dark blue team van enter the parking lot. He was standing in the gym lobby when they pulled up. The snow was still coming down when he stepped outside into the cold air. The team stretched and yawned as they unloaded from the van, and nobody noticed him as he approached.

Scotis was the first to see him. He looked at Ike, who was halfway across the parking lot, then looked back at the van. "What the…" he said. "Goodspeed, how in the Sam Hill did you get here before us?"

"You've got to want it coach," Ike said.

CONSUMMATION: 2004

Colleen Shaddox

Most of the passengers screamed, "Why? Why?" But as the elevator dropped down its fiery shaft, Jim O'Boyle simply thought, "Of course."

Not that Jim fancied himself the target of anyone's murderous rage. Jim O'Boyle had no enemies save the Universe, which he had just offended anew.

As Jim stepped on that elevator, he'd been thinking how the Red Sox had kept the season smoldering through September. He was thinking of the playoffs, the pennant, the series. He was happy, a condition in which the Universe does not allow Red Sox fans to linger.

He had been a Sox fan from the cradle, a cradle situated in South Boston. Under a baseball cap three sizes too big, Jim would sit by his father's side and try to make out the games through the snow of their black-and-white television. He learned to curse by listening to his dad's ninth inning exclamations.

He built elaborate fantasies about a World Series many years hence: Seventh game bottom of the ninth, Sox down by three with the bases loaded. Carl Yazstremski, in his final at bat before retirement, goes down swinging for the second out. "It's all up to you now, kid," he says to Jim O'Boyle, as the red-hot rookie steps into the box.

"I'll do my best, Yaz," Jim replies.

A called strike, a foul tip, and it comes down to one pitch. A bit high and outside, but that's how Jim likes them. He swings. The bat trembles at the impact as the ball sails on, on, and over the Green Monster.

Reality, needless to say, gave fantasy a wide berth. Jim was a baseball eunuch. He loved the game with a singled-minded passion, but could not perform. The pitch would come in, and Jim would know exactly where and when it would cross the plate. But somehow he could never get his bat there.

So he worshipped the game from afar, developing a knowledge of Red Sox trivia so extensive that his mother, upon learning of obsessive compulsive disorder from a *Reader's Digest* article, simply closed her magazine and said, "Jimmy." He knew Rick Miller's minor league stats. He knew how Ted Williams tied his fishing flies. He knew Tom Yawkey's shoe size.

It was sad, or so most people thought. But not Susan. No, not Susan.

Susan was the love of Jim O'Boyle's life, though they spent just a few hours together. As if they needed even that long to realize it. But their romance, like so many sweet dreams, was destroyed by a man named Russell Earl Dent.

Jim met Susan in a Boston bar in the year 1978. Not the television version of a Boston bar, where delightful eccentrics engage in witty banter. A real bar, where you can't hear a damn thing and your feet stick to the floor. Jim found a depressing fellowship there. It was the perfect spot to watch a game.

This was The Game, the playoff for the American League East Championship. Jim, ignorant of the heartbreak and humiliation to come, was letting hope soar within him.

He was surrounded by fellow Red Sox fans, each shouting commentary over the other shouted commentaries. Jim's attention was arrested by a young woman who brilliantly contrasted and compared the rookie performances of Jim Rice and Freddie Lynn to demonstrate the inevitability of Rice's greater success in the long run. As she went into insightful detail about how Lynn held his bat too far down on his shoulder, Jim O'Boyle fell in love.

He wanted this tawny-haired baseball queen to love him back. Jim knew better than to shout cold statistics with the rest. He waited, waited until the right opening presented itself. During a lull in the cacophony, Jim drifted to Susan's side.

"When the Sox finally win the World Series," he said, "I will lay down and die of joy."

"Careful what you say," Susan replied. "This could be the year."

"I can think of no cause for which I would rather give my life," Jim said.

She saw that he meant it.

They stood side-by-side watching the game together, exchanging smiles whenever Boston retired a Yankee. Six scoreless innings. It looked good. On any other day, Jim would have realized that it looked too good. But today, love made him disregard the lessons of a lifetime.

Then it happened: the cataclysmic moment when the Yankees' Bucky Dent, an absolutely unremarkable batsman, hit a three-run homer and changed the world, irrevocably changed the world for the worse.

When it was all over, Jim and Susan left hand-in-hand. They wandered the streets of Boston and instinctively ended up under the Citgo sign that peers expectantly into the Fenway outfield. They held each other in silence. Each knew they would never see the other again. It would only remind them.

They might have given their passion expression in the dark and deserted night. But this was a time of mourning, and they were not animals. Or Yankee fans. They parted at sunrise without a word or a kiss.

Now, rushing toward his death, Jim thought of Susan with a glad heart. Surely the Red Sox were going all the way this time. That was why he was on this God-forsaken elevator. If the BoSox were going down in flames, the Universe would have let him live, would have *made* him live to see it. It would not be a repeat of last year. This would be The Year, and Susan would think of him when victory finally came to pass.

He breathed deeply and waited for the everlasting embrace. In his mind's eye, he saw Carlton Fisk jumping up and down, waving the ball fair. He saw Fisk will himself that beautiful home run. He saw that ball fly past the foul pole on a stream of hope. Hope—the force that challenges the Universe itself, and that sometimes, when the wind is right, wins. Hope continued to soar within Jim O'Boyle as he sailed, like a long ball off the bat of Williams, Yazstremski, Rice, Ortiz and generations yet to come. He sailed on, on lifted by hope, hope that would not be dashed. He sailed on.

SPIDER-MAN VS. SUPERMAN

Jeanie Chung

The amazing, never-before-told story of Chicago's own prep basketball superhero battle! Get it while you can!

For generations, comic book aficionados have pondered this question: if Spider-Man and Superman were to face off in combat—a clash of the ages, an epic battle that would make the stars rock in the firmament—who would win?

Well, denizens of our fair city, this reader is a Marvel devotee, and so there can only be one answer: Spider-Man all the way. Who else represents the downtrodden masses huddled on Chicago's West Side? Surely not Superman, descendant of intergalactic royalty. And, for that matter, not Batman, scion of a multimillionaire family. But Spider-Man was no different from you or I, leading a simple life when—bam!—he was bitten by a radioactive spider *and* his uncle was murdered, leaving him, already an orphan, alone in the world with only his elderly auntie to take care of him. Well, and some superpowers—let's not forget those. But nonetheless, there he was: a man with secrets. A man beyond understanding. Who would ever know the trials he faced every day? Who would ever relate to his double identity?

This is a trip. For real. I don't even know how y'all hearin' me or nothin'. 'Cause I can't make words go like they supposed to, you know what I'm saying? I can't write 'em down right. I can talk, but, like, when it's my teachers or people like y'all, I got to talk real slow sometimes. I ain't stupid. But what's in my head don't come out my mouth or on a piece of paper. So I do like this: when I'm playing basketball—not, like, in a real game, but just messing around—or sometimes when I just be hanging, in my own head, I talk like I'm in a comic book. Then I sound smart. Like I could take over the world. It come real easy.

If only I could explain my own double identity to the heinous overlords behind the ACT.

Perhaps it's my spidey-sense. From the beginning of my own humble existence, I wanted all my friends to call me Spider-Man instead of JaRon, for that was how I appeared. Long arms, long legs. My spider-fingers ensnared any ball that came near. Woe to any man I covered on defense: he was powerless to get away from me. Zzzzzip! He was caught in my web. And, reader, don't think for a minute that it had anything to do with John "Spider" Salley. No self-respecting Chicago kid would aspire to be like a Piston.

In my possession to this day is the first comic book I ever got, given to me by my father when I was nine years old. Darius Watson was not exactly a ruler of the planet, or the owner of Wayne Manor, but he had at least the good fortune not to be dead like Spider-Man's father. Unfortunately, that was about all you could say for him. As I understood it, that fine spring day, I hadn't seen my father for a couple of years when he showed up saying he wanted "quality time" with me and my brother and sister. My mother slipped him some money and urged him to buy me some shoes. Instead, realizing the comic book was cheaper, he bought it for me and kept the extra cash for himself. At the time, I didn't know that, nor did I care that I had to tape my right shoe together in the front. I was captivated instead by all those colors and this cool red-and-blue motherfucker who could stop bad guys by shooting his web at them.

Eventually, I found out that there really was an epic battle between Superman and Spider-Man*, six years before my birth. But let us move forward in time to the winter of my senior year at Admiral Perry High School, when only two things mattered to me: beating Coolidge High, and getting my very own copy of "Superman vs. the Amazing Spider-Man." I knew that both tasks would require my mighty strength and every one of my superpowers. Even though I'd grown six inches in the last year and the talk of the local sports pages was the fact that our team had a chance to win state, doubtless you have already heard stories of mighty Coolidge and its own Superman, Roosevelt Rawls. Just as challenging was the fact that, as you might guess, there were not a lot of comic book stores in what we called the 'hood.

When we rejoin JaRon his senior year, eight years have gone by since he has last seen the man who was responsible for bringing him into this world, though not for keeping him in it. Darius' reappearance coincides with an anticipated event in the city of Chicago: the start of basketball season ...

Out of the shadows he stepped, still wearing that red Bulls jacket, ready to greet me after our first official practice of the year.

"Son."

"Darius. You musta heard the UCLA coach was here. He didn't give me any money, if that's what you're looking for."

"Show some respect for your father."

I shuffled my feet, looked at the ground.

"Boy, what you need college for anyway? What I hear, you ready for the league."

Wham! A blow straight to my heart. Surely he thought that flattery would win me over to his side. But I was not so easily swayed. "Coach says I need to play college ball first. I think it's better if I listen to somebody who's seen me grow up." Biff! Swatted him away.

So my father's reappearance remained a secret, one I planned to take to my grave. But of course, fate had other plans ...

"Look who's here," my sister Jelisa said when I returned from practice one night the next week. He was right there with her and my brother Jerell, laughing like old friends. With old friends like him ...

"I see." I turned to my father. "What do you want?"

"I'm just here to see my family," he said. "Look at that: my girl's all grown up, I got two big boys. And no grandchildren yet. Thank Jesus. I'm not ready." He laughed a crooked-teeth, red-mouth laugh.

"Come on. He's trying," Jelisa pleaded with her eyes.

Still looking at my sister, my father said, "You can forgive me, but maybe he can't." Before I could say anything else, he turned to me. "Remember that comic book I got you, son? Was it something about Spider-Man fights Superman?"

"*Superman vs. the Amazing Spider-Man*. And no, it wasn't that one." I took a closer look around him. "Do you have that one? Did you see it somewhere?"

How could he have known? In his hands was nothing but a plastic plate with a piece of pizza. He laughed, "Of course, I don't have it now. I'm going to go get it for you. Maybe next week. After your game?"

I would have to wait to find out.

The next week, we crushed those guys from Stony Island High—Kapow! Splat! I'd forgotten about the game almost as soon as it was over. The only thing on my mind was seeing my father and getting my hands on that comic book. Then I saw his face.

"I'm sorry, son," he said. "They said they had it at this one place, but I went over there and they sold it to somebody else. Long as we're here, though, let's go get us a hot dog."

When did he get a car? I wondered, then stopped. I didn't want to think too much about how he paid for it, whose car it was if it wasn't his, where he'd been, how long he'd be back, all those questions. Then again, they distracted me from how angry I was for being played for a fool. Again.

"Tell me about your life, son," he said. "How's basketball?"

If only he knew. "My life *is* basketball. That's all I do, that's all I want. You'd know that if you'd been around."

"You know, some of that time, I wanted to be here, but I couldn't."

"What about the time you weren't in jail? Huh? Where were you then?"

"It's, you know, son, some of that time your mom told me to stay away. I didn't want to make trouble for anybody." He stopped and stared for a minute at his hands in his lap. "OK, I fucked up. I should've been here more. Like Albert Rawls is for his son. But look at you. You turned out pretty good, right? As good as—no, no, *better* than Roosevelt."

I took a sip of my Coke. Who did he think he was dealing with, anyway? Spider-Man didn't fall for that kind of praise so easily. And if he did think I was better than Ro, he was the only one.

Flashback ...

Some superheroes are friends as well as rivals, but Roosevelt Rawls and I weren't like Peter Parker and Harry Osborn, or Superman and Lex Luthor: best friends who became mortal enemies. We were more like Peter Parker and one of the other kids he went to school with. Years ago, Roosevelt and I had played on the same AAU team. When we were around twelve, he started to grow, get stronger, play like a man. They were grooming him to be the next Kevin Garnett. Meanwhile, I was still chubby and a step slow, unworthy of the rarefied atmosphere of *real* club ball. Sure, they said, he can help any team out, be a good solid high school player eventually. His old man was pretty good back in the day. But he is not—they stopped to clear their throats—a difference-maker.

From then on, we saw each other around, but as far as teams, we were in two different universes. For high school, Ro and Albert looked at every school in the city, in search of the right place. At one point I had heard he was going to go to Fermi—he was smart enough for that school and their team was good enough for him. But when their coach didn't turn out to be old-school enough for Mr. Rawls, they chose the Knights of Coolidge.

As for me, I embraced what had surely been my destiny since birth: to go to Perry and follow in the footsteps of my father, one of the all-time greats to wear the Admiral blue and gold. It didn't matter to me then that by the time I started at Perry Darius Watson was just another loser hanging out on the playgrounds, talking about the 1980 city championship. The die had been cast, and, on the court at least, Roosevelt and I would fight for two different uniforms. Sure, Roosevelt kept getting better and better, but, to everyone's astonishment, so did I.

After that, it was more like he was a DC Comics character and I was a Marvel guy. We knew what the other one was doing, but we didn't hang out. After all, he was the one whose feats of athleticism were chronicled in 48-point type, in vivid color. The academic qualifier. The blue-chip recruit.

And back to the present day …

"Now," my father told me, "let's talk a little bit about what you're doing out on the court there. You're boxing out like you should. You take it strong to the hole. But what we got to work on is your defense and your outside shot. That's what's going to get you a scholarship."

Later that year …

To my surprise, he stayed like that—involved, interested—and was still in the picture at Christmas. He brought my sister a new coat and my brother some Xbox games. Brought me a new pair of Nikes and said he was going to bring my comic book when he came to see me at the Downstate Christmas tournament. He still wasn't working, so he had time.

We lost in the championship game, 72-70, to a Downstate team of hulking farm boys with square faces. Unlike Roosevelt, they actually looked like the real Superman, square-jawed, pink-skinned. Each one alone couldn't play like Superman, or like Roosevelt, but together they were as mighty as the Hall of Justice. I was disappointed we lost the game, but in my heart I knew we had bigger, more important battles to fight. Afterward, my father said he'd drive me back to Chicago if it was OK with Coach.

"Son, I'm sorry," he said when we got in the car. "They raised the price on that comic book. Those things are expensive. I thought I had enough, but with all the presents for everybody, I just didn't."

"It's all right," I said, surprised to hear real disappointment in my voice. "You did everything you could."

And in the stillness of that dark night, the two of us sheltered against the cold in that rattling car that I still didn't know if it was his, slashes of gray rain against the windshield, for two hours, my dad passed on his wisdom about defense. Once he even pulled off the road to get out and demonstrate the best way to set my feet. When he finished, he just kept talking. About the guys he used to play with, the jokes they played on each other, the games they won.

"That's what was so funny, son, when you started calling yourself Spider-Man," he said. "We, I mean, I guess it ain't that unusual, but we used to joke around that we were superheroes. This one little point guard, Eddie, he was the Flash. Our two guard, he was real talkative—he was our captain—he was Captain America. And me, I was the Green Lantern. Our uniforms were green, but the real reason they called me that was that he was the first black superhero. I mean, all of us was black, but the fact that they let me be the Green Lantern, that was special. That showed what they thought of me."

A week after New Year's, Darius has another surprise for JaRon …

He took me over to Madison Street and parked in front of a row of stores. They were open, but empty. "Close your eyes," he said, grabbing my arm and leading me.

I opened my eyes to find myself in a room with a chair, a table covered with needles and little bottles, and a smiling bald man. The table was across the room, or I would have knocked it over. I thought he was through with that stuff, though I did wonder why it would be so open, in a store and everything.

He and the man started laughing when they saw my expression. "We gonna get you a tattoo, son," he said, collapsing against the bald man's shoulder. "What did you think?"

On the back of a McDonald's receipt, my father had drawn a spider web with a basketball in the middle. He had made each one of the tiny, delicate lines of the web. It looked almost too pretty to be a tattoo.

"That's for you," he said. "A spider web don't look like nothin'. If you see it at all, it's just a little bitty thing. But if you're a fly? Shit. You need to fear the web. By the time you see that spider web, it's over. You're done. Just like you: you may not look like much, but you finna lay *waste* to some people out on that court."

Pretty as it was, the pain resulting from all those little lines was almost too much for a mere mortal. With my free arm, I reached out and grabbed my father's hand, squeezed it hard.

And there are more surprises ahead …

Two days before the epic battle against Coolidge, my father called to tell me that this time he had my comic book. For real. Fortune had still not smiled on him enough that he had his own place, but kind friends had taken him in, and it was OK for me to come over. I knew he was serious this time, and I had to give him credit. He got my comic book, which was no easy task, especially when you don't have the internet and have to search for it in stores. But he knew how much it meant to me. Knew it would be something special to take with me when I took on Roosevelt and Coolidge in combat. A father's legacy to his son.

But fate has other plans for this father and son:

That afternoon, as I was walking up the sidewalk toward an old house with porch steps that needed repainting, the scene before me stopped me cold. Two cops were taking my father away in handcuffs. They shoved him down the steps, dragged him along, but then when they got to the car, they put their hands over his head and guided him down gently, like they were putting a baby bird back in a nest, so he wouldn't hit his head.

My father: gone. Again. What could I do? Nothing? What did I do? I got out of there before the cops saw me. Even though I hadn't done anything wrong, like many superheroes I had an uneasy relationship with the police.

He called that night.

"I don't know if you heard, son," he said.

"Yeah."

"I'm not getting bond on this one, so I don't know when I'll see you again. But I want to tell you two things."

"OK."

"First of all, you're gonna be OK. You're gonna beat Coolidge. Remember, Roosevelt Rawls is just one man. He may be Superman, but you're Spider-Man. You got that … what is that? That extra thing in his mind?"

"Spidey-sense?"

"Yeah. Spidey-sense. Remember that."

"I'll try."

"Second of all, I left your comic book at the house where I was staying. I didn't get a chance to tell 'em it was special for you. They don't know about that kind of stuff. They might think it's junk. What I'm saying is, they might throw it away. It might be gone. And I'm sorry about that, son. I really am. All this time I wanted to do this nice thing for you."

"It's OK, Daddy."

Now, I knew what was going to happen Tuesday. I knew where my comic book was. Maybe. What I didn't know was whether my father was guilty. I could've asked, but I didn't.

The truth was that even then, I had no time to think about comic books, or even my father. Instead, I, like everyone else in the city of Chicago, was totally focused on our game against Coolidge. The next day was Monday, the game was Tuesday, and it seemed like no one—not the newspapers, the TV stations, or our schools—had talked about anything else for the past week.

The sports page headlines screamed:

"THIS ONE'S FOR KEEPS"

"WILL 'THE SHOW' GO ON?"

"SPIDER-MAN VS. SUPERMAN!"

For me, Spider-Man was just a nickname, but it seemed as though the city had come to believe that Roosevelt really was Superman. Even I felt that way. I'd watched him play in tournaments, and sometimes I'd swear, I really could see him with his face made of little dots, in a box with a yellow background. He'd soar through the air and throw it down, "BOOM! KAPOW!"

He'd block somebody's shot, "KER-RACK!"

And there'd be another box with all these people in the crowd, cheering, dancing, throwing back their heads and howling.

My first sight upon entering our gym on gameday was Albert Rawls behind the visitors' bench, smiling like he was about to watch a good movie where he already knew the ending. He never missed a game. Was it any wonder everything went right for Roosevelt, with his father helping him every step of the way? A superhero needs guidance. True, Superman didn't have Jor-El beside him as he fought against the forces of evil, but he did have those nice farm people who raised him.

As for me, who did I have in my corner? I looked up into the stands and saw some guys I knew from school. That was it. My mom was working. My brother and sister were working. And we already knew where my father was.

I looked over at the mural painted on the wall: Mark Pullman, a Perry graduate who became an NBA All-Star. The last real superhero we had. There he was in his Admirals uniform, flying through the air, ball in hand.

Of course, behind me I had fourteen teammates to lead into battle. Good guys. Strong, valiant men who fought to the death. But still, not like Roosevelt's team. Antrell Jones and Mo Chambers were both Division I recruits too. Superman had some of the X-Men with him today. All I had was Plasticman and Inspector Gadget.

Coach called me over.

"You ready, son?"

"Hell, yeah."

Mo got the tip and knocked it over to Antrell, who passed it to Ro, who laid it in. Not an auspicious start for us, but I knew we would not go down so easily. I looked over at Shon Taylor. He nodded at me, just a little bit. We went back up the court, and the first thing I did was get into position and set a pick on their big forward.

"OOF!" Shon was open for the shot. It was on.

We traded baskets for a while. Just as everyone expected, it was a classic. A game for the centuries. With a minute left, Coach told me, "Take it up strong. Mo's got four fouls. You'll either get an easy two—or he'll foul you and you'll get two easy free throws *and* he'll be out of the game."

That was what happened. They passed to me at the top of the key, and Mo was a little slow rotating over. Coach Rollins on the other bench was screaming for a charge, but even Mo knew it was a good call. If I made both free throws, it'd be a tie game.

Everyone knows that consistency is the key to free throws. It doesn't matter what you do—dribble three times, touch your elbow, stand on your head—just do the same thing every time and be ready when the whistle blows. Clear your mind of everything else except the vision of the ball going in the basket. Or, if you're trying to miss and get the rebound, you picture that. Sometimes I made it so I could see farther: us stealing the inbounds pass and scoring. Us winning the game. Me cutting down the net at the Final Four. It was my spidey-sense.

Just when I was walking to the line, a red jacket caught my eye. The man had braids, a red Bulls jacket, was a little lighter than me. How'd Darius get out of jail? I looked again and realized it wasn't him. And now wasn't the time. Focus. Back to the game. Then, in my mind, my spidey-sense showed me something else.

It was night, and my father was riding around with some other guys. He was in the passenger's seat, in the front. They saw a car parked in front of a house, didn't recognize it. They drove by and started throwing Disciples signs. The guys in the other car, they threw the signs back—upside down. Looked like one of them spit.

I bounced the ball from one hand to the other.

It was on. My father's car swung around the block, squealed its tires just enough so you could hear them. He and the other guys pulled guns from their waistbands.

I tugged on my waistband three times.

My father pulled out his gun, lifted it. The gun looked dark, hard to make out against the car and my father's black jacket, until a streetlight caught just a little tiny sparkle on the metal.

I took the ball, got in position, bent my knees.

Those guys in the other car were ready, they knew my father and his boys were coming back, but maybe they didn't know it would be so quick.

Everybody along the lane got ready to rebound.

The target was in sight. POW!

I got the ball back, bounced it from one hand to the other.

Someone else in the car pulled out a gun, and he lifted it.

I tugged on my waistband three times.

People started running from the parked car.

I took the ball, got in position, bent my knees.

POW! BANG! KAPOW!

The game was tied, and I was hustling to get back on defense, like my father would've wanted. Antrell brought the ball up for Coolidge and I was on Ro. I knew the best way to tell what he was going to do was to look into his eyes, not at his hands or his feet.

The comic book my father bought me was called "The Death of Spider-Man,"* and in it, one of the bad guys tells Spider-Man, "Great heroes inspire great villainy." I looked at Roosevelt, who wasn't on the yellow background with the word-balloon coming out his mouth anymore. He was sweating and sucking wind, like I was. He stank, like I did. He was tired, like I was. He was just a man, like I was. Except, right then, he had a father to talk to, after the game. He didn't need this, too.

My spidey-ears picked up the zip of the ball, this one time, just as it left Antrell's hands for Ro's. And just like I was throwing my web, I reached out and stole that ball. I ran—no, I flew—to the other end, and when Antrell caught up with me, I dished it off to Shon for three.

SWOOSH! The buzzer sounded.

In "The Death of Spider-Man," Spider-Man did actually die, but in the end, not only did he beat Thanos and come back from the dead, he brought back a little black girl who had died along with him. The last panel showed him cradling the girl in his arms as her grateful mother said, "Shush, girl, you're in God's hands again."

Meanwhile ...

"That's what I'm talking about!" my father yelled as soon as he saw me, ignoring the guard's demand that he pipe down. "Y'all see this boy right here?" He looked around at the other prisoners, the guards, the other visitors and made sure he had their attention before pointing at me. "He brought some *game* against that Roosevelt Rawls and them boys from Coolidge. That's my boy. Spider-Man. That's my *boy*."

I needed to go down to see my father: talk to him before his trial, even if it was through a piece of bulletproof glass. Actually, it framed his head perfectly, like he was in a comic-book panel.

"It was only three points," I said, once he picked up the phone.

"Don't matter, son. You tore 'em up. I *know* you did. My boy."

As I said before, "The Death of Spider-Man" was one of the few comic books I owned. There were so many things about Spider-Man, and spiders in general, that lay beyond my realm of knowledge at that time. For example, it wasn't so much the spider's web that made him dangerous. If you were caught in the web, you couldn't run away. Eventually, you'd starve to death. But usually it was the spider's bite that killed you. A real spider killed his prey by coming over and shooting poison into his blood. Notice how Spider-Man never did that? He could kill people, probably, because the spider that bit him probably gave him the poison too. Even if he had no toxic venom—surely he still could've carried a gun, right? But he didn't.

"Why'd you do it, Daddy?"

My father got quiet, shook his head. "Son, I can't say much right now. All's I wanna tell you is this: learn from my mistakes. You gonna make something of yourself. You gonna go to college."

Now, I thought he knew, but maybe it had never come up. He'd never mentioned it, at least. So I told him: I didn't have an 18 on the ACT. I couldn't play regular college ball until I got it, and I didn't know if I ever would. And shit, even Roosevelt Rawls didn't have much of a future without college.

His smile erased itself.

"What? Bullshit. We'll figure something out. We can—"

I interrupted him, so quietly he didn't hear exactly what I said. He asked me to repeat it, even though really, he already knew.

"I said, 'What do you mean, 'we?'"

He looked down at the table. "I'll, I'll talk to some people. I know some people, they maybe could help. Listen," he leaned toward me and whispered, even though that didn't matter through the phone, "you thought about getting somebody to take the test for you?"

I shook my head. "It's all right." Still, he had a point. It might be worth the risk of ending up like him.

After I left the jail, I went by the house where he'd been staying. A skinny lady with a T-shirt and a big Afro answered the door, or I guess you could say she was a lady. I don't know if she was older than I was.

"Did you—I know this is gonna sound weird, but did you see any, um comic book around here?"

"What, like Superman and shit? With the pictures?"

"Yeah."

"Baby, I don't know if I have ever seen anyone reading anything in this house, except maybe the want ads every once in a while. And those are starting to all be on the internet now anyway."

As I walked out, I found a ball of paper crumpled, wet, torn on the sidewalk. Thin paper, like newspaper. I flattened it out to find some criss-crossing lines on a red background, then black. On the other side it said, "Try It!" It easily could have been a page from my comic book. It also could have been a page from the newspaper. Surely my father would be reading about me in the newspaper. I'd brought him both papers when I went to visit him in jail. They had to tear the massage parlor ads off the bottom of the Chicago Express when they gave it to him, but he'd read the whole thing.

"Hey!" a voice boomed out, and, as soon as I looked up, said, "Aw hell, you Greenie's boy. The basketball star!"

"Greenie?"

"Yeah, because they used to call him the Green Lantern or some shit back in the day." For a man who only came up to my chest and looked like I could pick him up with one hand, he had a deep voice. "Anyway, that's you, right?"

I nodded, quiet. This man hadn't been in my free-throw-line vision of what happened with my father.

"I saw that game the other day. I went to Coolidge, you know." He turned to one of the three men with him, all of whom towered over him. "Your boy can *ball*." Turning back to me, he asked, "Where you finna play college?"

"Dunno. Gotta get the test scores first."

"Hmmm. Well, that's a shame." He looked at me, but past me, really. Through me, like I was made of glass and somebody more important was standing behind me. After a moment, he looked away from the imaginary person and back at me.

"I heard you and your daddy was just getting to know each other again. Now this happens. That ain't right." He shook his head.

I looked around. My hands felt twitchy, like I was waiting to grab something. I'd have felt more comfortable if I had a ball to dribble.

"Well, what you gonna do, you know what I'm saying?"

He smiled. "I do know. You probably feel alone now."

"I still got my mama and my brother and sister. My coach. My teammates. Just like always."

"Sure. But it ain't the same as having a father. And soon, you're gonna graduate."

"Yeah."

"What I'm saying is, we looked out for your daddy, as much as we could. We can look out for you, too. At the very least, we can provide you some, how can I put it? Options. If this college thing don't work out. Just think about it."

He turned on his heel and walked away. The other three men, who hadn't said anything, followed him, elbowing each other and laughing.

Will JaRon go to college? Or will he cross over to the dark side to avenge his father? Wait and see ...

The title, "Spider-Man vs. Superman," comes from a one-shot comic book that was a joint publication of Marvel and DC Comics, 1976.

*"The Death of Spider-Man" was the subtitle for Spider-Man #17, Marvel Comics, 1991

WINNING

Demian Entrekin

The divorce papers had been on file for over two weeks and the downstairs guest room was getting difficult to face.

A few years back, four years or maybe six, I don't remember anymore, we took out a home improvement loan and converted the garage into a guest room. We liked it at the time—it made the house seem better, or at least bigger.

The interest rates were good and that seemed important. Now it just felt like I was living in the garage. I could feel the slab of cold cement underneath the beige pile carpet.

Mornings, when I was jerked awake from the alarm buzzer on my travel clock, it would take me several moments to figure out where I was. Was I in a hotel somewhere? Then it would come back: the guest room. I was living in the guest room.

We had a bathroom put in with a toilet and sink and a small shower so at least I could pull myself together before going into the kitchen to sit with the boys and drink coffee and talk Star Wars before they went off to school.

Then I would head back into the guest room and try to clear my head. It was getting harder and harder to keep things clear, to see them as they were without them all getting jumbled together. Even my two children were starting to merge together into one source of uncontrollable energy.

On top of all of that, the weather had been terrible for weeks. Rain, wind, floods, hail, and all of it freezing. Then, finally, the rain stopped coming for one Sunday and the sun wandered out like a half-sober drunk. It was time to find a new place to live.

I got in the Subaru and backed out of the driveway with a vague notion of optimism. Or not optimism exactly—more like the brain unclenching just a bit. Or maybe even just an autonomic motor response to physical stagnation, the rumbling need of the body to make a move. I had a short list of places on the other side of town to check out.

I crossed the first few addresses off the list without even stopping to get out and look around. You can usually tell up front when a place won't even begin to work. Not enough trees. Bad colors. Too predictable. Or maybe simply dreary to the point of suicidal. You wonder "who in living hell would live there?" but someone usually does.

I finally pulled over and stopped at one place. It was up in the nicer part of town. It was advertised as a fully equipped guest house in a quiet neighborhood in the foothills. The guest house had its own driveway around the other side of the tree-lined hill and it shared a back yard with the main house.

According to the voicemail for the rental agent, the woman who owned the property was not available to show the place. I rang the bell anyway and looked in the front windows. The place was empty.

I went around the side of the house to check it out. The gate to the back yard was unlocked, and I soon found myself in an immaculate yard with a perfect lawn, a Jacuzzi and a bubbling bird bath. Someone was spending time or money on this yard. There wasn't a stray leaf or stick anywhere. The guest house was behind an oak tree on the other side of the pool.

There was a gravel path through a succulent garden to a free standing hammock. I noticed that there was another gate on the farthest end of the back yard fence. I found the path to the gate and pushed it open.

There, on the other side of a patchy wall of mulberry bushes, was an open field with a baseball diamond back in the far corner. Then I remembered that the rental listing said it was adjacent to a park.

I pushed my way through the bushes out to the baseball field and stood at the spot where the third base line met the outfield. It was still too early for any kids to be out playing or practicing. Despite the miserable weather, the infield was in perfect condition, brushed even and flat by the chains that get dragged across the dirt to even out the lumps. It was the kind of infield where you would always get a true bounce. Judging by the short distance to the outfield fences, the field was for Little League.

There's must be something permanent about Little League baseball, something that clings to you forever. Although I couldn't have known it at the time, one particular game turned out to be one of those moments that burn into your mind, permanently written there like a tattoo. But every time I looked back on that afternoon, I saw something different.

Maybe it's just the nature of the game in general, that the innings crawl along slowly and then there are short bursts of action and speed and chaos. I see it now with my own boys. Parents jerk their heads around and crane their necks in unison toward the bases, shield their eyes from the sun to see if their child has done something that needs to be noticed.

Then it all slows down again, sometimes to a standstill, while everyone tries to figure out what in the hell just happened. No one can really say for sure. Even the umpire might swivel his head back and forth and then call "time!" Even when you are one of the players, there's no certainty in the thing. Then the parents chuckle and go back to talking about how sports will build character.

Or maybe you just understand somehow that even during even the slowest moments, one of those crazed episodes is just around the corner so some part of you hangs there and waits for it. You are on slow alert, receptive. The players are goofing around, spitting in the dirt, yelling at the other team, staring into the outfield, waiting for their turn at the plate. Meanwhile, at least two or three of the parents maintain a steady flow of grumbling about the coach and how he doesn't know what he's doing, which of course is true.

There's one game in particular that comes back to me at different times, and it appears like a screen in the front of my mind, with colors and lights and sounds. The first time I remember that afternoon baseball game coming back so clearly was at my grandfather's funeral service. I had just turned 25 and it had been at least ten years since I played organized baseball of any kind.

We were sitting in the church listening to the minister deliver the eulogy about my grandfather, whose ashes were in a wooden box on the table next to a black-and-white picture of him as a young man in a pin-stripe suit. Inside the wooden box was a cardboard box, and inside the cardboard box was a zip-lock plastic bag. It was ridiculous that he could fit so efficiently into that little bag.

The church facility itself seemed to have borrowed several efficiency concepts from the local shopping malls. There were color-coded lines on the floor leading from one chapel to the other. There were glowing coke machines at regular intervals in the halls, and they all included Mr. Pibb and Tab. They had three different interconnected chapels in the campus and there was a full schedule of funeral services for that day. Apparently, a big batch of local people had been dying at the time, so efficiency was required.

We were scheduled in the southern facing wing for the 10 to 11:30 time slot. We were in the green chapel, and it was called the green chapel by the staff because it was at one end of the green line painted on the floor. It may have been the Mary chapel at one point, but it had become the green chapel as a response to the sheer convenience of the signage system.

By the time the service started, the group that had the next service, the 11:30 time slot, was already gathering outside in the parking lot, the adults standing around their shining cars in their nice clothes and the small children running around in circles and hopping up and down.

There were maybe 50 people sitting upright on the benches, the faces pointed up toward the lectern. I recognized about half of the faces there. The minister had vague blue-green eyes, shiny blond hair and a thin blond mustache. He wore a light gray suit with a Dodger blue tie. He had no lips to speak of. It was as if there was just a slit in his face between his nose and his narrow chin through which he spoke. There was a gold ring with a small ruby-colored stone on his left pinky.

He looked down at his notebook and then spoke about my grandfather. He talked about who my grandfather had been in his life and what he had meant to his family and his community. He spoke out in a soft high-pitched voice with professional sincerity. He had mustered the solemn note, but he was mispronouncing my grandfather's first name.

My grandfather's legal name was Erving, but everyone called him Ervin without the "g". He had lost the "g" at some point early in his life and never bothered to go back and retrieve it.

In the preparations for the service, my aunt Judy and I sat quietly in the minister's tidy, shoebox office. His assistant, a small stooped woman who moved across the room like a ghost, came and went leaving blue Post It notes on the screen of his laptop. From where I sat, the Post It notes didn't seem to have anything written on them. My aunt Judy was explaining how she wanted the service to be handled. Judy's face still looks like a slightly rounded copy of my grandfather's face, except that she is a woman, and that changes everything. He nodded, said "of course" several times and took notes in his notebook.

She handed the minister the check for the fees and then explained several times that his name had just naturally changed over time.

"Oh, and by the way, we will be bringing our own food for the reception in the dining hall so we have that part covered," she said. He wrote down a note in his notebook. He seemed very thorough in his note taking. The church offered a food and drink service but Judy didn't want to pay for that. There were plenty of regular volunteers who would bring something to eat. Many of these volunteers were ladies that came to most of the weekend funeral services held at the facility. Death had become their weekend outing.

"When you mention him by name, you should call him 'Ervin' without the 'g' since that's what we all called him," she said.

"Ervin without the 'g' is just fine," the minister said.

"No one can even remember calling him Erving," she said. I think she must have had some advanced warning about this minister. She seemed worried that he would not follow her wishes. "Without the 'g' is what we would like." I think the minister's name was Jeffries, Minister Jeffries.

"Got it," he said and winked at us both. "Erving without the 'g.'"

He seemed to have registered what we were asking, but when the service got rolling, the minister had forgotten Judy's instructions or hadn't been paying attention in the first place. Instead of taking notes, maybe he had been drawing pictures in the margins of his notebook. Neither one of us had the heart to stop the service and tell the man how to say it correctly.

After about five minutes of hearing that minister talk so sincerely and so knowingly about Erving with a "g", about how he was a caring father and friend and grandfather and a successful businessman, my aunt and I snuck a quick look at each other and then we both started spluttering with muffled laughter. We covered our mouths and tried to stop it. Our eyes were watering, and at first some of the others thought we were crying and they appeared to be moved by our tears, but then they seemed more confused than anything. We were both spitting through our fingers with laughter.

I decided I was happy that the minister didn't get the name right. He was talking about someone else after all, some caring guy named Erving. Pretty soon, Judy and I had to look away from each other or else we were going to bust out in howling laugher. I looked out the window at the sun coming through the poplar trees that lined the southern windows of the green chapel.

We loved that old man through and through, but he was none of the things that minister said about him. He was hard and mean and funny as hell. He was caring all right. He cared about keeping his three or four different lady friends in the dark about one another's existence. His idea of a fun time was to figure out some way to make you sick to your stomach and then laugh his head off. One night, when I was eight, he had me smoke a huge black cigar and as I turned green, he rolled around in his Lazy Boy chair and laughed.

When I looked out the chapel window, the laughter went away slowly and then I remembered standing at home plate looking out into left field. Most of the memories of my life are either vague or non-existent, but not this one.

The baseball diamond was at the end of a dirt road that just appeared out of nowhere. You drove along a hidden dirt road that snaked up the side of a hill and then suddenly there was a pristine baseball field surrounded by a chain link fence and a ring of trees.

It was an afternoon game and the sun was coming through the trees beyond the fence in left field. The entire outfield was submerged in solid shade, and the leafy shimmer of light and shadow through the tree tops was beginning to reach the edges of the pitcher's mound. I was at home plate holding the bat standing still in the bright sun. The pitcher was holding the baseball in his bare throwing hand and looking in my direction. I had just turned 10 years old and was one of the youngest players on the team. Since I was a big kid, I didn't look like I was as young on the outside as I was on the inside.

The sun was going down behind those trees, but I didn't know much about trees when I was ten. A tree was a tree. Some you could climb and some you couldn't. Now, looking back in my memory, I would guess that they were Eucalyptus trees. Those hills were covered with Eucalyptus trees and so that's as good a bet as any.

I couldn't quite make out the expression on the pitcher's face, but the dugouts from both teams were pretty loud. "Hey batta batta batta, hey!" It was an important moment in the game and I was at the plate.

Another time I went back to that one particular baseball game was the first time that I got fired from my job. I've been fired several times and now that I think about it, each time I've been fired I seem to go back to the same moment in that baseball game.

The first time I got fired, they didn't call it getting fired. They term they used was a RIFF, or a Reduction In Force. That was a new meaning for riff in my developing vocabulary. But I knew the real reason that I was one of the chosen ones to get cut loose was that I had been causing problems.

I had crossed that invisible line where you start to care just a bit too much about your work, which is a mistake worthy of either swift termination or prolonged punishment.

Once you cross that line, you fight and scratch and wrestle for what you think is right. You believe in something, you see something, you know something, and you are gunning for it. You are on the path, the righteous path, and you are committed. You believe that you should speak up, share your opinion openly, question the things that don't fit into your picture, and that can often exclude no one, even your boss and your boss's boss. Once you cross that line, it can be almost impossible to cross back to the other side, the side of restraint and patience and humor and the long silence, the side where you capture just the right amount of professional objectivity.

I could feel the end coming for days, long before they called me into the room, as if there was someone sneaking up behind me to take a whack at the back of my head with a large stick. I kept looking around behind me to see who was there but there never was anyone there. And then there's that surprise visit where your boss comes by and asks if you have a minute to discuss something, and you walk into the room to discover someone from HR in there as well. The air gets dry and your face gets warm.

There's no sensation quite like the feeling of being fired. The room will become drained of sound except for a far away voice that plinks away like it's coming out of a tin can. That voice is usually the voice of the person who is firing you and they are saying things that you cannot quite hear. You probably know the person, but all of a sudden they look like someone else. You can feel under your skin that you have already been jettisoned, cut loose from the dock to drift away as the current will take you. You can almost see them waving at you from the pier as they hand you the paperwork your hand will have to sign.

"So, it's certainly nothing personal. It's nothing personal. It's just that things aren't quite working out as we had hoped they would," says the voice. "We all gave it our best shot."

You look around the room at the strange surroundings, the room you've spent countless hours in up to this precise moment. You notice odd things about the room, like perhaps the carpet is dirty in one corner of the room and the chairs don't match and there are five blue pens and only one black pen.

"We hope the best for you in the next adventure. It's probably all for the best in the end anyway," says the voice. "It's really for the best."

At this point you mumble something incoherent.

"If you will please sign here we can provide you with the severance agreement and the check. It's a pretty generous offer actually, and should give you plenty of time to find that next opportunity," says the voice.

You sign the paperwork. Take your copy.

"Of course, you have seven days to change your mind. You should read this over carefully and make sure you agree. But we think you'll find that this is a pretty fair deal," says the voice. "It's a fair and proper deal."

You take the check, stand up you leave the room. Then perhaps you think of something else, something from the real world. In this case, as I walked to the elevator with my box of personal items, I remembered that one baseball game.

This time, I remembered the face of the coach as I approached the batter's box, the game on the line and runners leaning and twitching on all of the bases.

We were not a good team, and the coach had enough of losing. His back and his legs and his face had grown stiffer and stiffer with each loss. When we took the field at the beginning of our games, we knew vaguely that we would lose. It had become a habit. Even if we were playing well and were winning early on, we would eventually fold and the thing would fall apart. It was a cloud that hung over us and followed the team from game to game.

The coach's mouth was set and the muscles in his jaw were clenched. His cap will pulled down low but his brown eyes were hard beams of determination, as if this time he might somehow impact the outcome of the game with his own personal focus and energy. He wanted to win this goddam game, needed to win the thing. He glared at me from the his spot against the fence, arms crossed, his dark brown eyes filled with some unspeakable wish, a wish that only showed itself now as the need to win this one particular Little League baseball game. It was more than a baseball game now. It was bigger than that.

The problem was that I was not a good hitter. I had a terrific swing but I had a hard time making contact with the ball which tended to mean a quick strike-out. The coach had more or less given up on me and stuck me near the bottom of the lineup. But I could hardly blame him.

I stepped into the batter's box and tried to focus on the pitcher. His eyes were not like the eyes of the coach. The pitcher's eyes were blank and wide and filled up with the spectacle of it, which made us the same at that moment. He was to try to strike me out. I was to try to hit the ball. The only question at that point was which one of us was more terrified than the other. He fingered the ball and tried to gather his nerve to throw the pitch.

When he finally threw the first pitch, the sound of the players' screaming voices stopped. The pitcher lost his footing and started to fall to the ground. The ball came directly at me. I froze and the ball smacked against the side of my helmet with a loud crack. Then the ball rolled slowly out in front of me and stopped in the dirt.

My head was ringing and the coach was yelling. My getting smacked on the head with the ball meant that we had won the game. One run scored from third base. He ran right past me and into the dugout jumping up and down. The coach was jumping up and down. The players for the other team walked off the field. The game was over.

So there I was, standing at third base in the middle of an open field, and I decided that I was tired of losing. I suddenly understood why that coach had to win that game. The two of us had been on a slow collision course and I could not have known that we were joined in time. By now he was either dead or in a nursing home but that didn't matter. We were attached.

I didn't want to lose my wife and my kids and my house. I didn't want to start my life over, buy new furniture, new blankets. I didn't want to find a place to live by myself, and make new friends and get a new wife. I would go back to my house and explain that it was all my fault. That our last few years of fighting and silence were all my fault.

I would stand there and take it, take it all. I would soak it all in and own the thing. It was time. I would fix things and she would let me fix them. She would believe me, trust me, keep me. She would know that I was serious and capable of taking control of my life, capable of winning.

DIGGER

Frank Haberle

Just before practice, coach lost it on Booch.
    I was standing at center ice, smacking lappers against the box. The pucks cracked when they hit the boards. My new teammates skated in lazy circles around the rink. Their blades scraped across the ice. They checked their reflections in the glass and brushed their hair back under their helmets.

Coach was running Booch through goalie warm ups. He slapped his stick on the ice and yelled "Up! Down! Up! Down! Kick left! Kick Left! Up! Up! Our first game is in four days! Can you get up?"

Booch stayed down. He dropped his stick on the ice, shook off his waffle and pulled on the side of his leg pad.

"I think I broke another strap," he said. "These pads are all screwed up."

"You're all screwed up!" Coach yelled. "Get in the damn goal."

Booch's leg pads were a problem. He had outgrown his old ones. We drove to Southboro with my mom to buy him a used pair. They were too big; stitches were popping out of the sides. The straps kept breaking. I helped him patch them together with duct tape.

Coach blew his whistle. "Two lines!" He yelled. We massed in two rows at the blue line. Booch turned to face the first battery of warm up shots.

Richardson shot first. He launched the puck at Booch's neck. Booch flopped backward and slammed onto the ice. "Up! Up!" Coach yelled. Richardson made a face to his laughing friends, then took his place in line behind me.

"Nice lapper, Dickie," I said to him.

"The name is Richardson," he said. He was a full head taller than me; a black mane flowed out of the back of his helmet.

"You might want to keep it down, Dickie" I said. I spat on the ice in front of him. I stood up as tall as I could. "Booch's a friend of mine."

"He sucks," Richardson shrugged. "Screw you, townie, and your townie friend."

"I might," I said.

"Besides, coach called my friend in. Josh Fenton. He played goal with me at Manchester last year. He's coming to practice tomorrow. So you're friend Boochie's headed for the Benchie."

It was my turn to shoot. I let off a lapper at half-speed. It hit Booch's leg with a dull thud and skittered harmlessly into the corner.

From as long as I could remember it was me, Booch and Dingy playing under the shadow of the Bruins. We played squirts together, then pee wee, then bantam. Booch's dad, Mister Bouche, was the one who drove us to away games and tournaments. He found us used gear when we outgrew our gloves and skates. If he was working when we played, he slipped out to watch us for a few minutes. Somewhere in the second or third period we'd look up and see Mr. Bouche standing in the back row of the stands, in his worksuit covered with sawdust. He was a huge man with a buzz cut and a big smile. He'd yell "C'mon Booch! C'mon

Dingman!" His booming voice filled the quiet spaces of the rink, between the woops and the drop of the puck.

When we were 11 the Bruins won the cup. Mr. Bouche cleared out his garage and turned it into a mini Boston Garden. He painted white boards, a blue line and a red crease. A yellow Stanley Cup banner hung from the roof. We spent hours recreating the famous goal. Dingy was Bobby Orr, taking flight over the fallen goalie, stick up in the air; Booch was Glenn Hall, sprawled on the ice in defeat; I was Doug Harvey, just a step too late for the great one. After working it in slow motion we got down to drills: ten shot, pepper shot, dekes.

One afternoon Dingy bent his plastic street hockey stick a little too far. His slapshot cracked off one of Booch's front teeth. All three of us yelled. Booch started crying. Blood spurted onto the garage floor. His dad rushed out through the kitchen door.

"What's the matter with you!" he said to his son.

"He knocked out my toof!" Booch yelled.

"Jesus Christ." Mr. Bouche reached one of his huge hands into his own mouth. He pulled a set of dentures out. He grinned; there was a black hole where his front teeth used to be. Booch stopped crying. "Welcome to the team," Mr. Bouche said.

Our fourteen and under team made it to the state semifinals. We lost to Manchester. Mr. Bouche drove us home that night. He dropped Dingy off at his house. Booch was asleep next to his dad. I leaned against the back of the front seat, trying to listen to the radio. The Bruins were getting beaten up by the Black Hawks. Orr was out with his bum knee again.

"You played real good today," Mr. Bouche said to me.

"Dingy got both goals. Booch made some great saves."

"Yeah but you know something?" Mister Bouche said. He popped open another can of beer. The sweet smell filled the car. "Dingy and Booch, they get the limelight. But you're a real digger."

"A digger?"

"Yeah, you're always in the corners digging, kicking. You're hard headed. You know what I think? I think you're the one that's gonna end up on the Bruins."

"Me and Booch and Dingy," I said. "We're all gonna play for the Bruins."

"Well, first you gotta make the sixteen and under team next year," he said. The highway's two yellow lines drifted in the headlights from the left to the center of the windshield. Mr. Bouche eased the car back into the right lane. "It's real competitive at that level. They bring in kids from up and down the shore, like those kids you played tonight. You got to get invited, you got to try out, you gotta work hard to make the sixteens first. Then we'll see about the Bruins."

Two weeks later, my mom shook me awake at dawn. I have some bad news, she said. Mister Bouche died last night. He fell asleep at the wheel driving home on the turnpike. Dingy and I sat behind the Bouche's at the funeral, in a row of kids, all wearing our team jackets. A man got up and spoke. I'd never seen him before. He talked about Mr. Bouche, and then he turned to us. "You kids face a lot of difficult decisions at your age. When you need to make those decisions, I want you to think of Mr. Bouche and what he would have done. That will be the right thing to do."

Nine months later, I got the letter invitation to try out for the sixteen and under team. Booch got one too. Dingy was long gone; his parents had split up and he moved to Providence. Nobody'd heard from him since.

The day after my run-in with Richardson I was working on crossovers when the new goalie, Fenton, stepped onto the ice. His equipment was all brand new—white Bauers, cooper waffle and glove, spotless white tape around a brand new Sherwood. A blue and gold sunburst decorated his custom Higgins mask. He skated straight to the crease and started digging in at the net.

I skated for Booch, who sat on one knee on the ice, rewrapping a piece of tape under his skate. "What's up Booch," I asked.

"Hey," he said. He gave up on the tape and started packing some stuffing back into the side of his other pad.

Coach blew the whistle two times fast.

"You better get in goal, Booch," I said. "You know how coach is."

"Yeah," Booch said. I skated to my place in line. The new kid stayed in the net. I watched him move effortlessly, floating from one side of the net to the other, deflecting pucks away with little effort. His mother stood in the stands, clapping at each save. I put my first lapper in the upper left corner; at the last second he snapped his glove on it; then flipped the puck harmlessly away. Booch stood in the corner, chasing down the loose pucks and flicking them back out to the shooters.

As good as Fenton was, we lost our first five games. Near the end of the sixth I was on the bench, spitting up bubbles of blood. The bubbles made a series of pink rings on my white sleeve. I scraped a finger full of ice from my skate and held it up to my lip. I looked up and thought I saw Dingy in the stands. He was wearing an army coat. I'd never seen him in the winter without a team jacket. He had a big helmet of hair stuffed up under a Red Sox cap. He raised two fingers at me, like he was Christ. It was Dingy alright.

After the game, I stepped onto the carpet leading from the ice up to the dressing room. A gauntlet of parents waited for their kids. One of the fathers said 'Chin up boys! Good show.' At the end of the line Dingy held up an open hand. I smacked it with my glove. "Dingy!" I said. "What the hell are you doing."

"Visiting my Dad," he said. His eyes moved slowly down my arm, past the blue and gold elbow stripes, to the blood on my shirt. "You guys got wooped."

"We suck," I said. "We're 0 and 6."

Dingy looked out to the ice, where Booch was skating around aimlessly. "Old Booch's riding the bench huh?"

"Yeah, they got some dick from Manchester playing goal. They're all dicks."

"Booch was better than that guy. He finally lost it, huh."

"He didn't lose it," I said. "They just haven't given him a chance."

Booch came up the ramp. "Hey Booch!"

"Hey Dingy," Booch said.

"My mom's picking us up in an hour," I said. "You wanna hang out? Play a round of ten shot?"

"That all you ever think about? Smacking pucks around? Jesus."

When Booch and I got our gear off, we found Dingy in the parking lot, leaning on a car, smoking a cigarette.

"You see some of the cars these kid's parents drive? Jesus," Dingy said.

I watched him take a drag. "Those things will cut your wind."

"I don't need my wind. Get off."

"Go on," I said.

"I might."

Booch sat down on his bag next to us. He watched the last of the other kids climb into their cars with their fathers. I pulled my stick out, picked up one of the hundreds of balls of tape that littered the pavement, and zipped it at his head.

"Cut it out," he said.

I picked up another and aimed it at Dingy. "C'mon," I said. I zipped it at his ear.

"Do you have a jock on your head? Are you a jockhead?" He asked me.

"I'm just kidding around," I said. "What do you want to do?"

"If I had a doob I'd smoke it right here," he said.

"How's Providence?" Booch asked.

"It's just one big party, man. You gotta come down and party with me, Booch."

"You playing this year?" I asked him.

"You are a jockhead," Dingy said. "I'm done with hockey." He flicked his cigarette butt with his thumb and finger at a passing car. "I've moved on to the big leagues."

A week later, on the road, we were down four to one early in the third period. A big kid from the other team took two steps from the blue line and launched a lapper at Fenton's chest. A crack like a gunshot echoed through the rink. Fenton took four wild steps out of the crease. He dropped his gloves and ripped at his chest protector. He crumpled to the ice. His mother screamed. Coaches and referees rushed to get him up and off the ice, toward the locker room. Walking across the ice back toward the bench, coach waved a finger at Booch.

"Who me?" Booch said.

"You! Get in there," coach yelled.

Booch climbed over the boards. My line got on the ice with him. As he took his place in the crease, I smacked his pads with my stick.

"C'mon Booch," I said. "You can do it."

Booch looked up to the stands. He took a deep breath. "Yeah," he said. I took my position in the slot. The puck dropped. Ice sprayed in all directions. The big kid picked up the puck at the point and fired a low, hard shot. Booch kicked it out, sprawled on the ice. Another kid picked up the rebound and backhanded the puck up high. Booch smacked it into the air with his wrist, palmed it and covered up. The kid poked his stick at Booch's glove. I ran into him and gave him a leather sandwich.

"Break it up boys," the ref yelled, blowing his whistle sharply. I pulled my glove out of the kid's face and said: "don't mess with my goalie."

That night I called Dingy to tell him about Booch.

"He stopped 18 shots. Eighteen shots. They couldn't stuff it past him. He was flopping all over the place. Coach kept yelling 'get, up, get up! But he just sprawled over knocking down every shot, two, three in a row. Couldn't believe it. Booch was back."

"Yeah," Dingy said. Loud music blared in the background.

"It was just like old times."

"Old times, huh."

"And the other guy's out for a while," I said. "Cracked ribs. So Booch is starting Saturday. At home. Against Weymouth. They're undefeated."

"The Boochman." Dingy giggled.

"Can you come up? Are you doing anything?"

Dingy sniffed. "I got this party I was gonna go to."

"C'mon, do it for Booch. We'll get him fired up. Pepper him up at the garden."

"Nah."

"C'mon Dingy, you gotta come up. Just this once. Come up Friday night. We gotta help Booch. Do it for Booch."

"Alright, alright," Dingy said. "I'll see what I can do. I gotta go, jockman."

That Friday night I hurried home, wolfed down dinner, grabbed my street stick from the barrel in the garage and rushed to the Bouche's house. I walked the same route I'd walked for years, alongside the graveyard, past the church where they had Mister Bouche's funeral. As I walked past the church snow started falling. Things were coming around, I thought. Booch was back in goal; Dingy was back in town. We were going to hang out in the garden, drink cokes and laugh. We were going to pepper Booch, shoot at him for an hour, get him all worked up for tomorrow's game. Booch was going to be the hero again.

When I got to the Bouche's driveway I heard something crash in the garage. Dingy's laughter burst through the door. It was wild, out of control. I walked through the door and into a cloud of sour smoke. The street hockey goal and Booch's stick lay shattered at one end. Dingy was spray painting something on the Stanley Cup banner. Booch was lying in the middle of the floor gasping. His shirt was off. Beer cans littered the floor. A long blue glass pipe stood in the center of the face off circle.

"Booch," I said, standing over him, "what's going on?"

He blinked up at me. "I see hundreds of tiny sparkles," he said. "Why do I see hundreds of tiny sparkles?"

Dingy finished spray painting the words 'dream on' across the banner. He turned to see me standing over Booch. "Jockman," he said. "The jockoe. C'mon, do a hit with my friend and me."

"Booch, wake up, c'mon," I said, ignoring Dingy staggering toward me. I grabbed Booch's limp arm and tried to pull him up. I felt tears welling up in my eyes. "This is your big chance, Booch. We got Weymouth tomorrow."

Dingy got right in my face. "You know what your problem is?" He asked me. I punched him in the stomach. He'd always been bigger and stronger than me, but he crumpled without a sound. He lay on the floor next to Booch, giggling and crying at the same time. Booch lay still, staring at the roof. I turned and left them there.

It was freezing in the morning; at noon I hurried to the rink. I was always the first one into the dressing room. But that morning Booch got there before me. He was sitting in the corner, white-faced. His hands were shaking so badly that he couldn't tape his skates. He smelled like he'd just vomited. "Sorry," he said. "Sorry, sorry, sorry."

"It's okay, Booch," I said. I got down and helped strap his pads on. "You'll be okay. We'll get out there and skate it off in the warm ups."

On the ice I could see his legs shaking. He fell down twice during warm up shots and couldn't keep his stick down. The buzzer echoed through the rink to start the game.

Booch leaned up against the crossbar; he looked like he was going to get sick again. Then he got into position.

Soon after the first face off, Weymouth dropped the puck into our zone. Coach screamed at Booch to go get it. He stumbled in the corner and tripped. One of the Weymouth kids beat him to the puck and flipped it to a teammate in front of the net. A minute later, another kid wound up and shot from center ice. Booch swiped at it with his stick and missed; it clanged into the back of the net. When my line got on the ice, I skated over to him. "It's okay Booch," I said. "Just keep your stick on the ice." He looked down at his feet. On my shift I got knocked over trying to dig the puck out of our corner. Somebody banged my head hard against the glass. The rink started spinning. I lost track of the puck. One of their kids picked it up at the point and fired it at Booch. After the clang the rink went silent. Weymouth players started shooting from all directions. Four nothing, five nothing. The fans started screaming at Booch. "Wake up! Come on!" The kid who scored their sixth goal, 11 minutes into the first period, said something to Booch and laughed. He had the same long hair as Richardson. Coach called a timeout. He pointed to the new back up goalie, a small guy called up from the fourteens as an emergency back-up, to get into the goal. Booch skated back to the bench and climbed over the rail. He took one more look up into the stands, then lowered his head and started fidgeting with his pads.

My line got back onto the ice. The kid who taunted Booch was across from me. When I got the puck I dumped it slowly into the corner past him. When he turned his back I made a run for him. When I hit him he lost his footing; he slammed into the boards face-first and crumpled to the ice. The whistle blew. Players from both teams stopped and stared at me. The ref signaled me into the penalty box; ten-minute major misconduct. I skated by coach but he said nothing; didn't look at me or yell at me or nothing. When the buzzer sounded and the period ended, I walked up the ramp to the dressing room. A group of parents from the other team yelled at me. "That was a cheap shot!" One said. "Chicken shit!" yelled another.

Booch came into the dressing room and sat down across from me. He kept his mask on. Richardson entered behind him. "You suck!" he yelled, standing over Booch.

"You suck!" I said, standing up to face him.

"Yeah, well, uh, you suck worse," Richardson said, turning back to his friends.

I was about to go after him when coach came in.

He glared around the room at all of us. Then he spoke. "Apparently some people came to the rink today who didn't want to play." He paused, like he always did, giving it time to sink in. "Well, we got two more periods to get some of our self-respect back. So when we go out there for the second period, why don't those of us who don't want to play anymore just stay here, pack your bags, and go home. Because I only want players who want to play." He turned and walked out of the room.

We sat in silence until the zamboni left the ice. Richardson said "c'mon, let's go." The team followed him. The new goalie was the last to walk out.

Booch didn't move an inch; just sat staring blankly at the plywood in front of him. We sat across from each other until we heard the buzzer echo through the rink, beginning the new period. Then we took our skates off together.

Me and Booch walked home in silence, past the graves and the church. I dropped him off in front of his house. Then I walked back to the church. I looked out at the rows of crosses, where Mister Bouche was buried, and hundreds of Mister Bouches were buried in long rows all around him. I lay my stick and my bag down gently, and I sat down on the church steps. I put my face in my hands, and I tried to think real hard of what to do next.

THE PROMISED LAND

Carolyn P. Lawrence

It was sensory overload, it was risky—it was indeed madness. But having scrimped and saved for years for plane fare and a hotel room, not to mention game tickets, Minnie and Rose found their seats on the first tier, seats they had carefully selected to minimize climbing. After the afternoon's commotion of claiming their bags at the airport, checking in at the Holiday Inn Express, and hanging on to each other amid the jostling crowds at the arena, they were thankful to sit down. They fixed their eyes on their team practicing lay-ups below, and relished the noise: college pep bands blaring fight songs at opposite ends of the arena; people shouting at ushers and vendors; announcements booming over a loudspeaker; and cheerleaders warming up the fans. During the introductions of the two teams in this semi-final bracket, the ladies checked their programs, and they clapped and whooped with the rest of the crowd as each of their starters trotted onto the court. They put aside their latex foam "We're #1" fingers and hushed and stood while one of the bands played the national anthem. Finally, out of breath with excitement, Minnie and Rose settled into their seats for the tip-off. Like planets in a rare cosmic alignment, they and their favorite team had arrived at the same place at the same time—at the Final Four, the Promised Land of college basketball.

They savored all of it—and although Minnie needed opera glasses and Rose had to shut off her hearing aid, they still commented on the action as they always did when they watched games at home on TV: "Dee-fense! Foul! Boo! What a shot! Did you see that? Yessss!" And before they knew it, the first half ended and brought a welcome respite for their vocal chords.

The teams were tied, and the two ladies, unable to navigate the congested ways to concession stands, sucked mints from their purses. On the floor below, a couple of fans were trying to win a new car by heaving a ball from half-court into the hoop. One came close, and Minnie and Rose let out a simultaneous "Awwww" with the other fans in the stands. Then the dancers from each school pranced out for their respective routines, kicking their legs and shaking pom-poms.

"Sure are skimpy outfits," Rose remarked. She shifted her attention from the dancers' sequined tops and bare midriffs to her program where she'd been making notes. "I hope Coach makes appropriate adjustments," she said. "We're not getting enough in the low post. Our rebounding could be better—we need to box out a little more."

"Yeah, but we've had only two turnovers," Minnie answered. "And our bench is really producing. That kid from Philly is coming up big. Getting all those bodies in and out oughta keep us fresh in the second half."

And suddenly, it *was* the second half. The teams were back on the floor, passing and shooting and guarding and setting picks. Whistles blew and players fouled out and coaches substituted and the clock ran down and the star of their team sank a beauty at the buzzer. They won, and Rose high-fived a kid with studs in his nose who almost broke her hand and she dropped her cane in the process. It was delicious.

The kid with the nose studs handed Rose her cane, and she and Minnie collapsed into their seats and let the masses file out of the arena while the pleasure of the moment washed over them. They were exhausted.

"Only one more to go," Minnie said.

"Thank God we get a day to rest," Rose answered.

They found their way to an exit, flagged a taxi, and returned to the Holiday Inn Express. They always picked hotels that offered a free breakfast, and this one had the added charm of being close to the arena—too far to walk, but short enough that cab fare was manageable.

The next morning they slept late, had coffee, juice, and sweet rolls in the hotel's breakfast area and bought a couple of newspapers. Back in their room, they read accounts of last night's games and considered the views of various sports columnists.

"One of these guys thinks Jeffers is a shoo-in for Player-of-the-Year," Minnie said, referring to their team's point guard.

"Well, he oughta be," Rose answered, "but it would help a lot if we win."

The ladies spent the afternoon making up their own stat sheets from the articles and the tournament program and looked ahead to the final game.

"They're taller than we are," Minnie said, looking up from one of her sheets, "and their center is the best shot-blocker in the country."

"Yeah, but we're quicker, and we've been shooting lights out with three pointers all tournament," Rose answered. "I think you should call Big George."

"Okay," Minnie said. "How much?"

"How about two hundred?"

"Fine." Minnie picked up the telephone and dialed the maintenance man at their high-rise apartment building. Big George worked full-time as building superintendent and part-time as a bookie for tenants who liked to bet on sporting events.

"You gals enjoying yourselves?" Big George's voice bellowed over the phone line. "Increase your bet by two hundred? Done." Minnie, conscious of the phone bill, thanked Big George and hung up.

Other than venturing out to eat, the ladies stayed in their room until it was time to go back to the arena for the final game the next evening. They dressed in polyester pants, tee shirts sporting their team's colors and logo, and sweaters. Minnie carried a tote bag with their "We're #1" fingers, a couple of whistles, and their programs. Traffic was tight, and their taxi arrived with little time to spare. Minnie paid the fare while Rose struggled out of the cab. They went through the gate and joined the masses inside. That's when it happened.

She didn't know how—whether she was pushed or lost her balance or tripped—but in a flash Rose was on the floor, her cane clattering on the concrete and her face twisted in pain. A crowd gathered around her, and Minnie was trying vainly to help her stand. Someone said to find a doctor, and a few minutes later a man, who said he was a doctor, was kneeling beside her and feeling her ankle. He said he didn't think it was broken, but it was swelling badly and they ought to have an X-ray, and could somebody call 911, and they'd ice it down right away and get her to the hospital. And Rose yelled, "STOP! I've waited *years* for this game and I'm going to see it if I have to *crawl* in there." The doctor said she had a lot of spunk and helped her into a wheelchair. He found an ice pack for her ankle, gave her a couple of tablets for pain, rolled her onto the floor, and parked her at the end of her team's bench. And there, in the middle of the action, two ladies with blue-tinged curls watched the best basketball game they had ever seen.

Their savvy paid off, too, and they were glad because Rose needed every cent of her gambling profits to pay the medical bills that added up like points on a scoreboard in the weeks after they won the national championship.

TOP OF THE SIXTH

by William J. Francis

Jimmy paused long enough to look at the ticket stubs and then continued past section one-twenty-five. He could hear them talking behind him, their voices receding. Sighing, he slowed his pace so they might catch up. Eventually they did.

"Where's the fire?" Vicky asked. His wife raised her sunglasses, tilted them so they rested on top of her head, and put both hands on her hips. A single finger of sunlight slashed across the floral print of her tank top. She looked pretty standing there, frown and all.

"I just don't want to..." He glanced at the mammoth scoreboard. They'd already missed the first inning. "Damn." The taller woman standing next to his wife looked awkwardly at her own feet. Bright pink toenail polish. Flat brown sandals. Sarah. Jimmy's ears burned a little. Vicky cleared her throat and gave him a look, and Jimmy found he was unable to meet her gaze.

"You folks need any help finding your seats?" The man who spoke was tall with closely cropped hair. He was wearing a red and gold vest. An usher for the ballpark, the man was the second such employee who had stopped them since they'd entered the stadium.

"We're fine," said Jimmy.

"May I see your tickets?" the usher asked anyhow.

Great, Jimmy thought. Another delay. And how many ushers did they need at a minor league baseball game anyhow? Jimmy fanned out the tickets before the tall man, who nodded curtly and pointed in the direction Jimmy had been heading all along.

"Thanks," Jimmy said flatly.

"Just doing my job," the usher replied.

Jimmy and his two female companions walked on in silence. To Jimmy's relief their seats were at the end of an aisle. At least he wouldn't feel like a jackass trying to get by those fortunate enough to have made it for the opening pitch. He filed in, his wife behind him, and then Sarah. It was the bottom of the second when he sat down on the hard wooden seat and leaned forward, pressing his elbows to his knees. He pulled his thumb and forefinger over the stubble on his chin. The truth was he liked Sarah even if he had argued against bringing her along.

"We'll be late if we have to drive all the way out there to pick her up," he had said hoping that would be enough.

"She's having a rough time, Jim. The guy she was seeing dumped her and they are cutting back her hours at work. Besides, she likes you. You can't say that about most of my girlfriends."

The score was zero to three. The visiting team, the Kansas City Kings, were in the outfield. The pitcher wound up and let loose a wild pitch that nearly took off the batter's head.

"He's just nervous," announced a morbidly obese man sitting two rows down from Jimmy. The fat man shoved a handful of popcorn into his mouth. Directly in front of Jimmy, two young men lounged in their seats, a collection of empty cups stacked on the chair between them. "Have some more popcorn lard ass," one of them slurred. The guy who'd spoken was wearing a King's cap and he pulled it down tight on his skull before letting out a roar of a belch.

Jimmy had to give him credit, not everyone could tie one on before the second inning had even wrapped up.

Jimmy looked around expecting the ushers at any minute to swoop down and escort the drunks out of the park. But ushers seemed suddenly scarce. *Probably too busy checking tickets.* Jimmy couldn't remember seeing this many people in the stands before. A lot of families. But wasn't that what the park was going for these days? Affordable family fun.

There were two runners on base and two outs and the tall lean pitcher wasn't throwing anything over the low-eighties. *Of course he's nervous.* Jimmy turned to look in his wife's direction, though it was Sarah he found himself studying. Her dark eye shadow made her eyes look somehow gray.

Unlike the pitcher for the Kings, the athlete who climbed onto the mound at the top of the third was one cool cat. Everything about him wreaked of confidence—from the way he stood, with his hip cocked and his pitching thumb tucked into the band of his pants, to the way he spit, an impressive arc of dark liquid that he automatically rubbed into the dirt with his cleat.

The pitcher shook his head at the catcher, once, twice, and a third time. Jimmy was beginning to think the two would never agree on a pitch. But then the pitcher nodded and fired a rocket at home plate. The slap the ball made when it arrived in the catchers glove was unmistakable, like the crack of a wet towel. *Untouchable.*

"I've never been to a minor league game before," said Sarah. Jimmy felt his wife nudge his arm and still it took a moment before he found his voice.

"I'm not a big fan of the minor clubs myself," he said.

"Oh, when Vicky said you two were going I just thought you must be."

"Jim has a man-crush on the pitcher," Vicky announced. She reached out and lightly stroked the back of his neck.

A low buzz coursed through him, like when he was a kid being pushed on a swing, higher and higher until the chain buckled and he could actually feel the seat drop out from under him. Jimmy cleared his throat and scooted forward in his chair until her hand fell away.

"The pitcher for Texas, Donnie Jacobs, is a major leaguer, probably the best pitcher playing ball in the world right now."

"Well, what's he doing playing for the Tigers?" Sarah asked. "I've never even heard of them."

The Kings were fielding again, and their pitcher was still struggling to find his groove. Probably all the pressure, thought Jimmy. The guy had to know he had gotten himself in over his head. The catcher walked out to the mound and the two players exchanged a few words. Judging from the way the catcher stomped off, Jimmy guessed they weren't discussing where to go grab a beer after the game.

"Jacobs dislocated his shoulder in the spring," Jimmy explained. "He lost his temper or something at practice and did a number on one of his teammates. Truth is, he's a hot head and if it were anybody else in the league, he would have been suspended."

"So he got demoted to the minors?" Sarah asked.

"God, no. He's just recovering. He has to play a couple double A games to show he's got his arm back. Actually, in another farm he'd probably be playing single A but the Tigers are close enough, he can play with them and practice with his regular team."

The pitcher floated an ugly ball right over home plate. A thwack of wood meeting leather echoed through the stadium, and the crowd was on their feet. A man in plaid shorts and a polo shirt hoisted his daughter up onto his shoulders. The ball catapulted out of the park and both runners plus the batter came in.

"How about a drink?" Vicky asked. "Sure," Jimmy said. "Let me flag down the beer man."

Vicky turned to Sarah. "Do you want a beer?"

"A beer sounds great."

"She's just trying to be polite," Vicky said.

"No really, I'm fine with a beer."

"Jim, you don't mind finding us something else do you?"

Jimmy looked at his wife in dismay. First they were late and now she wanted him to go find them drinks?

"Please, honey?" Vicky asked in the same way she asked if he'd rub her back or occasionally something other than her back.

"Fine," Jimmy said. Both women stood to let him out. In front of him, the drunk in the King's cap looked back and mouthed something. "What was that?" Jimmy asked, but the guy was already facing forward again, laughing loudly and reaching for his beer. Jimmy squeezed past his wife. Sarah stepped into the aisle and put her hand on his arm. The fine hairs on the back of his neck stood up.

"Thanks," she said. Then the stands suddenly filled with jeers and Jimmy knew the pitcher for KC had walked another batter. "I'll give you the highlights when you get back," Sarah called to Jimmy over the ruckus.

At the top of the stairs Jimmy hung a right. He remembered seeing a sign as they were coming in advertising margaritas. One of the ushers, this one a woman, spotted him and began heading his way. He looked away, picking up his pace before she had a chance to stop him for a body cavity search. As he walked he ran the tips of his fingers across his bristly chin and wondered if he looked like a terrorist.

Jimmy found what was he was looking for near the restrooms. The attendant standing behind the cart was a heavy black man with a salt and pepper beard that hid most of his face.

"What can I do you for partner?" the vendor asked pronouncing his "T"s like "D"s. "Let's see," Jimmy said. He pointed behind the cart where a stainless steel machine was churning a neon green concoction. "I guess I'll get two of those and a bottle of Miller."

As the man stooped to retrieve a couple plastic cups he said, "Two lady friends, eh?"

"It's not like that," Jimmy answered. "I'm married to one of them."

With his back to Jimmy, the vendor spoke as he topped off the plastic cups. "You'll get no sympathy from me, partner. The only girls that flirt with a fat man selling alcohol at a minor league baseball game are the ones who aren't old enough to buy what I'm selling."

When Jimmy returned with the drinks, Sarah began talking to him before he was close enough to make out what she was saying.

"I can't hear you" Jimmy said, holding out the cardboard drink carrier. The women each took one of the cups and moved down one seat so that Jimmy was left on the end.

"You missed a phenomenal catch at third," Sarah said. "That pitcher, the tall skinny one, he seems to be getting better." Sarah turned to Vicky. "Wanna trade?"

"Trust me, I sit next to him plenty," Vicky said with a smirk. Jimmy turned toward his wife and scratched his forehead with his middle finger. She ran the tip of her tongue over her teeth and suddenly he was back on the playground. *Higher, push me higher.*

Jimmy took a swig of his beer and swallowed hard. Somewhere behind him a child was crying. "The pitcher for KC just needed to calm down," Jimmy said. He pushed the empty cardboard carton under the seat and plunked down in the chair, sneaking a peek at the pair in front of them. One of the guys had a beer in each hand, while the mouthy one had both hands cupped to his face.

"We want a pitcher not a belly itcher," the drunk brayed.

"Calm down?" Sarah asked.

"Yeah," Jimmy said. "He's nervous. He's bit off more than he can chew tonight." Jimmy turned slightly in Sarah's direction, telling himself he was trying to get an unobstructed view of the first base coach. He placed his palm against his knee. Sarah was wearing khaki shorts, her smooth, long legs only inches from his hand.

Number four in the red, that's Donny Jacobs, right?" Sarah leaned into Jimmy, brushing him with her elbow. It was ninety degrees out but she smelled like winter—like Christmas morning.

"That's right," Vicky answered for him. Jimmy turned to see his wife tilt up her cup and swallow the last of the drink. "That's the guy my Jimmy has the hots for."

"How's your drink?" Jimmy asked.

"Tastes like cat pee," Vicky said. "But I love you for going and getting it any way."

"Mine's okay," Sarah said quickly.

Jimmy raised his eyebrows.

"Trust me," Vicky said. "Hers tastes God-awful too. If she knew you a little better she'd tell you."

Jimmy thought of the last time he'd seen Sarah. Fourth of July. The company barbecue. The three of them had ridden together that time as well, and Vicky had gotten so plastered she'd passed out. They'd all had too much to drink that night. In the end, Sarah had spent the night on their couch to save him the long drive. Jimmy remembered how Sarah kept going on about how lucky Vicky was as they struggled to get his inebriated spouse undressed and into bed. He took a long pull from his beer and found himself wishing he was sitting beside his wife. He almost asked Sarah to switch but couldn't bring himself to do it.

"So how many of these minor leagues are there anyway?" Vicky asked.

Jimmy perked up. Sometimes he wished Vicky was more interested in baseball. "There are three leagues in the double A circuit—Eastern, Southern, and Texas. Texas started its own league because they insisted playing on larger fields." Jimmy was about to go on and tell Sarah how a player worked his way through the minors but his wife cut him short.

"You Texas boys." Vicky chuckled. "Such a bad case of penis envy."

Jimmy tried to concentrate on the game. The count was two and two. The pitcher threw a real zinger right over home place. The batter never stood a chance.

"Strike three!" shouted the umpire.

"You're fucking blind!" shouted the buddy of the man who'd razzed Jimmy about the drinks. The guy was wearing a Hawaiian shirt, something like Tom Selleck probably burned the moment he got word Magnum PI was canceled. Jimmy clenched his jaw. The man who had put his little girl up on his shoulders earlier glanced back briefly. Jimmy looked around. Of course, the damn ticket Gestapos were no where in sight.

"He's talking to the ref, Baby," Vicky said.

"Ump," Jimmy corrected. "And I don't care who they are talking too." He raised his voice. "These guys are ridiculous."   Jimmy put his beer down on the concrete. He stood. He balled his right hand into a fist. The two drunks had turned their attention from the field and were staring right at him. Behind him he heard someone say: "Honey go find one of the security guards."

"Something on your mind, Chief?" asked the one in the cap.

From his peripheral vision, Jimmy sensed Sarah getting to her feet. He could already see how this was going to go down. The drunk let his empty cup fall, reached up, and turned his cap around backwards. The one in the Magnum PI shirt was smiling, but Jimmy could see the taut chords in his neck.

Jimmy parted his lips and sucked in a breath between closed teeth. The guy in the Hawaiian shirt was bigger, but the one in the baseball cap looked wiry. *Eeeny Meany Miney Moe.* Jimmy felt a hand on his shoulder. He turned to tell Sarah it would be fine but she wasn't looking at him. He followed her gaze to the monster digital display above third base. There was a swell of cheers and clapping and shouts and AC/DC's *You Shook Me All Night Long* started up over the PA system.

On the sixty-foot screen Jimmy saw himself, Sarah, and the infamous cheesy pink heart graphic. A spinning white font paraded around the jumbo-tron announcing proudly: "Texas Tiger's Kiss Cam." In a heartbeat the crowd seemed to organize and took up a chant. *Kiss her. Kiss her. Kiss her.*

Jimmy tore his gaze from the image on the screen only to find himself staring at Sarah. There was less than a foot between them. Her high cheek bones. The freckles on her nose. Pale pink lips. He looked into her eyes—dangerous and gray and full of want. She flipped back her blond hair and laughed nervously, and Jimmy could see her slender hand was shaking. He could do it here and now in front of everyone. Hell, they expected him to. What could his wife say? What could anyone say?

Then from the stands rose a series of boos, first unsure, but quickly gaining confidence as whatever artificial time limits get placed on these moments had apparently passed.

"Pussy," shouted the drunk as he turned his King's cap back around and pulled the bill down over his eyes.
Jimmy watched as his image on the giant display was replaced by a humorous graphic of a chubby little cupid being shot out of the sky. Then the camera panned the stadium and selected its next victims, an older couple who wasted no time throwing their arms around one another and kissing, much to the delight of the fans.

The baseball police showed up then. There were three of them, including the tall one who'd insisted on seeing Jimmy's tickets. The ushers paused, first at Jimmy's seat, then looking up to a man and his wife who were pointing, went down one more row to the King's fans and their pyramid of empties. Jimmy was expecting the worst but both the drunks went without any trouble. As if being thrown out of the game had been their goal all along. A few people clapped for the ushers. Jimmy wasn't one of them.

"Oh my God," Vicky said. "I can't believe that just happened."

Jimmy thought she was talking about the fight, or maybe those two clowns being tossed.

"You two looked like you were going to die," Vicky said. "Or make out. I wasn't sure which." When no one else said anything she laughed. "I guess that will teach me to let another woman sit beside my husband."

"How about another cup of cat urine?" Sarah asked.

"Sure," Vicky said. "I'll go with you."

Sarah shook her head. "You caught me." She reached into her purse and pulled out her cell phone. "I want to make a quick call."

Vicky nodded.

Sarah had only been gone a few minutes when Jimmy turned to his wife.

"Sorry, Hon, but I've got to take a leak."

He found Sarah sitting with her back against the wall near the little shop that sold Tiger hoodies and those big foam fingers. Her purse was on the ground. She was hugging her knees, head down. He wasn't sure what to say.

When he returned from the bathroom, Jimmy scanned the stadium. Except for the hardcore fans, or those who had come to see Donny Jacobs, the stands were quickly clearing out. It had been a blowout and now, at the bottom of the seventh inning, the opposing team was changing out the pitcher.

Jimmy wondered what the lanky lefty was thinking as he moped off the field, never looking up. Sure he was tired, but Jimmy knew it was more than that. The pitcher was mentally fatigued, the pressure of being observed and judged. Doing his best to fight the good fight and knowing that in the end it wasn't enough.

"You were gone a long time," Vicky said.

He nodded and took the seat next to his wife.

"Did you see Sarah?"

He nodded again.

"And?"

"She just got something in her eye."

"Is it serious?"

"It'll be fine," he said. He hoped he was right.

WELCOME, ANYBODY

Jen McConnell

Jim sat in the dining room, bouncing a quarter across the table. It missed the juice glass, crashing into the pile of change off to the side. The house was quiet except for the sound of the grandfather clock gearing up to strike noon. The next quarter clinked into the pulp-streaked glass. Jim thought about the afternoon's baseball game. Now he was free to go.

As the clock chimed, Jim heard the garage door open. A moment later, Nancy came through the kitchen door, bringing in a combination of perfume and car exhaust. Jim fished out the sticky quarter and pushed it into the pile.

Nancy stood in the doorway. Jim pictured her in the car a moment ago, checking her hair in the mirror and thinking over details of the Reverend's party. She squinted at Jim as if he were somebody else.

"What is it?" she asked.

Jim thought about lying to her—just for a day or two—while he figured things out.

"Jim?"

"They let me go." He motioned for her to sit down, but she crossed her arms. "Company's restructuring. There'd been rumors. But I'll get something else," Jim continued, "before you know it."

Nancy's eyelids flickered. "Why didn't you tell me?"

"Thought it wouldn't happen to me," he said.

"But it did."

Jim kept talking, trying to reassure her. The severance was fair and he was paid out his vacation. They had some savings. Nancy turned pale when he mentioned filing for unemployment.

"You don't seem upset," she said.

He shrugged. When Morris, his supervisor, made the announcement, Jim was more worried about being left to clean up the mess than being fired. He was almost relieved when Morris called his name. Denise Rudnick cried and even Kevin Stannard, who hated the company, had a wild look in his eye. Jim simply packed up his desk and left. Strange how easy it was—how satisfying—to walk out in the middle of things. It wasn't until Jim entered the quiet house that he felt the edges of panic.

"I'll take care of it." Jim pushed the termination packet across the table but Nancy ignored it. "Besides, I can catch Daniel's game today. Surprise him."

He thought of Daniel on the pitcher's mound. The brown dirt and the chalky resin bag; Daniel's face peering in for the sign; and Jim's father, the Reverend, in the bleachers. The Reverend had been to every game this season. Jim wiped his hands on his pants.

"Maybe this is what I need," he said. "Chance to try something new. Maybe this'll be good for me and Daniel."

"There's nothing wrong between you two!" Nancy burst out. She looked around the house as if she'd lost something. "Should I cancel the party?" she asked.

"It means so much to you."

"He's your father."

Jim slammed his hand on the table. "No one needs to know about this, okay?"

"He could be helpful, you know." Nancy's voice was thin.

She always defended the Reverend. Sometimes the three of them—Nancy, the Reverend, and Jim's mother, Gertrude—acted as if Nancy was their daughter and Jim had married in. Gertrude hadn't asked Jim to help plan the Reverend's retirement party. One day she called up Nancy and that was that. Jim knew the details only from overhearing his wife on the phone. The clock struck the half hour. He reached for Nancy but she moved to the sliding glass door.

"Nothing to worry about." She placed her hands on the glass and stared out.

"Just act normal," Jim replied. "We'll talk about it tonight."

"This is anything but normal."

Her voice was calm, betrayed only by the hitch in her shoulders. Jim longed to embrace her but even moving in his chair made her shake her head. She would come to terms with it in her own way. They'd been married long enough for him to know that.

"Just do what you normally would today, sweetie," he said. "Why did you come home, anyway?"

"I picked up the invitations." She peered up at the sky. "Whether you agree with him or not, you have to admire his dedication. He believes what he believes, you know?" She turned back to Jim, the wistfulness gone from her voice as quickly as it had appeared. "Invitations need to go out tomorrow. Will you stuff the envelopes?"

"Didn't the store do all that?"

"Cheaper." Her voice was apologetic. "If you stuff them this afternoon, tonight the three of us can order pizza and address them." She stood still until Jim nodded his head. "And, if you don't mind, maybe you could drop the deposit off at the caterers?"

Back at the table, Nancy handed Jim an envelope from her purse. She let him clasp her hand for a moment before pulling away. Jim followed her into the kitchen, where she took a can of soda from the refrigerator.

"Stay for lunch?"

"I'll take it to go." She grabbed an apple from the fruit bowl.

When she walked by, Jim hugged her but she didn't soften against him. He kissed the top of her hair, wishing he could do something more. How many nights she quieted his mind with her smooth legs, her tender hands that found his before sleep. How many mornings he woke to find her hand still resting in his. Those were always the best days.

"I'm sorry," he said.

"I believe you," she whispered.

Jim stuffed the celery-green invitations into their envelopes for twenty minutes before taking a break. He drank a glass of tap water and wandered from room to room, careful not to disturb the stillness.

Upstairs in Daniel's room, Jim knelt on the twin bed and studied the Xavier schedule taped to the wall. Why shouldn't he go? He was the one practicing with Daniel in the middle of winter, not the Reverend. He taught Daniel to throw the curve. When the season began, Jim tried to schedule around Daniel's games but it didn't work out.

The phone rang as he left the room.

"Hello?"

"James?" the voice asked.

"Mother?"

"What's wrong?"

Jim affected a cough. "A little under the weather today. Thought maybe I'd catch Daniel's game."

"Well, which is it?"

"More of the second, I guess."

"Just like your father. He postponed the ladies' guild until tomorrow so he could go."

"Nancy's not here," Jim said.

"I know. I was calling to leave two more names on the answering machine."

She gave Jim the names and addresses. As he was about to hang up, she stopped him. He heard the Reverend's voice in the background, then his mother came back on the line.

"Will you drive your father to the game?" she asked. "He'd love your company."

Jim smiled despite himself. How she came to believe what she did, he'd never know.

"I'll swing by at two-thirty," he said.

"He says two-fifteen." She laughed. "Afraid it'll sell out."

Jim hung up, thinking of the time that stretched between now and the game, between the job he no longer held and whatever the next one might be.

At the harbor, Jim bought coffee at a kiosk, surprised at the number of people walking around. No one looked in a hurry to go anywhere. *Don't these people have jobs?* he wondered.

The blond at the register smiled as he placed the money in her hand, conscious of the crispness of each bill. They didn't live like kings but he'd done okay. With Nancy's recent promotion, they managed to take an extra trip this year—a long weekend in Ensenada—but they couldn't live on her salary alone.

Jim walked along the boardwalk, gazing at the boats in the bay. Above him, the sun was high into the cloudless sky and a slight breeze had picked up. Ideal baseball weather. Jim caught his reflection in a window, pleased that he had changed from slacks into shorts and his old Xavier hat. Maybe he would grow a mustache. Start jogging again. Rent a boat and spend a week on Mission Bay.

Jim dropped off the check at the caterer's office, forbidding himself to look at the amount. He didn't want to be tempted to interfere just because he had the time. After the caterers, he stopped in front of a cigarette shop and looked at his watch. Still half an hour before he had to pick up the Reverend.

He glanced up at the wooden sign above the shop door. It read *Welcome Anybody* in wood-block letters bordered by a dozen tiny flags painted in primary colors. He stared at the sign for a few minutes, then peered inside the shop. A man leaned against the counter reading a paperback, his thin hands cradling his chin. A horn sounded somewhere behind Jim, prompting him to step into the store.

Before he could think of a reason not to, Jim bought a pack of cigarettes. The man handed Jim the change and looked at him expectantly. Jim wanted to ask him a question—what he was reading, how business was doing, if he owned a boat—but hurried out, feeling the man wanted more than Jim could give.

Outside, Jim stood under the sign and rubbed the package between his fingers. He hadn't smoked in five years. He unwrapped the package, savoring the sound of the cellophane crinkling and the sharp smell of tobacco.

When he put the cigarette between his lips, the earthy feel of the paper was almost enough. Jim imagined his throat and lungs tightening, the taste of the smoke, trying to feel as if he'd already smoked it, but the pleasure wasn't there.

Finally, Jim lit the cigarette. It was as good as he remembered—the deep breath, the exhale, the sharp, immediate buzz. He smoked quickly, berating himself to slow down. Fumbling for a second cigarette, he dropped the pack. He felt the women walking by stare at his shaking hands. He lit the cigarette, shoved the pack into his pocket and walked away, coming to rest on a bench on the edge of the harbor.

He watched a boat nose its way around the jetty to the open sea while the others rocked in the dock. It was unnatural to live in San Diego and not own a boat. He might have forgiven the Reverend for bringing them to California if he had bought a boat, even a kayak. Fortunately, Uncle Frank, Gertrude's brother, visited during the summers that Jim was in high school and rented the same silver motorboat each year.

Uncle Frank took Jim onto the warm waters of Mission Bay three summers in a row. During the day, Jim steered through the water skiers and the hydro-boats from Sea World, practicing his turns and smiling at girls. At night they docked and remained on board long past sunset, eating charred hot dogs and listening to the Padres on a portable radio. Uncle Frank taught Jim how to smoke and how to hide it from the Reverend. For those summers, away from everyone's gaze, Jim pretended Uncle Frank was his father.

Jim drove along the coast, the steering wheel warm in his hands. He loved being on the edge of the world. He could be anybody here, different than at the beach in North Carolina, where, even beyond the breakers in the cold Atlantic water, he couldn't escape being the Reverend's son.

In 1962, the Reverend had been on track to become pastor of St. Andrew's in Asheville, where he served as junior deacon. One rainy January afternoon when Jim returned from school, the Reverend was sitting on the front porch.

"Reverend Harris is not retiring after all, son," he said when Jim climbed the steps and stood before him. "But there's an opportunity for us in California. St. Anne's-by-the-Sea. Just a different ocean."

Jim hated San Diego. The only solace he found was riding his bike to the beach and flinging himself into the sea. The shock of the water, and the knowledge that no one knew where he was, made him invisible. The kids he met on the beach taught him to surf. He began to slip out of church on Sunday mornings, first to surf and later to play baseball. Jim didn't tell his new friends about the Reverend and they didn't ask.

When the Reverend discovered Jim was skipping church, he wasn't angry, which annoyed Jim. Normal fathers yelled at their sons. Instead, the Reverend didn't speak to Jim for nearly a week, then delivered a lecture that lasted six nights. The Reverend spoke relentlessly about the grace of God, the call to service, the meek of the earth and the damned. One night, the Reverend began the story of how he was called to be a minister. Jim had heard it many times and stood up to leave. The Reverend grabbed him by the arm.

"You're smart, son," the Reverend said. "I resisted for so long. I don't want you to go through that."

"I'm not going to be a minister."

"I know that," he said, "but a man without faith is doomed. Like walking a tightrope with no net. Faith is a seatbelt. Don't you understand? God is speaking to you, but you have to listen. You can't listen if you're playing baseball."

"I don't want to listen to God. I want to play baseball." Jim pulled his arm away.

"You can do more than one thing."

"Then why can't you?"

When the Reverend hesitated, Jim left the family room, walking past his mother in the kitchen. Since then, Jim had rarely been inside a church. Even Daniel's baptism in St. Anne's was painful under the Reverend's gaze.

After that, the Reverend gave up on Jim and turned his attention to Daniel. And now, fourteen years later, it seemed to be working. Lately, Daniel was leaving the house early on Sundays for services at St. Anne's. Jim had to hand it to the Reverend: he never gave up.

When Jim turned into his parents' driveway, the Reverend was waiting on the porch. Jim tried to shake off the familiar dread as the Reverend got into the car and buckled up. In his wrinkled black shirt, stiff white collar and Xavier cap, the Reverend looked less imposing than Jim remembered. Jim wanted to ask if he had lost weight but lapsed into his habit of waiting for the Reverend to speak first.

"Wait 'til you see him, James, you won't believe it."

"I see him every day," Jim said. "I coached him during tryouts, remember?"

"This is different." The Reverend waved his hands in the air. "He's so grown up out there. So confident. He doesn't even hear the catcalls from the stands. And he's a natural hitter."

"You only saw three games."

"You should have been there."

"Dad."

"He even drew me a diagram of their pitch strategies. You know, what to throw with a runner on first and one out."

"I played for four years, remember? I know about pitch strategies."

"I don't know if he should really be a pitcher, though. He's got a great swing."

"Of course he's a pitcher." Jim moved the car into the fast lane. If he could manage it, they would only be alone for another ten minutes. "Why would you say that?"

"Anything can happen."

"Yes."

"That's all I'm saying. He needs to keep his options open." The Reverend was silent for a few minutes. "Why aren't you at work?"

"Sick."

When the Reverend didn't answer, Jim glanced at him. He was holding the caterer's receipt Jim had left on the seat.

"Nancy knows what I like," he said. "Shrimp cocktail, calamari."

"What are you talking about?" he asked.

"Daniel's a good boy but he doesn't keep a secret very well."

"Well, don't let on. It's a big deal to Nancy."

"But not to you."

Jim didn't answer. He reached into his shirt pocket, fished out a cigarette and put it to his lips.

"You're not—" the Reverend began.

"I'm not."

They didn't speak the rest of the way. Soon, the road dead-ended and the green, glorious baseball field lay in front of them.

Jim left the Reverend at the first-base bleachers. They were ten minutes early and Jim was too nervous to entertain the Reverend, so he wandered through the deserted campus. Jim had been to Xavier many times since his own graduation but now it was Daniel's school.

As a starter, Jim had been ten and four, including a win in the first game of the state championships his senior year. But those were ancient memories to anyone Daniel's age, kids who were much bigger and stronger than Jim and his teammates had ever been. Jim had watched Daniel eat his cereal in the morning, back when it was like every other morning. Daniel's legs, too long for the rest of his body, stretched underneath the entire length of the dining room table, kicking Jim every time he moved.

Jim went into the boys' bathroom near the front office and stood in the third stall, searching for the initials he carved into the ceiling years ago. After a few minutes, he located them, amazed they were still there. Jim lit another cigarette, thinking of all the uneasiness he smoked away in high school. Back then he fantasized about playing college baseball and making the majors but no scout ever called.

After graduating, Jim enrolled at junior college. At first he was content to disappear in the anonymity he craved his whole life. No one knew or cared who he was. He didn't realize until he met Nancy that he had grown used to everyone looking past him. She was the first person in years that looked directly into his face and smiled. He often told her that he married her because of that first smile.

Jim called her as he walked back to the bleachers.

"I wanted to hear your voice," he said. "It's about to start."

"Things are going to be okay," she said.

"Things are going to be okay," he repeated.

"Cheer for me, too," she said.

At the top of the bleachers, Jim reached the Reverend just as he stood up. Somewhere below them, a recording of the national anthem began. Jim removed his cap and turned to the field. The grass was a deep, healthy green and an electronic scoreboard, new since Jim's time, was hoisted above the right-field fence.

"He's number eighteen." The Reverend said as they sat down.

"I know." Jim's throat tightened.

When Daniel trotted to the mound, Jim stood and put his hands up to his mouth, preparing to shout. The Reverend pulled him down to the bench.

"Don't," he said. "He doesn't want to know we're here." The Reverend gestured to Xavier's dugout. "The coach, Mr. Martinez, expects Daniel to go far. I talked to him last game. He said if today goes well, Daniel might start against La Jolla."

"Daniel told me."

"Did you know he's batting sixth, not ninth, like most pitchers?"

"What do you think, Dad, I don't know my own son's business?"

The Reverend looked away, his chin lifted. *Good*, Jim thought. They sat in silence for a few minutes, cracking peanuts shells and flicking the red skins off their fingertips.

"Mr. Martinez says his curveball's the best he's seen in a long time," the Reverend said.

"Really?" Jim squinted toward Daniel, trying to discern which pitch he was throwing from that distance. Next time, he'd bring binoculars. "I taught him that curve, you know."

"You didn't throw a curve," the Reverend said.

"Of course I did."

Jim was preparing to lay into the Reverend, but pictured Nancy's face and took a deep breath. He exhaled the anger. The Reverend recited the Xavier players' names to him, their batting order and their stats. Jim was impressed with how much he knew. Maybe instead of attending service, Daniel and the Reverend sat in the sacristy talking ball. He saw them: the Reverend in his white robes and purple bands cloistered with Daniel in the tiny room, heads bent over the playbook as the choir sang in the church. Jim would have gone to church, too, if it had been like that.

He took out a cigarette and rolled it between his fingers. The Reverend raised his silver eyebrows but Jim waved him off. He looked back at Daniel, who pushed and pulled at the brim of his cap. The Vista batter stepped in. Daniel's first pitch sailed far right and rattled against the backstop. He pounded his fist into his glove and picked up the resin bag. His next three pitches were balls and the Vista bench hooted as the batter jogged to first.

"Double 'em up, Saints," Jim called out.

Daniel pitched and the batter hit a grounder to the third baseman who started a double play. Jim saw Daniel's shoulders relax. On the follow-through of the next pitch his rear leg kicked high, like normal. Daniel struck out the next batter on three pitches. The Reverend turned to Jim as Vista took the field.

"So what is it?" he asked. "You're home, you're smoking?"

Jim took off his cap and wiped the sweat from his hairline. The Xavier lead-off hitter stepped up to the plate.

"Well?"

"It's none of your business."

"Tell me."

"Fine. You want to know?" Jim stood up, his anger bubbling over. "Downsizing, outsourcing, restructuring, expendable middle management, lay-offs, pink-slips, severance package, human resources, exit-interview." Two girls sitting nearby shot Jim looks as his voice grew louder. "How about unemployment insurance, career counseling, update resume, forty-six-year-old unemployed father of today's starting pitcher having to look for a new job. Is that what you want to know?" The girls yelled at Jim to shut up but it felt good to heap it all on the Reverend, who didn't blink or twitch a muscle. Jim slumped back against the warm metal railing.

"And Nancy?" The Reverend's voice was thick with pity.

Jim nodded.

"Daniel?"

"Not yet."

The Reverend pulled Jim down to the bench. "If there's anything I can do."

Jim looked at the Reverend but he had turned back to the game, his face indiscernible. The Reverend leaned against Jim, their shoulders just touching. Jim could feel his strength, a rigidity that seemed to work in the Reverend's favor.

"If you kept an eye out for me," Jim said, "that'd be okay."

The Reverend held out the bag of peanuts. Jim dug in.

Xavier maintained their lead through the sixth. In the bottom of the inning, Jim bought sodas from the boosters' table behind the bleachers, then peeked at Daniel in the dugout. He sat in the middle of his teammates with his windbreaker pulled over his right arm, grinning and blowing small bubbles of gum. Jim realized with relief that Daniel was enjoying himself. He was pitching because he wanted to, not because Jim had encouraged him. For a moment, everything felt right. If only Nancy were there to see it: Jim and the Reverend sitting together, Daniel mowing down the opponents, and the sun shimmering off the outfield grass.

In the seventh inning, Vista tied the score by hitting back-to-back doubles off Daniel. Jim pulled his hat down over his eyes. In the bottom of the inning, with two outs and a runner on second, Daniel got his first hit of the game by beating out an infield grounder. That started a rally that pushed Xavier ahead by four runs. Jim's heart was full as he watched Daniel in the center of it all.

After giving up two runs in the bottom of the eighth, Coach Martinez pulled Daniel and put in a hulking blond-haired boy to protect Xavier's diminishing lead. The boy retired the final batter and then the bottom of the ninth in order, saving the game for Daniel. Jim and the Reverend made their way to Xavier's jubilant dugout.

"You're here," Daniel shouted.

Jim hugged him, feeling the boy's taut muscles through the sweat-soaked jersey.

Did you see me?"

"You were great, son," Jim said. "First rate. I counted five K's."

"Six." The Reverend slapped his palm against a score sheet. "Here, autograph it for me."

"See, Granddad." He took the sheet. "I needed that extra practice on Sunday."

Jim looked from his son to his father. "You skipped church for baseball?"

"No big deal, Dad. Hey." Daniel became excited again. "I was trying to remember every pitch I threw so I could tell you later. Mike, over there," he pointed at a boy in a leg cast, "is supposed to keep track but he never does. Did you see me beat out that infield ball? They scored it a hit, not an error. I'm three for six." He glanced at Jim, then at the Reverend. "Did you come together?"

Jim avoided the Reverend's eye. "Can you come with us now or do you have to shower here?"

"He showers here," the Reverend said.

"I'll be home soon as I can," Daniel said. "Can't wait to tell Mom."

"We're getting pizza for dinner."

"Double pepperoni, please." Daniel handed Jim a baseball. "It's the game ball. That's number two."

When Daniel left for the showers, Jim and the Reverend walked back to the car. The sun was heading downward and a cool breeze swept over Jim's legs. The wind on Mission Bay would be perfect.

TWILIGHT

William Torgerson

Joe Larkin stood in the u-shaped driveway that ran in front of the clubhouse of Moses Park Golf Course in Queens, New York. It was a heavily wooded area just across from a cemetery and connected to New York City's second largest park. Located a quarter mile from the nearest bus stop and even further to any train, the neighborhood was just the sort of place in New York City which Joe hadn't realized existed before he moved from Indiana to Long Island City because of a job his wife had gotten in publishing. He'd always imagined New York a concrete slab with high rises.

Over by the large maple tree near the first fairway, the course's adopted cat—everyone called her Cans—sniffed her way through several torn containers of Chinese take out. These had gone unnoticed all day, probably dragged there by the raccoon that raided the oil-drum trash receptacles every night. A teacher by trade, Joe needed the job because his first paycheck was two months away. It was the day before Independence Day and the blue lights from a squad car in the drive thumped into Joe's eyes like tiny punches, so much so that he had trouble seeing the face of the police officer who questioned him.

"You better be more sure than that," the officer said. "That's a pretty serious accusation you're making."

From under the canopy of trees that arched over the entrance to the course, Joe took a deep breath and surveyed the driveway: a guy with the last name Kim—he was Asian—sat in the back of a squad car, head down while a second man with the last name Conrad—he was white—lay on a stretcher as he was loaded into an ambulance. Just a half hour before, Kim had hit Conrad with his Calloway Big Bertha driver breaking Conrad's nose and maybe even his arm. The officer, who was a few years younger than Joe, puffy faced and round bellied, cleared his throat and leaned in close enough that Joe thought he could smell peanuts on his breath. Joe turned his gaze down to the blacktop, thrust his hands into his pants pockets, and hoped the officer wouldn't see how badly his hands were still shaking.

That morning Joe had begun what was to be his first day working alone at the cash register in the pro shop. Just as soon as he woke up, Joe knew it was no day for a first day. On previous mornings Joe had woke drenched in a sheen of sweat because of the heat, but now Joe felt a cool breeze blow in through his open window. It was practically chilly outside.

During Joe's two days of training at the golf course—one with Becky the boss's daughter and the other with Perry who was getting divorced and moving to Florida—there hadn't been much to do at work besides complain about the smell of urine that wafted up from the basement restrooms. Most of Queen's golfers hadn't been willing to endure the heat. But the temperature was likely now in the low seventies, and as soon as Joe arrived to the golf course, the phone began ringing with golfers who wanted to be added to the twilight list. This meant that they were in line to play golf starting at four o'clock, when the rate for play dropped from thirty-two dollars all the way down to $16.75.

Course policy stated that a golfer had to be present on the course to be put on the list, a procedure closely observed by Perry the divorcee, but discarded by Becky the boss's daughter. She'd informed Joe that her dad wanted happy customers first, at least to the point where the golf course made enough money to get their lease renewed by the city. Joe sided with Becky and thus his overall work philosophy was born: happy customers but no stealing from the bosses. The stealing part of that came from the constant freebies or discounts that the golfers continually angled for: free pull carts, green fee price reductions, or two people riding in a cart for the price of one.

On the day Joe had trained with Becky, a golfer had asked for the Korean Special, something he explained was a sandwich with a drink, green fees, and a gas cart for twenty dollars. "The Korean Special," Becky had scoffed, "now that's how you run a golf course into the ground." She meant the previous management, which had been Korean, and depending on who you talked to, had either disappeared into the night or been fired by the city.

On Joe's other training day, the one with Perry, he'd been offered a warning: *watch them push*. According to Perry, if you allowed the Koreans to tee off five minutes early one day, they'd want twenty minutes the next. Right after he said that, a Korean man carrying a Bloomingdale's bag of refreshments came to the counter at 3:15 and asked to tee off for the twilight rate. This was forty-five minutes early, and Perry promptly and curtly told the man no. Joe wondered if it were a custom of the Korean culture to recycle department store bags, or if that was something New Yorkers of all backgrounds did.

Although Joe did give Perry credit for the way he stuck to his guns and denied people of all colors and creeds early twilight golf, Joe thought he might detect an extra glint of pleasure in Perry's eye when he told the Koreans no. *Watch them push*, Perry had repeated as the man with the

Bloomingdale's bag went outside to the practice putting green to wait for four o'clock. Joe felt uncomfortable with the way Perry said *Koreans*, as if they were all the same, the way one might remind a friend to watch out for ticks in the woods.

Joe had little experience with cultures other than his own; in fact, he'd only ever known one Korean, a friend of a friend who used to have beers with the teachers on Thursday nights. She was young and pretty, and what Joe remembered about her was that she'd first introduced herself as Bo-Bae, but within a few weeks she'd begun to tell people to call her Mellissa. Joe suspected that if he moved to Korea, no one would expect him to drop his name and choose a more culturally appropriate one.

The golfer named Kim—he hadn't hit Conrad with his driver yet—arrived at Moses Park at 2:30 excited to see that there were only four people waiting outside. Golf had been steady all day, but there had never been much of a wait on the first tee. What Kim didn't realize as he sat down under the giant shade tree halfway along the first fairway, was that all afternoon Joe had been taking calls and putting people on the Twilight list. When Kim entered the double-glass doors to the clubhouse, Joe remembered him from his first training day. The man spoke more confident English than many of his Korean counterparts, and he made much more eye contact. When Joe informed Kim of his position on the twilight list, Kim responded by demanding how in the hell there could be twenty-four golfers ahead of him when no one else was around. Joe explained how as a courtesy to the golfers he allowed people to sign up via telephone.

"That's not what Perry does," Kim said. No doubt Perry had axed his hopes for early sign up at least once. Kim's anger hung like a heavy chain on his voice. He gave a little puff of disgust and walked a few steps over to where used golf clubs were for sale and lined up along the wall. There was a print of Augusta's Amen Corner and also a photograph of the golf pro—a man Joe had never met—who was seen pictured standing happily next to the professional golfer K.J. Choi. Kim turned the clubs over in his hands, but he wasn't really looking at them. He was thinking. Joe anticipated that he would have more to say, probably not pleasant.

"It's just bad business," Kim said, "and no way to run a golf course: different rules on different days." Joe tended to agree with Kim's observation. There were several ways the course worked that Joe would change, but this was his first day and already he found himself dreaming of the day he could quit. The goal of *happy golfers* was likely unattainable. The world had happy people in it, some in the middle, and others who were quite determined to be unhappy—and a person working the register at a golf course cash register had little power to alter these psychological states. Joe thought Kim was a man who allowed the light breezes (or gale force winds) of the circumstantial kind to alter his emotional weather.

Joe asked Kim if he still wanted to play, that is if he still wanted his name added to the list. The golfers came in ones, twos, and threes, but everyone had to go off in a foursome, and so Joe had decided he would keep two lists: the original where he first took the players' names as they showed up at the course, and a second one into which he puzzled the golfers into their actual playing groups. Because sometimes there were disagreements about who was to tee off when, Joe had also been writing little notes to the side of the golfers' names so he could distinguish them from one another. Kim said he indeed did want to be put on the list, and so when Joe added his name, he did not write the phrase *angry Korean*—although this was what first popped into his mind—but instead he wrote the words *orange shirt*.

A group of four police officers came into the pro shop next. They were not dressed for work, but they all got their badges out, and Joe thought he saw a gun under one man's un-tucked shirt. The smell of beer accompanied them to the counter and the men looked different parts of a recreational league football team: quarterback, linebacker, tailback, and maybe one tight end.

"What do you think?" the quarterback cop asked. He had a crew cut and his golf shirt was tight, meant to show others how big his chest and biceps were. "Give us the twilight rate right now?" Joe imagined almost every golfer who came to the course mentally working through how they were going to twist the man at the register into some sort of discount. Joe paused at the cop's request—just for a second—a time during which he considered saying yes. The cop pushed a little harder. "C'mon man, for all we do?"

Joe had seen an article in the *Times* about how much money the cops made—it was even worse than a teacher's salary—but then he told the guy that he wished he could let them go, that if it were his course he would, but that the golf wasn't his to give away. Joe nodded up to behind the men where a camera was pointed right at the register. He didn't tell them it didn't have sound.

One of the other cops—this one had a scruffier look to him—told Joe that he *could* let them go no problem, but that he just got off on telling cops no. "Why don't you have a couple beers?" he said. "Then we'll see you out on the road." Another one told the mouthy one to take it easy, and a third picked up the giant tub of used golf balls for sale on the counter and said he would just take them for compensation. The cop's hair was spiked up in one of those fauxhawks, and he had on several gold chains, just the sort of look Joe had expected from all New Yorkers before moving to the city. He'd known a guy from Brooklyn once, a man who was usually clad in a shiny Fila sweat suit and never seen without his gold necklace with a matching *Jets* charm dangling on his chest. Of course Joe had learned New Yorkers looked all sorts of ways, and it was the diversity of Queens—that there were over a hundred languages spoken in the borough—that had been an even bigger surprise than the tree-lined streets.

"Ha, ha—just for laughs," the cop said as he pushed his back up against one of the glass doors. What would Joe do if the guy carried the tub of balls outside? Call the police? Eventually the quarterback cop suggested they head over to the bar and get some beers. The men exited the clubhouse out on the patio and left the tub of golf balls sitting on the floor of the pro shop. Joe went around the counter and put them back up where they belonged.

Just a few minutes before four o'clock—the beginning of twilight tee times—Joe left the register and went out onto the stone patio—it was nice out there with lots of tables shaded by new umbrellas. All the seats were full, and golfers lined the concrete wall separating the deck from the cart path, others gathered under the giant shade tree, and more stood on or around the putting green practicing or talking. A three-story high net ran from the back of the first tee to just beyond the gate, protection for others from being beaned by errant tee shots. Down by the red ladies tees, there was a slice of an entryway in the net, a spot where Randy the starter sat in a gas golf cart. It was Randy's job to take the receipts Joe gave the golfers, look at the number Joe wrote on them, and then announce each group when it was their turn to play. Randy was a pony-tailed Texan, his cheeks always red as if he'd just had a couple of *coldies*—that's what Randy called beer. He knew a lot of jokes—most of them disrespectful to women—and he was tight with Matt the golf course manager, a retired telephone company guy who said he managed the course to keep himself away from the horse track. Both days that Joe had worked, Randy and Matt had shared a couple beers after the twilight rush. The only other employee around was Luisa, who according to the time sheet hanging by the computer, had already logged nearly sixty hours in the kitchen for the week.

Standing on the patio just outside the doors to the clubhouse, Joe hollered with his big voice for everyone to come inside and pay; it was what Perry and Becky had said to do. Then he turned and went inside to the register, followed by fifty or so golfers. With only one small window air conditioner, the pro shop heated up fast and the golfers bumped against one another like five-thirty on the subway. Joe called out the first couple of names on the list, and after the two golfers struggled through the crowd to get to the register, Joe rang up two twilight fees. His mouth went dry as soon as he saw the total: $147.

The last group to pay full price had been just after the time the cops had come in: two Korean women, fairly young and attractive—they had brand new everything (pink bags, Nike clubs, even outfits that matched their bags and clubs) and they had charged the golf: two regular green fees plus a gas cart. Although Joe didn't realize it yet, he'd forgot to open and close the register door, an unnatural act since no cash had exchanged hands, but nevertheless something required of him to clear the register.

The men on the other side of the counter laughed. "Well that's not right," one of them said. Joe hit the *clear* button, but when he rang up the twilights again, the golf totaled $175. Joe then chose to have faith in his actions when there was no reason for it. He went through the process again, only to find that he'd added to what was already a ridiculous amount. Like the smell of the urinals on a hot summer day, grumbles began to rise up from the crowd and Joe heard someone ask: "Where do they find these guys?" Joe thought *Craig's List* but didn't say anything.

The first tee was open and ready for play; Joe's actions were extending what was already going to be a long wait. By the time the last golfers went off, they would be lucky to finish before dark. Tension thickened like traffic on the Long Island Expressway, and Joe's hands shook so badly that when he tried to call Matt the manager for help, he fumbled his cell phone to the green indoor/outdoor carpet on the floor.

Nearly twenty minutes passed before Matt the manager was able to get to the pro shop and clear the register. He wore gruffness and violence like a suit of armor against the customers, attire that Joe realized many of the residents of Queens felt compelled to don. As Matt rang up the golfers, some of them complained, and he told more than one of them to *go to hell*. It was Matt's initial response to any gripe, and if it wasn't that one, then it was an invitation for the golfer to take his or her game to a different course.

"Go to hell," Matt told the next golfer who complained about having a fourth added to his group. Joe wrote numbers on each receipt, something he returned to the golfers so they could deliver it to Randy out by the first hole. Also, Joe continued to write himself little notes on the tee sheet so he could remember who was who: black Ping shirt, married couple, knee-high socks, Taylor Made visor, and so on. His blood pressure began to return to normal as Matt's mean-spirited attitude backed off the aggressiveness of the crowd. Joe could tell that many of the golfers were sympathetic to his plight, that they realized the course was extra busy and understaffed, but there were others who waited to bite into any mistake like the raccoon that worked the garbage at night. Joe transferred Kim's name from his notes to the official tee sheet and copied the phrase *orange shirt* next to his name.

At five o'clock a cart ran out of gas and so Matt needed to leave and go get it. "You okay?" he asked Joe, a look of genuine concern on his face. Joe felt sick to his stomach to be left alone in the pro shop, but he told Matt that he ought to be fine, and then he made a joke about remembering to cash out any charges.

"What?" Matt asked. He was hard of hearing and wouldn't admit it. Joe shook his head, *never mind,* and Matt left the pro shop. Joe rang up several more green fees but as the line continued to grow, he thought maybe he should start turning away golfers. The course was full. There was bound to be nearly a two hour wait for anyone who paid now.

"You've got two seven's," Randy the Texan starter said, poking his head inside one of the glass doors that led out to the patio. He waved a receipt as if it were a tiny flag of surrender to Joe's ignorance. *Shit*, thought Joe, *I've done it again*. What Randy meant was that Joe had used the same number for two receipts. "It's either four cops or a group with a Korean named Kim," Randy said. "He told me you'd remember him?" Joe leaned over the podium next to the register with the tee sheet clipped to it. Of course he remembered him but who had come in first, Kim or the police officers? As it turned out, there had been several groups who'd used the name Kim, and Joe didn't see the one with the phrase *orange shirt* written next to it.

"Tall with an orange shirt?" Joe asked, not because he needed to know the information but just to buy himself some more time.

"Hell," Randy said, "I don't know what color his shirt is. Do you want me to go look?" Joe located two groups with the name Kim—he felt the will of those in line hurry him—but neither *Kim* name was followed by the phrase *orange shirt*. Joe thought maybe he'd forgotten to copy it over from the first sheet, but because he was so flustered, he was no longer sure of what he had written when, which receipts he'd given out, what buttons he'd pushed, or if he'd even returned change to the customer who stood before him. Both of the groups denoted by the name Kim appeared after the group of police officers, but Joe wanted to be sure. He felt Kim would expect him to let the white cops go first. But there were the names Kim, definitely below the group Joe had marked with the letters *NYPD*.

"Kim is after the police officers," Joe said, trying to sound confident.

"Fine." Randy balled the receipt into his fist. "That's what I'll tell him. It's ten minutes either way—like it matters on a day like this." Randy pushed through the golfers and headed back to the first tee.

Joe took a deep breath and tried to collect himself. "Who's next?" he asked, and then a woman holding a book with an image of a woman golfer's pretty legs came to the counter. Joe couldn't really imagine someone playing golf in a skirt as short at the one pictured on the cover, but he did admire the sight of legs. He wondered about the book, and whether or not the woman at the counter read it only while she waited to tee off, or if she might actually carry it down the fairway with her. If one came to the course without any playing partners, a round of golf at Moses Park could be a fairly long and lonely event.

"C'mon," a man behind the woman with the book said. He meant for Joe to hurry up. Joe gave the reading golfer her change and looked down into his drawer, where there was a dollar bill and three quarters. The standard twilight transaction was that the customer gave Joe a twenty, and he returned $3.25 in change. He told the men next in line to wait a second, that he needed to get some change. A bearded man in one of the Titleist caps sold by Moses Park—he'd chosen the Mets version—cursed and left. Joe used his cell phone to call Matt so he could come get him some singles and quarters out of the safe. There were ten or so golfers remaining in the clubhouse.

The Kim in the orange shirt came into the pro shop holding his driver. Joe was thinking that the time should have arrived for Kim to tee off, but Kim came hurrying over to the counter where he slapped his receipt down so hard that Joe half expected for the glass to break.

"You stupid people," Kim said to Joe, his mouth frothing up when he talked. Kim was so angry that Joe almost didn't recognize him. "All you have to do is look at the time." Joe's heart beat fast; he knew he'd screwed up—didn't know how—but was sure that Kim's anger must have been his fault.

"What do you mean look at the time?" Joe glanced to the clock on the back wall.

"The time is on the receipt," Kim said. "I'm sure the time on mine is before the group on the tee. It's just simple logic; all the ranger had to do was look at the ticket and let me go. When he brought it in here to show you, what did you tell him?"

Randy hadn't mentioned anything about looking at the time on the receipt. Why hadn't he done that? Joe thought Kim's solution about the time stamp was brilliant—brilliant to the degree that they didn't even need to number the receipts. Joe looked over his shoulder to the first tee where the fauxhawked cop had just teed off. It was too late to tell Randy to let Kim go first.

"I looked on my clipboard," Joe said. "Your name is right here." He pointed to Kim's name and turned the sheet to him so he could read it. Kim squinted at the chart and then nearly broke his finger on the board when he jabbed it into a name several spaces above the police officers. "Kim," he yelled. "That's me, Kim! Orange shirt, remember?" There it was; Joe had remembered to write *orange shirt* after all. "You've got three Kim's there. It's like your Smith."

"I'm sorry," Joe said. "I made a mistake. This is my fault." Kim smiled strangely, looked from Joe to the people in line waiting to pay, and then he nodded as if he finally recognized a conspiracy, one to which he was going to lose to, at least for today.

"But you're not going to do anything about it are you?"

"What can I do? They'll be heading down the first fairway any second."

"Just give me a refund," Kim said, but Joe definitely couldn't do that—*absolutely no cash from the register*—it was the first thing Becky's dad had said right after introducing himself. "Hi, I'm Bob. Don't give anyone any cash out of the register." It had been funny at the time but now Joe could see Bob's point of view clearly.

Since Kim hadn't played a stroke of golf, he thought it a perfectly reasonable request to want his money back. This Joe tended to agree with; but again, it wasn't his call and if he returned the money his receipts wouldn't match, and Bob came by every night to do the totals right in front of whoever had worked the register that day. For a moment, Joe thought he saw volcanoes bubbling up in Kim's eyes ready to erupt upon him, but the glass door to the patio opened and Randy came halfway in.

"Kim, you want to play golf?" Randy asked. Kim dropped his head and put both hands on the glass of the counter. His mood changed; he no longer looked angry, but just terribly frustrated, as if he might cry.

"I just want to go home," he said, so soft that only Joe could hear. "Golf is ruined."

"Kim, your group is on the tee," Randy said. "You want me to give your spot away?"

"I'll take it," a man in a Notre Dame hat said from over where he'd been eyeing the handicap postings taped to the wall. Kim seemed to buck himself up, standing taller, seemingly inflating his will. Joe hoped he would decide to play, hit a nice first drive, and maybe score so well that by the time his round was over his spirits would lift. Golf has that sort of power; if only a long putt would drop for a birdie or a mid-iron shot bounce up tight to the flagstick, then Kim's entire outlook on the day, maybe even the week could change and send him off the course anxious to return, this when only hours before he'd noted golf was ruined. Joe remembered his dad's friend Cuppie, who back in Horseshoe, Indiana had thrown his bag into the pond on fourteen and never played again.

Kim thumped his fist on the glass hard enough that once again Joe was surprised it didn't spider into a break. But then Kim magically transformed himself with a deep breath. Almost enthusiastically, he headed for the door with his driver. The man next in line—he had white hair that haloed out from under his Key West hat—said something which was at least at first inaudible to Joe. This was the man who turned out be named Conrad, and the men around him laughed at whatever he'd said.

"Two twilights," Conrad said, and as Joe took the money from his hand, somewhere in his mind rose the word *gook*. It happened a good three seconds after Conrad had stepped up to the register, the way sometimes one understands what someone has said right after asking, "What?" Joe didn't even know why he knew such a word; maybe he'd heard it once in a war movie? He thought of that old TV show *M.A.S.H.* but didn't think the word was probably allowed on television.

Joe didn't even consider challenging the man in front of him about what he'd said, and as he fumbled in the register for change, he didn't see Kim turn and swing his driver. He did, however, hear it connect with Conrad's arm, making a thud that Joe thought sounded like the time his own father had missed a ball in the rough and thumped his rescue wood into an unseen log. Joe surprised himself as he came over the counter. It would have only been a couple extra feet to go around. His legs knocked the tub of balls to the floor, and Kim's second swing shattered the graphite shaft of his club across Conrad's nose. With Kim's big swing uncoiled, he was left as powerless as a three iron with a cracked head. Joe wrapped Kim up in his arms and then stumbled on the spilled golf balls. The two men went down. Quickly, Conrad's friends began to stomp their golf shoes onto Kim's forearms, which he'd put up to protect his face. The men adjusted their aim to Kim's exposed middle, occasionally missing and catching Joe. Squinting through the churning legs, Joe swept his foot and took one man down. With surprising quickness, Matt the manager came through the doors from the patio. Many years before Matt had been an athlete, a second baseman at Rutgers, and it was with some degree of agility—something like he'd done turning double plays—that he hopped over Joe and Kim, falling into the stomping men who he knocked into the used golf clubs that were for sale along the wall. Like dominoes; men, bags, and clubs tumbled to the floor—even the rickety closet door fell from its hinges onto the men who would have completed Conrad's foursome.

The fight escalated quickly, could have continued, but almost immediately the room filled with regret. Most of the men were used to muttering their prejudices quietly to those of their own kind, but not accustomed to the overt physical violence that had manifested itself in the clubhouse. Blood flowed from Conrad's nose like water from one of the green Gatorade coolers spread out on the course. A woman golfer who'd just been entering the clubhouse, ran outside and used her cell phone to call the police.

And now authentic twilight—not the artificial sort suggested by the rate—had finally stopped the tide of new golfers from coming to the course. Joe still hadn't responded to the police officer's question. "So it seems to me," the cop pushed, "that you couldn't *think* you heard that. Either Conrad called Kim a 'gook' or he didn't."

Joe felt the pressure of testifying in the distance. He wasn't sure what Conrad had said, and he didn't know what Kim's story had been to the police. Joe thought maybe when he heard the laughing of Conrad's friends, he'd just assumed that they were prejudiced and so it was possible that his own imagination had supplied the word. It would be much easier for Joe to tell the police officer that he couldn't be sure at what had been said. This, in fact, would be the truth, and if he said that, his involvement with the situation would likely end. But Joe wondered what would happen to Kim if according to the law he'd just assaulted Conrad because he lost his temper. Certainly Kim had not been a pleasant customer for Joe to deal with. Why should he help him? Joe remembered the men's laughter, something they'd already told the police officer came from Kim's obvious frustration. Sure, they were sorry for that, it had been mean spirited but surely it didn't warrant being cracked by somebody's driver. *We were just waiting like everyone else,* the men had said, *but the guy was a maniac.* Joe thought if Mr. Conrad hadn't said *gook,* that Kim's frustrations wouldn't have been enough reason for him to crack Conrad with the club. In fact, hadn't Kim appeared utterly calm before the attack? If anything, Kim should have hit Joe, but that was obviously not his intent.

"Mr. Conrad," Joe said to the officer, "called Mr. Kim a gook."

Joe's first day working the register ended after that: the ambulance eased out onto Moses Boulevard; the police car followed—lights off—and Kim rode in the back seat, leaning forward to take some of the pressure off of his handcuffed wrists. Bob the big boss, who'd arrived shortly after the police, told Joe to go on home, take a couple days off, and they'd talk at the end of the week. There was a lot that needed to be cleared up. Three quiet hours later, emboldened as it always was by the coming of darkness, the raccoon from the night before re-emerged from the trees that lined the first fairway. He hissed Cans the golf course cat away from where she licked at some tuna salad. After the raccoon ate that, it dove into one of the trash barrels and feasted on stale bread, half-eaten hot dogs, and the two-day old remnants of Perry's Chinese takeout leftovers.

MY AMERICAN SOCCER SEASON

Lee Ann Robins

If I can take the ball away from Yellow Shoes, I don't care if I get a warning or even a yellow card. He is an asshole. He has fouled me three or four times and the referee hasn't called it, so if I get close, I'm going to hurt him. James is in passing position, but if Gato and Eli can get the ball to me, I'm scoring, Yellow Shoes or not. James will get up to the goal and not shoot, or he will shoot it right into their keeper's hands, so it is my play. I can hear some stupid kids on the side are screaming, "Go, Cesar!" so I guess that is Yellow Shoes' name.

Gato kicks the ball right out from under Yellow Shoes, dribbles it around, passes to Eli, and Eli brings it up for me to score; I am much faster than their defenders, so it's only Yellow Shoes at midfield I have to watch for. I scored two times already in this game, and if I can just score one more, we will be ahead by one goal and only three minutes left. I think Juan can block their forwards and then we will be in the finals for the tournament. Here he comes, Yellow Shoes, and his groupies are screaming again. He tries to take the ball from me and his cleats slam into the top of my foot. I know it would hurt if I could feel anything right now, but

I have too much adrenaline rush. For him to do that pisses me off though, and so when this Cesar comes in too close to me, I become his Brutus, throw up my elbow and get him in the throat. I hit his neck hard and he makes big choking sound. He falls down, all crying like a baby, clutching his throat so ref will give the yellow card, and Cesar's groupies start booing me.

I remember how great player Zinadou Zidane ended his career with a red card in 2006 World Cup. I was only fourteen, and had already been playing since I was five, so my father and I were watching final match together. Already there was talk of me making it all the way in our new UEFA league, and we were both dreaming Serbia would make it to the next World Cup and maybe I would be there. When I saw Zidane head butt-the Italian, I understood him. It's temper, like how when Yellow Shoes kicked me, I just threw my elbow at this throat. All football players have temper, I think. The Italian player grabbed Zidane's shirt, and Zizou said he'd give it to him after game if he wanted it so bad. When the Italian said "I'd rather take your sister's shirt off, you son of a terrorist whore," that's when Zidane head-butted Materazzi, and a second later, Materazzi went down on the field just like Cesar did. I knew how Zidane's blood was pumping, how he was high from his penalty kick ,and how he knew it was last seconds of World Cup, and the whole world was watching.

I'm not Zizou, not world-famous yet, but I did score 23 goals in ten games that year, my team was featured in the Beograde paper, and there was an article just about me and my background. My father thought it was better for me to come to America as exchange student and try to get scholarship to an American college. That'swhy Coach has video camera tonight, for the University and scholarship, so I will not go home. My parents always wanted everything for me—they want American education, American career, American wealth, and this is why I am here. For me, all I care about right now is to get by Yellow Shoes and score .

"You see him kick me? Ref!" I screamed at him because Yellow Shoes didn't even kick the ball, he kicked my foot instead on purpose, to hurt me, and didn't get a yellow card, and cost me a goal maybe. I would have head-butted him like Zizou myself if he had not fallen down on the field and I would have taken red card, too. So I say to myself, as I try to wait for what is going to happen, it would not crush me to be going back to Serbia and leaving the U.S., even though I want to go to college here, too. What I thought was I would sell my motorcycle to pay living expenses if they would just give me a football scholarship, but Yellow Shoes' faking could keep that from happening.

Also, in the eight months I have been here, going to high school and living with my second host family because the first one wimped out on having exchange student, it is old. I feel like I can't stand another minute sometimes, with the little kids of my new host family running around and screaming at 6 in the morning when I just went to bed at 5. I hid a bottle of vodka in my suitcase because I can't go to clubs here. Over here they pay attention to drinking laws and there are no good clubs to go to anyway. All they listen to is rap and country music, and those things make me want to go back so bad. But my father, he says the street is long and dark, you should know that the world is yours, the world is ours, don't ever give up, you must try your best. So I stay here, I try for college in America, and I know they will probably want me for my football. But now all I can see is the ref running up to me and I know yellow card is coming. Right now I hate him for maybe taking all my plans away and I hate the sissies on the other team.

All their parents on the sidelines and their friends are yelling for them, so I yell, too. I yell nothing, just nonsense sounds, right into Yellow Shoes' face while he lies on ground pretending and grabbing his throat. The ref looks at him, and I know the yellow card is for sure and maybe red card. If I get thrown out of game, there's no chance of us winning and there will be no sending my tape. I open my mouth to argue, but "Dusan, shut up!" Coach is yelling from the sidelines. "Dusan," Gato says, right in my ear and puts hand on my shoulder. "You can't get sent off. We'll lose." So I shut my mouth and turn my back. Ref reaches in his pocket and Gato gets right in ref's face and says to him, "He's an exchange student-he doesn't know better." Ref gets look on his face like all Americans when they are feeling superior, which I hate more than anything, so that's it—I just say fuck off and fuck you, too, American peasants. Then I realize I said it not just in my head but loud and everyone heard.

Cesar's middle school groupies, who don't know football from what, volleyball, all start jumping and screaming, "Throw him out! Throw him out!" All they care about is getting attention. No Americans can name any football player but David Beckham, and if you call it "soccer" you don't know anything anyway. American teenagers are so spoiled, always talking about their X-boxes and Facebook. The parents are overprotective of their kids, kids grow up to be babies, like the ones in my host family. In my country, we fight for ourselves. My parents say, "You got yourself in trouble; get yourself out," because that's what we have had to do for so long as Serbs, fight for what is ours, and Americans, they don't even know how. So I just say "Fuck you" again, to Yellow Shoes, to groupies, for all condescending American peasants, and I spit, right beside Yellow Shoes' face, because I have nothing to lose now. Ref comes out with red card in his hand still with that stupid superiority look on his face and I want to spit at him, too. Yeah, I wanted another goal and I wanted to make it to finals in this tournament, but I'm too angry now. Angry at Cesar for kicking my foot and pretending to be so hurt, mad at Cesar's groupies for watching, mad at the fascists in my country who ruined the economy, mad at my father for wanting me to come. I'm mad for losing my temper and blowing this whole season. I know I don't have control now

Lee Ann Robins

and I don't know what I'll do, so I run off field past coach and the rest of the team on bench.

Guys all are saying things to me, but I need to get out before I hit something or scream more curse words; it will get us in more trouble. I walk away from the field and over to parking lot. Coach should have taken me out ten minutes ago, when I got so mad at that jerk and put Jano in then; maybe I wouldn't have hit Yellow Shoes or said that to the referee and been thrown out. But Jano is stupid slow; we would have lost anyway. I think about how Coach is partly to blame for not taking me out, about Gato and Eli having to play with Jano as forward, and it makes me so angry, I ball my hand into a fist and punch a big American Jeep Cherokee right in the quarter panel, not caring if I break my hand. I rub blood on my jersey and if stains I don't give a shit. I take some deep breaths and try to hear what's going on. Cesar's groupies are shrieking and screaming more now, so his school must have scored another goal. I can't watch. I know exactly how Zidane felt and Anelka. Even though Zidane's a freaking Muslim, I understand him.

I think how it could be a relief to go home and see my friends and speak my own language, go clubbing and drink. I won't have host family parents telling me I shouldn't have so many Cokes or coffee or sleep so late and no little brats to wake me up too early. I wonder how the story in the paper will say about this tournament and why my school lost, after they ran a picture of us after the first round when we beat everyone in our bracket. In America, they think you are already great at football, soccer they call it, if you are from Europe, but the newspaper photographer is here tonight, and I don't know if he maybe took a picture of me fouling Yellow Shoes. He could have, sure.

I remember newspaper headline after Beckham's red card in 1998 World Cup said, "Ten heroic lions, one stupid boy," and they burned models of him all around Britain. Just this year, when the French team's forward Anelka refused to apologize for insulting his coach and got thrown off the team, French football president resigned in shame. Zidane, in moment after he head-butted Materazzi, pulled off his captain's armband and did not argue, but Italians won 2006 World Cup, and FIFA disciplined him anyway. When you get angry on the pitch, no price is too big—not the match, not your team, not fame from the world, not even World Cup title.

I look across parking lot at scoreboard, and now it says "Home 2, Visitors 4" so Yellow Shoes' team has scored twice since I got kicked out. It could be Juan's clumsiness, but Gato and Eli have probably given up like they did if we started losing at beginning of season. I listen more, and I hear Gato yelling directions. I hear, "Venga!" probably at James. Then I hear "Chuta!" That's Juan at the keeper's box, "Chuta!" again and then silence, so James either missed or choked and didn't shoot. And I realize they have gone back to talking to each other in Mexican, which was like the first of the season before we started winning.

It was when we started passing to each other and having strategy that we won and we got in the tournament, but now it's all gone to hell and they're playing like everybody hates each other. I did hate them at first, most of them kiss-up Mexicans. They skipped practice and they always talked to each other so I couldn't understand. All I heard in English from them the first month was "Get off the field! Go home!" But after we played four or five games, we learned to be team. They saw I could handle the ball, and they started defending me and passing to me. I see I screwed up my American scholarship, but I also screwed up my team for stupid reason. Yellow Shoes didn't call me "son of a terrorist whore" and ref didn't even say a word. It was me thinking that scoring 23 goals would be enough to get me what I want, always knowing inside Americans are so prudish. This makes the only game I didn't score in. I hear the whistle, and the match is over.

So Yellow Shoes' team goes to finals. Coach waves at me to go on to the bus so I don't have to shake hands with other captain, but I will go back and do it. I take one more deep breath of American air and come out of the dark parking lot, back to the field where the ref I said "Fuck you" to is watching me come along with Gato and Eli and coaches. He is watching me come across the field for the end of my American soccer season, and something about their all watching me makes me laugh.

A minute ago I thought I would cry, but already in my head I am getting on the plane next week and leaving the U.S. behind, flying toward my homeland and the whole fuck you of trying to get a future there and it just is funny. Americans don't understand—not Kosovo or Milosevic or NATO aggression. Yellow Shoes couldn't understand or ref or Coach. Even Gato, Eli, and Juan, not American citizens either, they don't understand. My father might, but who knows. Myself, I understand some things. I control dribbling the ball down to goal and sending it past the keeper. I control the ball and how we set up to play, but I have not enough control over my anger. Next week at home, other things will be out of my control, and I will be wondering if I will ever come back. I'm wondering if Zizou and Anelka or Beckham wanted to go back and do things different or even if they could have. Or if I could—I know my friends at home would have booed the refs and would have said the same thing I did. But I think about how Gato told me to calm down and put his hand on my shoulder, and so I join the team and shake hands with Yellow Shoes' team, even him, and then I pick up my bag and get on the bus behind Gato, Eli and Juan. I have the bus ride home to think which way is better.

If I had kept my temper, if Beckham, Zizou, or Anelka had kept theirs, would anything have been different? I think about some pretty dream world, a world with me and Eli and Gato and Juan playing in the World Cup, all on the same team even, a world where refs always make good calls, a world where Americans don't think they are so superior. I think about a world where Yugoslavia still exists, but I can't envision such a world any more, not after everything I've seen and everything my father's told me about 1992, the year I was born in Serbia. Maybe nothing will ever be different in this world, or maybe someday everything will. In the seat next to me, I see that Gato has put his headphones on to listen to his iPod and has his eyes closed, so I look out the bus windows. I watch at the dark of the U.S. slipping past, and know that it will be a long time before I can get to sleep.

THE YEAR THE PADRES WON THE PENNANT

J. Weintraub

One summer, many years ago, before any of the other clubs realized what was happening, the Chicago Cubs finished on top of what was then the Eastern Division of the National League.

Even more surprising, they were heavily favored to defeat their Western Division opponents, the San Diego Padres, in the upcoming best-of-five playoff series. Certainly, every Cubs fan viewed the playoffs as a lock, a minor hurdle for their team on their way to a classic confrontation with the powerful Tigers in the World Series, and I was astonished when Dana, whom I assumed had been successfully transplanted from San Diego, revealed an unexpected affection for her local team.

"The lions in front of the Art Institute are wearing Cubs caps," I announced one evening as the city prepared itself for the playoffs.

"I think that's disgusting," she said.

"The Picasso, too."

"That's worse."

"Come on, Dana, be a sport. This is our year."

"Our? You know, there might be one or two people in this town who don't consider the Cubs the greatest thing in the world since sliced bread!"

"Only someone from southern California would think that sliced bread was great."

She was about to reply but managed to restrain herself. The following night, however, she could not contain her anger when a local commentator began to assess the Cubs' chances against Detroit.

"They've got to beat the Padres first, you asshole!" she shouted at the screen.

"Only a minor technicality."

"You're just like everyone else in this town," she said, turning her anger on me now. "You don't know a thing about the Padres because you've closed your minds to everything else but those stupid Cubs!""

"The Padres have a rookie first baseman in left, two overpaid has-beens at the corners, a head case at short, and has their starting rotation ever completed a game?"

"They were good enough to win the West, weren't they?"

"The weakest division in baseball. But why are you getting so worked up about this? You're a football fan. You haven't been following the Padres at all this year."

"How can I? All your papers ever talk about are the Cubs! I never before thought of Chicago as bush league, but I'm beginning to understand now why they call you the Second City!"

This time I was the one who bit his tongue. Dana and I occasionally quibbled over sports, and the tension between us was especially thick one Monday night when the San Diego Chargers humiliated the Bears. But usually we confined our arguments to what was going on between the foul lines. Now, however, we both seemed intent on introducing extraneous issues, and on the eve of the playoffs I could not prevent myself from mentioning that a quarter of the Padres' pitching staff were card-carrying members of the John Birch Society.

"So what's your point?" asked Dana, not at all flustered by this revelation. "I suppose the Cubs are all registered Democrats?"

"My point is that only a Californian, a southern Californian, could ever stomach a team like the Padres."

She didn't back off this time. "You know, I'm just about fed up with you always hitting on California. We've been married for almost six years, and I don't think a day has gone by without you putting down the West Coast at least once."

"There's so much material, you can hardly blame me."

"It wouldn't be so bad if it were just with me, but at least you could have the sense to keep your trap shut when you're with my family."

"What's the matter? Your old man doesn't appreciate the Jew in the family shooting off his mouth?"

Her face turned red, and I realized I had once again entered forbidden territory. In our first years of marriage, Dana rarely took issue with anything I might say about her parents. As a teenager she had twice fled to San Francisco to escape what she called their "rampant materialism and primeval politics," and instead of enrolling at Cal-San Diego or U.S.C., she matriculated at Wisconsin, living in Madison with her aunt for the entire four years. After graduation she settled in Chicago, where we met and were married.

But in recent years, following the death of her aunt, Dana seemed intent on drawing closer to her parents, and even though her trips home aggravated old family wounds and opened new ones, her face now turned red with shame and disappointment whenever I complained about the behavior of my in-laws, as if I were contributing to her consistent failure to revive a bond that, as far as I could tell, had never existed in the first place.

"It really hurts when you say stuff like that, Dave," she finally replied.

"It's close enough to the truth, though, isn't it?"

"It doesn't have to be. Sometimes I think you push Mom and Dad into it."

"For instance?"

"For instance in February. At Mom and Dad's fortieth. It was such a glorious day, and everything was turning out so wonderfully . . . "

"Until you started that fight with your brother-in-law over abortion."

" . . . and still you had to find something to fuss over. Such fine weather, you said, made southern Californians complacent. What we needed was some good Midwestern slush to make us a little more human. Well, I know just what my mother was thinking when she heard you say that."

"Which was?"

"The same thing she asked me the previous day when you were griping about suntans or defense contracts or something just as silly. 'Why,' she wanted to know, 'do Jewish people have to be so negative . . . '"

"Well, we were kicked out of the Promised Land for close to two thousand years."

" . . . and yet act so superior."

"Still, we are the Chosen People."

"Anyway, if it means anything to you, that's what she must've been thinking about the day of their anniversary. And I'm beginning to think there's some truth in it, too."

"Really? The dark, negative Jew versus the blonde, positive Aryan. I suppose the Nazis had it right after all. Is that where your mother's coming from?"

"I didn't mean Jews in general. I meant you. You're the negative one. You're the superior one. And my mother's not a Nazi!"

She was probably right, and I apologized.

"Let's go to bed," I said, and I kissed her on the cheek.

"I'll be right behind you," but I was asleep by the time she joined me beneath the covers.

One of my coworkers brought a television set into the office the next day for the first game of the playoffs, and our entire department gathered around it for the opening pitch. When the leadoff batter for the Cubs homered, I couldn't resist calling Dana. Perhaps I wanted to bring our difference of the previous night back into perspective, a harmless rivalry over home teams.

Her phone rang half-a-dozen times before she answered. "Hey, hey!" I cried as soon as she picked it up.

"You're being childish, Dave. It doesn't become you."

"But that's what it's all about, Dana. We should be childish, not take everything so seriously, like you're doing, as if it really meant something . . . " An explosion of cheers resounded from around our TV set, and there was a distant shout from her end of the line, too.

"Hold it a second, Dana," and with one hand over the receiver, I called over to our publicity manager. "What happened?"

"Sarge just belted another one out of the park!"

"Hey, hey!" I yelled back into the phone, mimicking the triumphant cheer of a former Cubs announcer.

There was no response from the other side. "Dana, are you there?" I asked, but the line was dead.

The Cubs won that first game, 13 to 0, behind Rick Sutcliffe, the best pitcher in baseball that year.

They won the second game, too, and when they traveled to San Diego, they needed only one victory out of the next three to wrap up the playoffs.

"Look at the headline on this paper!" complained Dana, displaying the morning edition of the *Sun-Times*. "World War III wouldn't get a treatment the size of this! And I can't turn on the radio or the local news without hearing someone yapping about the Cubs, Cubs, Cubs! You're always accusing San Diego of being a backwater, but I don't think I've ever seen such provincialism in all my life!"

I was ready for her this time. "You have to understand, Dana. The Cubs are much bigger than Chicago. They're broadcast over WGN, and WGN is picked up all over the country. There are millions of fans who live and die with the Cubs every day. More than any other ball club, the Cubs are America's team."

"In that case, I'm for the Tigers in the Series."

"Giving up on your Padres already?" and then I added sarcastically, "Of course, they could sweep the last three games—even though it's never been done before."

"I'm for the Tigers."

"You once told me you hated the Tigers. Worse than the Yankees, you said."

"The Tigers," she repeated, glaring at me as if she herself were a jungle cat, ready to pounce, and I knew that the tension tightening between us would not slacken until the last out of the season had been made.

The Padres won the first game in San Diego, the Cubs playing as if they expected the ripe fruit of victory to fall into their laps while they waited below, doing nothing, and as I watched, an uneasy premonition migrated into my stomach. Two Alka Seltzers helped me endure the final three innings.

"They'll go with Sutcliffe tomorrow," I predicted. "He'll shut the door in their faces."

"That's ridiculous," said Dana, who throughout the entire game had buried herself in silence. "They'll save him for Sunday."

"What do you mean 'ridiculous'? There's a dozen good reasons for him to start tomorrow, not the least of which is that it'll shift the pressure back onto the Padres where it belongs!"

She didn't reply, descending once more into silence.

The next morning Jim Frey, the Cubs manager, announced that he would rest Sutcliffe another day, saving him for the fifth game, should it be necessary.

"Stupid! Stupid! Stupid!" I exclaimed, slamming the sports page down onto the breakfast table. "They should go with him today!"

But before I could again defend my position, Dana arose. "I don't want to hear any more. I've had enough. What do you know about it, anyway?"

What did I know about it! While she was still in diapers, I was calculating ERAs and slugging percentages. While my friends were reading *Boys Life* and Marvel Comics, I was subscribing to *The Sporting News*, and I could still recite the opening-day lineups for every Cubs team that took the field from 1957 to 1961. What did I know about it, indeed!

"Maybe I don't know anything," I said. "But you should have the sense to realize that our idiot manager just handed your team momentum on a silver platter!"

"Why don't you call him up and tell him, then? Better yet, why don't you apply for his job? I'm sure they'd be impressed with your resume. In the meantime, I probably won't be here to see how right you really are. Our art director screwed up again, and I've got to go into work today. I won't be home until late."

"Good," I said, and after she slammed the kitchen door shut, I swept half the dishes off the table, leaving them on the floor for her return. I then invited myself over to Peter's house to watch the game with him and Michaela.

Peter Lipschitz and his wife both had roots in Chicago predating Mrs. O'Leary's cow, and I could count on the two of them to travel to Wrigleyville with me for the celebration that was sure to erupt outside the empty stadium once the Cubs won. On the other hand, should my doubts about Frey's pitching rotation prove correct, I would need the sympathy only fellow sufferers could provide.

None of us, however, could have foreseen the agony that was to come as Steve Garvey—whom we all despised for his smug southern Californian brand of cockiness—drove in five runs, the final two with a homer to win the game in the bottom of the ninth.

Before he even rounded the bases, the phone rang. "It's for you," said Michaela. "Dana," and she extended the receiver toward me.

"Don't say it," I said.

"Hey, hey," Dana replied. Her voice was flat, and instead of joy or enthusiasm, it conveyed only arrogance and spite, as if Garvey had homered primarily to vindicate her. I hung up, and then I invited Peter and Michaela to join us at our house for the deciding game of the playoffs the next afternoon. Fortunately, they accepted, for I doubted that I could endure the pressure without sympathetic company. In fact, had I the power to cancel the game—declaring an armistice that would enable both teams to abandon the field with their honor intact—I would have used it without hesitation.

Peter and I sat drinking in his kitchen until long after midnight, trying to convince each other that the Cubs of '84 were a different breed, had far more character than the team that had folded in '69 (both of us, that year, living and dying with Kenny Holtzman's every pitch). When I finally decided to leave, Peter held the door open for me and raised his fist into the air. "Sutcliffe," he declared.

"Sutcliffe," I repeated, saluting him in return, praying that Frey had been right. After all, Sutcliffe had slammed the lid shut in the opener and, with a full four-days' rest, he should do it again. I was more than willing to admit I was wrong, to sacrifice my own self-esteem, for a Cubs' victory.

I entered our house through the back door, noticing at once that the kitchen floor had been cleared of the mess I had left. As I ventured into the bedroom and undressed, I could hear Dana rustling beneath the blanket.

"You asleep?" I asked.

"No," she said, her reply clear and brittle. She had apparently been awake for some time.

"You know what I need tonight?" I said, swaying slightly and clutching the bureau for support.

"It's almost morning."

"I need to . . . I'd like to make love to you," but perhaps I was tired or had drunk too much, for my appeal was edgy, demanding, and Dana probably suspected that the purpose of my desire was not to give her pleasure.

"What for?" she asked.

"What do you mean, 'what for'?"

"What good is it, anyway? You don't want any kids yet. You've already made that quite clear to me."

"It was your decision, too."

"I don't even know why we continue sleeping together."

"Neither do I," I said, grabbing a blanket from the closet. What was left of the night, I slept away on the living-room couch.

Peter and Michaela arrived as the lineups were being announced, looking as if they had been summoned to their own executions. Apparently they shared my dark premonitions, and although they both tried to disguise their fears—twice during the National Anthem Peter raised his fist and proclaimed "Sutcliffe"—we knew that our Cubs were doomed.

From the first inning it was apparent that Sutcliffe didn't have his good stuff, and even though we took an early lead, the outcome for us seasoned Cub watchers was never in doubt. But we still watched in fascination and horror, as if we were witnessing from afar an express train hurtling toward a collapsed bridge, powerless to stop it yet unable to avert our eyes from the impending disaster. Late in the game, when all hope was gone and Steve Garvey emerged from the dugout for his final at-bat, I observed that a fastball between the eyes would not be an unwelcome sight. "I'd really like to see that," I said. "Wipe that surfer cockiness right off that tanned mug of his."

Peter and Michaela nodded glumly in assent. Dana, however, who sat huddled in one corner of the couch throughout the entire game—remote, her arms wrapped around her legs, her chin propped on top of her knees—suddenly, like a spring held compressed for too long, unwound, and with her lips now almost touching my ear, she said, "You know, Dave, you're a real bastard. I never realized until this week what a fucking ignorant bastard you really are."

Dana rarely used such language, and even though the bitterness in her voice was almost palpable, neither of my two friends seemed to have heard her. They were too stunned by what had happened on the screen in front of them to notice that our marriage had been crumbling along with the Cubs' chances to win their first pennant in forty years.

The divorce was an amicable one, and although Dana accepted a position in her agency's L.A. office shortly thereafter, we always had lunch together whenever she was in town for business. In fact, I was one of the first to hear—after her mother, anyway—about her engagement to her agency's Financial Officer, a widower with two children. I congratulated her.

"Is he a sports fan?" I asked.

"He hates sports," she said. "At least the spectator kind. He's fond of swimming, though, and he loves ballet."

"Ballet seems safe enough," I said, and I wished her the best, sincerely hoping that she and her new husband would never stumble into one of those subterranean byways from which a man and a woman could hardly emerge together unscathed.

The Series, incidentally, went to the Tigers in five, just as I had predicted.

IN DREAMS BEGIN

Philip Gerard

Last night I had the dream again.

I'm sitting in the stands at Yankee Stadium, where I've never been in real life, and on the field a hubbub begins. A grizzled guy who looks like Yogi Berra points at me and the umpire and the other players all stare. "Me?" I say. Like I always say. They're too far away, so I pantomime, pointing to myself, and they pantomime back, waving me down out of the stands. All the other spectators make way for me. The ushers clear a path. I climb down onto the field. Berra throws a heavy arm around my shoulder, says, "We've got a situation here. Nettles is injured. How'd you like to play third base?"

I say, like I say every time, "I didn't bring my glove."

"We'll get you a glove."

"I didn't bring any cleats."

"We'll give you cleats, a cap, the whole uniform. You don't play, we got to forfeit."

So I play nine innings, go three for five at the plate with two singles and a double off the wall in left that drives in a couple of runs, and make all my chances in the field. We win 5-4. As we're walking through the tunnel back to the clubhouse, just a bunch of winners joshing with each other and the crowd noise fading, I wake up—gently rising from the depths of sleep to the surface of a sunny Saturday morning in bed beside my wife Joan, who looks haggard and sunken-eyed, like she hasn't slept a wink.

"Don't tell me," she says.

"Yep," I say. "Three for five at the plate, two RBI's. We won."

"Five to four," she says. "I know. You always win five to four. Which position did you play this time?"

"Third base."

The thing is, I haven't played baseball since Little League, and I was never very good. Haven't watched a major league game in probably fifteen years. But the dream energizes me, makes me feel like a talented kid, leaves me with a kind of afterglow of contentment, almost like sex. I snuggle close to her and stroke her bare arm. "How about you?"

She sits up and smoothes her copper hair back from her temples. "I spent the night roaming around a parking garage in Buenos Aires looking for a rental car I couldn't remember the color of because I was late for a speech I was supposed to give on quantum physics—in Portuguese, naturally. Oh, and did I mention I was naked and being chased by big rats and some creepy guy in a trench coat?"

My wife doesn't know anything about physics, but you knew that. And she speaks fluent German, but not a word of Portuguese. I'm not sure they even speak Portuguese in Buenos Aires.

Last week she was lost in a deserted warehouse in Berlin, a maze of wooden crates and pallets stacked to the ceiling, and she had to get to the airport to catch the last plane to London. And she was naked. A few nights before that, she was late for a class she couldn't find to take an exam she hadn't studied for in a subject she had never heard of. At Beijing University. Naked.

She spends her nights that way—chasing something she can never quite grasp, responsible for things she has no control over, missing flights and blowing exams and screwing up speeches, foolish and crying and vulnerable and always in vague danger, wandering in foreign places, lost, late, confused, worried, frustrated, scared, stymied, inadequate, unprepared, baffled, alone, and naked.

She's the executive secretary to the partners of a small engineering firm that for years has mismanaged itself onto the edge of bankruptcy. They've been doing all sorts of sketchy accounting lately, and Joan keeps telling them they're going to get into trouble and they just smile and make passes at her. It's not an ideal situation, she'd rather be in a bigger city, but she makes decent money—much more than I do painting houses. We need her income. I don't do all that well. Joan doesn't believe a guy with a Ph.D. in philosophy ought to be a housepainter, but I like the work, gives me time to think. She doesn't bring it up any more.

We fuss around the house all Saturday morning, lazy and slack, then roam the outdoor mall downtown for a couple hours in the afternoon. To lift her spirits, I say I'll treat her to Chinese, which is her favorite. So we have a late lunch at a franchise place called Chow Fats, eggrolls and rice beer, and when the fortune cookies arrive I crack mine open immediately. I love the secret promise of fortune cookies, the anticipation of great good things ahead. I feel the same flutter in my stomach as I do when I flip the mailbox open to see what good news awaits me. My wife dreads the arrival of mail, but then she's the one who writes out the checks to pay all the bills.

I unscroll my fortune and read it. "In Dreams Begin."

"That's it?" she says. "What's that supposed to mean?"

"I don't have a clue." But in my mind I'm already gliding effortlessly to the foul line, scooping up a hot grounder, whipping it sidearm across the long hypotenuse of the infield to nail the runner at first by a step, and my teammates all slap their fists into their gloves and say, "Way to go!"

"Let's see yours."

She breaks open the cookie and there is no fortune. Nothing, not even a blank slip of paper. She gasps and dashes the halves of the cookie onto the table, where they crumble into pieces.

"It's just a fortune cookie," I say, holding her hand. "Don't get so upset."

I flag the waiter and order two new cookies. "These are defective," I explain, and he looks baffled, but in a moment brings us two fresh cookies.

"Pick whichever one you want," I say.

She eenie-meenie-minie-moes and picks up a cookie, cracks it open. Again, no fortune.

My fortune reads, you guessed it: "In Dreams Begin."

"A defective batch, " I say. "Somebody's idea of a bad joke at the cookie plant."

Joan says, "Last August, Erin's friend Dana got a cookie without a fortune, and she got killed in a car crash a week later."

"Oh, come on—you don't believe that."

But she's so upset I take her straight home and brew her a cup of lemon zinger tea and we sit on the back porch not talking, just watching the light go gray and listening to the birds make a racket and finally going inside to watch a little TV and then go to bed.

And now I lie awake, resisting sleep, my eyelids heavy, my body tired from the tension of the day. Somehow if I can stay awake until Joan falls asleep, I have this feeling that she'll be all right tonight, that she won't spend the dark hours wandering parking garages on faraway continents being pursued by spectral figures who want to do her harm while she misses her chance at whatever urgent thing she must accomplish.

At last her breathing is regular and her slim body is still. I move closer to her, inhale her sweet warmth, wanting to touch her curvy hips and the small of her back but wary of waking her, this woman without a fortune.

Before I drift off, I already know how it is going to be. Tonight I am pitching—it is the only position I haven't played. My arm feels loose and good, my body nimble and strong as sleep overtakes me by gentle degrees. Tonight I have it in me to pitch a no-hitter. I feel this with certainty. A perfect game, maybe. But even though we were meant for each other, no man and woman were ever more perfectly joined, I cannot protect the women I love in the dark hours, cannot hold onto her when she retreats into her own troubled imagination, into the unconscious weight of the disappointing life I have given her, into the unsettling stuff of her dreams. She is beyond me then, out of reach, as lonely as a person can ever be in this life.

In my last willful moment before I float into my seat at Yankee Stadium, I wish hard for her to join me there. To be at my side, happy and safe, both of us in the same dream. I have two tickets tonight, box seats, and, just once, I want her to be exactly where she belongs, right where she's supposed to be, best seat in the house, with a ticket stub in her pocket to prove it, and the soundtrack of her dream to be the roaring cheers of the crowd, not a deadline clock counting down to panic.

And just once, just once, I want her to see me play.

GOLF IN PAKISTAN

Charles Blackburn

"Ever played golf in Pakistan?" Frank Donovan asked me.

"Can't say that I have."

A 25-year veteran of the oil industry in China, India and East Africa, Frank Donovan had caught tigers in red weather, and his stories never lacked point. He was one of my favorite people long before he decided to make me rich.

It was the autumn of 1977, and we were driving down to Morehead City, North Carolina, with his old friend Donald McClanahan to inspect the site on the Sampit River where Tar Heel Refining & Distributing, Inc., planned to build the first of four small oil refineries on the East Coast. Frank was founder and president of the company. My father and uncle, who practiced law in Henderson, were both vice presidents and had logged many a mile with Frank in pursuit of this dream.

Once financing for the first refinery had been arranged, I was to quit my vagabond newspaper career and become head of public relations for the firm, at roughly five times my salary as associate editor of the *Weekly Instigation*. The refineries were to be jolly little money mills, each producing daily $660,000 worth of gasoline, kerosene, home heating oil, propane, coke, and sulfur. Even with a price tag of $100 million apiece, they would pay for themselves in five years.

Living on the verge of fabulous wealth had done wonders for my outlook. It made even the withering tedium of school board and city council meetings almost bearable. As the county commissioners, whose average age exceeded par at the local country club, pontificated about all matters foreign and domestic, with the notable exception of the public's business, and the clock's hands verged on midnight, and the dull ache of fatigue gnawed between my shoulder blades, I had to restrain myself to keep from laughing hysterically. The creaky wheels of small town government were certain to seem laughably irrelevant to life, liberty, and the pursuit of happiness when viewed from the lofty heights of the upper tax brackets. This too shall pass, I scrawled in my reporter's notebook and bided my time.

At this point in my career, a flat tire represented fiscal calamity. Mine was a chronically hand-to-mouth existence. I didn't have a savings account. Nothing to put in it. So I was fully prepared to admire and esteem Donald McClanahan from the moment we met. Since his days with Frank Donovan in India two decades earlier, McClanahan had become right-hand man to the biggest junk dealer in the world, which made him a hot prospect to help bankroll our project. Frank had assured me his old pal had the Midas touch. "When Donald gives a thing his blessing," he said, "bank vault doors all across America swing open like the door to Ali Baba's cave."

McClanahan's boss had made his initial fortune by buying up abandoned oil refineries for five cents on the dollar from spontaneous governments in Latin America. It was customary for revolutionaries to nationalize foreign-owned assets and then, in the case of oil refineries, run off all the foreign devils who knew how to operate them. And there the refineries sat, waiting for McClanahan to come in with crews to hack off the vines, dismantle them and ship them to Arabia, where they were sold at a premium to the Saudis. As a result of dealing in junk on a global scale, McClanahan's boss now owned a fleet of freighters, office buildings in Manhattan, a chain of resort hotels, a thoroughbred horse farm in Kentucky, a professional basketball team and a sunny tropical island in the Caribbean. He had built refineries of his own in Venezuela, Taiwan, Scotland and Tobago, ranging in cost from $20 million to $400 million, and Donald McClanahan was his chief of project development.

It was my job on that sunny autumn morning to chauffeur them from Raleigh down to Morehead City, providing, along the way, a fresh audience for their reminiscences.

"But you've been to the Middle East?" Frank Donovan asked, on learning that golf in Pakistan wasn't on my résumé.

"That's right."

"Then you may have noticed," he continued, "that human life is not valued as highly in the East as it is here in the West. You've read Kipling?"

"*The Man Who Would Be King* is one of my favorite stories."

"Then you know about the Khyber Pass," Donovan said. "It's thirty miles long and runs between Afghanistan and Pakistan through the Safed Koh mountain range, as desolate and forbidding as anything this side of the moon.

"Twenty years ago the government transport service ran buses at irregular intervals through the pass between Peshawar and Kabul. They were old British-made buses, each with a maximum seating capacity of 50. But every trip, twice that and more rode them, wedging themselves in three and four to a seat, clutching their goats and chickens, their ragged parcels and filthy children.

"Those not lucky enough to get a seat stood in the aisle. A dozen more rode on the roof with the baggage. Another score perched on foot rails along the outside of the bus, or stood on the rear bumper, or on the running board at the door. By this distribution, the bus could accommodate upwards of 100 passengers, plus livestock.

"Naturally, that kind of load puts a strain on an engine on a steep grade, especially if the engine has seen better days. This was not long after Independence, and God only knows what they did for spare parts. At times the buses were lucky to make five miles an hour laboring up through the pass. To decrease the load, those perched on the roof and sides got off and walked until the bus was over the hump.

"For the ride down, the driver could rely on the lower gears to control his speed. But if the bus stalled during the ascent, the brakes weren't strong enough to hold it. The code of the road dictated that those standing on the rear bumper be ever vigilant. Should the bus stop for any reason, it was their duty to throw chocks under the rear tires. Because if the bus rolled backwards and gained speed... Well, there were no guardrails in the Khyber Pass then. Probably aren't any now. And to say the chasm is deep conveys no true idea of the thing. Here and there, the narrow serpentine road seems to hang on the edge of forever.

"One day such a bus was lumbering up through the pass when the unthinkable occurred. It stalled on the steepest part of the grade. The driver hit the brake, clutch, and starter in one instinctive motion, but the engine wouldn't crank, and the brakes couldn't hold. True to their calling, the rear guard threw the chocks under the tires, but they were a heartbeat too slow about it, and the bus had gained a perilous momentum. They held their breaths as the rear wheels rolled to the very top of the blocks and pause there for an agonizing moment. The sudden jolt that followed—the terrible meaning of it—could be read on the horrified faces of the passengers inside. The bus began rolling backwards.

"It was instant bedlam on board. They kicked and trampled one another. They tore each other's clothing and flesh trying to claw their way to the exit. Meanwhile, outside, the pedestrians trotted beside the bus in a state of disbelief. From every window, hands reached out to them, imploring their assistance, but there was nothing they could do. A woman thrust her baby out a window into waiting arms. Several people tumbled out the door. But as for the rest of 'em, their fate was sealed by dint of their numbers. In their blind panic, they had become a frantic knot of humanity. Try as they may, they could not untangle themselves.

"Above the screams and curses and the bleating of livestock, a man shouted a name and address over and over. Seated by a window, a dignified, white-haired old Indian gentleman in European attire calmly blessed the turbaned fellow running beside the bus and handed him his gold pocket watch. 'It keeps imperfect time,' the old man apologized. The runner fell behind and trotted to a halt, the watch swinging idly from the chain in his hand, his face a study in consternation. No one could keep pace with the bus now, and it was still gaining speed.

"The squealing breaks reached a crescendo of alarm as smoke poured from the brake housings. Two more passengers tumbled out the door. Then another. The bus lurched crazily this way and that. Then a heavy black military boot broke through the windshield, and here came the driver, rolling and tumbling out over the hood. He landed on his feet in the roadway just in time to watch the bus and its cargo hurtle over the side, with a swelling chorus of shrieks, and disappear into the void. Moments later, a chicken flew up out of the windswept silence, trailing loose feathers like confetti. It plopped down on the road at the driver's feet and issued an agitated squawk."

Donovan paused for a moment to allow me to contemplate the full horror of the accident, then added, "Four days later the headline in *The Bombay Mail* read: TRAGEDY

IN KHYBER PASS; ONE HUNDRED PRESUMED DEAD. Presumed. No one went down to look. No one ever did."

There was a big natural gas strike (Donovan continued) near Hairpur, northeast of Sylhet on the Assam border, in what was then Eastern Pakistan—they call it Bangladesh now. McClanahan and I were stationed in Calcutta at the time, working for CalTex. By a stroke of luck, he was at the telegraph office when the official dispatch came tap, tap, tapping on the key. He had learned Morse code in the Navy during the war, never dreaming it would be of any practical use, beyond saving his miserable hide and vanquishing the foes of democracy. We hopped the train for Dacca ahead of all comers.

Next day, the news hit the papers and started a stampede among oil company agents eager to acquire drilling rights. We got a three-day jump on 'em, because those who followed missed the connection in Dacca. There wasn't another train for the border for 24 hours, and once they got to Chhatak, they had to cool their heels another day waiting for the steamer to come chugging back from up-river. The roads were impossible or nonexistent, and there was nowhere around Hairpur to land an airplane.

Patty went along for a change of scene. She had wearied of Calcutta society and threatened to divorce me if I left her behind. She's always been a good traveler: cheerful, uncomplaining. The trip from Dacca was the worst of it. The wheezing old steam engine traveled a rough road. We sat on wooden benches as hard on the backside as any church pew. The heat presented a difficult choice. We tried riding with the windows of the car thrown open, but the smoke and cinders from the engine poured in, and with the windows closed, it was as sweltering as a sauna.

At points along the line, the train stopped to take on fuel and water, and the grateful passengers filed out, as hollow-eyed as zombies, men to the left of the water tank, women to the right, to outdoor communal shower stalls, where we stripped and bathed in tepid water. It was a little embarrassing for the sahibs. The Pakistanis are a well-hung people and were greatly amused by our comparative shortcomings. The fact that McClanahan's hair was red everywhere was an additional source of fun.

Donald stood there, in all his glory, grinning demonically, arms spread wide. "Feast your eyes, you filthy buggers!" he cordially invited our grinning brown brethren. "One day when we are rich, we shall buy this train and throw every one of your nasty arses off it!" He laughed heartily at his own joke, and the Pakistanis laughed with him. None of them spoke a word of English.

The last leg of the journey involved a 20-mile railway trip from the district headquarters to Chhatak and a 30-mile run up the Surma River on a rusty government steamer. After the train ride, the fresh air of the wheelhouse deck came as a relief. With our luggage piled around us, we staked out three deck chairs and settled in. As if by magic, McClanahan produced three tumblers from his suitcase, plus the necessary ingredients for gin fizzes.

"Emergency rations," he said.

"Your stock just went up five points," Patty told him.

We sat back and watched the river. Native boats, their high sterns painted brilliant colors, crowded the waterway, their decks swarming with small brown-skinned men wearing nothing but sarongs knotted around their waists. The songs they sang captured the essence of the mysterious East. It was the stuff of Kipling, Conrad, and Maugham. We were young, we had recently won a world war and were living a life far removed from brownstone and briefcase.

Sunamganj sat on a bend in the river like a jewel on a necklace. Oh, it was a filthy, squalid gem of a place, all right. The stench of it drifted down river to us before we ever laid eyes on it, and a glance was all it took to know that teeming Sunamganj town was a place of crushing poverty, even by Pakistani standards.

"The hell of it is," McClanahan observed, "this gas strike will mean about as much to these poor blighters as the Alaskan Gold Rush did to their grandfathers."

The young man who met us at the dock had curly black hair, a black mustache, rotten teeth and the yellow tinge of jaundice in his eyes. He was indistinguishable from millions of his countrymen, but something about him brought to mind that disarming old notion that angels sometimes appear in the guise of men to test human virtue.

"Greetings, upper class passengers," he said. "If you could be giving me one modicum of attention it would be frightfully outlandish. Refreshments are available if you are needful. Some privately managed tea stalls and restaurants are also functioning here. Sunamganj is a very old place, and the history of this place is very ancient. Shall I assist and guide you, noting such factuals as may elevate your journey?"

He smiled at the conclusion of this little speech. His gums and lips were bright red from chewing pan, a concoction of betel nut and lime.

"As you wish," I told him in Bengali, so he wouldn't mistake us for tourists. "But we haven't any money."

Evidently, this was the best joke he'd heard all week. His high, bird-like laugh echoed in the marketplace. "Never have I known sahibs without money," he declared. "No matter. My name is Satya Ram Datta. But you may please to call me Zia. I shall serve you faithfully and well."

"Then mind you keep an eye on that crate," McClanahan told him, pointing to the wooden box in the middle of our luggage.

"It is valuable, sahib?"

"It is worth your life," I told him in Bengali.

"Then it is rare beyond price," he replied in English, his dark eyes twinkling.

Zia secured the town's only carriage, a rickety contraption drawn by what looked like a half-starved Alabama mule, and loaded it with our things. He proved to be a loquacious guide, a likable fellow, full of high spirits, and he told us very much more than we ever wanted to know about dirty old Sunamganj.

Our intelligence had it that the man we wanted to see, the man who had his fingers on the pulse of Sylhet District, who knew who to bribe and who to flatter and who to bully, lived in the highlands north of town. A minor British official before Independence, he stayed on after the sun had set on the Empire and everybody else went home.

We found him sitting on the verandah of a big white house on a hill in the middle of what to all intents and purposes resembled an English village, such as you might see in Dorset or Kent, complete with thatched-roofed, stone cottages and a small gothic chapel. But it was certain that this far-flung corner of the globe would not remain forever England. When the place had been fully staffed and occupied, the unruly jungle had, no doubt, been kept at bay, but now, despite an abundance of cheap labor, the jungle was encroaching upon the settlement in every direction. One of the outlying buildings, whose roof had collapsed, had been completely overgrown.

Our host was glad to see us. He was a solid citizen, fond of his tucker, with a round florid face and sparkling blue eyes. His bushy eyebrows resembled two black woolly worms, and his mustache looked like a third, only it was pasted flat across his upper lip as though it had been run over by a wagon wheel. He had a regal bearing. It later occurred to me that he bore a passing resemblance to some Roman emperor or another on a coin my great aunt Effie Ola had given me years ago as a souvenir of her trip to the Holy Land.

"I knew this gas strike would bring me a bit of society," he said. "Come up and have a drink. Reginald Fortesque-Pitt at your service. Reggie to my friends."

He gave me a firm, if somewhat damp, handshake. I made the introductions. By then the carriage was being unloaded, and Fortesque-Pitt's eyes fell on the wooden crate that Zia gingerly cradled in his arms.

"I say," he said. "That's not what it appears to be?"

McClanahan confirmed his suspicions. "A case of Glendronach."

"Merciful God! You don't know how lucky you are," Fortesque-Pitt told us. "Can't get good Scotch around here, you know. Can't even get bad Scotch, if there is such a thing. Don't suppose you could spare a bottle? I'd pay handsomely for it."

"My dear fellow," McClanahan said. "It's for you. As a token of our esteem."

"A case of Glendronach!" he exclaimed.

"Absolutely," I concurred.

"You leave me speechless," Fortesque-Pitt said. His expressive blue eyes misted over visibly. He wiped a thick hand across them and cleared his throat, choking back the tears. Then he beamed broadly and said, "By all means call me Reggie. You are the dearest friends I have on this Earth."

"Tomar kaje ami khusi aci," I told Zia, which means "I am pleased with your work," and I gave him 10 anna.

"Blessings upon thee and thine," he responded.

"Run along then, Zia," Reggie said in a no-nonsense tone. As soon as the Pakistani was out of earshot Fortesque-Pitt chided me for my extravagance. "It wasn't worth more than five," he said quietly. "Doesn't do to spoil them."

"I didn't mean to undermine the local economy," I replied under my breath, as his servants took charge of our things.

"Not a joking matter, I assure you," Reggie said, exercising his eyebrows.

"Henceforth, I shall govern my purse."

"There's a good fellow." He was all smiles again. "You'll want a bath after traveling on that steaming rust-bucket. I think you'll find our spring water here refreshing. Just ring the bell if you need anything. The staff is most attentive. You and Patty take the front room. It gets a good breeze at night, and you have a fine view. The sunsets here are something to write home about. Donald is down the hall. A siesta could be in order. I leave that to you. Come to the study when you're ready to sample some of that Scotch, but forgive me if I don't wait for you. A case of Glendronach! Christmas will seem very dull this year."

It was a fine, spacious house, filled with treasures of the subcontinent, a testimonial to how far a government pension would go in that impoverished land. McClanahan met us in the hallway after we'd bathed and caught 40 winks.

"Gone a bit overboard for Gunputty," Donald remarked. "I counted 16 in my room."

"He's cornered the market," Patty agreed. "Must be two dozen in ours."

They were everywhere, in every corner and alcove, on every table and bookshelf, cast in brass, carved in ivory, stone and wood, some small and relatively plain, others three or four feet high and wonderfully ornate. Ganesha, the elephant god. Good old Gunputty.

"There are worse vices," I noted. "He's probably got 50 bucks tied up in the whole business."

Fortesque-Pitt's study was paneled in enough mahogany to veneer every cupboard in Hoboken. He had a fine collection of antique maps, a beautifully carved ivory chess set of Indian motif and a cultural hodgepodge of furniture that suggested its owner lived betwixt and between two very different worlds. He greeted us from the throne-like vantage of a rattan peacock chair.

"There you are. Feeling better, I trust?"

"Much," Patty replied.

"Traveling in this part of the world is an ordeal, even under the best of circumstances," Reggie said, filling his pipe, which was carved in the shape of an elephant's head. "I make it a point never to go anywhere I don't have to. Help yourselves to a drink," he said, gesturing with his meerschaum toward the bar table. "I think you'll find everything you need. There's a pitcher of water. But no ice, I'm afraid."

"We didn't come all this way to desecrate good whisky," McClanahan demurred, reaching for the open bottle.

"Forgive me," Reggie said. "I was under the impression Americans took their whisky over ice. As you are the first I've met, I had to see if there was anything to it. Should have known better. The chap who told me that was a perfect ass in so many ways."

McClanahan finished pouring the drinks, and Fortesque-Pitt said, "I'd forgotten how good Glendronach is. Not as smoky as some of the other single malts."

"They age it in sherry casks," I said.

"Lovely stuff," Reggie said.

"There must be a story in these." Patty was referring to a series of publicity posters on the wall touting the feats of an acrobatic troop called "The Flying Tysons." They showed the family performing various kinds of balancing acts on high wires.

"I was a child star in a circus back in dear old England," Reggie explained. "That's me at the top of that human pyramid. You might say I outgrew the act," he drolly confessed, patting himself on his ample stomach. He related several amusing stories about life in the circus.

"I see you're a devotee of Gunputty," McClanahan ventured. "How many do you suppose you have?"

"I couldn't tell you," Reggie said. "Four or five hundred. The accumulation of 30 years. Can you ever have too much wisdom and prudence?"

"He's also the remover of obstacles," I reminded him. "Rumor has it that you perform that function in this district."

"You've come to the right chap," Reggie confirmed. "I know who's in and who's out, the gods they worship, what gives 'em the jimjams, and what they think money's worth. Hard currency goes a long way here. They tend to regard contracts as empty promises. Can't say as I blame them. I don't suppose you came undercapitalized?"

"We have brought sacks full of money," I assured him.

"Splendid. Then we're in business." He lit his pipe, sat back in his peacock chair, closed his eyes and savored the first draw of tobacco. "My services do not come cheaply," he said, his eyes still closed, "but I believe in delivering value for the money. What you save your company by working through me will make heroes of you in the home office. By the way, I have a copy of the state geologist's report that may be of interest." He opened his eyes, and his black wooly worm eyebrows leapt up. "Which of you is the geologist?"

"That's me," McClanahan said.

"Right." Reggie closed his eyes again, his eyebrows reclining once more above them. "I think you will find it fascinating bedtime reading. It came my way at some expense, which, naturally, I shall expect to recoup. I am sure we can come to terms after dinner. There's no hurry about that. What I am most eager to discover," he opened his eyes, "is whether you play golf."

"A six handicap," McClanahan replied.

"I don't slow up a foursome too much," I told him, "but Patty's first rate. Championship Flight in the last Calcutta Club ladies' tournament."

Reggie closed his eyes again and smiled with sublime contentment. "Splendid. You can't imagine how long it's been since I had a decent game. We don't get many visitors up this way, and the locals haven't any feel for it. They go at it like they were chopping wood. They're excellent caddies, though. You'll see tomorrow."

"You have a course, then?" Patty asked.

"It was once the pride of the district. A bit ratty now, I suppose, but a full 18." He opened his eyes. "I think you'll find it a sporting little course."

"But we didn't bring our clubs," Patty pointed out.

"No matter. We've got plenty here. I cannot tell you how much I am looking forward to it. I go out practically every day, but it lacks the competitive edge, if you follow me. The bloody wogs have no appreciation for the game. It might as well be a Masonic ritual for all they care. I knocked down a wedge from 80 yards the other day, and it excited no comment whatever. They don't seem to see the point of it. Can you imagine? Depressing, I tell you."

"That reminds me of a story," McClanahan said, refilling his glass at the bar. "Saint Peter went to God one day and said, 'There's this fellow in Chicago who's so sinful I don't think you ought to wait for the afterlife to punish him.' God said, 'Fine. Does he play golf?' Saint Peter replied in the affirmative. 'Watch what happens tomorrow,' God told him.

"Next day, the fellow goes to his club early in the morning. There isn't anyone about, so he goes off alone. Has the course to himself. The first hole is a 340-yard par four, and he hits a booming drive. To his amazement, the ball keeps rolling and rolling, up onto the green and into the cup for a hole in one. He can't believe it. He looks around to see if anyone else has witnessed this miracle. But there's not a soul there.

"Number Two is a par three. He outs with a four iron, hits a marvelous shot straight at the flag. It sails bang into the cup on the fly for another hole in one. 'Wait a minute,' Saint Peter says to God. 'I thought you were going to punish this guy, and here you've let him hit back-to-back holes in one.' God said, 'That's right, and the rest of his round will go the same way. He's going to shoot an 18, and he won't be able to tell a living soul.'"

Reggie chuckled and sipped his Scotch. He stared wistfully into the middle distance, sucking on his pipe. After a heaving a heavy sigh, he said, with a tinge of sorrow, "That pretty much sums up my situation."

"You're forgetting this gas strike," McClanahan consoled him. "It signals the return of white men to the district."

"A steady stream of engineers, geologists, and whatnot," I concurred.

The gleam returned to Reggie's eyes. "With the occasional look-in from the company brass?"

Patty added, "We are merely the advance party."

Reggie cast a hungry eye upon her, as though she were a freshly baked strudel. "I could not possibly hope for more charming emissaries," he declared, fairly radiating masculine charm from his peacock chair. Just then his Head Man appeared, an imposing physical specimen with a great bristling white beard. "Dinner is served," the servant intoned, his smile revealing a gold front tooth.

"Right-o," Reggie replied. "Come along then."

It was quite a spread. The groaning board, as it were: fresh fruit, lamb roasted on skewers, baked fish, curried chicken, mutton curry, rice, coconut and mango chutneys, a green salad, and Pakistani pudding. Our host consumed everything within arm's reach, pausing only long enough to order his small army of servants to fetch him more. These well-starched Pakistanis were not nearly as gaunt as those we had seen in town, and as they hurried to and fro, bringing a plate of this and a bowl of that, they reminded me of sharp-eyed pilot fish who swim in the company of a shark and dine on the scraps he overlooks. After supper, we adjourned to the study for brandy and cigars and haggled over drilling rights into the small hours. About two a.m. we came to a satisfactory arrangement and pushed off for bed.

Soon after sunrise there was a timid knock on the bedroom door. It opened just enough to admit Reggie's large head. "Frightfully sorry to wake you, Frank," he apologized, "but we'd best tee off before the sun gets too high, if you follow me."

It wasn't until we joined him in the dining room that we got the full effect. Reggie was a golfer's fashion plate, resplendent in plus fours, with a jaunty green Tam O'Shanter on his head.

"You'll have to forgive me," he said. "I'm like a nipper at Christmas. Couldn't sleep a wink last night. It was all I could do to keep from rousting you out at first light."

Standing at his sideboard, we gulped down a breakfast of lamb chops, biscuits and honey, and "gunfire" tea—very strong and very sweet. I was still gnawing on a lamb bone when Reggie turned abruptly to Patty and offered his arm.

"Shall we hie unto the links?" he purred.

The golf course was a short walk from the house. "The man has style," McClanahan said softly as we trailed in Reggie's broad wake.

"Argyle socks," I noted. "In this heat."

The first tee was elevated and afforded a magnificent view of the steamer-ghat on the river, the fertilizer factory, the swamp, and the forests of Raghunandan against the blue line of the Khasi Hills. A tall, massive masonry column next to the tee had been erected, as its legend proclaimed, in memory of a Mr. Inglis, founder of the fertilizer factory.

"This monument," Reggie announced, "cracked in three places during the earthquake of 1897."

"You don't say," I said.

"Do you think it's safe?" Patty asked.

"How's that?"

"Couldn't it fall on someone?"

"Fall on someone?" Reggie exclaimed. "I doubt anyone has ever considered that. I bloody well suppose it could, now that you mention it. Right! Well, we're off then. No waiting for a tee time. We set par according to course conditions. In fair weather, like today, par for Number One is eight."

A crowd of no less than 50 ragged beggars had gathered around us, each one holding a golf club. It might have been a menacing sight except they were such a scurvy, malnourished lot, they appeared incapable of mustering enough strength to bruise an earthworm. The Head Man strode among them, a giant among pigmies, his voice booming like thunder, exhorting them to do their duty or suffer the consequences.

"Glad we didn't have to tangle with that one," McClanahan nodded at him, "in order to go to college on the GI Bill."

"Amen," I agreed.

His eyes were black as coal, and that bristling white beard and devilish gold tooth, flashing in sun, made him look a proper pirate, even though his khaki uniform was more reminiscent of the fusiliers.

"What's that on his turban?" McClanahan muttered.

"Rotary Club pin," I replied.

"We've had to adapt the game somewhat to satisfy local custom," Reggie announced. "These are our caddies. Instead of the usual one per player, you have one per club. Dao!" he said, pointing to a skinny little man in a turban who carried a driver. The man came over and presented the club, bowing solicitously.

"They don't understand that each club has a purpose," Reggie said, teeing up a ball on a little pile of sand. "To them, club selection is your way of honoring them personally. For the sake of harmony, try to use them all."

"But what are all those people doing out in the fairway?" McClanahan asked him, gesturing to the liberal disbursement of ragtag and bobtail spread out over the terrain. Here and there, the morning sun flashed on unidentifiable metal objects some of them carried.

"Those are the fore and side caddies," Reggie explained. "Here, I'll show you." He took a couple of practice swings and then hauled off and struck the ball a mighty blow. It sailed into the blue straight as an arrow for about 150 yards and then took a sharp left turn.

"Damned hook!" he exclaimed. The ball kicked up a little cloud of dust and skidded into a clump of undergrowth beside a wild orange tree. One of the side caddies scurried over, found the ball, brought it out into the fairway and teed it up on an ant hill. "That's what they do," our host remarked.

"But aren't you afraid you'll hit one of them?" Patty asked.

"Not a bit. They're quite nimble, actually. Have no fear. Fire away."

So off we went, escorted by a small army of beggars, 100 strong, out for a morning round of golf. The Head Man led the foursome in an open rickshaw, shading himself with a colorful parasol. In lieu of golf carts, we each had a covered sedan chair. It took eight of the poor buggers to haul old Fortesque-Pitt about, and not one of them as big around as his leg. He had lashed the case of Scotch to the stern and applied its contents liberally throughout the proceedings.

"Don't dare let it out of my sight," he confided. "The pilferage here is something fierce. They take things they don't even know what they are. I've seen 'em use a camshaft to hold a pot over a fire."

As we advanced up the fairway, the fore caddies began to make a fearful racket, beating on old gasoline cans, scraps of tin, cast off pots and pans. Several of them heralded our march with deep-throated trumpets that sounded like the cry of constipated cattle in extremis. "The caddies double as beaters," our host shouted to us. "Just a precaution. Never know what might be lurking about." The three gun bearers by his side each carried a heavy Mauser.

It was, as advertised, a sporting little course. It had been hacked out of the jungle, and everywhere the jungle was endeavoring to take it back. The greens were sand, and after each putt, a couple of caddies smoothed the surface with what looked like big toothless rakes. If any of the other players had a similar line, the trail of the ball through the sand showed you the way.

The first time I called for a three iron, I was greeted by the smiling face of our friend and guide Zia. "It is an honor to be servicing you, sahib," he said, handing me the club.

"Dhonnobad," I replied. "Thanks." As I took a practice swing, I added under my breath, "Be gentle, old love."

The Head Man tended the pin on each hole, performing this duty with almost military precision. He was the sort of servant that had made the Empire great. More British than the British, as the saying goes. It had become his religion, a fact that impressed itself upon us when I was putting for birdie on Number Three.

After calculating the break as best I could, I addressed the ball, adjusted my feet and prepared to tap it homeward, when out of the corner of my eye I saw a small snake making its way out of the hole. Its black and pale yellow bands gave me a chill, even in the tropical heat. It was a banded krait—a youngster, but no less poisonous. It twined itself around the flagstick and began climbing. You may recognize this little fellow from a Kipling story called The Return of Imray, in which a servant sticks his toe in the snake's mouth to commit suicide. It's known as a two-step snake. It bites you, you take two steps, and you're dead. It began making its way up the flagstick toward the Head Man's hand. The other caddies murmured in alarm.

"Steady, Frank," Reggie said. The deadly snake was halfway up the pole, but the Head Man stood there like a statue, tending the flag for all he was worth. Reggie hastened to add, "I'm afraid he won't move until you putt, Frank."

Before his words were out, I had sent the ball on its way, and when it neared the hole, the Head Man calmly withdrew the flag and watched it roll by, leaving its trail in the sand. He bowed slightly to me, flashed that gold-toothed grin, and walked unhurriedly over to the edge of the green, where he gently shook the snake onto the grass. Instantly, two caddies fell on it with sticks and beat it to a bloody paste.

"The old boy seems to take the game seriously enough," I remarked to Fortesque-Pitt. "He's the only one with any sense of decorum."

Before we could hit our approach shots on Number Four, the caddies had to shoo away a couple of peacocks that were strutting about on the green. On Number Six, McClanahan sliced his tee shot into the right rough, which was nothing but jungle. Even the side caddies couldn't find it. McClanahan went in to help them out, swinging an iron at the foliage in the time-honored fashion.

"I wouldn't linger, Donald," our host called from his sedan chair over the din and trumpeting of the beaters. "A man-eater's been reported in the district. We wouldn't want to break up the foursome."

"Talk about rough," McClanahan said, finding himself suddenly light-headed and nearly overcome by the sickly sweet smell of the resin from the weeds he'd been chopping. He came reeling out of the bush.

"I'm as boiled as an owl," he declared.

"No wonder," I said. "Look what you've been flogging. Cannabis."

"Marijuana?"

"Exactly."

"Should've warned you about that," our host apologized. "The stuff's pretty thick around here. What say we give him a stoke this hole, Frank? Patty? Ami har manlum!" he shouted at his bearers, who immediately righted his chair, which had been listing to starboard.

We came to Number Eight. It was a blind shot from the tee. A dry, dusty hill rose before us. The green was out of sight on the other side. "A par five," Reggie advised. "A little left of center will do it."

The fore caddies, likewise, were out of view.

"I'm still worried about hitting the fore caddies," Patty confessed. "Shouldn't we send someone ahead to wave them out of the way?"

"Not necessary, I assure you," Reggie maintained. "They have a sixth sense about it. To my knowledge not one has been beaned in the history of the club."

Nonetheless, when we rode over the hill to see whither our shots had strayed, we were greeted by the sight of the fore caddies convened in a circle around something in the fairway. They were looking down at it silently, whatever it was.

"I knew it," Patty said. "We've hit one of them."

The Head Man leapt out of his rickshaw and boldly advanced through the crowd, cuffing caddies left and right for daring to interfere with his progress. Thus the circle parted to admit us, and we beheld the object of their attention.

It was a body. None too fresh, judging from the flies. Male. Of indeterminate age. A wooden-handled fish knife protruding from his ribcage. The black bloodstain on his shirt was roughly the shape of West Virginia. He stared at us with the whites of his eyes, the balls having rolled back in their sockets. On the ground beside him, two inches from his right shoulder, was another white orb that appeared to have been gouged out of somebody's head.

"That's a bit much," I said, turning toward Patty to shield her view.

To my astonishment, McClanahan bent over and picked the damned thing up. "A Slazenger Two," he announced, putting it back precisely where it had been, with a fastidiousness only golfers could appreciate.

"Right," Patty said, looking a shade queasy. "Only, I thought..."

"Me too," I said, giving her a wink, along with my handkerchief.

"How perfectly ghastly," our host said, his eyebrows wiggling like two woolly worms. He removed his cap, as though out of respect for the dead. "Can't apologize enough," he said, looking down at the body, which was eclipsed by his shadow. The apology was meant for his guests, not the deceased. There was an awkward silence. A large drop of sweat rolled off Reggie's nose and fell into the dust beside the flyblown corpse.

"What should we do?" Patty asked, holding the handkerchief over her nose. There was another awkward silence. I hastened to fill it.

"I believe the rule is a club length."

"Right you are!" Reggie stoutly agreed, placing his tam back on his large head. "He's beyond help now. We'll report it when we get back to the clubhouse."

Patty had lived in China and India and knew the score. The poor wretch was as dead as he was ever going to be. "Dao!" she said, calling for a four iron. With it, she calmly measured off a club length from the corpse's head, took a drop, and proceeded to hit a lovely shot pin high, about 10 feet from the cup.

"Oh, I say, well struck," Reggie declared, with admiration. "Well struck, indeed."

"That's my girl," I told her.

"You really know how to turn up the pressure," McClanahan congratulated her.

We had an early lunch in the clubhouse at the turn. It was built like a series of connected pavilions, light and airy, and vaguely suggestive of Brighton Palace. "Could do with a coat of paint," Reggie noted, "but such is life." During lunch our host confessed to having once committed "the unholy act of matrimony."

"Her cat came between us," he explained. "It wasn't an unpleasant animal. No pedigree to speak of, but a decent, law-abiding cat. Adele was mortally afraid it would end up in some wog's curry bowl. And it was rather a plump morsel.

She doted on it, wouldn't let it out of her sight. Insisted on walking it on a leash. A painful sight, that!"

"You might as well walk a lobster," Patty commiserated.

"Just so," Reggie nodded in approval. "I say. That does conjure an image."

"The French poet Verlaine did," I threw in. "Walk a lobster, I mean. Or was it Valery? On a long red ribbon. On the sidewalks of Paris."

"You don't say," Reggie said. "That's the French for you. Anyway, one day I told Adele, 'If you gave me half as much affection as you lavish on that cat, I'd be a happy man.' She gave me a wounded look and said, 'But I do, Reggie. I do. I give you exactly half as much.' It was all over in 18 months."

"Eighteen months," echoed McClanahan, a confirmed bachelor at the time. "Well, nobody can say you didn't give it a try."

Our host downed the last of his lemon squash. "Best get back to it if we want to avoid sun stroke."

On Number Twelve, a par 10 dogleg to the left, I shanked my fifth shot out of bounds into the ancient, vine-covered ruins of a temple.

"Rotten luck, Frank," Reggie said. "You'll have to take a drop. The place is crawling with cobras. Even the caddies won't go near it."

It proved a disastrous hole for me. The green was guarded by bunkers of harrowing depth. I spent four strokes in one of them and was happy to card a 14.

"Don't punish yourself, Frank," Reggie consoled me. "Take a gentleman's 12." On we went, until finally we came to the 17th, a long par seven, the green protected by a stream-fed pond. Prudence dictated laying up short of the pond on the third shot, a strategy that was adopted universally. McClanahan was away for the fourth.

"Dao!" he said, pointing to the man who carried his wedge, which he received ceremoniously.

Reggie cheered him on. "Show us how it's done, Donald."

McClanahan addressed the ball, looking in that wild place every inch a golfer. He executed a picture-perfect swing. Unfortunately, he hit it fat, lofting up a pie-sized piece of turf along with the ball, which sailed up toward the green, up and up, but never had the distance. It began its descent far short, plummeting out of the ether into the middle of a dozen water buffalo that were hunkered down out of the heat. Nothing but their eyes, horns, and muzzles showed above the water.

"Damn!" McClanahan said.

"Hard cheese!" Reggie sympathized.

"Do not distress yourself, sahib. I shall rescue it."

It was our friend and guide, Zia. He jumped into the waist-deep water and trudged out to get the ball, heedless of the water buffalo. When he got among them, the ox-like beasts began to stir, not welcoming the intrusion. One by one, they raised their massive muzzles and snorted. Meanwhile, Zia dove repeatedly in their midst looking for the golf ball.

"I hope he knows what he's doing," I said to no one in particular.

"I don't like the look of it," Reggie agreed. "Come along!" he shouted at the caddie. "Leave it!"

But Zia didn't hear him. Their peace destroyed, the water buffalo rose up and decamped. We watched them lumber downstream, a dozen or more, with their droopy necks and swept-back horns, each weighing upwards of a thousand pounds. It was nothing like a stampede. They weren't frightened or annoyed. They merely got up and moved on.

"Hello?" Reggie said. "Where's the caddie?"

We had lost sight of Zia. In departing, the water buffalo must have trampled him, because he was nowhere to be seen. There wasn't any trace of him. We watched the ripples caused by the retreating buffalo spread out across the unbroken surface of the pond.

"Joldi koro!" the Head Man shouted—"Hurry up!" And the rest of the caddies plunged into the pond to begin dragging operations. I felt a hand on my arm. It was Patty's. Given the circumstances, it may have been an odd moment for such a revelation, but it struck me that her face, though clouded with concern and a bit smudged and damp from the heat, was exquisitely lovely.

"If they get to him in time," I tried to reassure her, "there's a chance we can bring him around."

"There's always a chance," she said, without conviction.

"I feel awful." McClanahan stood with us at water's edge, looking grimly at the club in his hand as though it were a murder weapon.

"Nonsense," our host said. "Couldn't be helped. The damned fool lost his head."

Our eyes were riveted on the pond. The water was boiling with humanity. They searched frantically until, at last, a joyous shout brought an end to the commotion, and all eyes turned to behold the most fortunate of men. A stranger to us, he waved his hand triumphantly overhead and sang a song of thanksgiving, for surely he alone among his people was praiseworthy in the eyes of the sahibs. The search was over. His fellow caddies headed back to shore. For in his waving, outstretched hand he held McClanahan's wayward golf ball.

SOCCER MOMS

Jane St. Clair

Believe me, Boulder is a beautiful place. Our mountains are angular, stable and interesting. We have a wonderful university. We take on a liberal, hip attitude so often that our town is called the Peoples' Republic of Boulder. Everyone knows about JonBenet Ramsey and Columbine High School, but not about Boulder. We don't eat our children. We are soccer moms like everywhere else.

My eleven-year-old son David plays defense for the Cooncats, a private club team that travels outside of Boulder for tournaments. Larry Lindsay is the head coach, and his assistant is George Carroll.

Coach George is so young we call him Boy George, but Coach Larry is about fifty. When he is around, there is lots of sex in the air. He is sensual with a full head of grey hair and a small grey mustache. In high school he wanted to be a priest, so he's had two years in seminary. Larry works for some kind of altruistic thing with handicapped children during the day. He talks about community all the time, about developing our sense of community and building our Village. His wife makes more money than he does but that is not a threat to Larry. He is typically tie-dyed Boulder, and this appeals to women.

He called me for lunch the day he asked David to join the Cooncats. The idea of going out with him was exciting. I was some married suburban woman with short hair, driving a minivan full of kids. No one was asking me out these days. It didn't matter: I would not go. Some things are best kept fantasy. Living in a mansion on Ramsey Row and having dates with Coach Larry are fantasies; rooting for the Cooncats is my life.

During the first game of our season, my son came up to my husband and me during half-time.

"They're going to take Eric Carroll out of the game," David said, gulping down water and orange slices.

"Good," my husband replied. "Eric's too small to play forward."

"No, the other team's going to take him out."

The whistle blew and the game resumed. I watched Boy George's son Eric instead of David—the other team was beating up on him.

"He's a shrimp," my husband said. "They have no business playing him as forward."

Within minutes Eric fell and an opposition player stepped on his face, causing his braces to fuse with his lips. The ref called time, as Boy George lifted his son off the field.

Coach Larry put in Misty's son, Tristan, as forward, and I looked at my husband in disbelief. I felt angry because the other team had cheated and gotten away with it, and because now we were subbing Tristan who was as tiny as Eric.

We were sitting in the bleachers next to the Blooms, who had been on the team since it started two years ago. We and the Blooms seemed to be the only ones paying attention—most of the other parents were watching the game while trying to grade school papers, write legal briefs or talk on cell phones. That kind of thing was chic: in fact, stress was very chic among our parents, especially combined with allergies. These days everyone put Claritin up their noses.

The Blooms were adorable and had been married forever. They had met at a peace march during Viet Nam, and then they went through college and law school together. They remained cutely liberal, and defended President Clinton no matter what. Private life was private; you can be a great president, coach or whatever, regardless of your private life. Most of the other parents took cues from the Blooms.

"Why are they subbing Tristan?" I asked Nancy Bloom.

"Coach Larry likes Tristan's mom," she replied matter-of-factly. "After all, she went out to lunch with him."

We lost that game, but at our team meeting afterward, Coach Larry told everyone how fairly we had played. Nancy Bloom got up and said she would not want her son on a team that cheated. We took a phone call from Boy George at the Emergency Room: he said Eric was going to be all right.

Misty Peck took over the after-game meeting. She was the team mom and it was her job to keep our Village together. She talked about how great our coaches were, and how great our kids were, and she congratulated us for raising such great kids.

I couldn't stand Misty. She was noisy and all psyched up about sports, like a cheerleader. She had big poufy black hair that pinged from hair spray, and long red fingernails that got in her way. Misty did the cell phone/posturing thing, even though she was just selling Avon out of her house.

Our next game was at 7 a.m. on the other side of Boulder. David and I left the house at 5:30 a.m. to be there in time. It was dark and drizzly. I sat in our Bronco with my Abercrombie and Fitch thermos of coffee, as Coach Larry ran laps with the boys in deep mud. He still had physique which he showed off with silk boxers and a big Rockies jersey. Now he was standing under the ramada and drinking hot chocolate as Misty held the mug for him. She was looking at him goggle-eyed, peering out from under the hood of her L.L. Bean rainjacket.

They looked like something out of a woman's secret romance life: the fantasy of being a mom and sexual at the same time. There's a McDonald's ad like that, in which the mother of a toddler flirts with a man sitting in the next booth. There's also a car ad like that too: I may just be a soccer mom, but the music says—"I'm too sexy … I'm too sexy for the grocery … I'm too sexy for the carpool …" The ads make a lot of sense in a world where forty is old, married is boring, and Asingle mom@ is the best of both worlds.

I was just thinking about those ads when Boy George knocked on my car door. I let him climb out of the rain and sit in the passenger seat next to me. He was very good-looking with big saucer eyes, only late twenties at most. It felt intimate sitting in the car in the rain, with the radio playing make-out music, all alone with a man not my husband. A Cooncat grandmother, who was visiting from Massachusetts, stared at me in disapproval. I looked away from her and kept flirting, only to be disappointed and forty again when he tried to sell me Amway.

We got out of my Bronco and stood in the line-up with the other Cooncat parents. We were all dressed in Land's End or Eddie Bauer sun-resistant shirts and pants, brimmed Museum Expedition hats, and high-tech shoes meant for Michael Jordan-caliber athletes. We looked like we were going to hike the Tetons, but instead we were watching a kiddie soccer game. The other team's parents looked like us too, like New West people, coming here from somewhere else, to turn the old West into highways, subdivisions and shopping malls, and to form makeshift villages that only last long enough to raise our children. We came without letters of introduction or family ties, so acceptance was all about clothes, jobs, cars, having enough money and saying the right things and getting all the cues.

We lost that game 7 to 0. Coach Larry again stressed how well our Cats had played, and singled out several players, including his son, Kevin, for individual praise. Misty

Peck talked about the upcoming Fort Lowell tournament in Tucson, Arizona, where some 5,000 players would participate. She stood next to Coach Larry and there was sex all around them.

My son was upset all the way home, and said Tristan Peck was a jerk and a show-off who got special privileges on the team.

The Fort Lowell Shoot-Out had a colorful eclectic quality, like a medieval festival with a tournament of Lilliputian knights. We arrived as a group on Friday night. There was a big parade with bands, jumping castles, and food booths. Decorated cars and people in team colors were everywhere. Players with green and red jerseys had matching green and red hair. There were team banners and balloons, and adults wearing team shirts. Each team had a mascot, including a pit-bull dressed in a soccer shirt and a seven-foot paper mache chicken. There were things to buy, things commemorating the event. The kids were high but the adults looked bored in this their quality time together.

On Friday night sometime around 9:30 p.m. Caroline Rogers and her son went out to the parking lot to get jackets from their car. She saw Coach Larry and Misty Peck making love in the back seat of Larry's Explorer. The car was high off the ground, but she said there was no mistaking what she had seen.

Caroline came back to our group and said she was worried that Tristan Peck and Kevin Lindsay were being left around the park unsupervised while their parents occupied the Explorer.

That was the thing that went too far, that two boys were left alone at night in a large public place. There was talk of asking Misty to leave our team, but the next day, everyone dropped all that. Outside of wanting to win this soccer tournament, we did not really agree on much important except the importance of being nonjudgmental about other people's lives. Besides that, Misty and Larry were doing all the volunteer work for the team.

The games started on Saturday in a double elimination tournament. Last year the Cooncats finished in a mediocre place, but this year we had an advantage. We were in the Age 9 to 11 division, and most of our players had already turned eleven. We were also silver-flighted, which meant we were in the second or easier level of competition, not the first or gold flight.

Every one of the Cooncat parents would say they only want what the kids want, which is to have fun. But each of us wanted to win the Fort Lowell Shoot-Out, if only to justify the absurdity of all the times we spent rising at dawn to drive to some obscure park to watch little kids play soccer.

On Saturday we played first thing in the morning, but something was different with us. Misty sat by herself in the bleachers, and even the Blooms stood away from her on the boundary line. No one asked her to leave. No one said anything to her. Coach Larry kept her son in as forward, but what little game he had in him was gone.

The old Massachusetts grandmother finally said something. She said it loudly but to no one in particular.

AIn my day,@ she said, Amarried was married. And the President got respect.@

We nodded politely as the Greatest Generation struck out again in their perpetual disapproval of Baby Boomers.

We lost our second and final game to a team from Nevada. We had no business losing to them.

Afterwards Misty passed out little meaningless store-brought trophies to each wonderful Cooncat player. Coach Larry made speeches about each boy, but they did not amount to anything real. We were not together as a team and it showed; some of us could not look the others of us in the eye.

The Blooms said privately that what happened should not be taken out on Kevin Lindsay or Tristan Peck, that our kids were everything, and that the whole soccer thing was for our kids. Their words rang hollow. We had finished the

Shoot-Out second to last, in what should have been our win. Instead our main hometown rivals, the Big Green Machine, took Fort Lowell. We were looking to blame something for dividing us, and though it was left unspoken, we blamed the thing with Misty and Larry, the thing that had gone too far. Coach Larry had been our leader and Misty had led the cheers, but no one was following them anymore.

Misty organized a car wash to raise money for our next tournament, but only she, the two coaches, and the Blooms showed up. The rest of us paid our way out of the volunteer work by chipping in $150 each. We didn't party together anymore, and no one cared if we all stayed at the same hotel when we traveled. We were more or less just dropping the boys off for practices and not lingering to talk.

We had an 11 and 0 losing record by Christmas, when we traveled to a California tournament. By then Misty's husband filed for divorce. Coach Larry's wife started to come to everything, even though it was hard because she owned a company that had a lot of crises. She was on the phone in a Zen posture of there but not there. I watched her and all of us and saw the constant disconnection of our lives. People were traveling in separate orbits, husbands and wives at separate tables, children playing video games all day all by themselves, no one connecting, no one communicating, no one being a team player or even a family member, everyone worshiping at the Temple of the Mall, and sex was just a search for the easiest, simplest, most elemental coupling. It was too cynical to be a true epiphany.

In California we played a team from Beverly Hills. The Beverly Hills team had gone to soccer camp together; they had hired a professional coach, and they were good. They played preppie-fair with superior passing skills. They had matching leather gym bags and shoes. They stayed at an expensive resort where they rented horses for their boys to ride. Everyone got along and smiled all the time. Everything about them was what we wanted to become. They made our appetite for material things worse: we only had to look at them and see what big money could mean to our kids. On that we could agree: rich was better than upper-middle.

Coach Larry's wife actually brought matching gym bags for the Cooncats, and we raised money for monogrammed warm-up suits. Boy George found a semi-professional coach whom we paid $400 a month to lead our practices. None of the kids liked him but we adults agreed that our boys would eventually have more fun if they won some games.

In March we were scrimmaging with local teams as practice for the big final state tournament that led to international competition. We played a team that had Brent Davis on it—last year he had been a Cooncat. Our parents acted strangely in terms of body language around Brent; there were murmurs and sniffs and even some uncontrollable laughter. I was clueless until Nancy Bloom told me that Francine Davis and Coach Larry had a thing together last year, and that Francine and Brent Davis had been asked to leave the team.

We lost that game 17 to 1; something was bizarre about us and our players picked it up and let it ruin their game.

After that it was all over between Misty and Coach Larry. He started to call different mothers on the team to ask them out for lunch. He called me, but lately I had begun to appreciate my husband, especially compared to what Hillary was enduring.

Meanwhile Misty moved toward Boy George. These days George Carroll and his wife were irritable, distant and stressed, especially about money. There was a rumor they had undergone an abortion. Misty moved right into that.

Caroline Rogers talked about saying something to Linda Carroll about what was going on between her husband and Misty. I said she should say something to George, not to Linda, because why should women pay the price? Why should Francine have to quit the Cooncats and why is Monica considered a slut? But we all knew that marriages can go stale and that we were living in a forgiving age. After all there had been three divorces on our team in three years. In that case, in the end, no one said anything to anyone. Private lives do not affect performance.

Then those two boys went crazy on a shooting spree at Columbine High School. The people involved in it were too much like us and we needed immediate insulation from such a thing, and reassurance that our boys were not like them and therefore safe. We Cooncats made a big deal out of the fact that we were involved with our kids and they were into sports. We spend all kinds of quality time watching them play soccer and getting to know the parents of their friends. But later it said in the paper that the Columbine boys had been soccer players too.

Two of our players quit that May, and two new ones came on, including a boy named Mike with an attractive blonde divorced mother in her early thirties. After she started going to lunch with Coach Larry, her son replaced Tristan Peck as forward.

Mike was not only klutzy, he was dumb. Coach Larry put him in the big state tournament when he did not even know the rules. In the first game of the tournament, he passed the ball to the opposition team, and they scored against us. None of the Cooncat parents were mean enough to complain about some little kid's honest mistake, but it was maddening to watch, after all the practices, the professional coaching, the gym bags, the car washes—after all of that.

We were in the final game of the state tournament against the Big Green Machine. They were playing smoothly and fairly. They had no stars but played like an efficient passing machine that moved and passed the ball in a choreographed ballet designed to score goals. By the end of the first quarter, the score was 6-0, and our goalie, Coach Larry's boy, was crying.

One of our better players, Kyle Rogers, could not control his emotions anymore and went crying to his mother that he wanted to quit the team now, not at the end of the season as his mother had promised. He was crying hysterically in a rage against the other team and then against the Cooncats themselves.

"I'm better than Eric! I should play forward! They keep him in because he's the coach's son!" He was loud enough for everyone to hear and his parents were embarrassed. Coach Larry made him sit out for poor sportsmanship.

Our boys went back in for more torture, and just a moment or two after the second half began, Eric Carroll tripped on a shoelace and fell on the ground where he just lay crying hysterically. He was hysterical because he was a little boy in a game where big boys win, and for trying so hard in a game that was against him. Eric cried that the other team had tripped him, and George Carroll and his wife and the three other Carroll sons agreed. There seemed to be Carrolls everywhere crying foul, demanding red cards against the other team. The Carrolls united in a ferocious family way so that even Coach Larry could not stop them.

One of the Machine team's fathers was a doctor, and he looked at Eric's foot and said it was just a slight sprain, and that enraged the Carrolls all the more.

After Eric was taken out, his father got even more angry and demanded to see birth certificates from each of players on the Machine. They were too big to be under twelve, and George knew cheating when he saw it. They had gotten away with cheating his son out of playing, but he was not going to stand around and let them cheat and take the tournament. His wife stood beside him and they yelled and screamed together.

The ref told us that these certificates had already been checked prior to the tournament. Boy George grew so intense, the ref gave us a yellow card and then permanently removed him from the tournament. It took four of our fathers to quiet George Carroll and escort him from the field—he was so angry.

The game resumed and Coach Larry put the blonde's son in as forward, replacing Eric. I began to wonder if private lives mattered after all. My son was angry and depressed during the break at third quarter. He told me it wasn't fair—all the coaches' sons and their favorites got the best positions, and the Cooncats were a bunch of losers.

Then our kids were all over each other. Misty's son got into a fist fight with Coach Larry's boy. Our semi-professional coach first threatened to leave the game because of our behavior, and then he did.

Some of the teams we had once called low class and dirty were watching us. They said we deserved to lose: we could never compete against Japanese or European teams. They were laughing at us, at our pettiness, our poor sportsmanship, and our big point loss. We did not finish that game, because Coach Larry got into a fight with the ref. Our parents were too far gone by the time the score was 13 to 0. We walked off as a group, which could have been dramatic and maybe even satisfying and unifying, if the refs had not decided to award the Green Machine the big trophy immediately and in front of us.

After a while, it settled down, and the Cooncat parents later agreed that the refs had been unfair and we did not really want to participate in rigged games like that. We went to a pizza place but only the kids ate.

My son did not buy a word of what went down. We lost because Kevin and Tristan and Mike and Eric stink. Kevin and Tristan were always digging at the other boys and lording things over them, because they were coaches' sons. Mike the Mentally-Challenged didn't even know how to play soccer, for Cripe's sake. All the other boys were taking sides against each other. Everyone hates everyone else. The Cooncats are a lousy team, even if all the parents get along so well.

YANKS

Gaynell Gavin

What can I tell you, kid? Gotta roll with the punches, that's all. I get to go home from the hospital tomorrow. Be laid up for a while, but it won't be so bad since it's baseball season.

I don't like the ways the game's changed—not what it used to be. The Yankees would ride all night from New York to St. Louis in a train with no air conditioning. Then they'd get off that train and play ball in the hundred-degree sun. No night games in those days. Baseball players were tough then. Take the Babe. There'll never be anybody like the Babe again.

It was different then. By the time I was eighteen, I was a man. By ten or eleven, my brothers and I knew what it was to put in a day of hard work in the hot sun, cutting yards, fifteen cents a yard. Or we'd gather scrap metal, burn the insulation off the wires, try to sell the copper to the junk yard. Winters, for heat, we'd pick up coal that fell off the coal cars. We'd spend a nickel on a movie now and then, maybe get a little popcorn. We had hunting, fishing, football, softball, baseball.

Walt, Percival, and I were the closest in age, with me right in between, a year younger than Walt, a year older than Percy. Sometimes we'd walk the Bluffton railroad bridge across the Mississippi to Missouri, hoping no train would come. The spaces between ties on the bridge were big enough so we had to be careful not to fall through. That river was deep and wide with a fast current, and it was a long way down. When we got to Missouri, we'd hitchhike to a ball game, but it could be hard for three guys to get a ride. We had our ways of getting in to the game if we got there. Once we couldn't get a ride either way, so we walked to St. Louis and back to Illinois, probably walked fifty miles. The worst time, though, was June of 1930. Yankees came to play the St. Louis Browns. When we walked off the bridge in Missouri, a cop was waiting, ordered us to turn around and walk back. There was nothing else to do, so we didn't get to see the Yankees win. I turned fourteen later that summer.

By eighteen, I was working at the Midwestern Cartridge Company, engaging .22 shells, and I saw Jeannie for the first time. Supervisor brought her over from the other side of the plant for some reason. I remember her exactly. She was wearing a black skirt, little gold cross necklace, and a white blouse, all her wavy dark hair brushing against that white blouse collar. I looked at her and said to myself, "I'm gonna marry that girl."

Almost all of us worked over at the Midwestern. Mom worked in the factory. I don't remember Dad working there, but I was so little when he died, I don't remember him too well. My two older sisters were machine operators, met husbands there. Percy had the most dangerous job of us all. He carried the cans of fulmonite. He carried them alone, in case they blew up, and he put the powder into shotgun shells.

My brother, Larry, died at the Midwestern during the Depression, and my oldest brother, Hank, worked there all his life, repaired machines. Larry collapsed on the night shift, got taken to first aid, revived, sent back to work, collapsed again, and died. He was twenty. Hank made it to sixty, died of TB.

I remember wanting a baseball glove so much, knowing we couldn't afford it. Somehow Larry got me that glove shortly before he died. I was seven.

Now the one who never worked at the Midwestern was Walt. He was always in the rag business, as we called it. What happened was Morris Goldenberg was looking for a salesman. He was a smart Jewish businessman, married an Italian Catholic girl. A Catholic and a Jew getting married was just not something people did then, at least not in Bluffton. Anyway, Walt and I were in school at Holy Ghost High. I played football and graduated Holy Ghost, but Walt left his junior year cause Morris Goldenberg went to Monsignor O'Connell and asked him to send a kid who'd make a good salesman. Monsignor sent Walt.

Percy and I went to the service, him to the army, me to the navy. Walt went to the navy too but not overseas. The Depression was good preparation for the military, kid. A lot of the hardships weren't too different from our civilian lives. I got transferred from the fore to aft boiler room the week before we were torpedoed. We took everything as it came, but that bomb came into the front boiler room and killed everybody there—they could never have survived being scalded by the boiler water. I was in the Atlantic six or seven hours and thought that was it for me, but another ship picked me up.

On land, Percy faced a Panzer division with a handful of men who knew they'd be killed or captured. He figured that was his last day on earth, went into a German POW camp weighing 180. Six months later, when he got out of the hospital where they put a little weight back on him, he weighed 116 pounds. I never talked about the war with anyone but him, and there's a lot even we never talked about.

We came home from overseas and went back to work at Midwestern. Walt came home from California and went back to Morris Goldenberg's. Walt never hunted with me, and Percy wouldn't anymore after we got home—said he'd had enough of it in the war.

I'd married Jeanne when we were twenty, and we started with nothing, rented a little two-room apartment. I'd wake up in the morning and walk to work at Midwestern. Then, after the war, Walt found a partner to help him open their own clothing store, Percy started selling insurance, and I got on at the fire department.

Let me tell you something, kid. Coffee and cigarettes? That's what we did at the fire department all day long. Smoked cigarettes, drank coffee. All this talk about addiction, well, I smoked three packs a day for thirty-five years. Loved it. Loved those things. Nothing like sitting down after work to watch a baseball game with a Winston and a cold beer. Jeanne would say she didn't think I'd ever be able to quit smoking. I'd say, "Hon, if I decide to quit, I'll just quit."

After I retired from the fire department, I was sitting at home one morning, and by ten o'clock, I'd finished a pot of coffee and a pack of cigarettes. "Okay," I told myself, "this has gone on long enough." I took the other pack of Winstons I'd been about to open out of my shirt pocket, threw it in the trash, cut back to a cup of coffee or two in the morning, that's it. Now if all that stuff is so addictive, you tell me how I could turn away from it just like that. And another thing— all these scientists telling us everything that's bad for us—I don't see them living any longer than I've lived. You know what? It's all in the noodle, kid, all in the noodle.

That's what I liked about Ronald Reagan. He knew you couldn't protect everybody from everything. He didn't want a country of sissies. First I became a Reagan Democrat. Then I became a Republican, which almost caused a hard break between Walt and me. He said after being a New Deal Democrat, our mother was probably turning in her grave. Well, we still had the Fighting Irish and the Yankees in common. I could say more, but since family's family, I'm not gonna say it.

After the fire department, I worked part-time at a liquor store. Got robbed twice. With one of those robberies, I had to do a voice ID of the guy. I didn't see his face cause it was covered. I picked that guy's voice right out of a lineup. He did it all right. After the robberies, I didn't miss that job at all when it was gone.

I was married to Jeanne for forty-eight years, and it was beautiful. Near the end, she'd been real sick for a long time, been through chemo, everything. When she got out of the hospital and was feeling stronger, she was right back at her volunteer work at the hospital gift shop and the women's shelter thrift store.

One Sunday night, I was coming down with a cold and said, "Hon, maybe you should sleep in the front bedroom. Last thing you need is to catch a cold from me."

Next morning, I slept later than usual—almost never do that. The phone woke me up, and one of her friends said, "Isn't Jeannie coming to work at the thrift store today?"

I got to that bedroom door and knew what I'd find when I opened it. She was on the floor. That bothers me a lot. What if she was trying to come to me to tell me something? What if she had something to say to me she didn't get to say? I found a note she wrote and put in a wooden box on my dresser. Our son made that box in high-school shop class for Father's Day 1965. It's made from different kinds of dark, medium, and light polished woods. The note said, "I know you always believe what I tell you, but sometimes I don't think you understand what I'm telling you." Maybe she'd been trying to tell me she was dying.

Jeanne told one of her friends—that Schwegel girl, Patsy, married one of the Ryan boys—about when we were shopping the Friday before she died. Told her if she hadn't been holding on to that cart, she'd have fallen over, so that girl says, "Well, why didn't you tell Richie?" Turns out Jeanne was afraid I'd take her back to the hospital, and she didn't want to go. Why'd she think that? Hell, I wouldn't have made her go back if she didn't want to go. I wouldn't have done that.

Look who's in the hospital now. I've had a shoulder replacement, a knee replacement, diabetes, dehydrated and damned near starved to death because of these ulcers. No kidding. I lost so much weight so fast, it's not funny. They think the knee surgery medication caused the ulcers. I don't even have my own teeth anymore, and just before I got put in the hospital, what did I do? Fell on those stone steps in front of St. Mary Magdalene's right after eleven o'clock mass and tore a rotator cuff. So now when I get strong enough, I've gotta have surgery on the shoulder that wasn't replaced. It's like this, kid. I'll get better or I won't, but I had a marriage that made my life beautiful, and I don't know if too many people can say that. No complaints. I've had a good life—wouldn't change it.

Now it's baseball season, and what's better than baseball season? Maybe what comes next. Football. Notre Dame. What I say is, once a Fighting Irish fan, always a Fighting Irish fan, once a Yankees fan, always a Yankees fan.

Well, thanks for listening to an old man. Don't worry about me, kid. I'm not afraid to die.

THE TOOLS OF IGNORANCE

Anthony Bukoski

1.
THE VOICES I HEARD

I wipe beer glasses at the bar of Heartbreak Hotel in Superior. I turn the radio dial. I wonder where do the short, sweet years go to? Last season I got free drinks and Shrimp-Busters at Herby K's, got my muffler fixed free at Mufflers of Shreveport, got autograph requests all up and down Lousiana Avenue. That's before the bartender at Herby K's and the waiters at the Hayride Kitchen in Shreveport turned their backs on me. It is a story of loss and regret that has brought me home to Wisconsin.

Now who do I have to listen to but Pete Katzmarck in the corner of the bar staring at the hands of the Hamm's Beer clock? I tell him, "You're pickled. Go on home, you *gaboosh*, Pete."

"You go home, Augie," Pete says to me. "If I couldn't hit no better'n you, I'd never sign a contract. Bitter, bitter disappointment, *gorzki*."

"*Starość nieradość*," this other old guy, Władziu, moans in Polish. "Old age ain't no fun."

Somebody plugs in the jukebox. Eddie Blazonczyk's band comes on. Horns and accordions begin. On the phonograph record a guy yells:

Polka Time! Polka Time!
We're all fine at Polka Time!

I turn down the baseball game playing on the radio. Since it is growing dark, I flick on the switch to light the outdoor sign. Even the blue neon is heartbroken. Sizzling a little, only parts come on: HEARTBREAK OTEL.

I look in the mirror in back of the bar. Everywhere I see myself. Behind the bottle of *Jeżynowka* blackberry brandy it's me Augie, barkeep. Bum. Loser. I see me in Pete's face...in the old guys' faces slobbering over bowls of beer. Losers. Derelicts. Gabooshes.

"*You* go home!" Pete says.

"I've got nothing there but my ma waiting, Petie. What'll I do at home? I'm better off here. Either way I'm washed up. Jeezus, I threw my life away. I should've married this gal I knew down in Shreveport. What do I got now when I can't do nothing but think about her? I'm twenty-five. I'm through. No more baseball except what I play to embarrass myself on Sundays."

"You look like shit on Sundays," someone calls from the other end of the bar.

Over the cloudy jar of pickled pigs' feet, I stare in the mirror, wishing a storm would come to steam up the mirror and blow out the neon sign in front so I could serve the guys by flashlight or candlelight. Then you couldn't see our ceiling that's turned orange from seventy years of smoke or the mirror or the nicks in the long wood bar.

I've got to get a better job, or someday I'll be a washed-up geezer taking Pete's spot at the bar. I can't get over Shreveport, though. My heart's in Shreveport on the Red River because of what happened. Was it the night we returned from Jackson and Ellie Pleasaunt was waiting at the players' entrance to the stadium? Somehow I got tangled up in something very serious in Shreveport that was partly the result of my foolishness and pride and partly my disregarding someone who loved me. It eats at me every night, so that when I look in the mirror behind the bar now and ask myself (above the polkas and schottisches), "Did you really love her?" the answer is still "yes" from my broken heart up north in the Yankeeland of Superior, Wisconsin.

Why I didn't listen to the Voice of the Shreveport Captains and keep from coming back to such a miserable place of heartbreak as the East End is a two-year history of bus trips, doubleheaders, and rain delays. In this, Augie Wyzinski's true-life chronicle of lost love, I'll get the record-book stuff over first. Like how in high school I lined a "blue darter" into the screen that protects the windows of a paper mill in Menasha, Wisconsin—430 feet into the wind off Lake Winnebago. Like how after the Oshkosh game in college, with the season I had my junior year, the Giants signed me. The *Evening Telegram* of my hometown here had on its front page: "LOCAL BOY SIGNS." My ma, Uncle Louie, and I couldn't finish our dinner at The Polish Hearth for all the commotion. The Duluth paper wanted an interview, too. Bennett Stodill, the sports editor, wouldn't let me touch my cabbage rolls. "You're going to make it. I know that," he said. My ma smiled, my uncle patted my shoulder. "See?" Ma said as the future lit up for me.

The Giants assigned me to Clinton, Iowa. I tore up the league—Cedar Rapids, Kane County, Burlington. Ma sent clippings: "FUTURE BRIGHT FOR SIGNEE WYZINSKI. BIG CLUB TO PROMOTE LOCAL TO AA AFTER FULL SEASON IN IOWA. FRISCO NEXT?"

I wasn't going to toil in the low minors long, I told myself.

From Clinton the next season I went to Shreveport, Double-A. The first month there, April, I hit six homers, four doubles. After I tossed out my fifteenth base runner trying to steal, I couldn't walk into a clothing store or nightclub on

Louisiana Avenue without someone buying me a shirt or a drink just so they could be near me. You've heard of such phenoms as me.

Everything was great. ("Everytink great," the old gabooshes would say.) Things like this happen. Guys get lucky. I come out of college, I come out of northern Wisconsin. At the right moment, success and love strike me. Maybe no one from here will ever again catch on like this. Uncle Louie would talk about a "Hurricane" Bob Hazle that rose out of nowhere late one season in the '50s to help the Milwaukee Braves win a pennant. Then he was gone into oblivion like me. Now I'll explain how I, Augie, oblivious Augie, ended up at Heartbreak Hotel where "the bellhop's tears keep flowin'" and show why I, Augie, forgotten Augie, wear a baggy wool uniform these days on Sundays in Superior instead of the one with the orange and black SF of the big club, San Francisco. This is where the voice I should have listened to comes in. There were fifty thousand watts of power behind that voice.

2.
GIANTS' SIGNEE ADVERTISES GOODY'S HEADACHE POWDERS

Who'd argue with fifty thousand watts or question Biff Barton, the radio Voice of the Shreveport Captains? Mr. Barton had a full head of black hair he used Vitalis in. But in front, it was like you could see each strand where it grew out of a white scalp. His forehead and face were tanned. He wore tinted glasses that turned darker if the room or the press box was dark. Who'd argue with the power of that God-like voice? "Howdy, Louuu-ee-siana," he'd say over the airwaves with fifty thousand watts to back him up.

He studied us, studied statistics, talked about us. "You know," Mr. Barton would say when I saw him at Shooter's

Smokehouse Cafe in Shreveport, "it's a great game I hope you stick with, kid." I knew he had faith in me. He interviewed me on the field after a Tulsa game. "Those were king-size homers last night," he said. "Your throwing arm is a rifle, too."

"I'm seeing the ball good, Mr. Barton," I said into the microphone as I looked into his dark glasses.

"I'll say it's early in the season. Kid, you don't know your strength. You're soon going to be living on the West Coast. Fans in the Ark-La-Tex listening to this broadcast: Come out-chere to have a look. He's liable to be gone soon."

"Keep your nose clean," he said to me afterward.

"Don't worry," I said. "No smoking. No drinking."

In Tulsa I threw out three more runners. I knocked in six runs in one game, five in another. In El Paso I hit a scorcher off the flagpole at Dudley Field. At Smith-Willis Stadium in Jackson, Miss., I got two doubles. Sportswriters called it a "meteoric" rise.

"Keeping my nose clean," I'd say when I saw Mr. Barton before games.

I kept on hitting and playing defense like the Milwaukee Braves' "Hurricane" Bob Hazle Uncle Louie told me about. June went by. "Everything was good then, wasn't it, Augie?" I ask myself in the mirror behind the bar now, recalling a four-for-four day game with San Antonio and the night that followed with Ellie, this woman who adored me. She was a lonely, lovesick fan. Before I met her I was out every night after games pulling hijinks at the Sports Page in Shreve Square, at Forrest and Lulu Longrie's Dugout Saloon on Line Ave., at the Cove on Cross Lake. So many women love a hard-hitting catcher that you can fill out different lineup cards every night. Once in a motel room after a twi-night doubleheader with Beaumont, a rookie named Denise, naked, wore my chest protector, crouched, and gave me a signal for a fast ball. Another time in my apartment after a tight home game with Midland, I wore the catcher's mask through the whole act of "coytis." But one moonlit night after gunning down four base runners and going two-for-three against the Arkansas Travelers, I got even luckier; I came home and pulled off a triple play with three gorgeous roommates who loved my swing. Then her, Ellie. She fell for me right away. We met at the Captains' Booster Club Pig Roast when I brought her a paper plate of coleslaw, pig meat, and Jo Jo's. Despite what sportswriters called my "furious pace," something was missing in my life and career like it was in Ellie's, I guess.

On the night I think of now, Ellie and I'd been going out a couple weeks. Her loneliness and the pressure on me of my sudden fame in the South, all of it—I don't know—came together that very night in the quiet of my apartment when we kissed each other's shoulders and hair. "I think I'm in 'like' with you," I told her, looking into the shadows of her face. You don't say such things to women on the first date. But it was three weeks we'd been dating, and I could honestly tell her I liked her and partially commit myself to her—except for when I felt the urge to go on the prowl, drinking and looking for women who appreciated my star quality.

"I'm deeply in 'like' with you too, Augie," she said, looking up. "I'd give you my heart."

I buried myself in her neck and hair then.

The two of us lying there, I said her profile reminded me of a picture I'd seen of an ancient Egyptian queen, Never-Titty.

"I want you to feel like her husband," Ellie said.

"I wasn't alive back in ancient times before the designated hitter rule," I said.

"I was just teasing," she said. "I've been buried and you woke me and I'm in love. Nefertiti's in love." She moved a wisp of hair from her beautiful white forehead with the blue vein in her left temple. Like Never-Titty's, her nose had this very attractive bend. To me she was a goddess.

"We're not going to sleep this night," I said, "but I'm sure happy and don't give a darn. Lookit the homers I got today."

After all this baseball stardom, then Nefertiti's giving me her heart, regret and misfortune had to follow. It just seems like whenever I'm on a roll I always do something dumb to mess things up. Maybe it's part of my personality that I don't know how to hold on to the good things. Maybe I got what's called "low self-esteem." Now I have come to be counseled by winos and gabooshes with a real high regard for themselves who, when I say "I ain't any good anymore," they say, "You're right."

"But I once was, wasn't I, boys?" I ask.

"You no good ever. You were lousy. You stunk. We seen you play in the old-timers' basebull league on Sunday, too. You stink."

But once not so long ago I was in Shreveport under blue Louisiana skies, and there I had a fine time and there I met a woman named Nefertiti. When I look in the mirror, I still see her, heartbroken, looking back. *When you said you'd give me your heart that night, Ellie, I looked into your eyes and said I would not hurt you, and later you carried my baby. On the night you gave me your love, I didn't know how much I would fail you. But I did fail you, Ellie Pleasaunt, because I could not accept your open, innocent love, because I did not have it in me.*

A month after the Tulsa interview I was Biff's guest again—this time when he was promoting Goody's at Winn-Dixie Grocery. "Anybody who's had a headache," Biff Barton said over 71 KEEL-Radio, "get down to Jewella Avenue. Meet the Voice of the Shreveport Captains and Biff's very special interview guest today." While Ellie called her ma to say, "Turn on KEEL, quick!", Biff had me practice what he'd written on a scrap of paper. "Catching's hard work," I was saying nervously over the airwaves before I knew it. "When I get home with sore muscles, what do I reach for?"

Here Mr. Barton held out the microphone. "GOODY'S!" the customers in Aisle 7 shouted.

Every night last summer the Voice of the Shreveport Captains, the Old Testament God Biff Barton's voice, came over the Big Thicket Country (as it does tonight when I am working in a bar in Superior a thousand miles away). You'd look up through the smoke haze in the late innings at Beaumont last year, see him in the little square lighted press box, see him at V.J. Keefe Stadium in San Antone, at Windham in Little Rock, looking down through his tinted glasses at the way we were carrying on. You'd pull into Marshall, Texas, and hear Mr. Biff, who influenced our manager's decisions. You might live on the bayou in Homer, Louisiana, or be up in Helena, Arkansas, fixing your car, and you'd hear Biff's scouting report and interview show from down on the field. *Did you pass Ellie Pleasaunt on your road trips, Mr. Barton? Did you see her crying when she learned we were going to have a baby?*

3.
TEXAS LEAGUE HOME RUN KING

My whole name is August Joseph Wyzinski. Old guys call me "Owgoost." I was famous for a couple months, but I began wondering about my future when our manager, we called him the skipper, stopped looking me in the eye and benched me in Midland-Odessa in mid-July when I'd dropped a foul tip for strike three.

"Bet you'd go for a Polee sausage," the skipper'd say and spit tobacco. Sometimes pronouncing it "Pulley sausage," he'd ask on the field, "What you Yankees up north call that stuff you eat."

"Kielbasa."

"Well, from now on you're Augie Kielbasa with them sausage hands that can't hold onto a baseball."

Pete, you spilled your beer," I say a year later. "Here's a bar rag. Wash your face while you're at it."

"You looking in the mirror. What d'you know about my face?"

"I know. That's what I'm saying. I'll wipe mine, too."

Wipe my face with a bar rag because I have been a fool, Pete.

"Was I any good ever at anything, you guys?" I ask.

"No good. Right from the start, no good."

"Thanks."

"You welcome, Augie."

"Ah, who wants a bowl of beer on me? Why not play me for a fool? I've thrown it all away. But what's the use of telling you gabooshes? Just remind me I didn't deserve her and that I'm a fool. Tell me, Pete, was I a fool?"

"Sure, Augie."

"But why? I want to know."

"Because you are and you're no good with a baseball."

"Ah, you're right, Pete and you guys. That's what I don't understand about myself, how I can come so close to the good things and blow it every time. That's why I can't see any future for me. All I can do is think about the past. What kind of life is that to have?"

4.
"OW-GOOST'S" NIGHT OF TERROR OR HOW "OW-GOOST" ALWAYS MANAGES TO SCREW THINGS UP

One night last year we'd gone extra innings at home against the Beaumont Golden Gators, and though I hadn't caught, I was still tired. I'd been warming the bench, eating peanuts, thinking about my late nights with Ellie Pleasaunt and what I'd gotten into with her. I missed the night life—drinking, carousing, trading off of your fame to see how far you could get with a gal.

After Mr. Barton's stirring account of the game, KEEL-Radio had gone back to regular programming. Life was boring again. The parking lot was still burning from sixteen hours of Caddo Parish heat when all cleaned up I came out of the clubhouse with nowhere to go.

When you're famous and in a slump, you need something to cheer you up. You have a nice car from your signing bonus of a few years back and plenty of time after games. If you're short of dough, you fool gals who follow ballclubs by carrying a money clip with fifty bucks showing and a wad of one dollar bills beneath it. A few of the Captains have girlfriends in the Texas League towns. I had Ellie since I settled down from the wild days of April in Shreveport when I was out every night with Linda, D.J., Teri, and all the other women who came to watch me on the field and follow me off. Even so, I never promised Ellie Pleasaunt I'd be faithful. A star has a right to his fun.

Mostly, Ellie saw two or three games each homestand. When I hadn't seen her in the box seats, I thought she was home in Natchitoches with her folks. Sometimes after the game, she drove back the same night, sometimes stayed with her cousin Hattie in Shreveport, sometimes with me. I'd been to Cousin Hattie's with Ellie. She lived at the The Knolls Apartments on Jesuit Avenue.

I'd once visited Ellie's folks in Natchitoches, too.

"Come in, Mr. Wyz—," Ellie's ma had said the first time I showed up.

"Wyzinski, Mother," Ellie'd said. "He's Polish."

"Praise the Lord, you're as handsome, Mr. Wyzinski, as Ellie said. Pardon me, I was just cleaning up around here. Mr. Pleasaunt will be home soon and we can all sit down to get acquainted. Come right in, son."

Good people, Christians, but love counts for something, too. When we were alone, Ellie'd get over her reservations about sin, and we would be together in the name of love and ancient Egypt, and she got pregnant. This particular night, though, I needed time off from all the family stuff to figure how to get out of my slump. It was August. Things weren't so hot at the park. After a few times around the league, I'd stopped seeing the ball. My throws to second were off. Guys stole too easily on me. The skipper really started losing interest in me after my average dropped and my run production dried up because all the love and fame had jinxed me. If the weather didn't wear you down, then thinking of the women of April did. I figured maybe if I just got out on the town like I once did—meet some Louisiana gals, have some drinks—I'd be okay, get back my concentration, then settle in with the one who loved me.

Not ready for sleep, on this hot night I practiced my swing with the umbrella I'd gotten free at Hall Clothier and Bootery when I was the Prince of Lousiana Avenue. I was killing time in a parking lot swinging at bugs. I hit two moths for homers. "Dodgers' pitcher goes to the mound," I could imagine Vin Scully saying. "Wind blowing in tonight at venerable Candlestick Park. Wyzinski, the batter, steps in."

Around 11:30, with nothing to do, I pulled into a convenience store a thousand miles from the Heartbreak. "How you gals doin'?" I said to this lady and her friend running the place. Ready for some action I tried the money clip trick on them.

"Where you from?" one of them asked.

"Louisiana."

"You aren't with that funny accent," the other one said. Her name was "Honeydew." She was the store clerk. "You got 'America's Dairyland' license plates."

"I'm from Louisiconsin, a new state. Superior, Louisiconsin."

"I'm gonna stock the coolers, Joyce hon," Honeydew said, rolling her eyes.

"I'll have a Yoo-Hoo," I said.

Joyce rang one up the way I now ring up Stashu's vodka or Władziu's blackberry brandy at Heartbreak.

"My name's Race Gentry," I told her.

Honeydew came out to check on us.

"How you doing?" she asked.

"He wants to know how old I am. I rang up the Yoo-Hoo."

"You're twenty-seven, aren't you, Joyce?" asked Honeydew.

"Well how about making me an old lady. I swan, I'm not a day over twenty-six."

"I'd a guessed that," I said. "You look great to me."

Joyce wore these plastic shoes, just strips of white plastic. She had tan legs with little bumps in the skin around back of her thighs.

"Oh these?" she said when she noticed me looking. "Them's nothing. I 'loofah' them away. Look at my hairdo. People tell me I resemble Connie Stevens."

"Who?" I asked.

"The movie star. The actress that once married Eddie Fisher."

"Never heard of her," I said.

"Jeez, where you been hiding? Jeez, it's a hot night and lots of stars are out. Why don't we go over to your place and talk a little baseball, honey?"

When we were set to leave, Joyce opened the front milk cooler and hollered in to Honeydew, "We're going!"

"Have fun, Joycey. Call me tomorrow," Honeydew yelled from behind the 2%.

I got a Stroh's twelve pack for the ride. She followed me in her car. I cracked open a beer, turned up the radio, thought of what I'd do to Joyce. Things ain't so bad, I told myself.

She was giggling when she arrived. "I don't much watch sports," she said. "Say, I know where it was! I heard you on the radio. You know that Biff Barton guy you see around at groshery stores?"

"He's my agent."

"He was on radio advertising Goody's, wa'nt he?"

"Sure, I been on the radio with him. Why don't you whisper so we don't wake the neighbors."

"Thas where I heard you," she said.

After drinking two on the way over, I had ten beers left. Joyce carried a few with her. One can fell from her purse, broke open, fizzed. We were in the third-floor hallway of my apartment building. "I'm destined for the Polish-American Sports Hall of Fame, you know," I whispered, unlocking the door. "What you wearing under that blouse?"

"Oh hush," she said.

A Yoo-Hoo and three beers later and the blouse was on the floor. It was 1 A.M.; I figured Ellie was home, and Joyce, Honeydew's friend from the convenience store, was dancing to Merle Haggard's "Mama Tried" playing on the stereo. What was I doing? *Crazy with failure. Treadwell called me "Kielbasa"… "Sausage hands." I'd lost my hitting eye. I was trying to get it back with this Joyce lady.*

"What's the matter?" she asked when I didn't want to dance right off.

"Nothing. I want to drink. Ain't been feeling so hot lately and I just want another beer. Let's talk about something before we dance."

"Talk! What am I goin' to tell Honeydew? Oh yeah, Honeydew, he was a great guy. We just talked all night. Hon, I'm thirty years old. Well, twenty-nine. I've done enough talking. I want romance."

"Lemme just finish my beer."

"No, get up and dance with me. You must know them all. W-a-a-a Wa-Watusi."

"You know anything about ancient Egypt?" I said.

"Yeah, that you've got a mummy's curse put on you tonight. I've known guys like you all my life. Flashy big-with-the-talk-guys until you're alone. Then Boris Karloff. Look at me. Jeez, I've been told I'm beautiful."

When she lowered her head to my shoulder, I felt the stiff hair. It was peroxided blond, I guess it's called. When she tried to smile seductively, the skin on her face pulled tight. It was like her face couldn't do what her heart wanted.

"Jeez, don't put your hands on my face like you're testing it or something. Jeez, what do you think—I had a facelift? Jeez, why don't you kiss me at least?"

Her lips didn't move much when she talked. When I kissed them, she couldn't make them move either. She said her name was Joyce Gott.

"Hush a minute," she said between beers. "I thought I heard something."

"You musta just heard a car. Maybe it's my agent's."

"Someone's at the door."

"There's nothing," I said. "Let's dance. There's no one outside, Joyce. C'mon," I said real fast. "You know how to 'Limbo Rock?'"

"It's the '90s, hon. The Limbo went out when I was a teenager. I mean I heard it was a '60s dance. I think they play it on Oldies stations sometimes."

"I don't care. Turn up the music. Here, I'll find a song. Go ahead. Limbo. I'll hum it. How l-o-o-o-w can you go-o-o?"

"No. Listen! You got an 'Augie' here in this building? Is that you?" Joyce said.

"Augie?" the plaintive voice outside the door said.

"The hell!" Joyce said. "You told me Race. Who's this Augie"?

"I'm telling you, my name's Race Gentry. Lemme call my agent to see. There's no one at the door. There's an Augie upstairs, come to think of it. He's a bartender."

When Joyce, half naked, opened the door, I tried to push it shut. The neighbors were standing in bathrobes, angry, murmuring to each other. They'd been awakened by Ellie beating on doors calling mournfully for "Augie."

"Don't disturb me," I said to her as I stepped outside. "Get out of here now like you're supposed to do when I'm busy, Ellie. What you doing here? I had a hard day. Tell all these folks to go back in their apartments."

"I'm pregnant," Queen Nefertiti was saying. She was crying.

"Well I had a damn hard day. I'm trying to relax."

"Race, are you really an all-star?" Joyce was saying, popping her head out from inside the apartment. "Who's this weeping beauty?"

"An all-star with one homer? He's had one round-tripper in two months," said Mr. Youngblood from downstairs.

I thought Ellie was gonna faint.

"One?" Joyce said. "One home run?"

The other neighbors started in. When he wasn't ogling Joyce, Jack Wright said I was an all-star fool. When I looked back in, Joyce was fixing her blouse, grabbing her purse. "You told me the name Race Gentry meant fifty home runs. Who's this out here callin' for you? Are you married?" Joyce hissed.

Poor Ellie, pregnant, looked deathly white when Joyce rushed past.

Drunker than I thought, I tripped on the stairs, could've permanently hurt myself, hurt my throwing arm. "No one was here, Ellie," I was yelling. "I was alone. You're seeing things."

Jeezus, I thought, when I didn't have my car keys. By the time I fished them out of my pocket, both gals were gone. Driving as fast as I could, head spinning, I went by Corky's Townhouse South Restaurant, past Morgan Coffee, Shreve City Gulf. As I looked for Ellie and Joyce, I wondered what a Polack from Yankeeland was doing mixed up with Connie Stevens and Ellie Pleasaunt in Louisana. Why hadn't I been assigned to Triple-A International League Buffalo, a good Polish town, or Double-A Scranton-Wilkes-Barre?

Hung over, out of gas, I had on KEEL-Radio when the sun came up. I waited for Mr. Barton's voice over the radio to tell me what to do. If he'd said, "Go to Winn-Dixie, buy a hundred packages of Goody's," I would have. If he'd told me, "Go to Wal-Mart, greet people in my name," I would have done that. I had no one else now, and he knew how to call the Game of Life with fifty thousand watts behind him.

When I phoned, Ellie was at Hattie's.

"I'm out on King's Highway," I told Ellie when I got her to come to the phone. "It isn't what you think."

"I don't want to bother with you anymore," she said.

"What can I do all day without you?"

"I can't talk. Hattie's gotta get to work," she said hanging up.

When I got Joyce on the phone, she hung up, too. She'd telephoned around town. Made a lot of calls about me. Maybe she even called Fair Grounds Field. "I fooled you anyway, Augie Gentry or whatever your name is," Joyce said. "Because I'm pushing fifty and you didn't notice." She called me "Sausage Glove" and slammed down the phone.

Then it was just me, Augie Wyzinski, listening to the dial tone. I waited and waited for Mr. Biff Barton's voice over the radio, over the phone. Jesus, I needed the sound of him for a minute to straighten me out. Nothing came on the radio, just ads for Pamida, Farmer Brown's Chicken, a few country songs, more ads. Where was talk radio? I went through a tank of gas between 7 A.M. and 1 P.M. driving Louisiana Avenue, I-20, then on the Barksdale Highway to Bossier. "Do you know Biff Barton?" I asked anyone I saw. "Where can I find Biff, the Voice of the Captains?"

Messed up in the head as I was now, I remembered Ellie talking about gardenias that bloomed in front of her folks' house. On January days you could smell them through the window, she'd said.

"Mama was hinting you should come back here in winter. Come see us," I remember Ellie saying. "If you don't, I'll send you a gardenia up north." She took my hand then. "You'll have a gardenia in the snow to remind you of me."

I recalled it so well. What had happened in two months? Thinking of Ellie and her parents as I sat in the parking lot in the rising August heat broke my heart. They were only seventy miles away. I turned the radio on, listening for Biff Barton. Where was he, a voice that in summer came out of the very heart of the country where you were...a voice that told you there's this field under a blue sky where an organ can be heard, where people cheer, yell, and grow lonely in the late innings of losing games or toward the end of the season when autumn is coming? This same voice tells you a catcher has responsibilities. He backs up first on infield ground balls, blocks wild pitches, explodes from the crouch to gun down the base stealers of this world. But I couldn't do it, couldn't get it done on the field, and now I'd blown it with the only girl who ever mattered to me.

By two o'clock it was a hundred degrees out. It looked like rain. On the dirt road that leads to Bayou Clarence I listened to heat bugs...watched the cattle egrets stepping gently in the water. I was sick. I do not know why a man does such things as I'd done. Why he cannot be faithful to one who loves him. Is it the price of fame? When you think you're above every citizen of Caddo Parish, Louisiana, because you're on a record home run streak, can you hurt and disregard them?

"Kielbasa. From now on you're Augie Kielbasa," the skipper'd said a month earlier. "Why don't you wear a sausage to catch with? Wear one on your head while you're at it."

From that night in Little Rock, Midland, or wherever it was through the whole last half of the Texas League season, I meant nothing to Mr. Treadwell with my .060 average and twenty passed balls.

A Christian man, the skipper would always say, "Morals is important and my boys gotta be good men—on the diamond and off. Always cherish the temple. Honor the temple. You live right and good off the field, you'll play right and good on the field. Thas all we ask, boys. Don't let no weakness of soul or heart destroy you in this game and in the Game of Life."

I guess he knew why my game had suffered. I'd struggled to get my hitting eye back, but it was like everything else I'd done. Acting so crazy with women and drinking made me lose my edge. I'd forget what signal I just gave. A pitch in the dirt wouldn't get blocked. Thinking about it all made it worse. What about folks waiting for news of me in the *Evening Telegram* back home? How could I let them down?

By now it was 3:30. I was exhausted from the long day, not to mention the crazy night before. I missed Ellie so much. I turned the car around to head to the stadium for tonight's ball game against the Arkansas Travelers. I was done in with regret and shame. I feared for the future. What would come of me?

Since mid-July, when I'd become the bullpen catcher, I heard the skipper Treadwell and Biff Barton talking as I warmed up the pitcher before games. Today when I got to the park, the Voice of the Captains seemed to know I'd been searching the dial for his voice—but he spoke to the skip as if nothing had happened.

"After the weekend only six games left," Biff was saying.

"We'll probably have El Paso in the playoffs, Biffy," the skipper was saying. Turning to me, he said, "Kid, you're startin'. Les us get a game out of you tonight." Some of his tobacco spit landed by me.

"Looks plum wore out," said Biff Barton. "Keepin' your nose clean, kid?"

Feeling pretty ragged, I didn't say nothing back.

"It's gonna rain," said the skipper. "I cain't risk the new young kid come in last week. The big club when they sent us Siveney last week told us 'Go easy...don't hurt Siveney. Get him in his playing time, but don't hurt him. He's a real prospect.' Les us just see what Augie's got or ain't got. Dry off from the drizzle, Kielbasa-hands. You're startin' tonight. You aren't too tired, are you?"

"I had some trouble with my girlfriend last night."

"Moral trouble?" the skip said. "Baptist trouble?"

"How'd you know?"

"Don't they teach you how to play it straight up north?" he asked. "Thas a problem."

As he stared at me, the rain started. I strapped on shin guards, chest protector, mask...the so-called "tools of ignorance" because only a fool crouches behind home plate. The Voice of the Captains yelled to me he was going to transmit my name to thousands of fans. He hung out his banner. KEEL-Radio would simulcast in Polish and English, he said, the first-ever Polish-English broadcast of a Texas League game.

Then I heard the crowd, organist, vendors, and heard Mr. Barton start his broadcast with observations on the catcher, 00. And I knew all the members in the National Polish-American Sports Hall of Fame in Orchard Lake, Michigan, were listening, waiting for me to join them. I'd read about them, seen programs Uncle Louie sent from the induction ceremonies: Stan "the Man" Musial in 1973; Ted Kluszewski in '74; in '75, Aloysius Harry Szymanski (Simmons), who was voted MVP with the Philadelphia A's and the next year, 1930, won the batting crown; Stan (Kowalewski) Coveleski in '76...on and on, Eddie (Lopatynski) Lopat, Bill Mazeroski, Bill "Moose" Skowron, Tony Kubek...

5.
HOPEFUL FUTURE HALL OF FAMER SEES PLANS CHANGE

At 8:34 I struck out. It was the sixth inning. KEEL's every watt carried it. When Treadwell came out, the public address system switched to polkas. There was "Pennsylvania Polka," "She's Too Fat Polka," "Liechtensteiner Polka." Fans groaned and started chanting "Ban Polka! Ban Polka!"

"I cain't put in no one else before the playoffs because orders from the big club tell me to keep Siveney benched on rainy nights so he don't hurt his arm or twist his knee," the skipper said through the rain. "So what do I do? You're good for nothin', Kielbasa. Even your music stinks."

As the grounds crew unrolled the tarp in the rain that was falling harder now, Treadwell's face got redder and redder. Someone had told him what happened with Joyce. He didn't like embarrassment by his players. Rain dripping from his cap, he cussed, spit his tobacco. Was Biff analyzing my life-moves?

How do you go back to local programming, you wonder in the rain with the last polka playing? Some other night in years to come the skipper will be chewing tobacco, Biff Barton saying, "Good evening, Caps fans," the stadium vendors hawking their goods while cars and trucks on Highway I-20 outside the ballpark whip across America as usual. It's like nothing ever changes down there. What will Ellie be doing that night, talking to someone else about flowers? As she reads the paper, will her eye catch a story on the Shreveport Captains? Will her ma ask, "Ellie, do you ever think of that nice young man from up north? Your father asks about him from time to time." Will Ellie tell her, "No, Mama, not much anymore...But look how nice the gardenias are blooming." Now there was an empty stadium. The rain they'd predicted all day was forming puddles and streams behind home plate when I saw Ellie walking through the box seats of section C, blouse and pink summer sweater soaked.

"Why didn't I keep you a secret?" she was asking, wiping rain from her forehead. I knew she was no ghost. She was down on the field now. Only two other people were left in the ballpark.

"I shouldn't have taken you to meet my parents this summer." She was running her hands along the screen behind home; and I was thinking how, when I'd first gone to Natchitoches with Ellie, her mother and father had said, "Sit down, young man, we saved you a place." It'd all changed by late August. Ellie was saying, "I want to get away from here. I'll apologize at home to my folks, apologize to Hattie—"

The groundskeeper was talking to Mr. Barton. They surprised us. Standing in the shadows, they looked like a part of the ballpark.

"Leave the lights on for them?" the groundskeeper was asking.

"Sure," the Voice of the Captains said.

From under the umbrella the groundskeeper held for him, Biff Barton yelled over, "Kid, you know this might be it for you? If you were famous here and hitting .330, they'd forgive you for fooling around with all those women. But with the way you've gone...Next year fans are going to ask, '"Where's the Polish boy? We don't see 00. Where's Kielbasa Kid?' 'He got released,' I'll have to say."

"I know. Tell'em I'll tend bar up north or sweep floors at the flour mill like my dad does. I can practice my swing in the boiler room for the comeback. I'll get a tryout somewhere."

"You come live down here and straighten out," Mr. Barton was saying. "Stay here, kid. Start a life where you'll pause at the screen door after work...dream of what might've been if you'd gotten the extra base hit in Tulsa. Then you can go inside, see her fixing your supper and how beautiful she is no matter what she's doing, and be glad you have turned into a hardworking Christian who once had a shot at the big show. There's one decent thing to do, Wyzinski. Why not stay south here, work for the cotton oil plant or for that little college in Natchitoches? Cut grass for the college till you get settled. Maybe when the Caps release you, you can take responsibility—fix car radiators for Ates Radiator or something. We've all made mistakes."

"I wonder if I can, Mr. Barton. Maybe I could get into the insurance business," I said, thinking to myself that "moral prospects" is what the skip and Mr. Barton were wanting us to be—good players with clear consciences who didn't have defects of soul and heart, defects that would hurt them no matter what they did in life.

When I saw beautiful Ellie still standing in the rain, I believed there was hope if she'd give me a chance to change my life. She was smoothing the wet hair from her face, listening to Biff.

"Then you got a kid steps in like this one they protected, this straight-arrow, nondrinking, nonwomanizing prospect Siveney," Biff Barton was saying. "Kid, most folks aren't going anyplace in life but to the feed store, the insurance business, or the lumber mill day in and day out. They're just ordinary moral folks. It's raining tonight, so they're home. They've got families. Tomorrow they'll go to work, struggle along, pay the bills. Are you going to join us?"

"Sure," I said.

When Mr. Barton held his fingers like an umpire signaling the count, I was thinking how I'd once hit safely in eight straight games. That should mean something to God and the Blessed Virgin.

"Three and two. Runner at first is going," Mr. Barton said. "This pitch could decide it." When he said that, he turned on his heel and walked away.

The rain came so hard then I thought Ellie and I'd be washed off the field. She was looking at the frightening sky. "You shouldn't have come to Natchitoches. You got my folks believing in us," she said.

"Tell them I didn't want it to turn out wrong."

"It don't matter now," she said.

When she told me she never loved me—not even at the start—her voice breaking, too, I knew I'd had my chance, that she'd given me her heart and I'd broken it and that she would go away. I'd turn into an immoral gaboosh who'd work in places like the Heartbreak, recalling the might-have-beens Biff Barton told me about.

"Too much is wrong with you," she was saying, crying. I didn't hear what else she said as she opened the gate by the dugout where the sign on the fence says: No Pepper Games.

When the Voice of the Captains and the groundskeeper escorted her through the dark runway beneath the stands, nobody asking whether I could do better, nobody giving me a second chance, I realized what remained was for them to shut off the lights on my chances for happiness with Ellie and on my one chance at making the Polish-American Sports Hall of Fame.

I sat all night in the dark stadium, regretting what would become of me. Lots of people hurt and betray others. She didn't deserve it. I should've valued her the way I valued making the Hall of Fame. I didn't think or know much last season. But it hits me now that these memories are the tools of ignorance I am left with, so I put them on and I regret who I am.

6.
EX-MINOR LEAGUER JOINS COUNTY BEER LEAGUE

A season later, I wipe the bar at the Heartbreak and turn the radio dial when the jukebox is off. Over the airwaves of the South last year, signals were crisscrossing, bringing me together with folks like Mr. and Mrs. Pleasaunt, like Ellie, like Biff...good, ordinary folks. Folks who lived plain, quiet lives. A life in Louisiana would've been perfect for me, too: Captains broadcasts, the summer skies Biff Barton talked about, Ellie on walks by Cane River, reminding me of my hitting streaks and pulling out newspaper clippings she'd once saved about me. There'd be faithful church attendance and a baby to love and rear. Oh, Ellie, I've learned what I never knew last season: you were trusting and honest and I let you down. I looked for a flower this January, but you didn't send one.

Nowadays till someone at the end of the bar—till Pete, say—needs the services of a washed-up ballplayer (of a gaboosh like him), I imagine a voice a long ways off in the rain. I can hear you, Ellie, walking away with that voice from the radio I knew so well.

Nowadays, circling the bases in the Old Timers' League up here in Douglas County, wearing this wool uniform in Sunday's heat, I think of you. For each rocket I hit, the owner of Heartbreak buys me a Fitger's beer and a package of string cheese. My signing bonus was a job here and Sundays off to hit homers for you and me, the catcher and you, Ellie—who will never be together after last year's season of lies. I hit home runs of a kind never seen before. You can believe this. Home runs that tear out my heart, home runs that are talked about in this league of nobodies.

"Augie?"

"Yeah, Pete?" I say.

"What ya thinkin' about?"

"Nothing," I say. "A girl."

"Who?"

"I'll tell you later, but now I'm gonna think about runners I threw out in Jackson, of the great two-hit game I called for Tim Crow in Midland-Odessa. A catcher has responsibilities, you know, Pete."

I shake his hand as he slumps against the wall. I shake all their hands. My East End fans. The Hamm's clock ticks on, the sign sizzles. The gabooshes shuffle to the jukebox, the men's room, the pachinko game to try to roll a nickel down the right path. Things never change at Heartbreak Hotel.

"Thanks," I say to them, to ham-faced Władziu, to Stashu, to Benny.

"Thank you," they say. "You had a goot career in baseball."

"Thank you, Paul," I say.

"Yeah, Augie."

"Thank you, too, Casimir."

"You bet, Augie. Glad you're home."

"Thank you, John."

"Tank you, Augie. Strike three for you?"

"Here's a toast to all you guys for telling me how bad I was at the game," I say. "Next we're getting the neon sign fixed. I'll talk to the boss. We aren't heartbroke, so why should we have a broken sign? Well, maybe Pete is. Pete, you're pickled. Why don't you go home? Can you walk or should I call you a cab?

"You go home!"

"I can't. What would I do? Sit with my ma? Say the rosary with her? Anyway, if I looked in the mirror at home, I'd just see you guys. I might as well stay here where I got you in front of me. Go on, tell me I'm lousy. I got all night to listen to you guys with high self-esteem."

ABOUT THE CONTRIBUTORS

Charles Blackburn, Jr., Raleigh, NC
Charles Blackburn, Jr. grew up in Henderson, NC, attended UNC-Chapel Hill and Barton College. Early in his career, he roamed the state as a reporter and editor for four small-town newspapers. He has also been a bookshop owner and associate director of public relations at Duke University Medical Center. Since 1991, he has been communications manager for Sigma Xi, The Scientific Research Society. Blackburn is a past president of the NC Writers' Network and NC Writers Conference. His fiction, poetry, and features have appeared in many regional and national publications. He is a three-time winner of *Crucible*'s annual fiction award, the recipient of the Sam Ragan Award for Literature from St. Andrews Presbyterian College, and a literary fellowship in fiction from the NC Arts Council. Charles plays guitar in a rock band called When Cousins Marry.

Anthony Bukoski, Superior, WI
Anthony Bukoski is the author of five short-story collections. His stories have appeared in *New Letters*, *The Literary Review*, *New Orleans Review*, and elsewhere. His collection *Time Between Trains* (Southern Methodist University Press 2003) was named a Booklist Editor's Choice. After Liev Schreiber read the title story to a live audience at Symphony Space in New York City, the piece was broadcast on NPR's "Selected Shorts" program. A former Christopher Isherwood Foundation Fellowship winner, Bukoski's most recent books are *North of the Port* (SMU, 2008) and *Twelve Below Zero: New and Revised Edition* (Holy Cow! Press, 2008).

Jeanie Chung, Chicago, IL
Jeanie Chung's fiction and essays have appeared or are forthcoming in *Drunken Boat, upstreet, Numero Cinq, Stymie online* and elsewhere. This story is part of a novel-in-stories based on her time as a sportswriter covering high school and college basketball for the *Chicago Sun-Times*.

Michael Lunny Duffy, Morristown, NJ
Michael Lunny Duffy has an M.F.A., teaches writing at a university, and has published short stories in literary journals—*Cimarron Review, Beloit Fiction Journal*, and the *New Mexico Humanities Review*, among others.

Demian Entrekin, Oakland, CA
Demian Entrekin is a technology entrepreneur in the San Francisco Bay Area and has founded two successful software companies. He holds an M.A. in English from San Francisco State University and has published poems, stories and articles in journals and small press magazines. He authors an award-winning technology blog called *Future States* and has published numerous papers on software development and the software industry. He is also a regular contributor on Vator.tv, a website that covers entrepreneurial business and industry trends.

Mike Falcon, Los Angeles, CA
Mike Falcon was formerly the editor of *Max Muscle Magazine* and a columnist for both RichKern.com, the women's collegiate volleyball website, and *Spotlight Health*, which appeared in *USA Today*. He holds an MFA in Professional Writing from University of Southern California and a BA in English from Immaculate Heart College, where he studied under Mark Harris and Theodore Sturgeon. He lives in the Silver Lake section of Los Angeles.

William J. Francis, Dallas, TX
Lives outside of Dallas, TX with his son. Spends his free time writing short stories and working on a novel. His work has appeared in *The Cabinet of Dr. Casey*, *Tantalus Fire*, *Black Petals*, and the Pen Dragon Press anthology *Nasty Snips*.

Gaynell Gavin, Columbia, SC
Gaynell Gavin's poetry, creative nonfiction, and fiction have appeared in many literary journals and anthologies, including *Fourth Genre*, *The Main Street Rag*, *North Dakota Quarterly*, *Best New Poets 2006*, and *The Best of the Bellevue Literary Review*. Her essay, "What We Have," published in *Prairie Schooner*, was included among "Notable Essays " in *The Best American Essays 2009*. She was a finalist in the AWP Award Series in Creative Nonfiction, and her poetry chapbook, *Intersections*, was published by Main Street Rag. Originally from Illinois, she now lives with her husband and menagerie in Columbia, South Carolina. She is a faculty member at Claflin University.

Philip Gerard, Wilmington, NC

Philip Gerard is the author of three novels, four books of nonfiction, and numerous documentary scripts, essays, radio commentaries, and short stories. With Jill Gerard, he co-edits *Chautauqua*, the literary journal of Chautauqua Institution (NY). He chairs the Department of Creative Writing at University of North Carolina-Wilmington.

Frank Haberle, Brooklyn, NY

Frank Haberle's stories have appeared in numerous print and web-based journals including *So New Media's Necessary Fiction, Adirondack Review, L Magazine, Birmingham Arts Journal, Cantaraville, Broken Bridge Review, Taj Mahal Review, 34th Parallel, Hot Metal Press, Melic Review, Smokelong Quarterly, Johnny America, Starry Night Review, East Hampton Star* and *City Writers Review*. Frank is a professional grant writer and a Board member and workshop leader of the NY Writers Coalition, a nonprofit group committed to providing community writing opportunities for disenfranchised New Yorkers. Born in New York City and raised in New England, Frank migrated back to Brooklyn 25 years ago, where he lives with his wife and three children.

Atari Hadari, Hebden Bridge, UK

Atar Hadari was born in Israel, raised in England and won a scholarship to study poetry and playwrighting with Derek Walcott at Boston University. His *Songs from Bialik: Selected Poems of Hayim Nahman Bialik* (Syracuse University Press 2000) was a finalist for the American Literary Translator's Association Award 2001. Four times nominated for the Pushcart prize by magazines such as *New York Stories, Margin, Witness* and *Larcom Review*, his story "Deacon," merited honorable mention in the 2001 anthology. He won the Liverpool Literature Festival's "Pulp Idol" novelist competition by reading two minutes from his novel, *When We Were Saved*, of which his story, "Where is Lion," is a chapter.

Thomas E. Kennedy, Denmark

Thomas E. Kennedy's novel *Falling Sideways* was published by Bloomsbury in 2011, following *In the Company of Angels* (2010), the first two books of his Copenhagen Quartet, four independent novels about the seasons and souls of the Danish capital. Kennedy's 25+ books include novels, story and essay collections, literary criticism, translation and anthologies. His work appears regularly in American periodicals such as *New Letters*, *Glimmer Train*, *Ecotone*, *Epoch*, *The Literary Review*, *Serving House Journal* and many others and has won O. Henry and Pushcart prizes and a National Magazine Award (an "Ellie") in the essay genre. He teaches in the Fairleigh Dickinson University MFA Program, holds an MFA from Vermont College of Fine Arts and Ph.D. from the University of Copenhagen, and is co-publisher, with Walter Cummins, of ServingHouseBooks.

Carolyn P. Lawrence, Williamsburg, VA

Carolyn P. Lawrence is a retired religious educator and university campus minister who has won awards for both fiction and nonfiction. Her essays have appeared in *America*, *National Catholic Reporter*, *St. Anthony Messenger*, and the *Virginia Gazette*. A previous short story was published in *The MacGuffin*. She is an avid ACC basketball fan, loves "March Madness," and enjoys biking and traveling.

Jen McConnell, Rocky River, OH

Jen McConnell is a native of Southern California and moved to San Francisco in 1996. In 2001, she received an MFA in Creative Writing from Goddard College in Vermont. She has published seven of the short stories from her manuscript, *Welcome Anybody*, in literary journals including *Bacopa Literary Magazine*, *SNReview*, *Clackamas Literary Review*, and UC Santa Barbara's *Spectrum*. After living on both coasts for most of her life, she currently makes her home on the Lake Erie shore, though she escapes back to the Bay Area as often as possible (Go Giants!). and supports her writing habit by working in non-profit marketing and communications.

Deirdre Murray-Holmes, Tujunga, CA

Deirdre Murray-Holmes is a Los Angeles area producer and writer whose world view was framed by 70s pop music and the original *Star Trek* series. She spends her time making movies, watching baseball, and steadfastly awaiting her overdue deus ex machina.

Mark Pearson, Houston, TX

Mark Pearson's work was recently anthologized in *The Best American Sports Writing 2011*, and the short fiction collections *Altered States* and *Suicidally Beautiful*. His fiction and essays have appeared in or are forthcoming in *Aethlon*, *Blueline*, *Broken Bridge Review*, *Carve*, *Gray's Sporting Journal*, *Iron Horse Literary Review*, *North Dakota Quarterly*, *Short Story*, *Sport Literate*, and *Stories*. He attended the University of Michigan on a wrestling scholarship, and later, after working as a journalist, college wrestling coach, bouncer, and high school English teacher, earned a Ph.D. from the University of Georgia, an M.A. from the University of California, Davis, and an M.A. from St. John's College, Md. He teaches English and coaches wrestling at The Hill School in Pottstown, PA.

Charles Rammelkamp, Baltimore MD

Charles Rammelkamp lives and writes in Baltimore, MD. He is the author of a novel, *The Secretkeepers* (Red Hen Press), two collections of short fiction, *A Better Tomorrow* (PublishAmerica) and *Castleman in the Academy* (March Street Press), a full-length collection of poetry, *The Book of Life* (March Street Press) and half a dozen poetry chapbooks. For several years, Rammelkamp has been editing the online literary journal, *The Potomac* (http://thepotomacjournal.com) and has guest-edited several other online and print journals as well. He grew up in Michigan, a Detroit Tigers fan and rooted for the hapless Red Sox during much of the 1970's and 1980's when he lived in Boston. He and his wife moved to Baltimore in 1983, the last year the Orioles won the American League pennant and the World Series.

Lee Ann Robins, Monroe GA

Lee Ann Robins is from Meridian, Mississippi and received her BA in Journalism and Broadcasting from Mississippi State University. After working as a journalist and a photographer in New Orleans, she has taught English, Creative Writing, AP Literature, French, and Journalism in Mississippi, Tennessee, and Georgia. Her work has won awards from the Alabama Writers Conclave, *Meridian Community College Review*, and Tennessee High School Press Association. She has published articles and stories in *The Meridian Star*, *The Jackson Sun*, and *The West Tennessee Writing Project*. In 2001, she was chosen to represent Tennessee for the Al Neuharth Freedom Forum, and she has received fellowships from Quill and Scroll, the Journalism Education Association, and The American Society of Newspaper Editors.

Colleen Shaddox, Hamden, CT

Colleen Shaddox's work has been published by *The New York Times*, *The Washington Post*, *The Christian Science Monitor* and many national magazines. As a journalist, she's interviewed royalty, a Nobel Laureate and a bank robber (who confessed to her print). She lives in Connecticut, where she often finds herself surrounded by Yankee fans.

Jane St. Clair, Tucson, AZ

Jane St. Clair grew up in Chicago, and graduated from Northwestern University. She has been a staff member of the TV show *Sesame Street*, and a newspaper reporter for several newspapers, including the *Louisville Courier-Journal*. She is the author of 21 children's books and a novel entitled *Walk Me to Midnight*. Her short stories have appeared in literary magazines like the *Red Rock Review* and *Thema*, as well as several other anthologies. She is a soccer mom of four children in Tucson, Arizona.

Michael Stigman, Weston, MO

Born and raised in Minneapolis, MN, Michael Stigman cut his teeth on hockey sticks and skates, baseball gloves and bats, basketball and football. He has lived in Virginia, and in Lawrence, Kansas, where he earned a Ph.D. in English and Creative Writing at University of Kansas. His dissertation, which consists of fourteen stories, includes "Gunn and The Hammer." Stories he has written appear in *Sycamore Review*, *South Dakota Review*, *AGNI-Online*, *Zone 3*, and elsewhere. He lives with his wife and their three children in Weston, Missouri, and he teaches in the English department at Benedictine College in Atchison, Kansas.

William J. Torgerson, College Point, NY
William Torgerson teaches in the Institute For Writing Studies at St. John's University in Queens, New York. His novel *Love on the Big Screen* was released in 2011. He's adapted the novel for the screen and his script has been named a semi-finalist in the Rhode Island International Screen Festival writing competition. His work has appeared or is forthcoming in numerous journals, including NYU's *Anamesa*, Old Dominion University's *Barely South Review*, and *Sakura*. He blogs at *TheTorg.Com* and enjoys writing-related conversations on Facebook.

Gordon Weaver, Cedarburg, WI
Gordon Weaver is the author of four novels, ten collections of short stories, as well as a collection of poems. He was the founding editor of *Mississippi Review*, fiction editor and editor of *Cimarron Review*, managing editor of the AWP Award Series for Short Fiction, and General Editor of the Twayne Series for Short Fiction and has had more than a hundred of his stories published. Weaver's novel *Count a Lonely Cadence* was adapted for the movie *Cadence*. He has been awarded the St. Lawrence Award for Fiction (1973), the Quarterly West novella prize, two Pushcart Prizes, two NEA fellowships, Best American Short Stories (1980 for "Hog's Heart"), the O. Henry Award (1979), The Sherwood Anderson Award (1982), and the 2002 Andrew Lytle Fiction Prize. Father of three daughters, Weaver currently lives in Wisconsin.

J. Weintraub, Chicago, IL
J. Weintraub has published fiction, essays, translations, and poetry in *The New Criterion*, *Massachusetts Review*, *Michigan Quarterly Review*, *Crab Orchard Review*, *Chicago Reader*, *Modern Philology* and many other reviews and periodicals. He has received awards for writing from the Illinois and Barrington Art Councils, was an Around-the-Coyote poet, is currently a network

playwright at Chicago Dramatists, and has been a featured writer/reader in such well-known Chicago literary salons as the Red Lion Pub, the Uptown Writer's Space, and the Bourgeois Pig.

ABOUT THE EDITORS

Dennis F. Bormann, Columbia, SC.
Dennis F. Bormann was born 35 miles from NYC in Suffern, NY. Vermont College granted him a MFA in Creative Writing (Genre: Fiction). Continuing his education at Oklahoma State University with his mentor Gordon Weaver (who he met at VC) he received a Ph.D. in English. Besides his academic career, Bormann's been a gardener, house painter, bartender at a longshoreman's gin mill in NJ, delivered drugs (legally), house-roofer in Florida, and sold high fashion women's shoes in LA. He was even an investment banker in LA (people actually trusted him with their money-go figure.) The last seventeen years he's taught literature and creative writing at the oldest HBCU in South Carolina, Claflin University. Bormann has been a fiction editor for *Midlands Review, Cimarron Review, Short Story,* currently is the short story editor for MSR's literary magazine (*The Main Street Rag*). His novella, *Airboat*, was published by MSR in August 2011. He lives in Columbia, South Carolina with his wife Linda, and is the proud parent of a son and daughter, AJ and Katie.

Stephen Taylor, La Crescenta, CA.
Steve Taylor teaches at Glendale College where he has won a whole bunch of teaching awards due to a system he worked out where the students do all the work and give him all the credit. The stuff he writes has gotten him an L.A. Arts Council Literature Award, won him the 2004 Main Street Rag Short Fiction Contest, and made him a two-time finalist and

this year one of three Honorable Mentions in The Katherine Anne Porter Prize for Fiction given by Nimrod International Journal. Humoring him in this way has only increased his urge to write even more stuff.

Contributors